Windrush: Warriors of God

Windrush: Warriors of God

Jack Windrush Series – Book VI

Malcolm Archibald

Copyright (C) 2019 Malcolm Archibald
Layout design and Copyright (C) 2019 Creativia
Published 2019 by Creativia (www.creativia.org)
Edited by Wicked Words Editing
Cover art by Cover Mint
This book is a work of fiction. Names, characters, places, and incidents are the product of the author's imagination or are used fictitiously. Any resemblance to actual events, locales, or persons, living or dead, is purely coincidental.
All rights reserved. No part of this book may be reproduced or transmitted in any form or by any means, electronic or mechanical, including photocopying, recording, or by any information storage and retrieval system, without the author's permission.

Contents

Prelude   1

Chapter One   4

Chapter Two   17

Chapter Three   27

Chapter Four   35

Chapter Five   50

Chapter Six   59

Chapter Seven   79

Chapter Eight   90

Chapter Nine   111

Chapter Ten   125

Chapter Eleven   133

Chapter Twelve	146
Chapter Thirteen	153
Chapter Fourteen	163
Chapter Fifteen	180
Chapter Sixteen	189
Chapter Seventeen	205
Chapter Eighteen	224
Chapter Nineteen	235
Chapter Twenty	242
Chapter Twenty-One	265
Chapter Twenty-Two	275
Chapter Twenty-Three	285
Chapter Twenty-Four	294
Historical Notes	298
About the Author	303

For Cathy

First comes one Englishman, as a traveller or for shikar; then come two and make a map; then comes an army and takes the country. Therefore, it is better to kill the first Englishman.
Pashtun proverb

Prelude

Daffadar Habib Khan heard the tiny click through the sinister blanket of night. It could have been nothing, a stone dislodged by the wind, the noise made by a nocturnal animal, but Habib Khan was instantly alert. Born and bred to *Pakhtunwali*, the Pashtun way of life, he touched the shoulder of the sowar to his right, nodding in the direction of the sound. Immediately understanding, the sowar passed on the message until every man of the Guides patrol was alert.

A chill wind blew from the unseen heights of the Spin Ghar, the range of mountains otherwise known as the Safed Koh. Here, in Pakhtunkhwa, the unstable North-West Frontier between British India and the independent land of Afghanistan, every sound could mean danger.

When Habib Khan heard the slither of cloth on rock, he knew that a man was approaching. When he caught the slight whiff of gun oil, he knew that the man was armed. Every single sound or smell added to his knowledge so that within minutes Habib Khan had a complete picture of what was out there in the dark. He did not have to think; the instincts of generations of hillmen had been bred into him.

Twenty men, he told himself. *Ghilzais; they are moving into an ambush position.*

Lying prone, Habib Khan nestled his rifle behind a rock and got ready to fire. He did not have to load; any man who carried an empty firearm in Pakhtunkhwa was either a fool or dead. Habib Khan was not the former and had no desire to be the latter. There was no sound from his colleagues; they knew the danger as well as he did.

A horse whinnied behind them, the sound carrying far in the dark. It was a tiny incident but enough to preempt the Ghilzai tribesmen's attack. They rose as one, moving onto what they hoped would be a sleeping camp. Instead they walked into the fire of a dozen Guides' rifles.

The shots shattered the silence, echoing from the surrounding hills as each muzzle flash gave a tiny vignette of the scene. Habib Khan had a partial picture of a score of Ghilzais advancing through the night with Khyber Knives or pulwars naked in their hands and rifles slung across their backs. Then came sudden darkness as the firing stopped. The acrid reek of powder smoke drifted in the sharp air.

'What the devil…' Lieutenant Beattock, back with the main body of the Guides, shouted. 'What's happening up there, Daffadar?'

With no time to explain, Daffadar Habib Khan ordered his men to fix bayonets. The metallic snicks sounded sinister on the hushed hillside.

'Ready?' Habib Khan had no need to ask.

The Guides followed, feet silent in the dark as Habib Khan led them forward to meet the Ghilzais, men of their blood, men every bit as adept in hill-craft as themselves, men eager to meet their attack.

Bayonet to Khyber Knife, rifle butt to pulwar, the skirmish lasted only five minutes and ended with the Ghilzais melting back into the dark. Lieutenant Beattock scrambled up in time to see the final few seconds. 'Well done, Daffadar.' He looked around at the crumpled bodies of three Ghilzais while a single wounded Guide tried to hold his entrails in place. 'Take Khazi back down the hill and we'll get him attended to.'

'Yes, Beattock Sahib,' Habib Khan said.

'Halloa now.' Beattock turned over one of the Ghilzai dead. 'What have we here?' Removing the rifle from the man's back, Beattock held it up. 'Now here's mischief. Where did you get this from, my fine fellow?' Lifting the rifle to his shoulder, Beattock sighted along the barrel. 'You did very well, Daffadar, even better than you think.' He looked again at the dead Ghilzai, swore softly, and crouched down. 'We have trouble,' he said, pulling at the red cord the man sported on his right wrist. 'We could have major trouble.'

Chapter One

Gondabad, India, June 1863

'Have you seen this, Jack?' Mary tapped the relevant paragraph of the *Times* with her forefinger. 'It's about your brother.'

Captain Jack Windrush looked up from the fishing fly he was tying. 'I didn't know the papers had arrived. What's William doing now? Winning the Victoria Cross for bravely parading down Pall Mall?'

'He's making more babies,' Mary said. 'I'll read it out to you: "We are pleased to announce that Captain William Windrush of the Royal Malverns has been blessed with a child. The new arrival, William Crimea Windrush, came into this world on the 13th of January 1862. Mother and baby are both well. Captain William Windrush is already the proud father of a three-year-old girl, Helen Sevastopol Windrush."'

'I'm glad they are both well,' Jack said.

'You are glad that William's Helen is well even though Helen transferred her affections from you to William?' Mary reminded sweetly.

'That was a long time ago.' Jack did not enjoy the memory.

'Well, I am glad she did,' Mary said. 'It left you open for me.'

Jack grunted as he missed the knot. He began to tie the fly again. 'That was fortunate.'

Mary put the newspaper down. 'What does William's male child mean for your position, Jack?'

Jack considered for a moment, sighed, and put the fly aside. He knew he would not get any peace until Mary had exhausted the subject. 'I grew up thinking I was the heir to Wychwood Manor, as you know. It was not until my father died that I learned that, although I was the oldest, I was also illegitimate, with William the oldest legitimate son and, therefore, the heir.'

'I know that,' Mary said patiently.

Jack leaned back in his chair, swatting at a circling mosquito. 'When my mother, or rather my step-mother, told me that I was illegitimate, I was devastated.'

'I can imagine.' Mary did not remind Jack she had heard the story before. 'Your mother must be a cruel woman. Was she cruel?'

'No.' Jack shook his head. 'I have had years to think about this. When my step-mother first told me that I was illegitimate and would lose what I thought was my inheritance, I did believe she was cruel.' He looked away, reliving those dark days. 'I thought it was unfair that I should not join the family regiment, the Royal Malverns. I thought it wrong that I was only commissioned into the 113th, the lowest regiment in the army, with what I considered a pittance to live by.'

Mary listened. 'Do you still think the same, twelve years later?'

'No.' Jack shook his head. 'The family is not anything like as rich as I once thought we were. The Windrushes are only country gentry with a handful of acres, not some great landowners with a vast estate. With two legitimate sons to support as well as me, our land was insufficient to grant me a large allowance. In fact, Mother was more than generous giving me what she did. She could legally have thrown me out without a penny.'

'Did you ever speak to a lawyer about your position, Jack?'

'Not right away,' Jack said. 'I was young, foolish and angry. I wanted to make my name and get rapid promotion to show the world how clever I was.' He shook his head. 'When I think now of the risks I took!' He looked away. 'I despair of some of the young griffins I meet now, but I was worse than any of them.'

'Did you speak to a lawyer eventually?' Mary kept the subject on topic.

'Eventually,' Jack said. 'I consulted a Mr Stark in Calcutta. He told me that an illegitimate child, which I was, was not entitled to inherit anything unless the parents married each other after the child was born. In that case, the child could legally inherit wealth – movable assets.'

'I don't understand,' Mary said. 'What are movable assets?'

'Movable assets are money or possessions. The land or the house would only come to me if my father had specifically mentioned me in his will.'

'Did he?'

'He did not leave a will. He died of disease. I presume that he expected to live longer and may have intended to write a will later. As it happens…' Jack shrugged. 'I got nothing, as you are well aware. My father did not marry my mother. My half-brother William got the estate, and the commission into the Royal Malverns, with my other half-brother Adam having the right to live here plus inheriting half the movable assets.'

Mary sighed. 'It would have been good to have a base in England, somewhere to go Home when you retire from the Army.'

Jack said nothing until Mary prompted him. 'Do you miss Wychwood Manor?'

'I miss it because I always thought of it as Home, despite not being there much,' Jack said. 'I was in India until I was about five, although my memories are a bit vague. Father sent me to England, but I was at boarding school most of the time.' He leaned back as the memories returned. 'It's strange. I used to think that Wychwood Manor was huge until I went to India. Now I see that it's only a small country house, unpretentious and rather ugly, really.'

Mary patted his arm. 'I'm sure it's a lovely house. Will you show me sometime?'

'I'd like to,' Jack said. 'I'm due leave; in fact, I'm overdue leave.' Lighting a cheroot, he blew a slow cloud of smoke toward the mosquito, which reacted with an angry whine. 'I need a change, Mary. When I took this job with Colonel Hook, I believed it would be interesting. All I've done for the past four years has been routine and, quite frankly, dull.'

'I know what you have been doing,' Mary said. 'You've helped reorganise the country after the Mutiny; you've learned Pushtu and Urdu and some Persian; you've improved your horse-riding immeasurably.' Leaning forward, Mary took the cheroot from him and drew on it, smiling. 'Most importantly, you've been married to me, and we've created a child together.'

'I certainly don't regret that part of it.' Jack thought of young Andrew, sleeping in his cot with the ayah looking after him whenever Mary allowed. He did not mention to Mary that it would soon be time to send the lad back Home to be properly educated. After surviving the horrors of childhood disease, such partings of mother and child were the most heart-wrenching in the world. Taking his Home leave would enable them all to travel together and ease some of the pain.

'It was a wonderful day.' Mary handed back the cheroot, still smiling. Jack knew she was reliving the day of their marriage.

Jack had intended the wedding to be low-key affair, knowing that Mary was not a woman who sought to be the centre of attention. With his half-Indian mother, Jack was on the very margin of British respectability, while Mary as a Eurasian was on the opposite side of that definite social divide. He had not expected many guests.

They had married in the garrison church at Gondabad, with newly promoted Captain Arthur Elliot as best man and one of the mission teachers as maid of honour. Few of the officers of the 113th attended, for Colonel Snodgrass had made his disapproval evident. Only Ensigns Peake and Wilden, men who had marched with Windrush in the latter part of the Mutiny campaign, accompanied Elliot.

'The church is nearly empty.' Mary had tried to hide her disappointment as she surveyed the echoing interior.

'Your presence fills it all for me.' Jack was insufficiently skilled with words for his attempt at gallantry to succeed.

'Thank you, Jack.' Mary had looked beautiful dressed in white, with her veil pushed back and the white gloves extending almost to her elbows. She forced a smile for him. They had both turned around as the church door crashed open, with Jack instinctively reaching for his sword.

Mary had taken hold of his wrist. 'It's all right, Jack.'

'Sorry,' Jack had said. 'Old habits.'

Mary had released him. 'The Mutiny is over now. We're all at peace.'

'Sorry we're late, sir!' Dressed in his Number One uniform, Sergeant O'Neil had stridden into the church with a squad of men at his back. Jack had known who they would be even before he looked at them. There were Thorpe and Coleman, the Burma veterans, Riley the gentleman thief, and Logan, the diminutive Glaswegian with his face split into an uncharacteristic smile. There was Williams, limping from his recent wound, and Mackinnon who possessed some instinct that enabled him to sense danger. At the back was Parker, the quietly kind-hearted Liverpudlian.

'Thank you for coming, lads.' Jack had felt his words were inadequate. He knew his men would understand. 'I hope you don't get into any trouble for coming here.'

'No, sir.' Riley had said.

Jack had said no more. He could trust Riley to have thought of some dodge to subvert authority.

Mary had patted Jack's arm. She did not have to say anything. Her smile wrapped around the grinning men.

'Sir.' Sergeant O'Neill had thrown a thunderous salute as his boots crashed onto the paving stones that floored the church. 'We don't have much time, sir, but we all want to wish you and Mary … the future Mrs Windrush the best of all possible happiness, sir.'

'Thank you, Sergeant.' Jack had looked over his men. He could not quite believe that he was leaving the 113th. After sharing years of trials and bloody war, he would probably never see them again. *I'm getting foolishly emotional. Such partings are a soldier's lot.*

'The Church is quite full now with all your men there.' Mary's bright words had chased away his momentary gloom.

The ceremony had been brief. Elliot played his part with his usual efficiency, producing the ring at the required moment, and organising everything and everybody to an inch of their lives. Jack and Mary exchanged their vows without hesitation, with Jack wondering at the speed he transferred from a single man to a husband with responsibilities.

'I do,' he had said, and that was that. He was married for evermore. Looking at Mary, he had no regrets. It felt right, and there was no more to be said.

When Jack and Mary had marched back down the aisle as man and wife, their footsteps sounded hollow in the nearly empty church. O'Neill and his men had already left. Mary bit back her renewed disappointment.

'They probably had their duty to attend,' Jack had whispered. 'They would be here for you if it was humanly possible.' *All the same, I thought Elliot would have organised something.*

Mary's hand had squeezed his arm, gently reassuring. 'I know.'

All the same, I'd prefer the lads to be here for Mary's sake. She'll only have one wedding in her life. I hope.

The second they had stepped outside the gloom of the church into the bright Indian sunlight, Jack knew that he should have trusted Elliot. His men waited in a double row with their bayoneted rifles forming a triumphal arch under which Jack and Mary had to walk.

'Oh!' Mary had put a hand to her mouth. 'Oh, Jack!'

'All Elliot's doing.' Jack had renounced all responsibility. He resolved to buy Elliot a bottle of something suitable at the first opportunity. No price could adequately compensate for Mary's pleasure.

As they had marched beneath the glittering steel arch, Jack tried not to think of the times he had seen these same bayonets dripping with blood. Instead, he concentrated on the delight on Mary's face, and the loyalty of these rogues and badmashes he had fought beside for so many years.

'It's not the same without you, sir.' O'Neill had spoken awkwardly, as if he had not seen Jack in every state of dress and undress for the past decade.

'You have Elliot as Company Commander,' Jack had said. 'He's a good man.'

'Yes, sir,' O'Neill had agreed. He glanced at Mary, who gave an encouraging smile. 'Well, sir, me and the boys had a bit of a collection to help your marriage, sir, you and Mrs Windrush of course.'

'There's no need,' Jack had begun until Mary forestalled him by stepping forward.

'How delightful!' Mary had said. 'You are good men, all of you. Forgive me, Jack.' Without another word she planted a kiss on O'Neill's craggy face, following that by doing the same to each of the men. Jack watched in amazement as his bitter-eyed veterans responded with smiles, and even blushes.

'I'll never forget this,' Mary had said. 'Thank you, gentlemen.'

Elliot had marched up, caught Jack's eye and winked. 'I could not find a spare carriage,' he said. 'I'm sorry, Mrs Windrush. I had to get a native form of transport.'

'Oh, that's all right,' Mary had said. 'A bullock dak is fine by me.'

'There were no bullocks available,' Elliot had said. 'Forgive me.' Putting both fingers in his mouth, he gave a loud whistle.

Jack had not seen from where the elephant thundered. He only knew it was large and grey, with an elaborately decorated howdah. 'Well done, Arthur!'

With the grinning mahout dressed in splendid gold and red and tassels of the same colour swinging from the howdah, the elephant had been an impressive sight as it came to a halt in front of them. Mary's smile could not have been broader as the beast knelt down, to the cheers of O'Neill and the men of the 113th.

Feeling slightly self-conscious with so many people watching, Jack had helped his new wife into the howdah.

'General Baird supplied the elephant,' Elliot had said. 'That's the Rajah of Gondabad's general, in case you have forgotten.'

'My grandfather,' Jack had murmured. 'I'm hardly likely to forget.'

Elliot had nodded. 'The elephant will take you on a tour of the camp and city. It's not quite a carriage ride, I'm afraid, Mrs Windrush.'

'It's wonderful.' Mary had been nearly in tears with pleasure. 'Thank you, Arthur.'

'Thank you, Arthur,' Jack had echoed.

It had been strange to see Gondabad from the back of an elephant. It was not strange to have his new wife sitting opposite. Jack smiled across to her; it seemed perfectly natural to have Mary there, as if they had always belonged together and always would. There was no feeling of awkwardness, no embarrassment, just a sense of completion as if he had always known that Mary would come along, with his previous romantic encounters merely preparing him for the real thing. It had taken the blood and slaughter of the Mutiny to bring them together, so one good thing came out of that nightmare. Jack's eyes darkened for a moment, then he realised Mary was watching him and smiled. Pushing away the memories of the horrors the recent Mutiny had unleashed on India, Jack tried to contemplate the future.

With Mary being half-Indian, many regiments would not accept her in their Mess. Colonel Snodgrass of the 113th had given him an ultimatum: Mary or the regiment. Jack knew that by choosing Mary, he might have made himself an outcast, with his prospects of promotion blocked. He could be a captain forever, fortunate for any post that kept him from surviving on half pay in some dreary English coastal town.

'Jack?' Mary had leaned forward. 'We're here.'

The elephant had brought them back to their home, outside the lines of the 113th yet still within the British cantonment. Standing within its own grounds, the bungalow had no bad memories. It was a fresh start for their new life together.

'Come on, Mary.' Lifting her in both arms, Jack had carried her past the bewildered servants and over the threshold to deposit her on one of the broad wickerwork chairs. 'Welcome to our home, lady of the house.'

Mary had looked up at him, her eyes concerned. 'I hope you don't regret marrying me.'

'Don't be silly.' Jack had said with a grin. 'Anyway, it's too late now. There's no going back.' He gestured to the room next door. 'The wedding presents are in there. I suppose you want to wait a day or two before you look at them?' He grinned as Mary scampered across the floor.

Mary had no need to open Elliot's wedding present. The huge bed stood in the centre of the room. 'Oh.' She put a hand over her mouth.

'Well, even Arthur knows that we have to sleep somewhere,' Jack had said.

'It's a bit suggestive.' Mary had touched the carved footboard. 'I wonder where he got it.'

'He had it made especially for us,' Jack had said. 'What else is there?'

Smiling, Mary had turned to the large ivory chess set with its elephants and rajahs. 'That's unexpected. I did not know you were keen on chess, Jack.'

'That was Jayanti's chess set.' As the memories had rushed back, Jack pushed the set to one side. 'That should not be here. It's too soon.'

'Too soon?' A small frown had puckered Mary's forehead.

'I'll tell you sometime. What else can you find?'

With the colonel's displeasure hanging over them, the officers of the 113th had not been generous with their gifts. Mary sifted through the small pile of simple offerings. 'It was very good of them to give anything,' she said. 'They know what Colonel Snodgrass thinks of us.'

Jack grunted. 'We won't spoil the day by thinking of such things.'

'What's this?' Mary had walked to a chest that sat in the corner of the room. 'Is this yours? I haven't seen it before.'

'It's not mine.' Jack had guessed who it was from.

Heavily carved with elephants and monkeys, the chest was of teak, bound with brass. Turning the key in the lock, Mary had opened it and gasped. 'Who sent this?'

The chest was packed with clothes in the finest silk and cotton. Jack had stepped back as Mary lifted them out, one by one, exclaiming in wonder with each item.

'That should keep you going for a while,' Jack had said.

At the very bottom of the chest, the document had been folded into an oblong of parchment, yellowed with age and heavily sealed. Red ribbon crossed and re-crossed the parchment, enclosing a square of white paper with a short note in shaky handwriting.

'What's that?' Mary had taken her attention from the clothes long enough to glance at the document.

'I do not know.' Jack had read the note and handed it over. 'See what you think.'

'Dear Mary and Jack,' Mary had read. 'You know that I would have loved to attend your wedding, but circumstances did not allow. I do thank you for the very thoughtful invitation. As you know, I head the army of the Raja of Gondabad, a position which has a surfeit of prestige, but little in the way of portable remuneration.'

Mary had sighed. 'That means the rajah does not pay your grandfather very well,' she explained. 'Probably in case he returns Home.'

'Yes, Mary.' Jack had understood the letter when he read it. 'Carry on.'

'On the credit side, I have a fine group of women who are friendly with me.' Mary had frowned. 'Does that mean your grandfather has a harem?'

'I would think so,' Jack had said.

Mary had shaken her head. 'I would have thought he was a little old for that sort of thing.'

'I'll remind you of that when we are his age,' Jack had said.

Mary had lifted her eyebrows. 'I might hold you to that, Mister.'

'Each of my women has a clothing allowance, so it was an easy matter to obtain the enclosed for the use of Mary.'

Mary had lifted the clothes again. 'So these are clothes from a harem.' Her voice was thick with disapproval.

'Quality clothes from my grandfather,' Jack had said.

'I'm at the final two paragraphs.' Even as she read, Mary had not relinquished hold of the clothing. 'You will see that I have sealed the attached document. I have put it in your case and ask you not to open it until the event of my death. My days on this earth have been full, and it cannot be long before they come to an end. I will meet my Maker in a much happier frame of mind knowing that my only grandson has had the sense to marry such a beautiful lady as you, Mary.

I close this missive with the assurance of all the love I am capable of giving, and my blessings for a long, happy and fruitful marriage.

Yours aye

Jack Baird, Major, Bengal Fusiliers,

General, the Rajah of Gondabad's army.'

Mary's hand had shaken as she read the letter a second time and then lifted the sealed document. 'Should we open it?'

'No.' Jack had shaken his head. He took the parchment away. 'It will be the general's will and testament. We will honour his desire.'

Mary had snapped shut the chest. 'As you wish, Jack. There is also this.' She lifted the packet that O'Neill had handed over in the church.

'This means a lot to me.' Jack had lifted the packet. 'These men only get paid one shilling and a penny a week, and they have so many stoppages it's amazing they have anything left, let alone a surplus to raise money for us.'

'They have good hearts,' Mary had said. 'Rough tongues but good hearts.'

'They can have.' Jack had thought of all the dangers he had faced with the 113th. At that moment he despised the class system and the innate snobbery of Colonel Snodgrass and his kind. He handed over the sealed packet to Mary. 'You open it, Mary. They meant it for you anyway.'

'I feel guilty taking the men's money.' Mary had broken the simple seal. 'The parable of the widow's mite comes to mind.' She emptied the contents onto the table.

Half a dozen silver coins had clattered out, with three golden sovereigns and a thumb-nail sized packet.

'That's a lot of money from the men.' Jack had read the writing on the final packet. 'This has your name on it.'

'I'll open it later.' Mary had tucked it away inside her pocketbook. 'We have other things to do.'

'What's that?' Jack had asked.

'It's our wedding night.' Mary had extended her hand. 'And we have Arthur's bed to test out. Come with me, husband.'

* * *

Jack jerked back to the present. Marriage had undoubtedly hindered his advancement. When the war in China had broken out, Jack had applied to go, for success in active service was the best step towards promotion. With the troops sent from India, Sir Colin Campbell, now elevated to the peerage as Lord Clyde, chose the staff officers.

Jack's hopes had risen when Lord Clyde had sent for him.

'I know you, Windrush,' Lord Clyde had said, glowering through his crinkled, kindly face. 'You are a fair officer. Why the devil did you get married?'

'Because I fell in love, sir.'

'Hmm.' Lord Clyde surveyed Jack from under his bushy eyebrows. 'Well, congratulations on your marriage, Windrush. Permission to join the Chinese expedition withheld.'

'Sir?'

'I said permission withheld, Windrush. I'm not going to deny Mrs Windrush the pleasure of your company so soon after your wedding. I'll give the poor woman some happiness; God knows there are enough departures and loneliness in the life of a soldier's wife.'

Aye, Jack thought, *trust kind-hearted old Sir Colin to think of the women as well as the men. He is a one-off, is Sir Colin, but he has not done my career much good. I could have been a major by now if things had gone well in China. There is a lot of truth in the saying that marriage is ruinous to the prospects of a young officer. What was the mantra? A subaltern cannot marry, a lieutenant must not marry, a captain should not marry, a major may marry, and a colonel must marry. Well, I married as a captain, and my career has stalled as a result.*

'Jack?' Mary noticed his preoccupation. 'Are you all right?'

'Never better,' he said truthfully. He looked at Mary. He did not regret his decision. Lighting another cheroot, Jack discarded the memories and handed the cheroot to his wife. 'I have spent sufficient time being a glorified clerk. I am not suited to pushing papers around.'

'What's in your mind, Jack?' Mary puffed on Jack's cheroot.

'One of two things.' Jack leaned forward in his chair. 'Either I take the leave I'm due, or I look for a vacancy in a regiment, either British or one of the native pultans. The latter surely won't object to me having a half-Indian wife.'

'Why not do both?' Mary said.

'I could,' Jack mused. 'How do you fancy a trip Home? I could show you Wychwood Manor, London, Bath, maybe travel up to Scotland to see all the places Sir Walter Scott wrote about. When we're over there, I can visit Horse Guards and see about transferring.'

'I'd love to see Home,' Mary said.

'Good.' Jack kissed her on the forehead. 'I'll speak to Colonel Hook tomorrow.' He leaned back. He felt as if this peaceful chapter of his life was about to end. He had enjoyed his time with Mary but knew that it was false; something was missing. He had been waiting for his career to begin again.

Chapter Two

Gondabad, India July 1863

'Ah, Windrush!' Lieutenant-Colonel Hook marched forward with his hand extended, his hair still unfashionably long but his face remarkably unlined. 'I was about to send for you. I need your services for something more interesting than administration.'

'Yes, sir.' Jack saw his hopes of home leave begin to fade. 'What's happened, sir?'

'Now.' Hook perched on the edge of the table, sipping at a glass of brandy. He continued as if Jack had never spoken. 'You'll be wondering what this is all about, Windrush.'

'I am, sir.' Jack glanced around. Hook had taken up his quarters in the great fort of Gondabad, where the Rajah had become a staunch ally of Britain since the failure of the Mutiny. The room was empty except for the desk, a small, glass-fronted drinks cabinet, two deep leather armchairs, and what looked like a couple of brass-bound arms chests. A large map of North West India covered one wall, with handwritten annotations in various places.

'You'll find out in a minute or two.' Hook looked no older than he had when Jack had first met him. 'Ah, here he comes now.'

A short, heavily bearded major entered behind Jack.

'Ah, Kerr, do you know Windrush?'

'No, sir.' The major nodded to Jack.

Hook made the introductions. 'Major Kerr of the Guides, meet Captain Windrush, late of the 113th, now working for me. For the past few years, Kerr, Windrush has been busy reorganising India under the Queen's, rather than the Company's, rule.'

Standing with his back to the door, Kerr looked anything but impressed. His eyes bored into Jack with the intensity of gimlets.

Hook put down his brandy. 'Now I have another task for you, Windrush. One perhaps more fitted to your peculiar talents.'

Glancing at Kerr, Jack took a deep breath. He had promised Mary he would mention home leave to Hook. 'I am due home leave, sir.'

'I am aware of that,' Hook said. 'I'm afraid you'll have to wait. Duty comes first. Mary will understand.'

Jack nodded. He knew that Mary would understand, but that did not mean he wished to disappoint her. He hoped that Colonel Hook's task, whatever it was, would not take too long.

Hook stood up. 'The job I have in mind may be more important than any military post you have ever held, however distinguished your service may have been.'

'What is this job, sir?' Jack was acutely aware that the silent Kerr was listening to every word.

'I'll come back to that in a minute, Windrush. You know the northern Indian plains as well as any officer of your rank. How well do you know the North West Frontier?'

'Not at all, sir.' Jack looked past Hook to the giant map that was spread across the wall. Most of the annotations were along the North West. He wondered what they signified.

'Have you ever read Clausewitz, Windrush?'

'Yes, sir.' As a young ensign, Jack had striven to learn all he could about military theory. The book *On War* by the Prussian Carl Von Clausewitz had introduced him to the moral and political aspects of warfare. A decade of the reality, peppered by three wars and five savage campaigns, had taught him that theory and reality did not often coincide.

Hook grunted. He was not used to young officers who had spent time reading books. 'You'll be familiar with Clausewitz's phrase: "War is an act of violence pursued to the utmost."'

'Yes, sir.'

'Could you describe that, Windrush?'

Jack blinked. 'I am not sure what you mean, sir.'

'Could you describe an act of violence pursued to the utmost?' Hook sipped again at his brandy.

Jack considered for a minute. 'I presume Clausewitz was referring to a battle, sir.'

'What would you think of a people – and I choose that term carefully – what would you think of a people whose entire culture is based around violence? What would you think of a people who have resisted invasion for not hundreds but thousands of years, who have never been completely conquered, and who control the gateway to India?'

'They must be an impressive people, sir.' Jack felt Kerr stir behind him.

'They have been called many things, Windrush, usually by their enemies. They are a Semitic people, more devoutly Muslim than the Crusaders were Christian. They speak Pushtu, and we know them as Pathans, Paythans, Pakhtuns or Pashtuns.' Hook's smile should have acted as a warning to Jack. 'You are going to get to know them very well.'

Jack had already guessed that. 'Yes, sir.'

'Pour yourself a drink, sit back, and let me educate you,' Hook said. 'Major Kerr, please be seated and join in whenever you wish.'

'Whisky for me, sir, please.' Jack chose a Glenfiddich before he settled into one of the armchairs.

'Good choice,' Hook approved. 'Glenfiddich is her Majesty's tipple, I believe. Now, let me take you back in time a couple of hundred years or more to when the British first came to this land. We came as traders to Madras, Calcutta and Surat.'

Jack nodded. His family had been involved with India for generations.

'When the major local power, the Moghul Empire, gradually disintegrated, other Indian states rose in importance, some friendly to us, some friendly to our trade rivals, the French, some not caring about either, and everybody out for what they could get.' Hook paused, presumably to see how Jack was accepting his version of Indian history.

Jack nodded, wordless.

Hook continued. 'With so many rival states marching and countermarching their armies across India, Britain, or rather the Honourable East India Company, needed to protect their trading posts. The Company recruited local forces, well, you know the pattern. What had begun as a simple trading operation ended up in one of the most successful companies in the world. Our often less-than-Honourable Company expanded to control much of the Indian sub-continent. The Company's final war of expansion was against the Sikhs, which brought Company rule to this point here.'

For the first time, Hook stepped to the map of India. Lifting a pointer, he stroked it down the northwest of the sub-continent. 'Now that the Company has gone and the Crown has taken over India, the British Army is responsible for this North West Frontier.'

Jack felt a shiver run through him. The name seemed redolent of an ending, as if the ancient civilisations of India stopped at that frontier, and something much wilder, something dangerously untamed, began.

Hook tapped the map with his pointer. 'Here we have hundreds of miles of mountains, from beyond the Khyber Pass in the north to Baluchistan and the Bolan Pass in the south.' Hook stopped, ostensibly to sip at his brandy, but Jack suspected more likely for dramatic effect.

Jack stepped forward to examine the map. Although he had been born in India and Indian blood flowed through his veins, he had never served west of the Indus. The North West Frontier was unknown to him. 'It looks like an interesting area, sir.'

'These mountains are bleak beyond your imaginings, Windrush, with some of the wildest, most independent-minded, intractable people in the world.' Hook leaned back in his chair. 'It is certainly the most dangerous frontier of the Empire; it is arguably the most dangerous in the world.'

'Yes, sir.'

'It is a land of savage, bare mountains interspaced with narrow passes, like sabre slashes between high peaks. It has some green, beautiful valleys but more often is stark and bare beyond description, tormented by dust storms, bitter cold with snow in winter, scorched by the sun in summer.' Lifting his pointer, Hook pushed Jack out of the way and indicated the map. 'There are avenues into this area. We have the Kabul River, the Khyber Pass, the Kurrum River, the Tochi River, the Gomal River, and the Bolan. As a student of military history, which you are, Windrush, you will be aware that a British Army came badly unstuck in these passes back in '41.'

'I have heard of General Elphinstone's misfortune, sir.'

'Bear it in mind. It was undoubtedly the worst defeat the British Army has ever suffered in the East.' Hook continued his lecture. 'There are fertile valleys where crops are grown, there are fast-running rivers, there are ancient forts, hill villages, and there are the Pashtuns.' He looked up then, catching Jack's gaze. 'I believe you have a little experience of these gentlemen.'

'Yes, sir. A Pathan, sorry, a Pashtun named Batoor helped me during our last campaign in the Mutiny. I was glad he was on our side and not against us.'

Hook gave an enigmatic smile. 'The Pashtuns are the most obliging fellows imaginable, as long as it suits them. I am not sure if the Pashtuns are ever on anybody's side except their own. It might have happened that his needs coincided with yours on that occasion.'

'I believe that was the case, sir,' Jack agreed.

'Let's talk about these people.' Hook spoke so casually that Jack knew he was hiding something. 'The Pashtuns occupy a large area between British India and the independent nation of Afghanistan, spilling into both territories. They are divided into tribes who are as often as not mutually hostile, rather like the Scottish Highland clans or even more like the old reiving families of the Scottish-English Border. If you have read your Walter Scott, you'll know what I mean.'

'I am working my way through Scott's novels, sir, when I have free time.'

Hook gave a bleak smile. 'I am sure that Mary will guide you there.'

'Yes, sir.'

'Back to the Pashtuns,' Hook said. 'From the north, we have the Yusufzai, then the Mamunds, the Mohmand, the Afridi, the Waziri, and the Mahsud and Baluchis, who are slightly different but associated.'

Jack listened, wishing he had thought to bring a notepad and pencil. He guessed that such information was going to be important.

'Each tribe is divided into sub-tribes, which for the sake of clarity I will call clans. For example, the Yusufzai have the Bunerwals, the Ado Khel, the Babuzai, the Hassanzai, and many others. Often the clans are further split into family units. Do you get the idea?'

Jack nodded. 'Yes, sir.' He heard Kerr shift behind him.

Hook sipped at his brandy before continuing. 'Throughout history, the Pashtuns have existed, never thrived, by being semi-nomads, trying to farm their thin soil, grazing livestock in summer and raiding the richer plains of India to the East. The men are brought up to robbery, fighting and feuding; I'll come to that later.'

Jack nodded. No British soldier serving in India could fail to hear about the tribes of the North West Frontier.

'If the Pashtun families fall out, they live by the blood feud, again like the Scottish clans or Border reiving families.' Hook refilled his glass, offered Jack more whisky, and nodded when Jack refused. 'Very wise. You'll need all your faculties where I am sending you.'

'I gather that I'm going to the Frontier, sir.'

'Don't jump the gun, Windrush.' Hook sipped at his brandy again. 'The Pashtuns are adept at using their jezzails, their long muskets, as our men will all testify to. They live by Pakhtunwali, the way of the Pashtuns, and are dedicated to Islam.'

'Yes, sir.' Jack was beginning to feel as if he sat in a lecture theatre.

'Have you heard of the Five Pillars of Islam, Windrush?' Hook asked.

'I have, sir,' Jack said.

'Good. What are they?'

Jack had expected the question. 'They are: shahada, which is faith, salah or prayer, zakat or charity, sawm or fasting, and hajj, where every follower of Islam should endeavour to make the pilgrimage to Mecca at least once in his life.'

'Good man.' Hook approved. 'Well, there is an unofficial sixth to which the Pashtun can become addicted. That is Jihad: Holy War. It is a concept that sits on their shoulder at all times.'

'They sound like a formidable if quarrelsome people, sir. Yet I rather liked Batoor, the Pashtun I worked with.'

'I respect them beyond all other peoples I have ever met, Windrush, except perhaps the Sikhs. They have no mercy to the loser, offer hospitality to any traveller, follow blood feuds to the death, and keep their code. If you have a Pashtun for a friend, you have a friend for life, or until he decides otherwise.' Hook finished his brandy, looked at the decanter, shook his head in sorrow, and pushed it away. 'Now, you will be wondering what all this has to do with you.'

'I am, sir.'

'Open that first case.' Hook indicated the brass-bound case that sat on the floor.

The padlock was already open. The case contained a dozen Enfield rifles.

'Enfields, sir.'

'Exactly what we don't wish the Pashtun to own. Our patrols have been picking them up the length and breadth of the frontier; the Ghilzais of the Kurrum Valley, the Afridis of the Khyber, the Mohmands, and even the Bunerwals, who are a fairly peaceful tribe, by Frontier standards. In fact, they think themselves superior to all others, being religious and surprisingly honest.'

'Do we know how the Pashtuns are getting these weapons, sir?'

'No, Windrush.' Hook shook his head. 'We all know that the tribesmen are amongst the greatest thieves in the world. They can take a rifle from a man's hands while he is asleep, but that would only account for a few weapons. We have found dozens of these Enfields.'

'It's a bit worrying, sir.' Jack knew that the British Army had dominance over the native armies they had met through three things: discipline, strong leadership, and more modern arms and tactics. The wars with the Sikhs had been amongst the hardest fought in India because the Sikh Khalsa had both discipline and modern weapons. If they'd had better leadership, the wars could have taken quite another turn. The Pashtun had a plethora of capable commanders; with modern weapons, they represented a significant threat to the security of North West India.

'It is worrying,' Hook agreed. 'I've put notice out to all our political agents, the men who live with the tribes, to look out for these rifles. I have also sent a few trusted men into Pakhtunkhwa, tribal territory, to see what they can find.'

'To let you understand,' Hook pressed his point, 'some of our sepoy battalions still carry the Brunswick Rifle, which has a range of 250 yards. The Pashtuns' normal firearm is the locally manufactured jezzail, with a range of up to 400 yards. Our Enfield is sighted to over a thousand yards.'

'There was a problem with the cartridges, sir,' Jack reminded him.

'There was a problem with the grease that coated the cartridges,' Hook corrected. 'The sepoys believed the paper cartridges were coated with pig and cow fat, which was abhorrent to their religion. Now the cartridges are coated with *ghee*, butter, so are quite acceptable. However, that is not your problem.'

'Yes, sir.' Jack waited to find out his fate.

'I have an important role for you, Windrush.' Hook offered Jack a cheroot.

'Thank you, sir.' *Sugar to sweeten bitter medicine*, Jack thought. *I hope Mary is alright when she hears my leave is indefinitely postponed.*

'How are your language lessons coming along?' Hook's smile appeared genuine.

'Not bad, sir. I've had plenty of practice in Hindi, and my Pushtu is passable. Not so great in Persian.'

'Good man. You'll need all three.' Hook drew on his cheroot. 'Concentrate on Pushtu just now, Windrush, because you're going to the Frontier.'

'Yes, sir.' All prospect of going Home disappeared.

'I want you to find out where these Enfields are coming from. Do we have a rogue supplier in Britain? Do we have a gun runner on the Frontier? Or is there a regiment somewhere with a quartermaster who is storing up his pennies for a comfortable retirement, based on the blood of British soldiers and Indian civilians?'

'I'll see what I can do, sir.'

'Up to this point, Windrush, you have worked nearly exclusively with British infantry. Well,' Hook said and smiled, blowing smoke into the air, 'Major Kerr will introduce you to the Guides. You'll no longer be plodding along at the pace of a snail; you will be with the cream of the Indian Army, and that means you will be working with the best soldiers in the world. Is that not so, Kerr?'

'We like to think so, sir,' Kerr said. His accent was pure Ulster. 'We have the best soldiers. We need the best officers to command them. Not all make the grade.'

Is that a warning? Or a challenge?

'All right. Windrush, report to Major Kerr in Peshawar as soon as you can.'

'Yes, sir.' Windrush glanced at Kerr, who responded with a cold nod.

'Oh, there is one more thing, Windrush.' When Hook spoke in that casual tone, Jack knew that he was about to introduce something particularly unpleasant. 'Some of the Pashtuns who have been active against our men were wearing these on their right arms.' Opening the top drawer of his desk, Hook lifted a twisted red cord, which he dropped into Windrush's extended hand. 'Do you know what it is?'

Jack's mind leapt back to the advance on Bareilly during the Mutiny, when hundreds of swordsmen in green cummerbunds had charged at them. The swordsmen had broken the redoubtable 4th Punjab rifles before the 42nd and 113th had mown them down. Each swordsman had worn such a red cord.

'It's the mark of a Ghazi, sir, a fanatical Muslim fighter.'

'The Warriors of God,' Hook said softly. 'Warriors with modern weapons.' Something in his voice sent shivers down Windrush's spine.

'I'll watch out for them,' Jack promised.

'Well, the best of luck to you, Windrush.' Hook held out his hand. 'You'll be glad to be doing something active after so much desk work.'

As Jack left the room, he thought of Mary, sitting in their bungalow full of hope for their leave back Home.

Chapter Three

Peshawar July 1863

Peshawar. The last city before the Frontier and the final outpost of British rule; East of Peshawar stretched the hot Indian plains; West of Peshawar spread some of the most dangerous territory on the face of the Earth. The very name meant Frontier Town.

Jack reined up Colwall, his brown gelding, to survey the city. Allowing the dust of his passage to settle, he watched as a long caravan of camels plodded majestically out of the city gate. The caravan headed into India, with the camel bells tinkling, and the merchants eyeing Windrush with bold curiosity. If this had been India proper, Jack would have expected a salaam or two, an obsequious greeting. Here, so close to the Frontier, such things did not happen. These men were not inclined to be servile to anybody, much less a lone British officer travelling without a single servant.

As the caravan passed in choking dust, Windrush looked at Peshawar. Set in the fertile Vale of Peshawar with its orchards of plum, apple, peach and pear trees, its canals and its gardens, Peshawar had a wall some five miles long to protect it from the predators of the surrounding mountains. Jack was immediately aware of the aura of menace. Even the names were harsh. The range to the north was the Hindu Kush, the killer of Hindus, allegedly named for the thousands of Indians who had died on the passage west as captured slaves of Islamic conquerors. From Peshawar the road stretched westward to the Khyber Pass, built by the Mughal Babur, who had conquered northern India, updated only a few years previously by Lieutenant Alexander Taylor. That was the road of merchants, holy men, poets and conquerors. Beyond the Khyber was Kandahar, Kabul, and all of Afghanistan.

'Let's get on, boy,' Jack whispered to Colwall. He passed through the Lahori Gate with the atmosphere closing about him and the heat punishing as it rebounded from the pukka-brick walls of the houses. Three storeys high, with the lowest storey used as a shop, the building created channels of streets crowded with traders and women, beggars and water carriers. Jack pushed through, noting everything he could. He saw tall, rangy hill men in hairy poshteens with long jezzails slung across their backs. He saw clean-shaven Hazaurehs with conical hats, a handful of burqa-clad women, and a single patrol of sweating British soldiers in red serge tunics and a more wary air than Jack had experienced since the end of the Mutiny.

Hailing the officer who commanded the patrol, Jack enquired for the address Hook had given him.

'Just outside the Bala Hissar.' The lieutenant's eyes were never still, inspecting every man that passed. 'There is a Guide on duty outside.'

'Thank you, Lieutenant.'

'Are you new to the Frontier, Captain?'

'Is it that obvious?'

'Yes, Captain, with all due respect.' The lieutenant glanced over his shoulder as somebody shouted. One of his men shifted his rifle to the ready position until the sergeant snarled at him. 'British soldiers are not always made welcome here. Sometimes it's not best to travel alone.'

'I know India, if not the Frontier,' Windrush said. 'I am not a Griffin.' A Griffin was a man new to the East.

'Yes, Captain.' The lieutenant did not press the subject. 'Peshawar is not quite India, but the best of luck, Captain.' The patrol walked warily, the rear marker turning every few steps to check behind him. Jack watched them for a moment and then walked deeper into the city.

Jack saw the sentry standing at attention. He wore the khaki uniform of the Guides, with a blue turban, and did not move when Jack approached.

'I am Captain Jack Windrush. Is the sahib in?' Jack asked.

'Yes, sahib.' The Guide remained at his post, his face impassive.

'I wish to see him.'

'Kerr sahib may not wish to see you.' The Guide appeared less than impressed with Windrush's travel-battered uniform.

'Please tell him I am here.'

Without moving, the Guide bellowed something, and a young servant appeared at his elbow.

'Please tell Kerr Sahib that a Captain Windrush sahib is here,' Jack said.

Within a minute the young servant was back. He salaamed. 'Kerr Sahib will see you, Captain Windrush, sahib.'

The Guide edged aside to allow Jack bare access to the two-storey house.

'You made it then, Windrush?' Major Kerr surveyed Windrush through the hardest eyes Jack had ever seen.

'Yes, Major.'

'Don't Major me, off duty, Windrush. I'm Kerr.' The handshake was firm as Kerr's glance took in Windrush from his forage cap with the havelock to protect his neck to the dust on his boots. 'My boys will take care of your horse. How do you like Peshawar?'

'It's unlike any other city I've been in,' Jack said. 'Your guard at the gate was not keen to let me in. I am used to having sepoys jump to attention at even the sight of me.'

Kerr nodded. 'He is an Afridi, as different to the normal sepoy as a mountain is to a hill. You have to earn the respect of an Afridi. Have you had any dealings with them before?'

Jack thought of Batoor. 'I knew one Afridi very well.'

Kerr's level gaze did not falter. 'In that case, you will know that they are not a people to take lightly.'

'I found that out.'

'Do you know why Colonel Hook sent you here?' Kerr stood four-square in the centre of the room.

'Gun running, Major.' Jack did not remind Kerr he had been present at the interview.

'That is part of it,' Kerr said, 'and only for the servants. Anything said in Gondabad will be repeated in Kabul before the echo dies, and probably St Petersburg and Washington I shouldn't wonder.'

Jack waited.

'This is the Frontier, Windrush; there is always trouble brewing here.' Kerr walked to the window, which afforded him a fine view over Peshawar and to the west. 'You're going to be working for me out there.' He nodded towards the hills. 'I will warn you that it is the most dangerous posting in the British Empire. You will face extreme heat and chilling cold; you will be up against an enemy that can be your friend one minute and an enemy the next, with no thought of mercy or pity. If you are captured, they will certainly kill you and most probably torture you in ways so hideous even the thought will make your skin crawl.'

'Yes, Major,' Jack said.

'Do you now wish you had remained with the 113th?' Kerr asked.

Jack's anger was beginning to rise at this bitter-eyed major. 'Duty is duty, Kerr. Danger is part of the soldier's bargain.'

Kerr grunted. 'We will see if you still think that in six months if you are still alive.'

'I'll do my best to live,' Jack said.

'I have arranged for you to be temporarily transferred to the Guides.' Kerr's gaze never left Jack's face. 'If I feel, even for an instant, that you will disgrace the regiment or put any of my men in danger, I will send you back to Hook.'

'As you wish.' Jack was not offended at the suggested slight; he knew how protective good officers could be of their men.

'Are you wishing you could strike me?' Kerr's question took Jack by surprise. 'Come, man. Be honest! We have no room for fabrications in the Guides!'

'You are my superior officer, Kerr,' Jack said.

'If I were not your superior officer?' Kerr asked.

'In that case, the situation would not have arisen.'

When Kerr stepped abruptly forward, Jack put himself in a position of defence.

'Ah! So you are ready to fight me!' Kerr's grin further unbalanced Jack. 'Can you shoe a horse?'

'Major?' Jack did not hide his confusion.

'Can you shoe a horse? Come, man, it's a simple enough question. Well?'

'Yes, Kerr. I can,' Jack said.

'Good man. In the Guides, you will have to be more independent than in the Queen's regiments.' Kerr sat down, offering a cheroot. 'That's why I picked you. You have a reputation for operating with small, hard-hitting units. You are an unconventional officer, Windrush.'

'Yes, Kerr. I had not realised that you picked me.'

'I was looking for an officer who is not scared to operate outside the regimental system,' Kerr said. 'Colonel Hook made me aware of your exploits in the Crimea, and more recently in the Mutiny.'

'What am I to do?' Jack asked.

'I'll tell you en route to Hoti Mardan. I hope you are fit to travel. We don't count much on weariness in the Guides.' Kerr's eyes were still basilisk, but there was an underlying humour that Jack had not noticed before. 'Your horse has been fed and watered, so we will leave immediately.'

It was a forty-mile ride to Mardan, the headquarters of the Guides, with the sun hot above.

'You see, Windrush.' Kerr rode his horse as if he had been born to it, with an easy grace that ignored the miles. He spoke through the scarf that protected his mouth from the constant dust. 'We think there is something serious brewing on the Frontier, something much more dangerous than the usual raiding and feuding.'

'Why is that, Kerr?'

'When you've been out here for a few years, you get a feeling for that sort of thing.' Kerr lifted a hand to acknowledge two men with a string of camels. They met his eyes, tall, rangy men with twisted turbans on their heads. Both walked with long, lifting strides that covered the ground without apparent effort. One had a jezzail strapped across his back, the other a Minie rifle that could only have come from a British soldier, alive or dead.

'Have you heard about the Hindustani Fanatics?' Kerr asked.

'Only vague rumours,' Jack said.

'Forget the rumours,' Kerr said. 'They are as desperate a threat as we have faced since the Mutiny. We know them as the Hindustani Fanatics, while the Muhammadans call them the Mujahidin, the Warriors of God.'

'That's an interesting name.' Jack remembered that Hook had used the same phrase.

'You might know them better as Ghazis.'

'I've met them.' Jack mentioned the fight outside Bareilly as Kerr listened, nodding.

'Pray to the Lord you never meet them again,' Kerr said. 'Now imagine the Pashtuns joining the Ghazis. What a ferocious combination that would be.'

Jack watched a family group pass by. The men stared through kohl-rimmed eyes, each with a jezzail on his back and a ferocious Khyber knife at his belt. The women wore the long burqas that hid them entirely from view, except for a slit around the eyes. Only the young pre-pubescent female children had their faces uncovered. They watched the two British horsemen with curious eyes and big smiles.

'I can see the dangers,' Jack said.

'I am going to give you a history lesson,' Kerr said. 'Listen carefully. Back in the 1820s, a Ghazi named Sayyid Ahmad visited Mecca; you are aware that visiting Mecca is one of the pillars of Islam.'

'I am,' Jack said.

'Good. Inspired by his visit, Sayyid Ahmad came to Pakhtunkhwa with about a hundred followers and began preaching holy war, a jihad, to the Yusufzai.' Kerr lifted his hand to a bullock cart before he continued. 'In the 1820s, you will remember, the Sikhs controlled all this area. We were not involved. Sayyid Ahmad gathered thousands of Pashtun tribesmen to his standard. He was able to push back the Sikhs, besiege and capture Peshawar.'

Jack looked around. The mountains surrounded them, seeming to dominate everything. 'The Sikhs would not be pleased.'

'They were not,' Kerr said. 'Can you think of two more dangerous people to cross swords than the Sikhs and the Pashtuns? The Sikhs waited for a couple of years then sent an army from Lahore. They recaptured Peshawar, killed Sayyid Ahmad and a thousand or so of his Ghazis, and chased the rest into the hills.'

Jack nodded to show he was still listening.

'Those Mujahidin that remained settled in a small village named Sitana, hard by the Mahabun Mountains, on the west bank of the Indus maybe seventy-five miles northwest of Peshawar.'

Kerr moved aside to allow a string of mules to file past, each one attached to the beast behind. The two mule drivers neither looked up nor acknowledged the British officers.

'We're not in the India I know now,' Jack said.

'It's better not to even think that you are,' Kerr said. 'This is Pakhtunkhwa. The British are merely the next wave of invaders. To continue with my history lesson: a follower of Sayyid Ahmad by the name of Sayyid Akbar Shah owned the village of Sitana. Within a short time, the number of Mujahidin swelled. They amused themselves by looting and raiding the more settled lands. By the time the British came to this area, these Mujahidin Ghazis were a damned nuisance.'

Jack nodded. After the battles of the Mutiny and the Crimea, the antics of a few hundred fanatics did not seem as dangerous to him as they did to Kerr.

Kerr noticed Jack's air of scepticism. 'In 1852, after we had defeated the Sikhs and annexed the Punjab, Colonel Mackeson took a force to the Sitana area, captured the Mujahidins' Fort Kotla and withdrew. Before the last British soldier had left, the fanatics returned to their raiding ways, kidnapping merchants for ransom and making a general nuisance of themselves. The Mutiny was a boom time for them as hundreds if not thousands of malcontents joined them.'

'Were these new recruits defeated Mutineers?' Jack asked.

'Possibly, or just the usual ragtag and bobtail that wars throw up.'

Jack nodded as Kerr continued his story. 'With the end of the Mutiny we had time to sort them out again, and in 1858 Sir Sydney Cotton led five thousand men to scatter the Mujahidin. They ran to Malka, which is on the north of the Mahabun Mountains.'

'Are they still there?' Jack asked.

'The Mujahidin have reorganised once more,' Kerr said. 'Now they are infesting a mountain at Siri. We are at present blockading the tribes that allowed them to pass through their lands.' Kerr reined up. 'That's where you come in, Windrush.'

The hills were closer now, frowning upon them, seeming to listen to everything they said.

'What am I doing, Kerr?'

'There is an Afridi clan we know as the Rahmut Khel not too far from the Khyber. We know that they have a new Khan, a new leader; we don't know who he is. We think that the Rahmut Khel have allowed these Mujahidin through their lands.'

'I see.' Jack nodded.

'You are taking a patrol to the new Khan of the Rahmut Khel, Windrush, and you are going to persuade him not to allow these fanatics through his territory. While you are there, search for any sign of gunrunners.'

Jack nodded. 'Yes, Kerr.' He was back in the saddle again, going into the heart of Pakhtunkhwa to see an unknown Pashtun Khan. Mary and the prospect of Home leave seemed very far away.

Chapter Four

Mardan, India, July 1863

Jack was unsure what to expect at Hoti Mardan, the headquarters of the famous Guides. His first view of the squat, star-shaped fort that sat on the Yusufzai Plain was not inspiring. Shimmering under the frontier heat, it was functional rather than dramatic. A score of Guides infantry drilled on the *maidan* in front of the gate, marching back and forth with their khaki smocks and pyjama trousers looking slightly shabby, while their khaki turbans were untidy. The jemadar in charge was screaming at them in Pushtu, the words very similar to those any British sergeant would use to a platoon of privates.

The infantry stepped aside to allow a patrol of cavalry to return from the hills, indigo-blue turbans bobbing above horses that seemed better cared for than the riders. The men were handy enough, Jack allowed, remembering the British cavalry he had seen in the Crimea.

After they had eaten, Kerr showed Jack to his quarters, a tiny cubicle within the walls of Mardan, with an orderly with a face like Satan to cater for him.

'Early reveille tomorrow,' Kerr said. 'Hassan will look after you.'

Hassan glowered at Jack through narrow eyes.

'I'll be all right,' Jack dismissed him.

Grunting something that might have been a curse or a blessing, Hassan withdrew, leaving Jack alone with Kerr. 'One thing, Kerr,' Jack said.

'Do my men know how to fire Enfields? I want the best available if we are to go into Afridi country.'

'They will carry Enfields,' Kerr promised. 'And bayonets as well as their favoured sidearm.'

With his head spinning from days of travel, Jack barely undressed before throwing himself on his charpoy. The Pashtun voices seemed alien, with high-pitched laughter echoing around the fort. Although Jack had lived in India for six years, he was used to a British cantonment with British voices around him. He felt slightly uncomfortable spending the night surrounded by armed Pashtuns, whatever the colour of their uniforms.

Well, Mary, here we go again. Jack unpacked the Bible that Mary had handed him before he left Gondabad. *Once this mission is over, I will apply for leave and show you Home.* The thought of the soft green Malvern Hills brought a wistful smile. Jack shook his head, wishing that he was back with Mary.

Marriage has softened you, he told himself, placing his revolver under the pillow. He was sleeping before he closed his eyes.

* * *

Kerr inspected the men who were lined up outside the walls of Mardan. They stared back impassively, tall, bearded men with narrow eyes who looked capable of anything from murder to storming the Redan.

'Captain Windrush is going up the Khyber. Hassan is going with him.'

Jack tried to read the expression in Hassan's face. It was a mixture of disgust and resignation. *Now there's a man I will not trust.*

'I want another five volunteers. That's you, Zaman, Sawan, Ursulla, Fatteh and Alladad.'

All willing volunteers then, Jack thought. The names meant nothing to him.

'The rest of you, dismiss,' Kerr said.

The six picked men remained standing. They returned Jack's scrutiny, no doubt wondering who this officer was and why he was taking them into hostile territory when there were experienced Guides officers who could do the same job.

'Say a few words,' Kerr ordered. 'Let them hear your voice.'

'Well volunteered, men,' Jack said. 'I have heard good things about the Guides.' There was no reaction from the men. They stared at him, stone-faced. 'I'll soon see how good you are.' Still no reaction. 'We are going to Torkrud to speak to the Rahmut Khel.'

One man started at that.

'That troubles you, I see.' Jack focussed on the man. He was in his mid to late twenties, he judged, with a neat beard and bright brown eyes.

'I may not be welcome at Torkrud,' the man said.

'Why is that, Zaman?' Kerr was frowning.

'It is a family matter.' Zaman clamped shut his mouth. 'It is nothing.'

Kerr's frown deepened. 'I take it you have cut the wrong throat or slept with the wrong woman, Zaman.'

'It is of no importance,' Zaman said.

'I could leave you behind,' Jack offered. 'Many men would be willing to take your place.'

'No, sahib.' Zaman shook his head. 'It was Allah's will that Major Kerr sahib volunteered me.'

'Good man, Zaman,' Kerr said. 'You are a soldier of the queen and a trooper of the Guides. If anybody attacks you, they attack all of us.'

That might not be much consolation to Zaman if he is killed, Jack thought. *I'll keep an eye on that man.* This expedition showed signs of having as many complications as any other he had been on. All the same, Jack could not deny his tingle of excitement. He had lived all his life to be a soldier; maybe it was this thrill he had missed while enjoying the ease of married life.

'Hassan,' Kerr said. 'I've promoted you to daffadar.'

Although Hassan nodded, Jack was not sure if he looked pleased or not.

'Look after Windrush sahib,' Kerr said. 'He is not used to our ways yet.'

'Yes, Kerr sahib.' Hassan's glance at Windrush may have been meaningful or merely instinctive. Jack fought back his irritation. It was unusual for a major to ask a daffadar, the equivalent of a corporal, to look after an officer of Jack's experience, but the Guides were a unique formation.

'Captain Windrush.' Kerr dropped his voice. 'I've known Hassan for years. I would advise you to be guided by him. He knows the Frontier far better than you and I. Even if you don't agree with his advice, or it goes against the grain, trust him.'

Jack nodded. 'I will remember that, Major.'

'Good luck, gentlemen.' Kerr raised his voice again. 'May Allah guide you.'

That was the first time that Jack had heard a British officer say such a thing. He could only nod in return, check each man's equipment, and ensure they had food, water and ammunition for the expedition ahead.

* * *

They rode out of Mardan in the black of the pre-dawn with the air brisk and the horses lively beneath them. Jack looked over his men. He was unsure if Kerr had chosen them as willing volunteers or they had grudgingly accepted him. Either way, the die had been thrown; they were stuck with each other. Jack wondered if the evil-looking Hassan could be trusted and what secret Zaman was hiding. Moonlight glinted on the bugle that bounced at Fatteh's thigh. Jack grinned. *I wonder how Fatteh can use that with only half a dozen troopers? He must be proud of his position to display his bugle so prominently.*

Even a mile from Mardan, the tension was tangible. Jack felt as though the very air was electric, brittle with suspense. His Guides rode quietly, without the subdued chatter he would have expected from a similar patrol of British soldiers. Glancing over his shoulder, he saw that each man was alert, with their heads up and eyes never still as they constantly examined their surroundings.

Jack touched a hand to the butt of his revolver then checked the hilt of his sword. Although India was at peace since the repression of the Mutiny, he felt very much that he was on active service. Peace was relative on the Frontier.

They entered the Khyber exactly as the dawn rose angry-red in the east, tinging the harsh mountains to the colour of dark blood. Immediately, Jack felt the atmosphere alter once more. The air seemed harder, the Guides waiting for something to happen.

I have left India far behind now, Jack thought. *This is a different world to the sultry heat of my homeland.* He felt the tension in his men. They rode more alert, spread out slightly, and kept their rifles handy. Even the steady clump-clump of their horses' hooves seemed to echo, mocking their progress, while the vultures that circled above were hardly reassuring.

The road ascended, twisting in front of them. As the sun rose, the heights on either side became clearer, gaunt, dark-shadowed, like the bones of the earth shed of all flesh.

'When Allah made the world,' Hassan murmured in his ear, 'He had a pile of rocks left. "What shall I do with these?" he asked himself and fashioned them into Afghanistan, with Pakhtunkhwa as the remnants.'

Jack smiled. 'Is Afghanistan your country?'

'No, sahib. It is Pakhtunkhwa, the land of the Pashtun, who are watching us now.'

Jack peered into the dark. 'I can't see them.'

'No, sahib,' Hassan said. 'But they can see us.' He touched the lock of his Enfield. 'Although the British pay tribute to the tribes, a wayward youth may still take a shot at a British soldier just for *shikar*, for sport, or an old man to recall the pleasures of his youth.'

A string of camels passed them, walking toward India with the camel bells tinkling musically.

'*Salaam Alaikum* – greetings, good day,' the camel driver said with his gaze level with Jack's.

'*Salaam Alaikum*,' Jack replied.

'May you never tire.' The camel driver did not drop his gaze.

'May you never see poverty.' Jack had been schooled in the correct reply.

The camels swayed on, each one with two panniers full of fruits and Afghan carpets. The dust settled. Jack continued deeper into the pass.

At the defile of Bagiari, the heat was oppressive as it bounced from the cruel rocks. A small British garrison challenged their progress, with the Dogra sepoys holding rifles in sweating hands.

'Captain Windrush with a patrol of Guides.' Jack reined up, brushing dust from his uniform.

The lieutenant in charge of the post was about twenty-five, with the eyes of an old man. He looked wearily over the Guides. 'Be careful out there, Windrush. The Afridi are getting a bit restless these past few weeks.'

'We'll be careful,' Jack said.

'Where are you headed?' Lines of responsibility were deeply etched around the lieutenant's mouth.

'Torkrud,' Jack said, 'to speak to the new Khan of the Rahmut Khel.'

The lieutenant stiffened, glancing over Jack's escort. 'You might need to reconsider. That's bad country for such a small force, Windrush, if you don't mind me saying so.'

'Thank you for your advice, Lieutenant, but orders is orders.'

The lieutenant gave a faint smile. 'That's true, Windrush. Well, good luck, and may the Lord look after you.' He gestured to the west. 'We're the last British outpost. After us, you are all alone.'

That was not a comforting thought as Jack looked forward to the route to Afghanistan and the heartland of Pakhtunkhwa. He grinned. *Come on, Jack, I'm letting my imagination carry me away here. Nothing has happened, and probably nothing will happen.*

The pass narrowed as they approached Ali Masjid, where the fort glowered at them from its steep-sided hill.

'Sahib.' Hassan approached with more diffidence than usual. 'Some of the men have a request.'

'What is that, daffadar?'

'This is a holy place, sahib. There is a shrine here to Ali ibn Abi Talib, who was Mohammed's cousin and son-in-law. Some of the men wish to pray.'

Jack hesitated for only a moment. *Don't interfere with the men's religion.* 'As long as you're careful, Hassan. Keep two men on watch at all times.'

'Yes, sahib.' For the first time, Jack thought he saw a glimmer of respect in Hassan's face. He stood aside as his Guides prayed at the shrine. It was an example of the devotion of the Pashtun people that Jack had never experienced with ordinary British soldiers. He was unsure how he felt, but he knew that every little bit he learned about the Pashtun might help. Unsure how the Guides would feel if he watched, he rode fifty yards away to survey the route ahead.

The horseman appeared at the back of the shrine, an unkempt, barechested, shaggy-haired figure astride a horse that looked in no better condition than the rider. Jack watched the rider for a moment, saw he had a tabla drum but no weapon, and lost interest. India was full of strange people; it seemed that they also seeped into the Khyber Pass. A man with a drum was no threat to him.

'Captain Windrush, sahib.' Hassan threw a salute. 'We are ready.'

'Thank you, daffadar.'

Leaving Ali Masjid with its holy shrine and grim fortress, Jack led them through a narrow gorge and upward to the summit of the pass. He halted there, with the hills of Tirah to the south, and a valley on the north, gradually rising toward the Inzar Kandao Pass.

'Now we leave the Khyber,' he said.

'Yes, sahib.' Hassan said no more.

Jack glanced over his men. Most looked impassive. Zaman looked a little edgy, his eyes continually roving to the surrounding hills. Jack wondered what he was thinking. Until he earned the trust of these Guides, they would never open up their fears to him. Jack accepted that: British soldiers were the same.

Spread out and moving in a zig-zag to ensure they were a more difficult target for the jezzail men who Jack guessed would be watching them from the crags around, the Guides rode on. Fatteh was softly singing, his voice surprisingly melodious. Slightly off the road, tribal villages sheltered behind stone-and-mud walls, each village with a watchtower or fort. Men stood or sat on the flat roofs of each tower, watching Jack's patrol ride past. Some lifted a hand in acknowledgement. Most did not.

Jack consulted his map, trying to make sense of his surroundings. He noticed the riders cantering away to their right.

'Three men, moving fast,' Hassan said. 'Afridis.'

When the riders came within a few hundred yards of Jack, they abruptly altered direction, heading at right angles to their original route.

'They are nervous of us,' Jack said. 'They've seen that we are the Guides.'

'Yes, sahib,' Hassan said. 'Why should that make them nervous? Half a dozen Guides in the midst of Afridi territory? They could call on a hundred men in minutes.'

'That is true,' Jack agreed. 'Hassan, take a couple of men and bring these fellows to me. I want to know what they are afraid of.'

'Sahib!' Hassan signalled to Sawan and Fatteh to join him.

'Come on, lads.' Jack gave them a moment to draw ahead. 'This way.' Kicking in his heels, he followed the galloping Hassan.

The chase did not last long. Like many Pashtuns, Hassan was a superb horseman, while the fugitives evidently rode tired horses. Within ten minutes Hassan rounded them up and herded them back to Jack. For a moment, Jack thought the men would show fight, so he rode forward with what he hoped was a smile, removing the rifle from the man who appeared to be their leader.

'Salaam Alaikum,' he said, 'greetings, good day.'

'Salaam,' the man replied with ill grace, watching the Guides through nervous eyes.

'I wanted to apologise for frightening you.' Jack disarmed the man with an apology.

'We are not frightened,' the man denied.

'I am glad to hear that,' Jack said. 'You were riding so sedately until you saw us, and then you galloped away. What are you scared of?'

'This one is hiding something.' Hassan took hold of the oldest of the three men. 'What are you hiding?'

The man said nothing, while his hand slid toward the T-shaped *Choora* dagger at his waist. 'You will not need that.' Hassan took the dagger away. 'I will find out what you're hiding, cousin. Get off that horse.'

'Don't hurt the man,' Jack said. 'He has done us no harm.' He glanced around the surrounding heights, hoping the incident was not attracting too much attention. The flash of sunlight on steel confirmed that at least one man was watching them.

'Here.' Hassan pulled a folded note from inside the man's clothing. 'He is carrying a message. Who is this for, fellow?'

'Gulbaz of the Rahmut Khel,' the man said at once, spreading his hands in a gesture of innocence. 'It is only a message. It is of no importance to anybody except Gulbaz and the man who sent it.'

'Then why did you run and try to hide it?' Jack asked. 'Give it here.' The note was written in flowing Persian, the language used by the more educated of the Afghan and Pashtun tribal leaders.

Jack's language lessons had included basic Persian, but even so, he struggled with the terminology. 'This seems to be a legal document,' he said. 'It mentions a lawsuit, with the law agent being the most important person.'

'Yes, sahib,' the elderly man nodded eagerly. 'It is from a lawyer to Gulbaz of the Dagger Hand.'

'Can you read Persian, Hassan?' Jack wondered about Gulbaz's nickname.

'No, sahib.' Hassan shook his head.

'It seems perfectly innocent.' Jack handed back the note. 'I am sorry to break your journey.'

'He's not innocent, Windrush sahib,' Zaman said. 'Whatever he is, he is not innocent.'

'He is no threat to us,' Jack decided. 'Let these men go.'

Zaman grunted, stepping back.

Jack watched as the released men smiled and rode on in the same direction as Jack's party. 'I agree they are suspicious,' he said. 'But they have not attacked us, and the note seemed innocuous.'

Hassan frowned. 'They are trouble, sahib. I can feel the menace on them.'

'We should have asked them further.' Zaman touched the hilt of his bayonet. 'I know Gulbaz.'

'You know more about Torkrud than you are saying,' Jack said. 'Tell me about Gulbaz.'

'Gulbaz wishes to be Khan of the Rahmut Khel,' Zaman said.

'Tell me more,' Jack insisted.

'He is not a man you wish to cross.' Zaman again touched the hilt of his bayonet. 'If he wishes to meet you, he will come. If he does not, he will not.' Zaman pulled his horse around a prominent rock. 'He is watching us right now.'

'Where?' Jack looked around.

'Up there, just below the skyline.' Zaman nodded to the left. 'He is beside that group of pine trees.'

Lifting his binoculars, Jack focussed on the trees. Gulbaz made no attempt to hide. He sat astride a black horse with his left hand at his side. As soon as he saw Jack looking at him, he rode free of the pines and walked his horse slowly along the ridge.

'He's ensuring that we can see him,' Jack said.

'He is showing us that he is not afraid of us.' Hassan tapped the hilt of his sabre. 'I would be happier if Gulbaz was short of a head as well as his hand.'

'We cannot kill people merely because we don't like them,' Jack said. Perhaps these Pashtun can do that. What did Hassan mean, short of his hand? Moving his binoculars, Jack studied Gulbaz again. He grunted: Hassan was correct. Gulbaz had no right hand, which explained the strange way he rode his horse. He had a hook in place of his hand, with what looked like the sheath of a dagger protruding. The hook and dagger were attached to his stump by long strips of steel.

'Gulbaz looks like a formidable man,' Jack said. Gulbaz was a bear of a man with a great beard, a steel skull cap, and boots like a Cossack, from which thongs and rings dangled.

'He is,' Zaman said. 'I will kill him someday.'

Jack felt a chill run through him at the matter-of-fact way that Zaman said the words. He looked back over the rump of Colwall. 'Are you at feud with him?'

'Not yet.' Zaman's smile was a promise of future violence.

'Keep your feuding away from your duty,' Jack growled. 'You are a Guide before anything else.'

'Yes, Windrush, sahib.' Zaman's attempt to look innocent was a ludicrous failure. 'Torkrud is about half an hour's ride ahead,' Zaman said quietly. 'The khan of the Rahmut Khel will welcome us, or he will try to kill us.' His grin suggested he did not mind whichever choice the khan made.

'Thank you, Zaman. I suspect that you know Torkrud well.'

'I know it, sahib,' Zaman said.

The village was much like any of the others they had passed, except it was larger, with an arched doorway behind an array of dusty fields. The watchtower was taller and adorned with battlements.

Feeling like an alien in this environment, Jack took a deep breath. *I have my duty to do. Act as though you own the place.* 'Halloa!' He reined up outside the walls. 'I am Captain Jack Windrush of the Guides! I seek an audience with the Khan of Torkrud.' Even as he said them, Jack knew the words sounded melodramatic, as if he were playing a part in a pantomime rather than holding Her Majesty's commission. He stifled his smile. This whole place seemed like something out of the Arabian Nights, except the dust was real, as was the danger. The man in the watchtower looked down at him, spat betel-nut juice, and fired his jezzail into the air.

The shot set a dozen dogs barking.

'Now we will see.' Zaman lifted his rifle to a more comfortable position.

Hassan grunted. 'If Allah wills.'

As there seemed no response from Torkrud, Jack flicked his reins and walked Colwall through the arched gate. The Guides followed in single file, each man with his rifle held across the crupper of his horse.

Children crowded to watch the visitors, with a motley array of dogs emerging from corners to bark and snap at the horses. Jack kicked one persistent mongrel away as his Guides spoke to the children. An old man, his beard dyed bright red, came to the door of his house with a curved pulwar, the Pashtun sword, balanced across his shoulder. One woman in a white burqa scurried to the safety of a walled enclosure. A tall man in a twisted red turban watched from the corner of one of the high walls that delineated each family house. He fingered the pulwar that he wore around his waist, saying nothing as his eyes, kohl-rimmed, studied each of the Guides in turn before settling on Jack. The muzzle of a jezzail protruded from behind his left shoulder.

'There is trouble,' Hassan said quietly. 'Watch that man, sahib.'

'I see him,' Jack murmured, feeling for the butt of his revolver. He could nearly taste the suspicion in the air. *Any moment now the inhabitants of this place will attack us en masse.*

'Windrush!' The name boomed out across the village.

Jack saw the familiar figure striding towards him. The Pashtun wore a pakul, a woollen hat above a face with high cheekbones and a long beard. Alone of all the men who had appeared in doorways, the man did not carry a rifle, only a long Khyber knife at his belt, while a long-legged, hairy dog loped at his side. Despite his surroundings, Jack could not control the smile that spread across his face. 'Batoor! What are you doing here?'

'Did you bring my horse, Windrush?'

Batoor and Jack had fought together in the latter stages of the Mutiny when Batoor had freed Jack from captivity.

'I did not know you would be here, Batoor.' Jack dismounted at once, extending his hand in friendship. 'I wish I had! Do we meet in friendship or in war?'

'What's the difference?' Batoor asked. 'The Pashtun are only at peace when they are at war. You are welcome, Windrush, whatever your government says!' He raised his voice to a shout. 'Captain Windrush and his Guides are my guests!' The words echoed around the village.

Jack nodded. 'Thank you, Batoor.' He knew that by the laws of Pakhtunwali, the code by which the Pashtun people lived their lives, he and his men were now protected. If anybody attacked or even insulted them, Batoor was bound by his honour to avenge them. 'I hope your khan does not object. It is he I have come to see.'

Batoor looked suddenly solemn. 'Have you come to Torkud to meet the Khan of the Rahmut Khel?' He touched a hand to the hilt of his Khyber Knife in a gesture that Jack remembered well.

'I have.' Jack felt his Guides mustering behind him. He wondered if they would have to shoot their way out of Torkud, despite his having met an old friend here. He noticed Batoor's eyes narrow as he saw Zaman. *These two know each other.*

'Zaman is with me,' Jack spoke quietly. 'He is now one of your guests.'

Batoor's expression lifted as he looked about him. 'Have you heard about our new khan, Windrush? Have you heard how he came to power?'

'I know little about him,' Jack said. 'I have heard he is a powerful man.'

'Come with me, and I will introduce you,' Batoor said. 'He is a badmash indeed, a man with no scruples, a killer born to the saddle, a master of raid and rapine.'

Jack thought of Gulbaz of the dagger hand. Please God that Gulbaz is not the khan! 'A badmash and a killer? He sounds as if he would fit well in the 113th Foot!'

Batoor laughed again. 'He might, Windrush. Come with me and see for yourself.'

Jack knew that his men were listening to every word. 'My Guides will come with me.' He looked for the tall man with the red turban, but he had vanished.

'Your men will find their entertainment in Torkud,' Batoor said. 'They will be as safe in our *hujrah*, our guest house, as they would be in Mardan. Perhaps safer indeed, as the wicked Afridis of the Rahmut Khel will not snipe at them.'

Jack smiled at Batoor's roar of laughter. This was a new side to the highly efficient warrior that Jack had come to rely on. Batoor at home was a much more jovial man.

'Come with me, Windrush.' Taking Jack by the arm, Batoor led him into the heart of the village. 'Don't worry; your horse will be as well cared for as your men. Trust me.'

'I do trust you.' Jack told the truth. It was the unknown khan that he did not trust.

'The Khan lives in that building.' Batoor pointed to a walled compound, slightly larger than any of the others in the village. 'As you see, the gate is open. I will go ahead to announce you, Windrush. Follow me at a distance, and you will meet the Khan.' He paused for a significant moment. 'Be careful, Windrush. The Khan is a man of short temper and a long sword. Only he wears the silver sword of the Rahmut Khel.'

'The what?' Jack asked, but Batoor was already striding away. Wondering why most of the men of Torkud were laughing at him, Jack followed Batoor's instructions. Remembering the formidable appearance of Gulbaz, Jack felt his heartbeat increase. He touched the butt of his revolver for reassurance as he strode through the gate.

The walls must have been ten feet high, without a single window on the outside. Jack knew they were only partly for security; they were also to ensure the women were in *purdah*, privacy. The door was narrow, but once inside Jack saw there were three courtyards, one for animals, one for women and another for ordinary family life. The accommodation backed against the external mud walls, square and simple, while trees within the compound afforded shade.

'Halloa!' Jack stood within the first courtyard. 'I am Captain Jack Windrush of the Guides. I am looking for the Khan of the Rahmut Khel!' He heard various rustlings from the buildings behind him. 'Is there anybody here?'

'Only me, Captain Windrush.' Batoor strode in behind him, still grinning as if at a private joke. He had replaced his pakul with a karakul hat of Astrakhan fur, headgear often worn by a man of position.

Jack hid his irritation. 'I don't believe that your Khan wishes to talk to me.'

'The Khan of the Rahmut Khel is already talking to you,' Batoor said. He extended both hands. 'I am Batoor Khan, Windrush! I am the Khan of the Rahmut Khel!'

Chapter Five

'Batoor!' For a moment Jack was nonplussed. 'You are the Khan?'

Batoor placed his arm around Windrush's shoulder. 'Come, Windrush. Come into my home.'

'I am here on official business,' Jack reminded.

'Pleasure first, business later,' Batoor said. 'It must be four, five years since we parted outside the walls of Gondabad. Much has happened in that time. You have left your *pultan*, and I have become a Khan.' He touched the silver hilt of the pulwar that protruded from an ornate scabbard at his waist. 'As you see, I wear the silver sword of the Khan of the Rahmut Khel.'

'It is a beautiful sword.' Jack tried to make sense of this new development as Batoor led him toward the nearest building.

'Only the Khan can wear it.' Batoor seemed as proud of his sword as he was of his position as Khan. Drawing it with a single gesture, he rested the long, slightly curved blade on the palm of his left hand. The hilt was of ivory, inlaid with semi-precious stones, and the guard of chased silver. Sunlight gleamed on the flowing Persian inscriptions on the steel. 'It is at least two hundred years old, an example of Pashtun culture.'

Jack compared the pulwar with his own Wilkinson's blade. It looked longer and lighter. 'Is it sharp?'

In answer, Batoor took a square of silk from inside his loose perahan top. Lifting it high, he altered the angle of the pulwar so the blade was uppermost and allowed the silk to drop. The blade sliced the silk in half. 'You see, Windrush? Can you do the same with your Wilkinson's sword?'

Jack laughed. 'I won't even try,' he said. 'It's good to see you again, Batoor Khan! You can put your sword away now.'

'Batoor!' The red-turbaned man overtopped Batoor by two inches as he strode into the compound. 'This man is a feringhee.'

'This man is my guest, Ayub.' Batoor faced him, one hand on the hilt of his sword.

'A feringhee is not welcome in the lands of the Rahmut Khel.' Ayub ignored Jack. His gaze fixed on the silver sword of the Rahmut Khel.

Batoor straightened his shoulders. 'This man is my guest,' he repeated. 'He is under my protection, by Pakhtunwali.'

'There are more than you in the Rahmut Khel,' Ayub said.

'Ayub, my friend,' Batoor said, 'you do not wish to fall out with me over a solitary feringhee. There are many more in the world.'

Ayub glared at Jack through startlingly blue eyes. 'If I had my way,' he said, 'the skins of the feringhee and his companions would cover my floor, and their heads would decorate spikes along the wall of my house.'

Jack looked away. A private conversation between two old friends was none of his business. Turning aside, he flicked open the button of his holster.

'I will call a *Jirga* about this matter.' Ayub threw Jack a final baleful glare before storming out of the compound. 'Gulbaz will need to know about this.'

There is that name again. Gulbaz must be a man of some note.

'That was Ayub Beg,' Batoor said. 'He is a man with a large mouth and a small brain. You need not worry about him.'

'I won't,' Jack said. 'I might worry about somebody else. I have heard the name Gulbaz mentioned more than once. He watched us approach Torkud.'

'Gulbaz of the dagger hand, one of my last surviving cousins.' Batoor dismissed Gulbaz with a shrug. 'If he has offended you, tell me, and I will kill him. His absence will make the world a more pleasant place.'

'He seems a very forceful fellow.' Jack knew that Batoor's offer was genuine. 'You said Gulbaz was one of your last *surviving* cousins. What happened to your other cousins?'

'They did not survive.' Batoor's smile broadened. 'Come inside my house. I have warned my women.'

Unsure what to expect, Jack followed Batoor through a simple arched doorway into his house. It was neat, clean and comfortable rather than luxurious, with a gaggle of young children waiting to stare at the feringhee. Two women in full white burqas greeted Jack politely. Their eyes were friendly as they scrutinised him.

'Two of my wives,' Batoor explained, 'and some of my children.'

'You've been busy.' Jack counted five children. 'Two wives?'

'I have another somewhere.' Batoor sat down, inviting Jack to do the same. 'She will be organising the household, no doubt, ensuring that everybody does as she wishes. You know what women are like.'

Thinking of Mary, Jack nodded. 'They control us with their smiles.'

'And other things,' Batoor said. 'You will have heard the saying, a woman for business, a boy for pleasure, and a goat for choice?'

'I have heard people say that of the Pashtun,' Jack agreed cautiously.

'That is not my nature.' Batoor thanked the taller of his two wives for handing him a pipe. 'I prefer women to boys or goats.' He eyed Jack with an amused smile. 'Did you marry that woman of yours? Or shall I sing you the Zakhmi Dil?'

Jack knew the gist of that song: *There's a boy across the river with a bottom like a peach but alas I cannot swim.* He shook his head. 'There is no need to torment me with your singing, Batoor. And yes, I married Mary.'

'Good!' Batoor roared his delight. 'How many children has she borne you?'

'One. We have a son. Andrew.'

'Only one? You must marry another woman and get more sons,' Batoor gave his opinion.

'We are only allowed one wife,' Jack said.

Batoor was suddenly serious. 'You are strange people, feringhee. What will happen if she becomes barren?'

'More children will come in their own time.' It was something that Jack had often discussed with Mary, who hoped for a large family.

'It is the will of Allah the all-merciful.' Batoor clapped his hands. 'You'll be hungry, Windrush. Let's eat.'

A smooth-faced young man brought in a tray of tea, which was served to Jack first, as a guest, and then to Batoor and a group of elders who arrived with grave greetings and bright eyes. Jack tasted the mixture of milk, sugar and tea leaves that the youngest man carefully poured into small bowls. The sweet biscuits were delicious, as were the rice-flour-and-ghee cakes.

After the tea came the main meal. Jack was surprised at the quality of the food, chicken and eggs, flat leavened bread with a variety of vegetables including onions and spinach. As the Pashtun only ate meat on special occasions, Jack knew the chicken had been killed especially for him.

After the meal, the elderly men told stories, laughing as they recounted tales of fights against the British, scowling as they mentioned the far more bitter feuds with other Pashtun clans. 'The British are feringhees; they will pass in time. Our enemies of the Adam Khel will be here forever.'

'If you will excuse me, Batoor.' Jack stood. 'I had better leave you.'

'You must hear more, Windrush,' Batoor insisted. 'We have singing, dancing and stories.'

'Thank you, Batoor, but I will have to check on my men.' Jack gave a little bow. 'You know what trouble soldiers can get into.'

The Guides were in the hujra, sitting in a loose group, smoking, singing and talking, while their rifles were close at their sides. The building was large and airy, with a score of charpoys, wooden-framed beds, lining the walls.

When Hassan shouted an order, they leapt to attention.

'Stand easy, men,' Jack said. 'How are you being treated?'

'All well, Windrush sahib,' Hassan reported. He nodded to the tray of tea that sat on the ground.

'Keep your rifles handy.' Jack gave advice he knew the men did not need.

'Yes, Windrush sahib.'

Zaman wiped breadcrumbs from his beard. 'If Gulbaz comes in the night, do I have your permission to kill him, Windrush sahib?'

'If I don't give permission, you would kill him anyway,' Jack said. 'However, Zaman, he will not come. You are under the protection of Batoor Khan.' He could not read the expression on Zaman's face.

'Fatteh,' Jack spoke quietly. 'There will be no need for you to sound the last post with your bugle. It might irritate our hosts.' He saw the disappointment on the young man's face. 'There will be other opportunities.'

The Guides told stories or sang softly, with Fatteh producing a rubab, the Pashtun lute. His young voice had a certain beauty that Jack had not previously associated with these hills.

In some ways, Jack thought, the Pashtun were unlike any people he had met before, while in others, they were very similar. He shrugged: people were people with good and bad points. Today had been a success; tomorrow, when he discussed gun runners and the Mujahidin, things might be different.

As Jack settled to sleep, he heard the drumming, a slightly unsettling low throbbing that came from outside the village. He touched the butt of the revolver under his pillow and returned to sleep.

* * *

They stood in the middle of the village with Batoor stroking the throat of the laggar falcon that perched on his wrist. 'When I have this bird trained, Windrush, we can go hunting, you and I. Shikar is as good as war.'

'I would like that,' Jack said. 'I used to follow the hounds back in England when I had the chance.'

'Let me show you Torkud.' Batoor sounded as proud of his village as Fatteh was of his bugle. Within the outer barrier, a score of compounds rose, each one with high walls and a solid tower, eighteen or twenty feet tall.

'Why are the walls mainly of mud?' Jack asked. 'There is plenty of stone around.'

'The main watchtowers are of stone,' Batoor said. 'But in times of feud or war, the tribes destroy their enemy's houses. It is easier to rebuild a mud wall than one of stone.'

Jack nodded. He had heard the same sort of story from the Border wars between England and Scotland. The people along both sides of the Border had their peel-towers for defence, much like the watchtowers of these Pashtun villages. They built dry-stone cottages which could be replaced after the invaders of whichever nation returned over the Border. Jack understood the Pashtun point of view.

Wherever Batoor led Jack, women either scurried away from them or watched boldly through the slits in their burqas, while children laughed, joked and pointed to the strange feringhee. Groups of barechested boys played a hopping game, trying to knock each other down while balancing on one leg. Other boys, as young as five or six, played with large cleavers or eyed their elder brothers' rifles with real envy. *These are a martial people indeed.* Jack knew that the more he learned of them, the better, but he had his duty to do. 'How did you rise to become Khan, Batoor?'

'When I was with the feringhees,' Batoor seemed pleased to explain, 'I heard them talk about a process of elimination. That is how I became Khan.'

'Tell me more.'

'When I got back here after killing Jayanti, my uncle, the old Khan was dead. There was a Jirga, a meeting of the elders, to decide who should replace him.'

'Should it not be the eldest son?' Jack remembered the complications surrounding his own family.

'Perhaps,' Batoor said. 'My father had many sons by many women. It was hard to know who the eldest was. The Jirga decided that one of my brothers named Dilawar should be the khan, although Gulbaz and I pleaded our case, along with another man.'

Jack noted Batoor's reticence with the third name. 'Where is Dilawar now?'

Batoor stopped outside the ruins of what had once been a substantial house. Shattered stones lay amidst a heap of dry earth, with splinters of timber and pieces of what looked like rags. 'I accepted the Jirga's decision and invited Gulbaz, Dilawar, and his supporters to a peace meeting at my house.'

'That was the most honourable thing to do.' Jack knew that Batoor had more to add to his story.

Batoor pushed at one of the stones with his foot. 'They did not all come. Gulbaz turned down my kind offer.' Batoor's eyes were as calm as Jack had ever seen them. 'When Dilawar and his men arrived, I had two kegs of gunpowder waiting beneath the building, and I blew them all up!' Batoor roared with laughter at his cleverness. He indicated the ruined building beside him. 'There is the result. What remains of Dilawar is under there somewhere. Dig for him if you wish, Windrush.'

Jack nodded. 'I'll leave the digging to somebody else. Now you are the undisputed Khan except for Gulbaz and the third claimant you did not name.'

'Yes.' Batoor nodded. 'It is a pity that they were not here when I eliminated the others.' Batoor seemed to like that idea. 'Since Gulbaz returned, he has tried to depose me. I will have to kill him eventually.'

The cold-blooded statement shook Jack a little. 'Could the two of you not discuss things without bloodshed?'

'He wishes to be Khan,' Batoor said. 'I wish to be Khan. One of us will succeed, one will die.' He moved on, long-striding. 'There is another possibility, my other cousin, who may also return to stake his claim.'

Jack frowned. He guessed who this cousin might be. 'Where is this fellow now?'

'In the hujrah.' Batoor spoke without emotion.

'My Guides are in the hujrah,' Jack said.

'I know,' Batoor said softly.

'Is one of my men your cousin?' Jack wondered if Batoor's hospitality would extend to a rival for his position.

'Zaman.' Batoor confirmed Jack's suspicions.

'Is he safe? Will you harm him?' Jack stepped aside to give space to a smiling young man herding two buffalo.

'He is my guest. He is safe.' Batoor smiled. 'As long as he is within my lands, he is under my protection, unless he tries to kill me.'

Jack remembered Zaman's reluctance to come to Torkrud. 'He will not do that.'

'Then he is safe from me.' Batoor touched the silver hilt of his sword.

Every so often, Batoor stopped to talk to one of the many children or nod to a rifle-carrying man. All the time, Jack was looking at the rifles, checking for Enfields or any other British-made weapons.

'Could you not call a Jirga to decide who is khan?'

'We have, and the Jirga chose me. If they had not...' Batoor indicated the ruins behind him. 'That was in the past. More important for you, Gulbaz has called a Jirga over you and your Guides.'

'Has he? Why?'

'The British are not liked here. Many of our older men fought when the British invaded Afghanistan.'

'That was twenty years ago,' Jack said.

Batoor smiled. 'Twenty years, two hundred years, two thousand years. It does not matter. Our concepts of time are different from yours, Windrush.'

'The Pashtuns fought with us during the Mutiny,' Jack reminded him. 'You fought with us against the Mutineers.'

'I fought for my own hand, Windrush, as you know,' Batoor said. 'It happened that my cause coincided with yours at the time.'

'When is the Jirga?'

'Tomorrow,' Batoor said. 'They will decide if you and your men are guests, as I wish, or enemies, as Gulbaz wishes.'

So soon! Jack glanced around Torkrud. Armed men stood at every doorway, watching him, unsmiling. Some tapped the butts of their rifles; others had a hand on the hilt of Khyber knife or pulwar. 'What will happen if they decide as Gulbaz wants?'

'They will kill you,' Batoor said. 'It will be the will of the elders.' He lowered his voice. 'It will be the will of Allah. Come now, and we will try out my falcon.'

I will have to warn the men. I will have them prepared for any eventuality. What has Colonel Hook landed me in this time?

Chapter Six

Torkrud, north-west frontier July 1863

Jack heard the slow throbbing of the drum as he rode to the Jirga. He did not know if the drums were part of the proceedings or purely coincidental. He only knew that the sound added to his tension as he left the village for the knoll outside, where the elders of the Rahmut Khel gathered around a gnarled group of pine trees.

The men sat cross-legged in a great circle, some chewing betel-nuts, others smoking from hookahs or merely listening to the speeches. They looked dignified and serious, as befitted men who had survived many years in Pakhtunkhwa, men accustomed to making decisions for the benefit of their community. Jack stood some way apart with one hand on the butt of his revolver, aware that his life was being decided. In one way this seemed a very primitive method of determining what course to take, but in another, it was real democracy at work as each man had his say, while the others listened without interruption. Jack nodded, comparing proceedings to the bear-garden that was the House of Commons. *This Jirga is more polite than Westminster,* he thought. *It is similar to the Thinga parliaments of the Norse. People are far more alike than different.* Then he remembered that if the decision of the Jirga went against him, he could be dead before nightfall.

I've warned my Guides; they know what to do if things go wrong, but I'm damned if I will hide away.

'I have fought beside Windrush in the war with the mutinous sepoys.' Batoor was on his feet, talking. 'He is a man like us. He lives by the concept of *nang*, of honour. As Khushal Khan Khattak said: "I despise the man who does not guide his life by honour." Windrush keeps his word and defends his men. He is Pashtun in everything except blood and religion.'

There was a ripple of assent at that. As Jack had learned, the Pashtuns considered personal honour one of the highest virtues.

Ayub was no elder, but he stood next, pointing at Jack. 'This man is a feringhee. He cannot be trusted. We all know the proverb. First comes one Englishman, as a traveller or for shikar; then come two and make a map; then comes an army and takes the country. Therefore it is better to kill the first Englishman.' He sat down again, giving Jack a poisonous glare. He tapped the Khyber knife at his belt.

Some of the assembled men nodded ominous approval. One wiry old man with a henna-dyed beard stood next.

'I know the proverb. I also know Pakhtunwali, the way of the Pashtun. We have given this feringhee hospitality. By the law of *melmastia*, we are bound to shelter any traveller arriving at our village. If we break that tradition, we damage our *nang* and will forever be dishonoured. The feringhee and his men should stay in peace.'

Some of the assembled men mumbled agreement, others looked annoyed. Jack could not tell which feeling was in the majority. He stiffened when Gulbaz stood, with the sun catching the steel of his wickedly curved hook.

'I have no disagreement with Batoor over the feringhee's nang.' Gulbaz spoke quietly, with intensity. He pointed a finger at Batoor. 'I have no argument that Windrush and his men may be honourable, as far as a feringhee can have honour, and a Pashtun may retain his honour, while still accepting a feringhee's salt.'

There was a murmur of assent from the gathered elders. Jack wondered what the follow-up would be. He suspected that he and his Guides would have to fight their way clear of this village. He fingered his revolver once more. He was meant to find out about gun-running and the fanatics, not get involved in a firefight.

Gulbaz paused to give more weight to his words. 'I am sure that Batoor found Windrush a brave man while fighting those who eat pork and worship cattle.'

Gulbaz is going to try the religious angle, Jack thought. *That is clever.* He waited as Gulbaz paused, giving intensity to his next words.

'Why should we give hospitality to feringhees? We should wage jihad on them, as the Mujahidin wish!'

Jack grunted. Any mention of holy war or Mujahidin was troubling, especially with these Mujahidin now carrying modern rifles. He did not know how many Muhammadans there were in India, but many millions, surely. If they rose simultaneously and called on their religious brothers in Afghanistan, Persia or central Asia to join them, the under-strength British Army in India could be overwhelmed. The Waziris alone were said to have over a hundred thousand warriors.

'Why should we give hospitality?' An old man used a stick to help himself to his feet. A deep scar ran from his empty eye socket to the corner of his mouth. 'We are Pashtun. We follow Pakhtunwali. That is why we give hospitality to Windrush and his Guides. If we fail in our law, we fail as Pashtuns.'

Another ancient man rose, his face seamed by countless years but his eyes bright. His beard was white, streaked with red. 'Am I not a Pashtun?' he said and sat back down again with his contribution to the Jirga made.

Other men rose, some speaking in favour of Batoor, others arguing for Gulbaz. Jack noted who supported whom, while he mentally worked out his route of escape if Gulbaz won the day.

At last Batoor stood. 'Windrush and the Guides are my guests,' he stated. 'They are under my protection by our law of melmastia.' He stopped, looking around the Jirga, meeting the gaze of every man there. 'If anybody wants to dispute my right to have them as my guests, let him do so now.'

Jack held his breath as silence fell over the Jirga. Even Gulbaz held his peace.

'Very good,' Batoor said. 'We shall now vote.'

Jack slid a hand onto the butt of his revolver. He had told his Guides that he would fire three spaced shots if the Jirga decided against them. Now he wondered if he would have time to send such a warning.

The voting was surprisingly orderly, with a small majority of men agreeing with Batoor. Jack released his breath with relief as Batoor nodded.

'Windrush and the Guides are our guests,' Batoor said. 'That saves us the trouble of killing them.' Some of the assembled men smiled at that. 'It also saves us from fighting off another British column as it marches through the passes. If the feringhee come in peace, we should welcome them and learn all we can of their intentions. If they come in war…' He spread his arms. 'Well, "The Pashtun is never at peace, except when he is at war."'

'Will you accept the decision of the Jirga, Gulbaz?' the one-eyed oldster asked, stroking his beard.

'I will accept it as long as Batoor extends his hospitality, and I am not expected to be friendly to the feringhee.'

The one-eyed man smiled. 'Nobody expects you to share your bed with the feringhee; only to spare him your blade.'

The gathering laughed as the men returned to their homes. Only Gulbaz remained. He faced Jack, nodded slowly, touched the hilt of his knife, and strode away.

'You see?' Batoor said. 'You are welcome.'

'Gulbaz does not think so,' Jack said.

'Gulbaz will obey the will of the Jirga,' Batoor spoke softly. 'It is Pakhtunwali.'

'You did not obey the will of the Jirga,' Jack reminded. 'I will sleep with my revolver under my pillow.'

Batoor's laugh was as loud as Jack had ever heard it. 'That also is Pakhtunwali!'

Jack looked up. The drumming he had heard before the Jirga had started again, or perhaps it had never stopped. He saw a lone horseman riding along the hill flank to his right, near naked and with a tabla drum in front of him on the saddle. *I have seen that man before, at Ali Masjid.* 'Who is that?'

Batoor looked and frowned. 'That is a mullah, Windrush, an itinerant holy man. He could be doing good, or he could be doing evil. I will tell my sentinels to watch him.'

* * *

They sat inside Batoor's house with sunlight streaming through the open door to dapple the floor around them. Batoor grunted and passed over the hookah. 'I have asked about these Mujahidin. They have not come here yet, Windrush.'

'My Colonel Hook believes that you have allowed them through your tribal lands.' Jack smoked the hookah, finding it milder than most cheroots he used.

'It is worrying, Windrush,' Batoor said. 'Jihads are always worrying. They are started by holy men, mullahs such as you saw earlier. They do not understand the concept of war. They do not listen to the words of generals or warriors who have experience of fighting. They think that belief and the words of the Koran alone will win battles against rifles and artillery.'

'We have Christians with equal faith,' Jack said.

'Some of these mullahs tell the young men that if they wear the words of the Koran around their neck, the infidel's bullets will not harm them.' Batoor spoke quietly. 'Many young men die that way.' He shrugged. 'Maybe it is true. I have not tried it.'

'I would not advise it, Batoor. Would you let me know if you hear anything about a mullah talking Jihad?'

'I will watch for him,' Batoor said. 'I don't wish a Jihad. In our own hills, we can defeat you. In the plains, against your artillery and discipline, I am not so sure.' He lowered his voice. 'Do not tell my people I said that.'

'I won't,' Jack promised. 'You have not allowed these fanatics, or Mujahidin, to cross your lands, then?'

'I have not,' Batoor said.

'There is another thing.'

'With the British, there is always another thing.' Batoor was smiling. 'You are always pushing, striving, altering. What is it, Windrush?'

'Rifles,' Jack said. 'There have been many British Enfield rifles turning up all along the Frontier. I noticed that two of your men carried such rifles. Do you know where they got them?'

Batoor smiled. 'I am not their father. If two of my men have modern rifles, then that is their concern.'

Jack nodded. He knew better than to press further. If Batoor knew more, then he was keeping his knowledge to himself. 'Tonight,' he said, 'I will sleep in the hujrah with my men. I do not wish them to think I am neglecting them.'

That night, Jack heard the drumming again, insistent through the dark. Leaving the hujrah, he walked around the village, ignoring the barking of the dogs and the occasional noise from within the compounds. A scimitar moon shone above, with myriad stars pricking the void of the sky, showing the ragged edges of the surrounding mountains.

There is a rare beauty out here, Jack thought, *a wildness that the Romantic poets would find attractive. It is like the people, raw, untamed, and perhaps untameable.* Climbing to the flat roof of the hujrah, he peered over the walls of Torkrud, seeing the land ghost-lit by the moon. A shaft of moonlight caught the mullah as he rode his horse around the village. *That's three times I have seen that tabla mullah. He is trouble.* The mullah was nearly naked, with a mane of matted hair that descended past his shoulders. Using his knees to guide the horse, he beat his tabla drum with a monotonous rhythm as he slid out of the moonlight into the dark. The throbbing of the mullah's drum continued long after he was out of sight.

Pliny the Elder said Semper aliquid novi Africam adferre, Africa always brings something new, Jack said to himself. *Well, India is the same. What surprises is this fragmented sub-continent going to spring next?*

When a cloud slid across the moon, darkness closed down the landscape. Jack could see nothing. The drumming continued, wrapping its sound around all within the walls of Torkrud.

'Dear Lord in Heaven.' Jack touched the Bible that Mary had given him. 'Guide me in my hours of need.'

'Windrush sahib.' Hassan had appeared at his side. 'You are talking to yourself.'

'I am praying, Hassan,' Jack said.

'Ah.' Hassan nodded in complete understanding. 'I will leave you in peace. May Allah guide your words.'

'I hope He does, Hassan. I really hope that He does.'

Jack remained on the roof of the hujrah for another half hour, listening as the drumming continued. Eventually, he returned to bed with the throbbing of the drum constant in his head. *There is trouble in the wind. I can feel it.*

* * *

'Windrush sahib.' Hassan stood at the side of Jack's charpoy. 'Batoor Khan is leaving.'

Jack struggled awake. He could hardly make out Hassan's shape in the darkness. 'What's happening, Hassan?'

'The Khan is leaving.'

'The devil he is.' Jack got up and pulled on his trousers and jacket. 'Where is he?'

'This way, Windrush sahib.' Hassan was at the door with the other Guides behind him. Fully dressed, they all carried their rifles.

'Follow me.' Diving into the darkness, Jack nearly ran to Batoor's compound. The village was awake, with men on horse and on foot trotting in the same direction as Jack, muted voices through the night, and the ubiquitous barking of dogs.

'Batoor Khan!' Jack did not hesitate. 'What is happening, Batoor?'

'We have intruders on Rahmut Khel land,' Batoor said. 'They did not ask our permission, so we are going to challenge them. It is nothing to do with you, Windrush, or your Guides.'

Jack paused for a second. 'We are your guests, Batoor. Your enemies are our enemies.' That sounded very melodramatic. Jack wondered how Colonel Hook would react if he got involved in a private war, but being friends with the British had to be seen to have some advantages for the Rahmut Khel.

'I do not know who they are.' Batoor was not smiling as he checked the Khyber knife at his belt. As he spoke, he strapped a Minie rifle across his back. 'It may be your Mujahidin, or the Adam Khel. We will find out. This is not your quarrel.'

'We'll come with you,' Jack said. 'We'll help.'

'You are British soldiers,' Batoor said. 'If you fight alongside us, we may be seen as your allies.' His grin gleamed through the night. 'You have your duty to do. Stay safe, Windrush, and God save the Queen.' His laugh broke the tension.

'How long will you be?' Jack viewed the growing number of Rahmut Khel warriors. 'We still have much to discuss.'

Batoor touched the hilt of his Khyber knife. 'I will be back as soon as I have removed these intruders.' He raised his voice. 'Men of the Rahmut Khel, we belong to God, and unto God do we return!'

Lifting his hand, he trotted out of the village with his men following in disciplined silence. A band of horsemen led, and then a larger group of warriors on foot, running at the same speed as the cavalry.

When the dust cleared, Jack looked at his Guides. 'This could alter things.'

'Torkrud is stripped of fighting men,' Zaman said. 'Batoor Khan has taken them all with him except a handful of elders.' He took a deep breath. 'And those who still follow Gulbaz.'

'It would be a good time for a rival to try to become Khan.' Hassan looked at Zaman. 'Unless he was an honourable man, a man of nang.'

Zaman smiled. 'It is all right, daffadar. I am true to my salt. Where would you be without me? I am the best fighting man in the unit.'

'If not the most modest,' Jack said.

'You boast like a Sikh.' Hassan punctured Zaman's ego. 'This would also be a good time for the Adam Khel or the Yusufzai to raid, sahib. Unless it is them that Batoor is riding against.'

'I don't think it was the Yusufzai.' Jack remembered the mullah of the previous night. 'I believe it was the Mujahidin.' Suddenly he felt very isolated. He was in an Afridi village in the heart of tribal territory with a handful of men of a vastly different culture. All around were tribes who waited on a hair-trigger to take offence, start a feud or otherwise create mayhem. He shook the depression away, trying to use Hassan's words to his advantage.

'Whoever it was, Hassan, if they raid, we will defend this village to repay Batoor Khan's hospitality.' Jack looked around. The rising sun cast long shadows from the peaks to the east, darkening the village. 'You know the culture better than I do; will we be insulting the Rahmut Khel if we mount guard on Torkrud?'

Hassan grunted. 'Gulbaz will not like it, but Gulbaz will not approve of us until we are dead.'

'That is all the more reason to get ourselves in a defensive position,' Jack said. 'Everybody ensure they have their ammunition pouches to hand, full water bottles and as much food as they can carry. Alladad, go and check the horses, make sure they are fed, and ensure the saddles, bridles and reins are close to hand. We may have to mount and ride in a hurry.'

'Yes, Windrush sahib.' Alladad strode away.

'Windrush sahib.' Hassan lifted his head. 'He may not have time.'

'Why is that?'

'Listen, sahib.'

The chanting came from outside the walls of Torkrud, a low babble that steadily increased in volume.

'What's that all about?' Jack could not make out any of the words.

'They want you.' Hassan did not sound agitated. 'They want the feringhee, the foreigner.'

'Ah.' Jack felt the old familiar tension rise within him. He usually experienced that mixture of fear, apprehension and excitement before a battle, but always he had been supported by the men of his regiment. He did not know how these Guides would react. Could he trust Pashtuns, even if they wore the Queen's uniform, to fight alongside him against men of their own religion and race? The old memories of the Mutiny increased his tension, now augmented by a thrill of elation he had not expected. He was a soldier again, facing danger. Some small part of him was enjoying this sensation.

'I'd better speak to them.'

'They don't want to talk,' Zaman said. 'They want to kill you, sahib.'

'Well,' Jack said. 'Let's see, shall we? I'll go and talk to them, for I'm damned if I'll run from a mob I haven't even seen yet!' He felt, rather than saw, Hassan motion the Guides onward. 'I'll go myself. There's no sense any of you men putting yourself in danger.'

Stepping onward, Jack did not have far to go before he saw the mob. They walked slowly, fifty or sixty strong, with a variety of weapons from iron-shod lathes to pulwars and jezzails. Jack stood still with one hand on the butt of his revolver.

'I am Captain Jack Windrush of the Guides!' He had to shout to be heard above the roar of the crowd.

The first stone rattled off the ground a foot to his left. The next whizzed past his head.

'I am a guest of Batoor Khan!' Jack tried again.

'They know that, sahib.' Hassan had followed him. 'Gulbaz has gathered men from the villages all around. With Batoor's warriors away from Torkrud, Gulbaz is the next most important man in the Rahmut Khel.' The other Guides lined up behind Hassan.

Jack glanced over his shoulder at the Guides. How would Zaman react to this situation? Would he try his hand at becoming Khan?

Jack refused to duck as another stone flicked past. The crowd was getting closer, swelling by the minute. He saw Gulbaz in the centre, taller than most of the others, encouraging them on with his metal claw held high. While the majority of the mob seemed to be old men, boys, and badly armed farmers, the men who surrounded Gulbaz were undoubtedly warriors, tall, rangy, fully armed men.

The mob continued to advance. Jack could make out their chant: 'Kill the feringhee' – kill the foreigner. 'Kill the Guides.'

'Load.' Jack snapped the order as he drew his revolver.

'We're already loaded, sahib.' Hassan sounded calm. 'Shall we kill them?'

'No! Aim into the air. Shoot above their heads.' Jack had no wish to cause civilian casualties, particularly in Batoor's home village.

'That's a waste of ammunition, sahib,' Zaman reproved. 'Kerr Sahib does not like us to waste ammunition.'

'Above their heads!' Jack ignored the complaints. 'Fire!'

When all six rifles crashed out, the mob halted. The chanting died away. Gulbaz stepped forward, the sun glinting on his steel hook.

'Reload.' Jack had no need to give the order as the Guides quickly reloaded and capped their rifles. Somewhere above, a bird called, the sound strangely sweet in the crisp air.

'Kill the feringhee!' Gulbaz voice grated through the bird call. 'Before the Guides reload.'

The mob surged forward again. Swearing, Jack fired his revolver in the air, knowing he had to make a rapid decision. He could stay put and fight it out, six Guides and himself against an armed mob that was now a hundred strong, or he could run for a defensive position and hold them off.

'Sahib...' Hassan glanced at Jack. 'Shall we fire?'

'To the watchtower, lads,' Jack decided. 'We'll hold them off there.'

Jack was too experienced to sit in any place without having a plan of escape, while he knew the reputation of the Pashtun too well to not guard his back. He had reconnoitred the village as soon as he arrived, looking for escape routes and defensive sites. Twenty feet tall, the watchtower was at the northern side of Torkrud, grimly overlooking the valley. Once there, Jack knew they could hold out until he decided on their ultimate course of action. Also, the watchtower gave them a splendid field of fire over the village, while denying that advantage to the enemy.

The Guides withdrew in good order, but their retreat encouraged the mob, which followed at a run, stopping only to throw rocks.

Sawan staggered as a stone crashed above his ear. He swore, lifted his rifle to aim, changed his mind when Jack growled at him, and continued the withdrawal with a trickle of blood down the side of his head. Ursulla stopped to lift a stone and throw it back.

'Don't delay.' Jack acted as rearguard. 'Keep moving, lads.' He pointed his revolver in the general direction of the crowd, tempted to shoot at Gulbaz, knowing he would not fire at stone-throwing civilians.

Were these civilians? They were certainly not uniformed soldiers such as the Cossacks or mutinous sepoys he had faced previously. He could not fire at them unless they fired first. That would be against everything he stood for. Jack grunted as a fist-sized stone thudded on the ground at his side. An increasing number of armed men had joined the crowd, no different from the tribesmen he would meet in the passes. Remembering the attack on the British at Kabul that began the terrible retreat of 1841, Jack was well aware of the danger.

The fusillade of stones increased, bouncing from the road and the walled compounds on either side. Jack heard women's voices from the houses, screaming to encourage the men. A boy about eight years old appeared, wielding a long Khyber knife and gesticulating toward the Guides. Jack had never seen such an evil expression on the face of a child.

A single shot sounded, followed by another. Jack saw a man kneel to fire his jezzail, with the long barrel swinging to aim at him.

That's enough, fellow! Stones are one thing, bullets something else! Swearing, Jack levelled his revolver and fired a quick shot. The jezzail man did not flinch; he levelled his weapon, but before he could shoot a surge of the mob obstructed his aim.

'Nearly there, Sahib!' Fatteh was first to reach the watchtower. 'There's no door!'

'There's a ladder in that house.' Jack indicated the nearest compound. *Fatteh should know that many of these towers had no internal stairs. The man is not thinking straight.* 'Fatteh, with me. The rest of you, fix bayonets. Form a defensive line, lads; only fire if they fire!' He knew the sobering effect that a glittering line of bayonets had on any crowd. Most of the mob would be willing for others to charge forward; few would want to be at the forefront when a soldier of the Guides waited with his bayonet poised.

'Afridi pigs!' Alladad was a Yusufzai, no friend of the Afridi. He grinned across the sight of his rifle. 'Come and try a real man.' His finger curled over the trigger.

The mob had halted, threatening with words and gestures, gesticulating with pulwars, waiting for any sign of weakness from the Guides.

Unlike most of the buildings in Torkrud, the watchtower was mostly stone-built, loose boulders crudely put together with mud in place of mortar. Decorative architecture was not one of the qualities of the Pashtun people. Pragmatic building was.

Don't run, Jack told himself. *If you run, the rabble will think you are panicking. Walk.*

Jack marched to the door of the compound that held the ladder. For a moment he had an impulse to knock politely, and ask to borrow their ladder, but instead, he booted the door in and burst inside. A woman, minus her Burqa, shrieked in horror at the sight of an unrelated man. Ignoring her, Jack grabbed the simple ladder that lay on the ground and withdrew, dragging it behind him.

'Come on, Fatteh! Daffadar, take charge of the men!'

Jack and Fatteh propped the ladder against the wall of the tower. Although it did not quite reach the crenellated top, Jack knew it was the best they could do. A group of young boys ran forward, each one throwing stones that bounced from the wall. A shot rang out from the flat roof of one of the houses, with the drift of powder smoke the only sign of the shooter.

Jack returned to the short line of bayonets. 'Up the ladder with you, lads! Hassan, you go first! Guides, if you see anybody aiming at us, shoot him.'

The Guides swarmed up one at a time, with Jack last. He heard the deep boom of a jezzail and saw the heavy splash as a bullet thudded into the wall two feet from his side.

'Fire!'

An instant before Jack gave the order, the Guides opened up. Four rifles fired at once, followed by a deep laugh from Alladad. 'That's one Afridi who won't be raiding my village!'

'Good man!' Jack rolled onto the roof of the tower. 'Haul the ladder up!'

Jack looked around. The roof of the tower was flat, with a low, crenellated wall as a defence against attack. In the centre of the floor, a square hatch allowed access to whatever lay beneath. Stones were piled at various places on the roof. Like most things in Pakhtunkhwa, it was functional but basic.

'Keep watch,' Jack ordered.

The Guides were safe for the present, Jack reasoned. He did not wish to think of the reverse; although Gulbaz's men could not get up, neither could the Guides get down. The watchtower could only be a temporary refuge.

'Sawan! Check down below; see if there is any food or water stored.'

'Yes, Sahib.' Sawan moved on Jack's final word.

With the Guides all in the same place, Gulbaz stepped forward from the mob. He lifted his metal hook, urging the crowd to the attack. They swirled ahead, throwing missiles.

'How many are there, sahib?' Zaman asked.

'I'm not sure.' The crowd was growing by the minute as men swarmed to Torkrud from the surrounding villages. 'At least a couple of hundred.'

'We can shoot them until our ammunition runs out.' Zaman sounded calm.

'They are your people.' Jack was surprised at Zaman's callousness.

'They are attacking us.' Zaman showed the pragmatism of the Pashtun.

'Don't fire unless they fire first.' Jack raised his voice. 'Check your ammunition! How many rounds do you have?'

'Seventy rounds each, sahib,' Hassan said. 'We are the Guides. We carry seventy rounds and eighty-five percussion caps.'

'Good man.' Jack was learning why the Guides were considered an elite fighting force. They were ready for whatever emergency the Frontier threw up.

Sawan swarmed up from the chamber below. 'There is neither food nor water, sahib,' he reported. 'Only some old clothes fit for rags, a few bits of broken weapons, some rubbish and barrels of mouldy gunpowder.'

We're sitting on barrels of explosives. That's not healthy. 'We can't stay here for long, then.' Jack had wondered if he could remain on the tower until Batoor returned. 'We only have whatever water is in our water bottles.'

'They're coming, sahib!' Hassan warned.

Now swollen to over 300 men, the mob surged forward, some firing at the Guides and others throwing stones.

'Fire at the men with muskets,' Jack ordered as a ball chipped the parapet beside him. Aiming his revolver, he loosed two shots without hitting his man. Rather than fire wildly as inexperienced men might have done, the Guides leant their rifles on the parapet, took careful aim, and squeezed their triggers. Two of the jezzail men crumpled, one to lie still as the other writhed, holding his stomach. A crowd of young boys began to clamber up the wall of the tower.

'Get rid of them, Sawar!' Jack ordered. 'Try not to hurt them. They're only children.'

'Yes, sahib.' Lifting one of the loose rocks that were scattered about the flat roof, Sawar leaned over the parapet. 'Here!' He dropped the rock. Three boys fell to the ground.

'I said don't hurt them.' Jack ducked as a bullet whined past his head. He saw a large part of the mob surge to the base of the tower and charge around, searching for an entry. Yelling and shaking crude weapons, they milled around the base.

'Leave them,' Jack said. 'I have no intention of starting a blood feud by killing virtually unarmed men. They can't do us any harm down there.'

'They can try,' Hassan said. 'Look. Gulbaz has them organised.'

With Gulbaz giving loud orders, dozens of men were hacking at the stonework at the base of the tower, sliding the blades of Khyber knives and pulwars between the stones to prise them free.

Jack swore. 'You're right, Hassan. If they take out enough stones, the tower will collapse.' He pointed to the closest pile of rocks. 'Copy Sawar; save ammunition by dropping stones on them.'

Hassan nodded. 'Yes, sahib.'

Laying aside their rifles, Hassan, Sawar and Fatteh rolled the largest of the rocks over to the edge of the roof. Beneath them, the crowd continued to work at the wall, cheering whenever they managed to work loose one of the stones.

'Ready?' Jack ducked as one of Gulbaz's men fired his jezzail. The sound was like a miniature cannon as a massive spurt of smoke jetted from the barrel. The shot crashed against the parapet, crumbling the solid mud. 'Drop!'

Grinning, Hassan toppled the rock.

The men working on the wall glanced up; one pointed upwards, too late. The rock landed in the middle of the pack, killing one man outright and injuring three others. One crawled away with his leg at a terrible angle; another held a shattered arm. The others scattered, shouting.

'Now fire!' Jack said softly. Gulbaz and his men were serious; it was time to properly retaliate. 'Try and drop Gulbaz.'

It was only an hour or so since Jack had doubted the loyalty of the Guides when facing fellow Pashtuns. He no longer had any misgivings as they opened rapid fire on Gulbaz's men so for a few moments the watchtower was the centre of a firefight. With their elevated position and better weapons, the Guides had the advantage, so their attackers withdrew to the cover of the various compounds. Glaring over his shoulder, Gulbaz joined them.

'Cease fire,' Jack ordered.

Powder-smoke drifted over the four Pashtun dead on the ground and the half dozen staggering or crawling wounded. The small boys continued to jeer; hiding behind a wall, they threw stones at the watchtower.

'We beat them back,' Hassan said.

'For now,' Jack agreed. 'But we can't stay up here forever. They will come again at night.'

'They will.' Hassan gave a small smile. 'The Guides can also fight at night.'

Jack hid his smile. It seemed that the Pashtun were as liable to regimental pride as any British regiment. 'Of course we can.' He emphasised the use of 'we.'

The day passed slowly, with Gulbaz's men keeping their distance but sniping when they could. Jack watched for the return of Batoor while trying to work out a plan to withdraw safely from the village. They ate half the bread they had brought with them drank from their water bottles, baked in the sun, and waited.

Evening came with its usual rush. The crisp darkness of the Frontier descended, brittle with tension as if the world held its breath. The chanting began again.

'They are saying, "kill the feringhee,"' Hassan said.

'They'll have to catch me first,' Jack said. "We'll take shifts. Two on watch, the others resting.' He raised his voice slightly. 'You men on watch; keep moving so the enemy cannot aim at you.'

'We know how to fight, sahib,' Hassan rebuked gently.

'I'm sure you do.' Jack glanced upward, where clouds obscured the night sky. 'No stars tonight, so we'll need artificial lights in case Gulbaz attacks.' He lowered his voice, knowing how far sound travelled at night. 'Fatteh: I have been told that you can find anything; find me a length of cloth. The rest of you, give me one of your cartridges.'

'Sahib?' The Guides looked confused.

'One cartridge from each man,' Jack said. 'Fatteh, have you found me that cloth yet?'

'There are old clothes below,' Sawan reminded him as Fatteh disappeared down the hatch.

Collecting the cartridges, Jack split them open and ground the gunpowder into the cloth Fatteh brought him. 'Fatteh; cut that into four, and put one piece on each side of the tower. Those are our lanterns if we need them.'

'Yes, sahib.' Sawan sounded confused.

'Now, unless you are on watch, grab as much sleep as you can. Either stay up here or go into the chamber below.' Jack contemplated remaining awake but knew he needed to keep alert, which meant resting while he could. Lying in the shadow of the parapet, Jack closed his eyes. Despite his best intentions, he could not sleep. He lay still, with ideas and images chasing each other through his mind. He saw the tabla mullah, and Batoor's friendly face, the children climbing up the wall of the tower, and Gulbaz with his iron claw, the long puff of smoke from a jezzail, and the scared face of the woman without a burqa.

He heard the noises an hour later, the furtive pad of feet on hard ground.

Jack nudged Zaman, the nearest Guide. There was no need to say anything. Zaman understood immediately, waking the man next to him. Moving more quietly than even Jack expected, the Guides took their posts behind the battlements of the tower.

The first of Gulbaz's men slid over the parapet in complete silence. A young, lithe man wearing a pakul hat and carrying a naked pulwar, he had only time to look around him before Zaman thrust his bayonet into his chest, so he died without a sound. The second man was naked except for a loin-cloth, and with a knife between his teeth. Alladad slit his throat, catching the sword he carried before it clattered onto the ground. The attackers climbed two sides at once, with the Guides disposing of them immediately as they arrived. Within three minutes there were five dead men on the top of the tower. Zaman had disposed of the final two men; they lay on top of the bloody pile with the Guides grinning at each other, satisfied with a job well done.

'Shall we throw the bodies over the wall, sahib?' Hassan asked.

About to give assent, Jack remembered their lack of water. 'No, Hassan,' he said. 'We'll hold on to them just now.'

'They'll stink when the sun rises,' Hassan said.

'They might come in useful.' Jack did not elaborate. His idea was still embryonic.

'I hear something,' Zaman whispered.

The Guides fell silent, listening. Zaman lifted his hand, fingers outstretched. He closed his fist and opened it again three times. *Fifteen men approaching*, Jack guessed.

Taking a packet of Lucifer matches from inside his jacket, Jack scratched one alight and placed the flame on the nearest length of cloth. The gunpowder sparked immediately, casting darting shadows across the roof of the tower.

Lifting the end of the cloth furthest from the flame, Jack threw it over the parapet. The burning rag floated down, twisting as the fire caught hold. The light flitted across the ground, revealing half a dozen men lying prone with lethal pesh-kabz daggers or Khyber knives in their hands. As soon as the light revealed them, they rose, moving swiftly forward.

'Shoot them,' Jack ordered. 'Don't waste ammunition. Only fire if you're certain of a hit.'

'Hassan, Alladad; check the other sides.' Jack sounded calmer than he felt. He moved around the roof, setting fire to the rags he had prepared. The Guides were firing, the time between each shot informing Jack they were carefully aimed.

'They're all around us.' Hassan's voice was calm.

'How many?' Jack did not have to ask. Zaman had reported fifteen attackers, so fifteen attackers there would be.

'There were fifteen,' Hassan said. 'We've killed some.' There was the sound of a shot. 'I think eleven now.'

The attackers broke before the Guide's rifle fire, running back to the shelter of the dark village.

'Cease fire.' Jack waved his hand to clear some of the powder-smoke. He ducked at the thud of a jezzail, the bullet slamming into the parapet. 'It's going to be a long night.'

The sobbing of a wounded man disturbed the hush.

Chapter Seven

Torkrud, north-west frontier July 1863

Dawn brought little relief as the heat rose with the sun, baking the handful of men who sheltered behind the stone-and-mud parapets on the lookout tower. With the sun came the flies, attracted by the blood on the pile of dead bodies. The sobbing of the wounded Pashtun had ceased. He lay a few yards from the tower, his twisted body furred with flies.

'We should throw them over the side.' Hassan nodded to the corpses. 'Soon they will stink.'

'Don't your people hold their dead in high esteem?' Jack asked. 'Don't they value men killed in battle?'

'That is true, sahib, but these men are not Guides.' Hassan dismissed the bodies as if they were so much carrion.

'We could cut off their heads.' Zaman added various other anatomical details that Jack preferred not to contemplate.

'Gulbaz may want his dead back.' Jack had noticed that parties of Gulbaz's men were creeping out to retrieve the dead from the previous night's skirmish.

'Is it your intention to give succour to the enemy?' Hassan looked unbelieving. 'It is not the Pashtun way.'

'I intend to barter with them,' Jack said. Raising his voice to a shout, he called out: 'Gulbaz! Can you hear me?'

After a few minutes, an answering hail came. 'I hear you, Windrush. If you surrender, I will supply an escort to take you and your men away from the lands of the Rahmut Khel.'

'Elphinstone sahib agreed to such terms,' Jack reminded him. 'The Afghans murdered all his men, with twelve thousand camp followers. I have another proposal for you.'

The silence was broken by the deep thud of a jezzail and the crunch of a bullet against the parapet.

'Speak, Windrush.' Gulbaz's voice was strangely musical.

'I propose that you surrender to me, and I will not desecrate the bodies of the men we have here.' Jack knew that Gulbaz would never agree to such a suggestion. He also knew that the relatives of the dead men would wish the bodies returned, so with luck he might spread dissension among the enemy.

Before Jack continued, Zaman shouted: 'We will castrate them, cut off the heads, and pour bacon grease into the mouths and bodies.'

Pigs were anathema to the followers of Islam. Zaman had given one of the worst insults he could imagine. He glanced at Jack, grinning.

'We have no bacon grease, sahib.' Ursulla was not the brightest of the Guides.

'Gulbaz does not know that.' Jack did not approve of Zaman's interference, but given the circumstances, he decided to say nothing. He expected Gulbaz's renewal of activity as half a dozen jezzails fired at once, with the bullets crashing into the battlements or whistling through the embrasures.

'We've got him angry, sahib.' Zaman was still grinning. 'Shall I throw him the head of one of his men?'

'Not yet,' Jack said.

'Shall I throw him something else, then?' Zaman made several suggestions, each one cruder than the previous.

'Not yet,' Jack repeated. 'Let's wait until he thinks about my proposal.'

'What do you have in mind, sahib?' Hassan asked.

'A trade,' Jack said. 'We need water and food; Gulbaz will want the bodies back.'

Hassan nodded. 'You are not as stupid as I thought you were, sahib.'

'Thank you, Hassan.'

The firing sputtered to a stop. 'Windrush!' Gulbaz shouted again. 'Leave us our dead, and you can go free.'

'I won't even answer that,' Jack said softly.

'Zaman had the best idea,' Hassan said. 'Throw Gulbaz a head or two, sahib.'

'Not yet,' Jack said. 'Ursulla, wrap up a rock in a piece of cloth. Make it look like a human head in cloth.'

'Yes, sahib.' Ursulla was apparently confused but was too good a soldier to question a direct order. He handed Jack a covered bundle that was roughly the size of a human head.

'Gulbaz!' Jack made to stand up until a marksman took a shot with a jezzail. Fortunately firing upward at a moving target seen through the aperture between irregular battlements did not help the marksman's aim. The shot flicked past Jack's shoulder. 'Here is a present for you, Gulbaz!' He threw the bundled rock as far as he could, watched it thud onto the hard ground, bounce once and roll. Almost immediately a man scurried out of cover to retrieve the bundle.

'Don't shoot him,' Jack ordered as Zaman levelled his rifle. He watched as Gulbaz's man scurried away with the bundle.

'That's a rock!' Gulbaz said a moment later.

'The next one won't be,' Jack promised.

'What do you want, Windrush?' Gulbaz did not appear from behind his sheltering wall.

'Water and food.' Jack decided to end the guessing game. 'Unless you wish to surrender.'

'You wish water and food in exchange for what?'

'I wish water and food in exchange for the return of your dead,' Jack said.

There was a pause. Jack guessed that Gulbaz was consulting his elders. 'I agree. Lower our dead, and we will bring you water and food.'

Jack grunted. He was making some progress. 'You bring out food and water, Gulbaz, and I will have some of your dead lowered.' He raised his voice. 'To show that I trust you, for I know an Afridi will never damage his honour by breaking his word, I will have one man lowered first.' He signalled to Hassan and Ursulla, who took hold of the hands and ankles of the topmost corpse.

'Lower him carefully,' Jack ordered.

'Yes, sahib.' Hassan hoisted the dead man above the parapet and let him go.

Ten minutes later, two of Gulbaz's men staggered into the open. Both carried heavy goatskin containers and baskets of bread.

'Stop there!' Jack commanded. 'Both of you.' The men were thin, nearly gaunt, and large-eyed. They stared as Jack stood with one foot on top of the battlements. 'Take a drink from the water.'

They stared at him. One lifted the skin to his mouth, dropped it, and ran away. The second followed quickly.

With his throat already parched from lack of water, Jack shouted, 'Try again, Gulbaz! Bring us water that you have not poisoned. This is your last chance!'

'Throw him a head, sahib,' Hassan urged.

'No,' Jack said. 'I won't stoop to such barbarity.'

'It may save all our lives,' Hassan said.

About to refuse permission, Jack remembered Kerr's advice to be guided by Hassan. 'All right, Hassan.'

God forgive me for the sacrilege.

Jack did not watch as Zaman cheerfully sawed off the head of the nearest fly-covered corpse.

'Here, Gulbaz. A gift for you.' Lifting the head by its hair, Zaman swung it back and forth before throwing it in a high, blood-spraying arc over the battlements. Jack saw the head bounce once before it rolled towards the nearest house.

'The feringhee officer is pouring pig fat over the body!' Zaman laughed as somebody in the village began to wail, a cry that was soon taken up by others.

After the expected fusillade of musketry, Gulbaz shouted again, 'Here is clean water, Windrush, and the bread is fresh.'

This time three veiled women brought the water and bread. When they appeared, Zaman aimed his rifle.

'Don't fire.' Jack pushed the barrel up.

The women stopped at the foot of the tower, placed the water-skins and baskets of bread on the ground, and gracefully returned with their long white burqas brushing the dirt.

Jack manoeuvred the ladder over the wall. 'I'll go down. Cover me.'

With his heart thumping inside his chest, Jack swarmed down the ladder and carefully sampled the water. 'It's sweet,' he announced. His head was throbbing from dehydration.

Expecting the thump of a jezzail bullet, Jack carried the water and food up the ladder. 'Throw the bodies over. Throw them as far as you can to clear the flies away.'

It was a relief to get the corpses with their buzzing cargo from the tower. Jack watched, licking dry lips as the men drank from the water-skins. When at last it was his turn, the goat-scented liquid tasted like nectar.

'We don't appreciate how precious water is back in England,' he said. The Guides looked at him, not comprehending.

'This bread is delicious.' Jack had not realised how hungry he had been.

Hassan nodded at that. 'We have a saying that Pashtun women make bread and children. They need do no more. They make the best bread and the strongest children.' He laughed, pointing to the surrounding landscape. 'They have to be the strongest, or they would not survive in a land such as ours.'

The moments the bodies were removed, the sniping began again. Every time one of the Guides showed his head in one of the embrasures a jezzail would fire. Fatteh swore as a splinter nicked the side of his face.

'Permission to fire back, sahib?'

'Only if you are certain of your target,' Jack said. 'Don't waste ammunition.' He kept careful watch over the village, seeing a steady trickle of men come in from the surrounding hills. 'The enemy's numbers are growing all the time.'

'They will starve us out,' Hassan said. 'Now we have nothing left to bargain with, and they know we are short of water and food. They will wait until we are weak and then charge the tower. Patience is a Pashtun virtue.'

Jack nodded. 'I have heard that your people can wait for days to ambush a single man.'

Hassan nodded. 'The feringhees hurry here, and hurry there; they do everything at a rush. Among the Pashtun, we have a proverb. The Pashtun who took revenge after a hundred years said: I took it quickly.'

Jack nodded. 'We have different ideas about time, Daffadar.'

With his 113th Foot, Jack would have not hesitated to ask the advice of an experienced sergeant. He did not know how the Guides would respond. Again, he remembered Kerr telling him to take Hassan's advice. 'We have choices to make, gentlemen. You all know the Pashtun better than I do, so I will welcome any comments, although I will make the final decision.'

The Guides nodded their acceptance. *Good.*

'Our first choice is that we remain on this tower in the hope that Batoor Khan returns soon. Our second choice is to slide away at night and hope to escape unseen. Our third is to fight our way out, hoping to cause so many casualties that Gulbaz is unwilling to follow us.'

The Guides listened, nodding. 'We do not know where Batoor Khan is,' Hassan pointed out. 'He could be defending the lands of the Rahmut Khel as he said, but if so, we have heard no gunfire.'

'That is true,' Jack conceded the point.

'In that case, Batoor Khan is far away, and we do not know how long he will be.'

Jack nodded. 'That is also true. The option of waiting for him is closed.' He ducked as a jezzail roared. The bullet smacked into the parapet, chipping away a sizeable chunk of stone.

'Gulbaz will expect us to sneak away at night,' Zaman pointed out. 'His men will be alert for that.'

Jack nodded. He knew that his Guides were expert at silent night movement, but so were the warriors of Gulbaz's Rahmut Khel.

Zaman patted the lock of his rifle. 'A break out will be honourable.'

'It will also be suicidal,' Hassan said.

Jack ducked as another jezzail bullet crashed into the parapet at his side. 'Sawan, you said there was no food or water stored below. Remind me what else there was.'

'Gunpowder, sahib,' Sawan replied at once. 'A few rusty pulwars that my grandfather would have thrown away, some old clothing...'

'Gunpowder? I forgot you mentioned that.'

'I said it was mouldy, sahib. It is not of good quality.'

'I'll have a look,' Jack said. 'Daffadar, you take over here. I'm going down below.'

The chamber was dark and dusty, with scorpions that scuttled away, tails erect, as Jack used a flaming rag for light. Wary of the gunpowder, he peered around. Sawan's assessment of the stores was correct. The pulwars were rusted and fragile-bladed, the clothing mostly rotted, and only a few of the barrels of gunpowder in reasonable condition.

Jack inspected the three best of the barrels; the British government markings stamped on the outside suggested that they had been stolen from some garrison, possibly during the Mutiny. Jack remembered his mission to search for stolen Enfields, briefly wondered if there was a connection, and dismissed the thought. His priority now was to get his men to safety. All other considerations were secondary.

He started as something crashed against the wall, realised that it was only a jezzail bullet, and rolled the powder kegs immediately beneath the hatch.

'Sawan! Drop me your bayonet!'

Using the tip of the blade, Jack made a hole in each of the barrels. The coarse-grained powder inside was dry but probably more volatile than he would have liked. Casting around for a fuse, he grabbed at the bundle of old clothes, swearing at the swarm of crawling insects that he released.

'That'll do.' He sliced a long strip of cloth, scattered gun powder over the top, and coiled it around the barrels. As an afterthought, he part-emptied each barrel, pouring the gunpowder into one of the small half-rotted goatskin bags that lay in an untidy pile in one corner of the chamber.

One can never have too much gunpowder, he told himself. *Although I do not at present know how I can use it.*

Aware of the Guides looking quizzically at him when he emerged from below, Jack took a quick swig from the already warm water. 'We're leaving an hour after sundown,' he said.

'Yes, sahib.' Having already voiced their concerns, the Guides would obey Jack's orders without question.

'We'll leave Gulbaz's men with a little souvenir of our visit,' Jack said. 'I'm afraid Batoor Khan will have to build another watchtower, as we're going to blow this one up.' He saw the glimmer of humour in the eyes of his men. 'We need a diversion.'

Splitting the remaining bread into two unequal portions, Jack spread around the smaller pile. 'Eat that,' he said. 'We'll need to keep our strength up.' The rest he divided into seven pieces and handed out to his men. 'This will have to feed us until we find a friendly village.'

'Yes, sahib.'

'Who amongst you is best at moving silently at night?' Jack knew that all Pashtun were expert at the arts of concealment and ambush, so the best of this patrol of Guides would be an expert.

'Alladad,' Hassan said without hesitation. 'He can walk through a thunderstorm disguised as a drop of rain without getting wet.'

Alladad was a supremely handsome man with kohl-rimmed eyes. He stroked his immaculate beard, evidently pleased at the praise.

'I have a job for you, Alladad, if you are willing,' Jack said. 'It is not an order; think of the implications before deciding.' Jack knew that his style of leadership, developed with the rogues of the 113th, was not what the Guides were used to. He hoped they would not take advantage of his flexibility.

'Speak, Sahib.'

'Could you slip through Torkud to retrieve our horses?'

Ignoring the almost obligatory jezzail shot, Alladad stood up, moving from side to side to put any marksman off his mark. He scanned the village, passing his gaze across the walled houses to where the horses were stabled. 'Yes, sahib.'

'The men of Torkud will be waiting for you.'

Alladad smiled. 'If Allah wills, I will succeed.'

'Can you all ride without saddles and bridles?' Jack asked.

'We are Pashtun.' Hassan's reply was calm as ever. 'And we are the Guides.'

'I expected nothing else,' Jack said with immense satisfaction. He bit back his concern for Alladad. The man was a soldier; he must accept danger.

The loud report startled Jack. The entire tower shook as something heavy crashed into the wall. 'That was no jezzail.' *Has Gulbaz found some artillery? Is the gun-runner dealing with more than just rifles?*

'That was a jingal.' Zaman sounded calm.

Jack saw the rising coil of smoke from deep inside Torkrud. *Of course, it was a jingal.* Jingals were large-calibre muskets or small, smooth-bore cannons, with a greater range than hand-held firearms. The deep boom sounded again, and another jingal ball crashed into the parapet, raising a great cloud of dust. 'I've faced them before,' Jack said. 'I thought they were normally mounted on the back of camels or elephants.'

'Gulbaz must have one somewhere in Torkrud.' Hassan pushed Fatteh further down. 'Keep down, Fatteh. I'm not going to kiss you better if Gulbaz puts a bullet through your arse.'

The jezzail ball crashed into the ground between Jack's feet, spreading splinters of rock. One sliced into his calf, tearing open a small cut. He grunted; that was another scar to add to his collection.

'Lie down,' Jack ordered. 'If you see any targets, shoot.' The Guides had been lucky so far, but with the volume of fire increasing, it was only a matter of time before they began to take casualties.

'The jingal is well concealed,' Hassan said quietly. 'Luckily it takes time to load. I hope they don't have much powder.'

I wonder if the powder kegs in this tower were for the jingal.

'We'll survive the day,' Jack said. 'Keep under cover as much as you can.' He ducked as the deep thud of the jingal sounded again. The ball crashed against the top of the parapet, destroying the stonework. 'I wish we could do something about that.'

Hassan nodded toward the drifting smoke. 'I could take two men across to find it.'

'In daylight?' Jack shook his head. 'Gulbaz will be waiting for that. Roll over the rocks to form a second barrier behind the parapet. Gulbaz is firing from a lower level, so hopefully, the jingal won't be able to reach us.'

It was the work of ten minutes to create a second barricade and pull the Guides behind it. The sniping continued, punctuated by the heavier boom of the jingal every fifteen minutes. 'There's no need for us all to lie so exposed,' Jack said. 'I'll stay up here with two men on watch. The rest go down below. It's safer. For God's sake, don't cause any sparks."

'Sahib,' Hassan said. 'It is best if you go below. We are used to the heat.'

'Thank you, Daffadar, but I'll stay here.' Jack knew the old adage that an officer should not order a man to do what he would not do himself. He would not leave men in danger while he hid below.

The jingal concentrated on one section of the tower, very slowly crumbling away the parapet and the corner of the roof that faced the village.

'They are trying to weaken us,' Jack said. 'They'll come at night with scaling ladders.'

'Yes, sahib,' Hassan said.

'We'll have to ensure that Alladad moves first,' Jack decided. He did not admit how worried he was. *A good officer must appear confident at all times, or his men will lose faith in him. Sometimes, only sometimes, I wish I was a ranker with no responsibilities except to myself. How easy a life a private soldier's must be, following orders and allowing others to make all the decisions.*

No! Jack shook his head. *I cannot think like that. I do have responsibilities; I have to look after these men, and I have Mary and Andrew waiting for me.* For a moment Jack thought what Mary's life would be like as the wife of an ordinary soldier. She would share a barrack room with a score of men with only a tattered blanket for privacy, with no security, half a man's rations, and always the possibility of being left behind when the regiment moved.

No.

'We have to stick it, Hassan.' Jack forced a grin.

We have to stick it.

Chapter Eight

Torkrud, north-west frontier July 1863

Lying behind a makeshift barricade under the sun, Jack watched as the jingal balls slowly crumbled their parapet away. He could do nothing except watch and wait.

I do not want Andrew to join the Army. Jack thought of his young son, helpless in his cot. *No, I want him to be a solicitor, or a banker, or a doctor, anything but a soldier. I don't want him to put himself in danger on a daily basis. I must tell Mary that when I get back. But first I have to get back.*

'Get ready, Alladad. It's nearly time.'

Stripped to only a loincloth, Alladad slipped through an embrasure at the back of the tower and vanished. Although Jack was only a few feet from him, he did not see him move. He peered into the dark.

The night was still. No wind; no sound, not even the barking of a dog or bleating of a goat. Jack felt the tension rise. Gulbaz had made a mistake; he should have kept the jezzail-men firing if only to keep the Guides occupied. He should have sent his storming party forward in the half-light before full dark when men were unsure what was real and what was not. That hesitation gave the attackers the advantage. *It's too late now, Gulbaz, too late now.*

Taking out his watch, Jack counted the seconds. Alladad had said he would need only five minutes to reach the stables. Jack allowed six, with each second hanging heavy as the minute hand slowly hovered above the next mark. He disliked sending a man into danger, for he firmly believed that an officer should never send a man to do what he would not do himself. However, Jack knew that Alladad was far better suited at freeing the horses than he would ever be. *God speed, Alladad, or Allah speed, if you prefer.*

'Time,' Jack said. Dropping through the hatch to the chamber below, he scratched a Lucifer and watched the flame grow for a moment before applying it to the end of the rag and scrambling back up.

'We've got less than three minutes.'

'We belong to God,' Hassan said, 'and to God do we return.'

Rather than everybody crowding on one ladder, Jack had them tie the old clothes together into makeshift ropes. With the top end fastened to the battlements where Alladad had climbed down, he dropped the ropes over the side, and the Guides slithered down, landing on the hard ground without a sound. They moved silently across to the corner of the building opposite, taking up defensive positions.

'Where's Alladad?' Jack thought of the fuse within the tower, quickly fizzing toward the kegs of gunpowder. He wished he had given it longer to burn.

'He's not here yet.' Hassan was as calm as if he was in barracks at Mardan.

The whole operation depends on Alladad. I should have gone myself, rather than sending a trooper. Jack glanced over his shoulder, thinking of the sparking fuse at the gunpowder. *Dear God, hurry, Alladad!*

'He's coming,' Zaman said. 'I heard the stable door open.'

Jack heard the horses' hooves a moment later, accompanied by a high yell that could only have been Alladad.

'Here he comes.' Jack swore as he heard the crackle of musketry. 'Get ready, lads!'

The horses erupted from the darkened village, a confusion of tossing manes and pounding hooves, with flaring nostrils and the occasional fearful high whinny.

'Grab your horse,' Jack ordered. 'Make for the gate! Hurry!' Waiting until all his men were mounted, Jack threw himself onto the last horse in the pack. He saw Colwall among the loose horses but had no time to reach for him. 'Well done, Alladad! Move now!'

Without glancing at his watch, Jack knew that time was up. The kegs of powder should have blown by now; the tower should be ablaze, giving them cover from the pursuit that was bound to occur. He hoped he had not taken too much powder from the kegs; he needed a massive explosion.

A horse whinnied shrilly as a bullet hit it. Blood spurted, half seen in the dark. Men rose beside them, slashing with pulwars and Khyber knives. Zaman roared, parried a pulwar swing with his Enfield, fired, and rode on.

The yelling increased as a hundred men burst from the buildings. Gulbaz must have timed his attack for that moment, for each man was armed and ready. Jack had time to fire a single round from his revolver before the mob was surging behind him.

'Spur, lads!'

That was when the gunpowder kegs blew up. Jack had experienced louder explosions during the siege of Sevastopol, and at Lucknow, but rarely had he been so close to a building that was so thoroughly destroyed. The gunpowder threw out the unmortared stones of the tower, so they splintered into small, deadly fragments that sprayed across the village, adding to the mayhem. Half a dozen of Gulbaz's men fell at once, with others ducking or throwing themselves to the ground to escape the flying debris. Fatteh fell from his horse, shook his head, and threw himself onto the nearest mount.

'Spur!' Temporarily deafened by the blast, Jack did not hear himself shout. As a youth, Jack had occasionally ridden bareback on the swelling slopes of the Malvern Hills. Back then it had been fun, an innocent feat of daring. Now, with scores of Pashtun warriors behind him, riding without a saddle, bridle or reins was far harder than he remembered. Clutching a handful of the horse's mane, Jack held on, shouting 'gallop, lads!' as loudly as he could.

The Guides did not have to be ordered to gallop. Jack was a good horseman; he had ridden point-to-point across Herefordshire and along the ridge of the Malvern Hills, yet he was awed by the skill of his men. Even without saddles or stirrups, they rode their horses like trained jockeys, ducking away from the flying splinters, driving onwards to the exit of the village.

Glancing over his shoulder, Jack saw Gulbaz's men as a mass of fierce, shouting faces and waving pulwars. He could not pick out individuals, even if he had wished to. By sheer determination, Jack forced himself to the front of his Guides to arrive at the gate a length ahead of his men.

The gate was closed and barred, with the white-bearded watchman staring in confusion at the flaming watchtower and the mass of horses charging towards him. Sensibly, he moved out of the way as Jack leapt from his horse, staggered, rolled and recovered. Grabbing the beam that closed the gate, Jack lifted it, poised, and threw it aside, nodding as Hassan joined him.

'Good man, Hassan!'

Working together, they thrust open the gate, with Jack waving through the Guides.

'I'll join you, Hassan!' Jack heard his voice as a distant croak. 'Get on your horse!'

'I won't leave you behind, sahib.' Hassan lifted his Enfield to cover Jack.

'I'm just coming!' Jack looked back at Torkrud. He had been welcomed here, yet left it a scene of smoking carnage. Othere than surrender, to face a grisly death by torture, there was nothing else he could have done.

Ten horses lay on the ground amidst the rubble of the watchtower and the bodies of men. In the dark, Jack was unsure if they were his Guides or the enemy. He hesitated, wondering if he had time to check. He saw Gulbaz's warriors surging forward and knew he had not.

'Come on, sahib. Your men are waiting for you.'

Jack looked around. Hassan was correct. His men were waiting, sitting astride their horses in line abreast. 'Come on, lads!' Kicking in his heels, he held on to the mane of his horse as they cantered into the dark with Gulbaz's men sending them away with a fusillade of shots.

Jack counted his men. By some miracle, they were all there, although one or two nursed minor wounds. That was on the credit side. On the debit side, his mission had ended in inglorious failure. He was no further forward in discovering the gun smugglers and had only gathered scanty information about the Mujahidin. Now he may have turned a potential British ally into an enemy. Jack pushed the black thoughts from his head. *No. He must concentrate on getting his men home. That was his principal duty; all the rest had to wait.*

'Kick on, boys, let's get away from here.'

That mad careen along the dark valley was something that Jack would long remember. His Guides took it all in their stride; riding bareback through potentially hostile territory without knowing the track seemed not to bother them. After fifteen minutes, Jack eased their pace and called them together.

'Well done, men,' he said. 'Now I have only one plan: get back to Mardan. We're stuck deep in tribal territory here, so it might be a bit sticky.'

'Every man's hand will be against us.' Fatteh looked around. Patchy clouds concealed the moon, but starlight glowed dimly behind the ragged peaks.

'We will have to fight our way through.' Zaman looked pleased with the prospect.

'If it is Allah's will, we will survive.' Alladad was struggling into his uniform.

'That is so.' Hassan nodded.

'We will ride faster with saddles,' Jack said. 'We can double back and pick up our own, or raid a village for them, although I don't like to take from innocent people.'

'These are only Afridis.' Alladad spoke with the contempt that the Yusufzai had for all other peoples. 'We need the saddles more than they do.'

'We double back.' Jack made his decision. 'We will lose distance, but Gulbaz won't expect that.'

'We will have to fight,' Hassan said.

'We have the advantage of surprise,' Jack reminded him. 'Ride hard, hit them, and return.'

There were no arguments. The Guides accepted Jack's decision. Leaving the spare horses tethered within a small copse of wind-stunted pines, they turned at once, galloping through the dark towards Torkrud. Jack knew he had no need to order the Guides to load their rifles; these men had been carrying weapons since they could walk.

'Look ahead, sahib!' Hassan pointed into the dark.

Jack had already heard the drumbeat of hooves on the path. Gulbaz had organised the pursuit with impressive speed, so now a score of mounted men hammered towards them.

Fight or flee? We are the Guides; we need saddles.

'Blast your way through,' Jack ordered. 'Fire when you have a target!' He knew that surprise was half the battle. Despite Gulbaz's men having the advantage of numbers and saddles, he knew that a sudden rush would catch them unawares. Movement always stimulated his brain; the idea came to him immediately.

'Fatteh! Do you have your bugle with you?'

'Yes, sahib!' Fatteh produced the instrument.

'When we are closer, play it. Sound the charge. Everybody, the instant that Fatteh plays, make as much noise as you can. Make Gulbaz believe that the entire Guides cavalry is here, aye and the Household Brigade and the Enniskillen dragoons as well. On my word, Fatteh!'

It was an old trick that Jack had used before in the fighting around Sebastopol. At best it could unsettle the enemy; at worst it was only a waste of Fatteh's breath.

A few of Gulbaz's horsemen slowed as they tried to ascertain who was charging towards them. A hail or two sounded through the dark.

Somebody fired a shot in the air. With a curtain of dust adding to the darkness, Jack drew his revolver, hoping he could retain his seat without stirrups.

'Now, Fatteh! Sound the charge!'

The brassy notes cut through the night, joined by the yells and cheers of the Guides.

'Forward the Guides!' Jack added his own voice to the noise. 'Number One troop, to the right. Number Two troop, guard the flanks! Number Three Troop, act as rearguard!' Leaning forward over his horse's neck, he fired two shots at the now confused Rahmut Khel. 'Follow me, Guides!'

The Guides hit Gulbaz's men hard, slicing into the hesitating horsemen and pushing through without pausing. Jack fired, seeing the mass part before him, heard a confusion of rifle fire in his wake, and kicked his horse on. He saw men turn aside, heard Zaman's high-pitched laugh, and then burst through to open ground with the Guides in arrowhead formation behind him.

Unsure of the number of men who had appeared so suddenly, the Rahmut Khel had little time to retaliate. Most of them scattered into the night, preferring the security of the dark to the uncertainty of fighting an unknown force.

As soon as they were clear of the Rahmut Khel, Jack pulled up. 'Is anybody missing?'

'No, sahib.' Hassan was not even out of breath.

'Kick on.' Jack guided his horse aside to count his men. *All present! Thank you, God.* He pushed onward, feeling the muscles of the horse between his legs. The gates of Torkrud were open, with a gaggle of ancient men and burqa-clad women clustered to see what the shooting meant. Riding through them without a word of explanation, Jack passed the smoking, still burning remnants of the watchtower to head straight for the stables.

'Zaman, you and Sawan guard the doors. The rest, grab saddles and bridles, get the horses ready.' Jack knew he had only minutes before Gulbaz reorganised his men. He had no wish to be trapped inside

Torkrud. 'I'll have Colwell back.' He exchanged horses with Sawan, wasting a few seconds to fondle his animal.

There was no resistance in the village. The men of Torkrud were either with Batoor or Gulbaz, while the women had scattered as soon as Jack rode into the village. The Guides stared as Jack grabbed half a dozen horse-blankets. 'We might need these,' he said.

'Yes, sahib.' Their expressions indicated their disbelief.

'Get the saddles on.' Jack decided that the time spent in putting on the saddles would be well-spent. If they had a serious encounter with Gulbaz, having the men properly mounted would be a major advantage. Only when he was satisfied that everybody was ready did he glance around the stable, with his men's bearded, hard faces half-seen in the dim light. 'Does anybody know this area well?'

'I know it.' Ursulla spoke after a few moments' hesitation. He was the quietest of Jack's men. 'I have raided here.'

'Is there another way out, one we can get back to the Khyber or Mardan?'

Ursulla considered carefully before replying. 'Yes, sahib. Over the hills.'

'Could you find it in the dark?'

Again Ursulla paused before replying. 'Yes, sahib.'

'Take us.' Jack made an instant decision. 'You lead; we will follow.'

Filling their water bottles from the well, the Guides followed Ursulla out of Torkrud.

'Watch for Gulbaz,' Jack said.

Ursulla did not hesitate as he led them around the walls of the village and up the slope behind, at right angles and to the north of the direction they rode previously. Ursulla did not speak; he rode at a slow trot, concentrating on his route.

After the first mile, the path faded, so the horses had to pick their way over a rough hillside in the dark. Jack glanced behind them. The flames from the watchtower had faded to a dull glow, barely seen through the night. Listening for sounds of pursuit, he heard nothing but the clack of the horses' hooves on loose stones.

'How far is it, Ursulla?'

'We will circle around the main path,' Ursulla said. 'We have to climb a bit later.'

'How far?'

Ursulla screwed up his face. 'About thirty miles before we reach the Khyber.' His grin highlighted the brightness of his brown eyes. 'You will see what other areas of Pakhtunkhwa are like, sahib.'

Jack nodded; he was gradually unravelling the mysteries of this land. 'That can only be a good thing, Ursulla.'

With the horses slowly picking their way up a hillside of slithering scree and broken rock, the Guides were silent, concentrating on moving rather than thinking about Gulbaz and his men. When Colwell began to struggle, Jack dismounted and walked beside him, wondering at the sure-footed Afghan horses his men rode.

'Kabul ponies,' Hassan told him. 'They are stout and strong horses, not fast, but surer-footed than anything the British have. They are best in the hills.' He shook his head. 'They are not good on the plains, though.'

After another two hours climbing, the sky began to lighten, with grey-orange bands streaking behind the mountains. Jack heard the low whinny of a horse behind them. 'I think we're being followed.'

'Shall I go and check, sahib?' Zaman tapped his rifle.

'No.' Jack did not want his men straggled all across the hills of Pakhtunkhwa. 'We'll stick together. Muffle the horses.' He showed them how to fasten cloth around the horse's hooves. Fast learners, the Guides understood at once.

'Is that why you brought the horse blankets?' Hassan asked.

'It is one reason,' Jack said.

The Guides moved on, as silently as possible through the lessening dark. Every time they stopped, Jack listened for the sounds of pursuit. An eagle called, high, shrill and thrilling. Jack glanced up; nature did not care about the stupid manoeuvrings of mankind. Each animal and bird lived its own life without any process of politics, religion or race. They were even more pragmatic than the Pashtun.

'Sahib,' Hassan said softly. 'There is one man very close behind us. Gulbaz will have sent his fastest man to ensure he does not lose us. That man will follow, leaving signs for the others to follow.'

'That's a neat trick.' Jack approved of Gulbaz's professionalism. He tapped Zaman on the shoulder. 'Did you hear all that, Zaman?'

'Yes, sahib. I know Gulbaz's methods.'

'Could you kill the man who is following us?' That seemed a very cold-blooded question.

'Yes, sahib.' Zaman's teeth gleamed behind his beard.

'Do you want somebody with you?'

'No, sahib.'

'Don't drop too far behind.' Jack contained his doubts about separating his command.

They moved on, slightly slower, with Jack leading Colwell and the Guides riding. Nobody spoke. Everybody listened for sounds of pursuit or the resounding thud of a jezzail. Only the call of the eagle disturbed the night.

It was half an hour before Zaman ghosted beside them. Grinning, he handed Jack a bloody package. 'Here are the man's ears, sahib. He was a youngster with no more guile than a feringhee.'

Jack shook his head at the gift. 'Do with them what you wish, Zaman.'

'I will make them into a necklace,' Zaman said.

'You'll not disgrace your uniform.' Hassan spoke first. 'Throw these things away, trooper.'

Zaman, the prospective Khan of the Rahmut Khel, glared at Daffadar Hassan, then at Jack before he tossed away the dripping ears.

'Enough time wasted,' Jack said. 'Come on.'

They moved on as dawn burst out in the east. They had reached an area of stark mountains, with razor-edged ridges and a plethora of crevasses and chasms. Their route took them to where a hand-wide ridge soared above perpendicular slopes that descended to shadow. The roar of a distant river rose and fell with the wind. 'Is this the best road, Ursulla?'

'Yes, sahib.'

The ridge led to a slope too steep even for Kabul ponies to ascend, so the Guides dismounted and led them, uncomplaining. Jack looked down into the dark crevasses, wiped sweat from his forehead, and carried on with the muscles of his legs screaming in protest and hunger gnawing at his stomach. As they reached each crest, he checked behind him, seeing nothing except a wilderness of rocky hills, the hammering sun reflecting on the rocks to increase the heat. The first time that a stone cracked in the heat, Jack started, believing that one of Gulbaz's men was firing at them. After the third occurrence, he accepted the sound as part of the landscape of the Frontier.

This is different soldiering from the humid heat of India. I have tales to tell my grandchildren if I survive that long.

Above them, a second eagle had joined the first; both circled, looking for something to kill.

'Are we still being followed?'

Hassan nodded. 'Yes, sahib. Gulbaz lost us when Zaman killed his scout, but he is back now. He must know this area as well as Ursulla.'

'I can't see anybody.' Jack peered over the route they had come.

'Forgive me, sahib.' Hassan took Jack by the shoulder. 'Do you see that rock? Use your binoculars.'

Jack did so. The rock looked no different from a thousand others.

'Look closely, sahib.'

Jack focussed. 'It's moving!'

'That is Gulbaz. Look for the sun reflecting on his hook. The rock to his right? Do you see?'

Jack altered the angle of his binoculars. 'Yes, I see. That is also a man.'

'They all are, sahib. When we passed that way, there were no rocks. Now there are a hundred. Gulbaz knows we are watching, so he has ordered his men to lie still and cover themselves with their *kameez*, their long shirts. With these and the *shalwar*, the baggy trousers, being the same colour as the hill from this distance, they appear like rocks.' Hassan was very patient with his explanation.

'By God, that man is clever.' Jack calculated the distance. In the clear mountain air, Gulbaz's men looked closer than they were. 'They are out of range. Push on.'

Leading the horses up inclines that had Jack panting for breath, the Guides continued, exchanging banter as Jack checked behind him every few moments. Now that he knew what he was looking for, he saw Gulbaz's men every time, flitting behind them, closing the gap.

'The horses are slowing us down, sahib,' Hassan said. 'If we release them, we can outpace these pigs.'

'We'll need them later,' Jack pointed out. 'I don't intend us to walk through the Khyber Pass.'

'If Gulbaz catches us, we won't be alive to walk through the Khyber.'

'We'll have to make sure he does not catch us, then. Increase the speed.' Jack ignored Hassan's frown. 'Come on, lads! Gulbaz is nearly on our heels!'

They negotiated another narrow ridge with the horses' hooves kicking at loose stones that clattered down a nearly vertical slope to an unseen valley hundreds of feet below. Beyond the ridge, a mountain rose, sun-tortured to the unforgiving sky.

'We have to cross that hill,' Ursulla said.

Jack looked up, his mind busy. The horses were flagging. 'Hassan, take the men on. Leave signs, so I know in which direction you have gone.'

'What are you going to do, sahib?'

Jack took Ursulla's rifle and ammunition. 'I am going to slow down Gulbaz.'

'It would be better if I did that,' Hassan said. 'I am faster in the mountains. I won't get lost.'

'I gave you an order, Hassan.' Although Jack knew that Hassan was correct, he would not order one of his men to remain in danger while he walked away.

The sun was high now, pouring its heat from a bright sky. Jack felt the sweat breaking out on his forehead, soaking his back. He grunted; he had experienced worse in the Indian plains.

Lying prone on the baking ground, Jack placed his cartridges and percussion caps handy beside him and built a crude sangar with a single aperture through which to shoot. This low position limited his view of the ridge, so Gulbaz's men would be closer than he liked when he opened fire, but on the other hand, they could not see him. Settling down to wait, Jack thought of the days he and the 113th had skirmished with the Cossacks outside Sevastopol. *I must be getting old*, he told himself, *living on past memories.*

A monitor lizard scurried past, eyed him curiously for a second, and moved on. The eagles above continued to circle. The overall silence magnified every sound, so Jack heard his men toiling up the hillside. When that sound faded, the quiet was oppressive. Jack remained still, trying to regulate his breathing. He did not know how much time had elapsed before he heard the soft slither of feet on the rocks.

The leading Afridi approached, moving frighteningly fast over the tortured ground. He was a young man with a twisted dun turban on his head and his mouth gaping open. Jack aimed for the centre of his body, the most extensive target, took a deep breath, let it out slowly and squeezed the trigger. The Enfield kicked, white smoke spurted, and the man fell.

It was as easy as that. It was eleven years since Jack first killed a man. The sensation was no more pleasant now than it had been then. It was so simple to end a life, so final. There was no glamour, no glory, only an ending. The echoes of the Enfield rebounded from the hills, gradually fading. One of the eagles called again.

Gulbaz's Rahmut Khel had vanished. Jack could only see the man he had shot, lying like an untidy bundle of rags with flies already exploring the blood. Jack knew that the others were there watching him with the uncanny patience of the Pashtun, waiting for him to move, perhaps crawling unseen across that stark landscape. He had had the advantage in that first shot; now the pendulum had swung. The shot and the drift of powder smoke gave away his position to the Afridis. At that moment there were a dozen or more jezzails waiting for him to move. He was as trapped as Gulbaz's men.

The monitor lizard ran past, heading for the new corpse. The powder smoke drifted away slowly. The sun tortured Jack, baking him as he lay unmoving amidst the rocks. *The longer I delay them, the further away my Guides would travel. Every minute increases their chances of success.*

Jack felt the sun scorching his back. He thought back to the Crimea again. The Cossacks had been a dangerous enemy; if anything these Rahmut Khel Afridis were more patient, even more skilled at moving unseen through a broken landscape. Using all his training from these days in the Crimean War, Jack peered through the tiny gap he had left in his sangar. The ridge looked empty of men. He could not see a single one of the hundred or so Rahmut Khel he knew were there. *I must use an old trick.*

Lifting a loose stone, and ensuring he remained behind the shelter of the sangar, Jack tossed it to his right. The stone landed with a distinct clatter that drew fire from a score of positions. Jack nodded, noting from where the white smoke jetted. The men of the Rahmut Khel were still there, watching, waiting for him to make a mistake, but now he knew where some of them lay. Jack snuggled his cheek beside the stock of his Enfield. The Afridi may well be patient stalkers of men; well, so was he. He had learned his trade in the jungles of Burma, in the biting cold of Inkerman Ridge, and on the humid plains of India.

Come on, lads. Let's be having you.

Flies already clustered around the man Jack had shot. They were like a black-furred blanket, rising and falling as they feasted. Jack lay still, trying to ignore the insects that explored him. A palm-sized spider emerged from a crack in the rocks at his elbow, scuttled toward him, walked across the stock of his rifle, and moved on to search for more interesting prey.

The man moved so slowly that Jack was unsure if it was his imagination. At first, he thought it might be a shimmer caused by the heat of the sun, then he knew it was not. One of the Rahmut Khel was crawling toward him, oh-so-slowly. Jack knew that if he altered his aim, even that tiny movement would alert the enemy. He schooled himself in patience, ignored the bead of sweat that hung on his left eyelid, and waited until the enemy moved into his line of sight.

I can see one. How many more are there? How many of the most devilish warriors in the world are creeping toward me at this second? Please God that they don't take me alive.

Jack remembered the tales he had heard of the Pashtun's treatment of prisoners. How they would routinely castrate their captives, skin them alive or hand them over to the women for prolonged torture.

Dear Lord, if I must die, make it clean and quick.

Waiting until the Afridi was in his direct line of fire, Jack squeezed the trigger. He saw the man jump as the bullet struck him full on the head, and then the Rahmut Khel responded. Half a dozen bullets slammed around Jack, spraying vicious splinters of stone. He rolled away, loading as rapidly as he could, replaced the percussion cap with his thumb, and returned to his position. Enfield rifles were not designed to be loaded from a prone position, so the time Jack had taken allowed a dozen of the Rahmut Khel to rise from cover. They advanced quickly, leaping across the broken rocks of the ridge.

I can shoot one. After that?

Unable to see Gulbaz in the press of faces, Jack sighted on the closest man. He fired, saw the man fall, and wished he had thought to borrow a bayonet as well as the rifle. Struggling to load, he knew he might get in another shot, with luck, and then it was the wildly inaccurate revolver and his sword.

Goodbye, Mary; I hope you find a better man. Goodbye, Andrew; I would have loved to see you grow up.

'Come on, you bastards! I am Jack Windrush of the Guides!' And then Jack yelled the old battle cry of the 113th, elongating the final syllable. 'Cry Havelock!'

The triple crack of Enfield rifles, so different from the deeper boom of the jezzail, startled him. Jack saw the puffs of smoke from higher up the slope, wondered how the Rahmut Khel had got behind him and heard Hassan's voice. 'Shoot them, brothers!'

Two of the Rahmut Khel fell. When two more Enfields fired, another Afridi fell, halting the advance. The nature of the ridge meant that they could only move in single file. With dead and dying men blocking their route, the Rahmut Khel lost their enthusiasm and took to ground.

'What the devil are you doing here, Hassan?' Jack greeted his rescuers with abuse. 'I ordered you to take the horses away!'

'We did, sahib.' Hassan looked as hurt as a Pashtun could. 'We took the horses away, and then came back for you.'

'I ordered you to get away!'

'Yes, sahib.' Hassan pulled Jack's head lower as Gulbaz's men began to snipe at them. 'But you must remember that Kerr sahib ordered me to look after you. He outranks you, so his orders are more important.' His grin was of pure triumph.

There was no arguing with a Pashtun. 'So now you have effectively trapped all my men here, Hassan, what do you plan next?' Jack hoped the sarcasm was evident.

'The horses are safe, sahib,' Hassan said. 'Fatteh is in charge of them. We have a surprise prepared for these Rahmut Khel further up the hill. All we need do is climb a little and not get shot.'

'Is that all?' Jack asked.

'Follow me, sahib, and ensure you keep a rock between your body and the sights of an Afridi jezzail. Gulbaz thinks he is only chasing a feringhee. He forgets that now you are one of the Guides.'

'Move in stages,' Jack ordered. 'I want one man to remain behind, watching Gulbaz's men. He will shoot at any movement. After five minutes, he moves up, and another man watches.'

Using all the skills he had learned stalking Cossacks in the Crimea, Jack traversed the hillside. The Guides had a natural ability at moving unseen, gliding uphill without a sign, moving from cover to cover.

Once Jack heard the crack of an Enfield, with every Guide remaining static until the echoes had died away. Twice Jack heard the sonorous thud of a jezzail, with a bullet flattening itself on the rocks a few inches from his head. He lay still, watching a small lizard scurry past his face until Hassan motioned him to continue.

'Come on, sahib. If you stay there much longer, you will grow roots.'

The slope seemed to stretch forever into the hard heat. Knowing that his men must think him a weak feringhee, Jack ignored the screaming agony of his muscles as he forced himself upward and ever upward.

'Be careful, sahib,' Hassan whispered. Jack had not seen Fatteh until he nearly stood on him. They had reached the summit plateau, with the horses tethered in the slight shade of an outcrop of rock. Flicking sweat from his forehead, Jack looked downward. He could not see the Rahmut Khel.

'Where are they?'

'Still on the ridge,' Hassan said. 'Zaman shot one who tried to leave. Now Gulbaz will have them wait until we are over the summit. He knows that you will station a man here to kill any who move.'

Jack grunted at Hassan's less-than-subtle advice. He had a lot to learn about fighting in this type of country. 'How long will Gulbaz have them follow us?'

'Until they have killed us all,' Hassan said.

That's reassuring. Thank you, Hassan.

'It is a long way to Mardan,' Jack said, 'through some very hostile country.' He glanced down the slope. 'It would be better to stop these Rahmut Khel now, so our rear is secure.'

'That is true, sahib,' Hassan agreed.

'Are there any villages at the base of this mountain?'

'Did you see any sahib? I did not.' Hassan was not smiling. 'There is no fertile land for crops or livestock.'

'There are no villages, then.' Jack accepted the implied rebuke. 'There are also plenty of loose boulders here.' He indicated the side of the plateau, which was lined with rocks of various sizes.

'Yes, sahib,' Hassan said patiently.

'We could wait until Gulbaz's men are part way up the slope, and then roll these boulders down. They might cause an avalanche and rid us of Gulbaz.'

'Yes, sahib. I said that we have a surprise waiting for them. We moved the rocks ready to drop on the Rahmut Khel.'

Still not used to the independent thinking of the Guides, Jack grunted his approval. 'Good thinking, Hassan, you exceeded your orders.'

'No, Windrush sahib. Kerr sahib ordered me to look after you.'

Jack hid his smile; he expected that Hassan would roll out that excuse for everything he did. 'Good man, Hassan. However, as you seem incapable of following my orders, I'll keep you under my direct command. We'll all stay together and roll rocks down the hill.'

Although Hassan nodded solemnly, Jack detected a gleam of humour in his eyes.

'Teach me how to spot them,' Jack asked. 'Continue with my lessons.'

Nodding, Hassan pointed to a rock a few yards up from the edge of the ridge. 'You see that rock, sahib?'

Jack nodded.

'Its neighbours are shimmering in the heat. It is not.'

'That's right,' Jack agreed.

'That is no rock, sahib. That is a man. Look for what is not there.'

Jack listened as Hassan explained the basics of fighting on the Frontier. 'Patience, sahib. A Pashtun can wait in one place for three days to make a single shot at a target. A British sahib,' he grinned and shook his head, 'he will rush. If we are in ambush, we sit still. If any young man makes a single move that might be seen, we leave.'

'That man has moved.' Jack indicated the man he had thought was a rock.

'Six men have moved since you joined me, sahib.' There was no expression on Hassan's face.

'We will wait until they are halfway up the slope,' Jack decided. 'That way there is less chance that any will escape.' *I have become more callous with every campaign I fight.*

The Guides sat, quite relaxed, behind the barrier of rocks. While most British soldiers might have played cards, or spoken in forced whispers, the Pashtuns were motionless, without speech or visible communication. Jack could not help but admire them.

These men are unlike any I have met before. Oh, they are thievish and predatory, fierce and bloodthirsty, but while they are reckless of the lives of others, they do not spare their own. They possess gallantry and courage; they are like us in so many ways. As our immediate enemy are also of this calibre, we will be up for a hard fight if anything significant develops on this Frontier.

After Hassan's schooling, Jack looked for small signs that he may have missed. *Is that a rock or a man? Is it different from its neighbours?* Jack focussed. He saw a hint of movement, concentrated and realised that what he had thought was a pebble was the end of a man's sandal. Gulbaz's men were moving much faster than Jack had expected, sliding up the slope virtually unseen. He could not make out faces yet. Far above, three vultures had replaced the eagles circling, as if they knew there would soon be pickings. Jack looked up, already hating these birds. He imagined what it must feel like to be lying injured on the ground with one of these devilish creatures swooping down, all beak, talons and predatory eyes. This Frontier certainly stimulated the imagination.

'It is time, Hassan,' Jack decided.

The Guides were at his side as soon as Jack spoke the last word. They looked at him, each man behind a rock, awaiting his order. Jack braced himself. 'Now.' He whispered the word even as he pushed.

Jack's rock teetered slightly on the edge of the plateau and then swung back toward him. He pushed again, harder, heard a small shower of stones slither down the slope, and the rock moved forward, nearly overbalancing him. He saw it begin a slow, lumbering roll, gathering a collection of small stones in its journey. The Guides had been busy, with their boulders also shifting downhill, accumulating others on their descent, so within thirty seconds a miniature avalanche was powering toward Gulbaz's men.

'Dear God,' Jack said. 'I had not realised it would be so bad.'

'It will sweep Gulbaz away.' Zaman sounded pleased.

The distinctive boom of a jezzail was unexpected among the rumble of the avalanche. Jack did not see where the shot went as his men ducked into cover.

'Even in death, the Afridi wolves bite,' Hassan said. 'They are men. They are true Pashtun.' He did not hide the respect in his voice.

'They are brave men,' Jack agreed. 'Now, we have a long way to go yet.'

The plateau ended in a long, shallow slope descending to another of the fast-flowing rivers that seamed this countryside. The Guides picked their way down cautiously, watching for ambush or stray herdsman who might give their position away.

There was no need to tell the Guides to water the horses first. They were born equestrians, as skilled horsemen as the Cossacks.

Jack looked around. The landscape was bleak beyond description, with areas of grey scree and shattered rocks that could provide cover for a score of marksmen. 'Zaman, keep on watch.'

'Yes, sahib.'

Only when the horses were filled did the Guides drink. Fortunately, there were a few patches of rough grass beside the river, so the horses could also feed.

'How far to the Khyber?' Jack asked.

'About twenty miles.'

Jack checked the sky. It was later than he thought, with the light already beginning to fade. 'We'll cross this river and find a place to bed down for the night. The horses need a rest. So do the men.'

'The men are hungry,' Hassan said. 'They have not eaten since Gulbaz's bread.'

'Are there fish in that river?' Jack's mind was working rapidly, searching for possibilities.

Hassan looked confused for a second. 'We have no nets to catch them with.'

'We have these.' Jack held out his hands. It was many years since he had poached fish as a boy, but he was sure he remembered the technique. The food at school had been as basic as the accommodation, so the boys had often resorted to the local river, chancing the trouble they would get into if the gamekeeper had caught them.

'Watch for Gulbaz's men, or anybody else.' Jack slipped off his tunic so he was in his shirt. Despite the heat of the sun, when he slid his arms into the water, it felt as if he was dipping into ice. All the same, he persevered, teaching the watching Guides the subtle art of fish-tickling, or guddling, as one of his classmates had called it.

'Not only have the Pashtuns had patience,' Jack said. The river was innocent of human presence, so within a few minutes a decent-sized fish swam between his fingers. He hauled it out with an impulsive shout. 'Kill it!'

He caught two more before his hands were too numb with cold to perform their task.

'What kind of fish are they?' One looked like a large catfish but with a pointed head and both eyes in front rather than on the side of its head. Jack glanced at its sharp teeth and decided not to try that method of fishing again. 'Never mind. Cook them; I'm not eating raw fish.'

The Guides looked at him with new respect. Hassan nearly smiled.

Posting a man high up the hillside, Jack had the fish gutted and cooked, with every man eating his share. It was not the best meal he had ever tasted, but far better than nothing.

Hassan provided the words of caution. 'The smell may warn Gulbaz if he is still alive.'

'Then we will keep the campfire burning,' Jack said. 'If he is around, it will attract him like a moth to a flame.' He pointed up the hillside. 'We'll stay the night up there and watch.' He took Hassan's nod as a sign of approval. Perhaps the Guides no longer looked on him as a Griffin in this type of warfare.

Chapter Nine

Pakhtunkhwa, July 1863

Jack had them moving before dawn, with horses and men rested and fed. Ursulla still led with Jack on his shoulder and some of the hills becoming familiar as they neared the Khyber.

'We have a tributary of the Kabul River to ford,' Ursulla said, 'and the Zargun Pass to get through before we are above Mardan.'

Jack nodded his satisfaction. Although he could never relax on this Frontier, his understanding was increasing daily. He no longer felt a novice amongst these hills.

'How far to the Zargun Pass?' Jack consulted his map. The pass was marked, but he knew that Ursulla knew the area better than any western mapmaker.

'Two hours,' Ursulla said.

The sound of the drumming came to Jack first.

'Tabla drum.' Hassan listened for a moment. 'I've heard that rhythm before.'

'At Torkrud,' Jack said. 'The mullah played it. And at Ali Masjid.'

Hassan glanced at Jack. 'That's correct, sahib.'

'I can remember a rhythm and a mullah.' Jack knew he had no reason to explain. He raised his voice slightly. 'Right, lads; muffle the horse's hooves again. There might be trouble ahead.'

Now in single file, they moved on, keeping a space between each man to reduce their mass as a target, watching the surrounding tree-dotted heights, keeping a finger on the trigger of their rifles.

'Sahib.' Fatteh saw them first, a group of men just below the skyline, flitting from tree to tree.

'Ursulla.' Jack called him over. 'How far now to the Zargun Pass?'

'When we round the spur of this hill,' Ursulla said, 'we'll find a ford of the river, with the pass rising on the far side. Once we are over the pass, we are only a half day's ride to Mardan.'

Taking out his binoculars, Jack focussed on the men on the hill slope. They looked like typical Pashtuns, with pakol hats, baggy clothing, and the ubiquitous jezzail strapped across their backs. Each man had a red cord on his right arm. 'Oh, dear God.'

'What is it, sahib?' Hassan was quick to detect Jack's change of mood.

'Take a look, Hassan.' Jack passed over the binoculars.

'Mujahidin,' Hassan said at once.

'Do they know who we are?' Jack wondered.

'He will know.' Hassan used his chin to point ahead, where the mullah sat on his horse. As Jack watched, the mullah began to play on his tabla drum.

Jack nodded. 'That fellow gets everywhere,' he said quietly. 'Move on, lads. There is no point in keeping silent now. That tabla mullah is staring straight at us.'

'Ride at attention!' Hassan ordered. 'Show them that we are the Guides.'

The mullah remained still until Jack's men were within fifty yards when he wheeled his horse and rode slowly back, beating his tabla drum. The group of men on the hill cantered toward him, forming a loose escort.

As they passed the hill spur, the mullah and his escort increased speed. 'Follow,' Jack ordered. 'Let's see what their hurry is.'

The Guides cantered around the spur, with Fatteh singing a Pashtun song, and the sound of the horses' hooves echoing from the rugged slopes. Within a few moments, the ground opened up to a small clearing. The Zargun Pass lay ahead, a definite cleft between two groups of hills with the slender thread of a track winding upwards into a mist. Between Jack's Guides and the pass, a broad river churned between surprisingly fertile grassland. In any other time, the area would have been noted as a place of beauty; the milling groups of armed men made it a place of extreme danger.

The mullah had stopped to address the men who gathered around him.

'Wait.' Jack held up his hand. 'The mullah is talking. I wish to hear.'

'Oh, Muslims.' The mullah had a surprisingly strong voice for such a scrawny man. 'I am not asking you to fight Afghans or Pashtuns, who are true believers, but to make ghaza. Therefore it is necessary that you should all obey my commands, which are those of God and his prophets. We are all God's slaves, but ghaza is the duty of us all.'

Jack looked at his Guides. They were listening, watching the mullah without expression.

'I inform you that I have come to release Pakhtunkhwa from the hands of the British. We should not let the country of true believers fall into the hands of the feringhees. If they gain our country, our reputation and honour will go, too. Hearken to my advice; if you will not listen, it is plainly my duty to make ghaza against you as infidels. Make up your mind either to be supporters of God and Mohammed or to be prepared for war against those who are.'

Jack looked over his men, wondering how they were taking the mullah's rhetoric. The mullah tapped his drum for a few moments and then continued.

'The kafirs have taken possession of all Islamic countries and, owing to the lack of spirit on the part of the people, are conquering every region. They have now reached the land of the Pashtuns. These people attack the kafirs day and night. Help from God awaits us, and victory is at hand. God willing, the time has come when the kafirs should disappear.'

The Guides listened in silence with the horses snorting, tails flicking.

'That looks unpleasant.' Jack scanned the waiting men with his binoculars. The mullah trotted over the river in a great show of spray, wheeling his horse on the far side to face Jack's men. The throbbing of his drum began again. 'Is there another way across?'

'No,' Hassan said. 'This is the only ford for twenty miles, and the Zargun Pass the only route. The Mullah has chosen well.'

'Well, they've seen us now, so there is no point in trying to hide.' Jack pointed to a small knoll. 'We'll form a camp there, build up sangars, and work out what to do next.' The Guides did not argue. Jack guessed that they were as bereft of ideas as he was himself. After escaping from Gulbaz, it seemed cruel fate to run across the mullah and his Mujahidin.

The slopes to the knoll were littered with rocks, while two wind-tormented pines surmounted the summit. Fortunately, there was a little grazing for the horses, if nothing for the men.

Hassan took charge of building the sangar as Jack surveyed the Mujahidin through his binoculars.

'Why don't they attack?' Jack asked. 'They far outnumber us.'

'They have no need to attack,' Hassan said. 'They know we are trapped. We cannot go back to Gulbaz, and we cannot go forward. All they have to do is wait as we weaken through lack of food.'

Jack nodded. There was that Pashtun pragmatism again. These people were a strange mixture of incredible bravery, patience and fanaticism. 'The mullah will tell them who we are.'

Hassan gave a small smile. 'They already know, Windrush sahib. The whole of Pakhtunkhwa will be aware that a British officer and a patrol of Guides are trying to get back to British territory.'

'I see.' Jack did not ask how they knew; he was already impressed by the efficiency of the Pashtun intelligence service. 'Keep strengthening our defences.' *I need time to think.*

Rain began to fall, grimly grey, shading the hills, slowly dripping from the turbans of the Guides. It continued into the night, part-shielding the campfires of the Mujahidin. Ascending one of the pines, Jack studied the enemy, listening to the drumming of the mullah and watching the figures flitting around the campfire.

'You must sleep, Windrush sahib,' Hassan said. 'The Mujahidin will be there tomorrow and the next day.'

Hassan was correct. Next morning the Mujahidin still waited at the ford of the river, the pass rising behind them between the twin hills. As the sun rose, hundreds of warriors scrambled up the slopes. The tabla mullah and a few men remained at the ford, inviting the Guides to cross.

'How many of them are there, would you say?' Jack asked.

'One hundred, two hundred,' Hassan said. 'Perhaps more. They will have more men that we cannot see.'

'That's a lot of men to deal with half a dozen Guides. They must have a very high opinion of us,' Jack said. *Either that or their presence here is pure bad luck. They must be here for another reason.*

Jack could see the Mujahidin's strategy. They would remain on the hillside during the day, with all the advantages of height and visibility, and return to ground level in the evening to cook their evening meal, blocking any access to the pass. Jack knew that if he led his men through the pass in daylight, the Mujahidin on the hillside would pick them off in minutes. At night, the hundreds of Mujahidin beside the ford made crossing impossible. The hills on either side were inaccessible to even the sure-footed Kabul ponies, while the longer he delayed, the more danger they were in from Gulbaz, if he had survived, and however many of the Rahmut Khel he had managed to collect.

Jack looked at his half-dozen Guides. He was responsible for the lives of these men. He had to get them back to Mardan.

We have to get over that pass. To do that we have to get past the enemy. We cannot force through, so we must either sneak through or remove them from our path. As they are Pashtuns, they will be alert to every move we make, which makes the first option nearly impossible. I have to resort to trickery; the old ways from the Crimea.

'Whoever is in charge does not know his job. They should attack us,' Jack said. 'They would overrun us by sheer numbers.'

'Yes, sahib,' Hassan agreed. 'The Pashtun are patient men, but if the mullah decides it is time, he will lead the Mujahidin across the ford and then...' He passed a finger across his throat.

'Strengthen the sangar,' Jack said. 'Dig a trench behind it, so we have more cover, and clear a field of fire all around; create a killing ground,' Jack ordered. 'I want to make them scared to attack us.'

Understanding at once, the Guides worked with a will, with Jack lending his muscles to the labouring. Officers should lead by example, not drive by words. They rolled boulders from the slopes to strengthen the sangar, hacked down the scrub, and placed sticks every fifty yards to act as range markers. Across the ford, the mullah beat his drum in a constant rhythm that got inside Jack's head. When he felt his position was as secure as he could make it, Jack nodded.

'That's better. Now if they come across the river to attack us, we can at least account for some of them.' Jack glanced at the hillside opposite, where the Mujahidin would be watching. 'They think they have trapped us,' Jack said. 'Let's make things hot for them.' Pouring half the gunpowder he had carried from the watchtower at Torkrud into spare water bottles, Jack made half a dozen small bombs.

'What are you planning, sahib?' Hassan asked.

'We bury these under an inch or so of dirt and mark the spot. When the enemy reaches our marker, we shoot the flask and boom, we blow them up.'

Hassan gave another of his bleak smiles. 'They will still kill us, sahib.'

'Perhaps,' Jack said. He would not merely wait to be attacked. He would take a more aggressive approach. Everybody had their weakness, and the Mujahidin were no exception. Swarming back up the tree, Jack stared across the ford, noting everything that was happening. After an hour, he saw a small group of men descend the hill, occasionally turning around as if to argue, with some of the Mujahidin shouting at them, brandishing their jezzails. As Jack watched, one of the Mujahidin slit the throat of a sheep. Focussing his binoculars, Jack saw the first group carried no weapons except stout staffs.

'Daffadar!' Jack called Hassan up the tree. 'Who are these men? They don't look like warriors to me.'

Hassan took the binoculars. 'Shepherds,' he said casually. 'They are shepherds without goats or sheep.'

'I thought they might be.' Jack's mind was working overtime. 'Now these lads up there,' Jack said to Hassan. 'The Mujahidin. What do they eat?'

Hassan looked puzzled. 'They eat whatever they carry with them.'

'I see.' Jack pointed to a thread of Mujahidin, negotiating the hill slopes. 'And what are these fellows carrying down the hill?'

'Dead sheep. You saw the shepherds.' Hassan was staring at Jack as if he was an imbecile.

'Exactly,' Jack said. 'We may be able to use that.'

Hassan frowned. 'The Mujahidin will not share their sheep with us, sahib.'

'No,' Jack said. 'Nor will they share with the proper owners.' He raised his voice. 'Sawan, bring these shepherds to me. I want to talk to them.'

'They're only shepherds, sahib.' Sawan looked as confused as Hassan was. 'Herdsmen. They are not of any interest.'

'Just do it,' Jack said. 'Will they cross by the ford?'

'Probably.' Sawan sounded doubtful.

'Wait until they cross and then grab them,' Jack said. 'Don't hurt them, and don't let the Mujahidin see you.'

The shepherds stared at Jack when Sawan brought them over. They were gaunt-faced men, perhaps in their late teens, one with kohl-rimmed eyes and lovelocks, the other with a tattered pakol decorated by an eagle's feather.

'They did not cross by the ford,' Sawan said. 'They used this.' He held up an inflated goatskin.

'Keep it,' Jack said briefly. 'You men.' Jack tried not to sound like an imperious British officer as he addressed the shepherds. 'Are you friends with the warriors on the hill?'

The shepherds glanced at Hassan, who ordered them to tell the truth. 'The sahib will not be pleased if you lie to him,' Hassan said. 'I will know, and I will tell him.'

Jack waited for a reply. 'No,' the shepherd with the lovelocks said. 'They are not our friends. They stole our sheep.' There was no hiding the bitterness in his voice.

'I thought not.' Jack played his hands slowly, one at a time. 'How much was your flock worth?'

The shepherds looked even more confused.

'Would this pay for them?' Producing a sovereign from his pocketbook, Jack held it up to the light.

The shepherd reached for the golden coin.

Jack pulled it away. 'How about two of them?' He pulled out another sovereign, holding them between his fingers, aware that Hassan was staring at him.

The shepherd looked disappointed when Jack closed his fist over the coins. 'We can make a deal,' he said. 'You have known these hills all your life, I think.'

The shepherd agreed, his gaze never straying from Jack's hand.

'You will know the best ways to the top.'

Again the shepherd agreed.

'Can you get to the summit of the hill in the dark without the warriors seeing you?'

The shepherd did not hesitate. 'Yes, if Allah wills.'

'Good. If you lead two of my men to the summit without being detected, I will give you one gold coin. If you lead two men to the summit without being detected and leave without the warriors knowing, I will give you both gold coins.'

The shepherd's looked pleased. 'That will be easy work.' They spoke to Hassan rather than Jack. 'If the men we lead are Pashtun.' The kohl-rimmed man glanced furtively at Jack. 'The feringhee are too clumsy. They make too much noise with their big feet and bands blowing.'

Jack frowned. He had intended to go up himself, yet the shepherd's words made sense. He might jeopardise everybody's life by the simple act of kicking a loose stone or gasping too loudly.

'The shepherd is correct,' Jack admitted, grudgingly. 'It is better if he takes up two Guides.' He felt his men give a silent sigh of relief. 'Are there any volunteers for what will be a hazardous mission?' He felt a surge of pride as all the Guides volunteered.

'Thank you, gentlemen,' Jack said. 'I only need two men: Fatteh, you and your bugle, and Alladad.' He had contemplated sending Hassan but knew that Alladad was the most skilled at night movement, while he had a use for Fatteh.

The two men looked pleased to be selected. Fatteh stepped forward. 'What do you wish us to do, sahib?'

'When it is dark, the Mujahidin will come down from the hill to the river. The shepherds will take you over the river with the goatskin and up the hill byways that only they know. The Mujahidin might leave a few men on the slopes; avoid them. I want no noise, nothing to alert the enemy of our presence.' Jack waited to ensure Fatteh and Alladad understood.

'Yes, sahib.' They nodded.

'When you get to the summit, make a sign; nothing large, just a single light to say you have arrived. We will be watching for it.' Again Jack waited.

'We understand, sahib.'

The Guides were quicker in the uptake than the majority of British soldiers would have been. The Pashtun could have been born for this type of guerrilla warfare, while even the 113th had to be trained.

'When I reply to your signal, I want you, Fatteh, to blow your bugle as hard as you can. I want you to blow every regimental call you know, and any others you think you know. Make the enemy think the entire Brigade of Guards is on top of the hill. You, Alladad, I want you to set off explosives to sound like artillery. I want the Mujahidin to believe the British Army has got behind them.'

Both men nodded, enjoying the deception. 'Yes, sahib,' Alladad said, 'except we don't have any explosives.'

'Yes, we do. I brought some from the watchtower in Torkrud, remember?'

'Yes, sahib. We used that to make these bombs in the ground.'

'I held some back for emergencies,' Jack said. 'All we need is a suitable receptacle.'

One of the shepherds carried a little earthenware pot of snuff, which Jack bought for half a rupee. 'That's a thief's bargain, my friend.' Filling the pot with gunpowder, he held it up. 'Can you find anything else suitable?'

Grinning, the shepherds unearthed more earthenware pots, although Jack did not want to think in what part of their filthy clothing they had been hidden. 'You'll have me destitute before this day's work is done,' Jack said as he tipped the last of the gunpowder into the pots before handing them to Alladad.

'Now we wait for dark,' he said. 'Hassan, make sure the shepherds stay with us and don't run off to warn the enemy.'

'Zaman is looking after them,' Hassan said. 'He has told them what he will do if they betray us.'

'I can imagine.' Jack did not ask any more. The Guides had their own way of doing things, not always in accordance with the wishes of the gentlemen at Horse Guards and perhaps all the more effective for that.

As on the previous day, the Mujahidin began to move half an hour before dark. Jack watched them descend the hill, so confident of their superiority in numbers they made no attempt at concealment.

'I've never seen Pashtuns so careless.'

'They know we are trapped,' Hassan said. 'They could destroy us if they wished.'

'I still don't understand why they don't,' Jack said.

Hassan tapped the stock of his rifle. 'Pashtuns enjoy shikar, the hunt. They treat us like sport. They are playing with us.'

'Not for long,' Jack said grimly. 'As soon as it's full dark, send up Alladad and Fatteh.'

'The shepherds will want to see their gold,' Hassan said.

Calling Fatteh over, Jack handed him one of his sovereigns, knowing the shepherds were watching. 'Give that to the shepherds when you reach the summit safely and undetected. If they seem likely to betray you to the Mujahidin, kill them.'

'Yes, Sahib,' Fatteh said without a trace of emotion.

'Tell the shepherds that they will get the second sovereign either when they return to me, or when we join them at the top.' Jack paused for a moment. 'Not a moment before.'

Already the Mujahidin were setting great fires on the other side of the river, while sounds of singing and merriment accompanied the scent of roasting mutton that tortured the hungry Guides.

'There's your sheep, boys,' Jack said to the shepherds. 'Don't forget.' He showed the second sovereign before replacing it in his pocketbook. 'Good luck, lads.' Jack sent Alladad and Fatteh up the hill. The lovelocked shepherd led the way with the other herding the Guides as if they were sheep.

Jack watched as the two Guides padded upstream and launched themselves into the fast current, one at a time, with each man paying out a cord from the goatskin so it could be retrieved for the next. Remembering the night-time encounters with the Plastun Cossacks outside the walls of Sevastopol, Jack wondered how his Guides would have fared. *Probably very well*, he thought. He looked up to the hill, unseen in the dark. *I hope these lads are all right up there. I hope this plan works.*

Time always passed slowly when Jack waited for something to happen. Even the river seemed to run slower, with the rippling louder, and the occasional splash of a fish making his nerves jump. The Mujahidin were singing, bouts of loud laughter reaching across the ford. Jack glanced at his watch for the fifth time. Each minute seemed an eternity.

'Your watch will not speed the passage of time, sahib,' Hassan said. 'It is Allah that decides our fate, not the ticking of a clock.'

'On that, we must agree, Hassan.' Jack checked the men. Hassan was on sentry duty, his eyes roving through the darkness. The others were asleep as if two of their number were not at that minute climbing a mountain in the face of the enemy, risking hideous torture if they were caught. These Pashtun were the most philosophical soldiers Jack had ever met.

The singing from across the river increased, with the figures of warriors silhouetted against the campfires. Jack wondered what would happen if he led his men into a night attack. The idea appealed, but the odds were too heavy even for the Guides. No, he had made his plan and must abide by it.

'Sahib.' Hassan touched his arm. 'Up on the hill.'

Jack looked up, unsure if Hassan was warning him of disaster or notifying him of success. The gleam of light showed, distinct in the dark. It flickered, flared up for a second, then died so completely that Jack wondered if he had ever seen it.

'They've made it.' Jack felt a surge of relief. 'Wake up the men, Hassan.' He heard the grimness in his voice as he struck a Lucifer and applied it to the torch of dried grass he had ready.

The sudden flare would be visible for miles. The men on the summit of the mountain could not fail to see it, while the Mujahidin across the river might wonder what he was doing.

Let them wonder, Jack thought. *With luck, they will have more on their minds in a minute than a handful of fugitive Guides.* 'Come on, Fatteh. You've wanted to blow that blasted bugle since I first met you; do your stuff.'

Shrill and distinctive, the bugle rang out a moment later. Jack stood upright. 'Well done, Fatteh!' Call followed call, with the sound echoing around the mountains. Jack peered across the ford, seeing increased movement against the flaring bonfires. The next stage took longer than Jack had expected, but eventually, he heard the sharp crack of an explosion as the first of his gunpowder flasks erupted.

Jack had not known what to expect from the Mujahidin. He heard the rising clamour from across the river as the second gunpowder flask exploded, followed by the third. He saw the muzzle flares as some of the enemy began firing wildly up the hill, then the Mujahidin's bonfires grew larger.

'They don't know what's happening, sahib,' Zaman said.

'That's the idea,' Jack said. 'Let's make things a little worse. Fire into them. Give them a few casualties to worry about.'

The Guides needed no encouragement. Lining the parapet of the sangar, they fired across the river as another of the gunpowder flasks exploded. That was followed by a familiar rumble.

'Avalanche.' Hassan sounded mildly excited. 'That last explosion has caused an avalanche.'

An avalanche was frightening in the day. At night, with the sound increasing, yet the extent invisible, it was terrifying. Jack nearly felt sorry for the enemy on the far side of the river.

'Ceasefire,' he said. 'Save our ammunition. Only shoot if any of the Mujahidin try to get across the ford.'

Fatteh's bugle sounded again, the notes thin against the rumble of shifting rocks. It faded away and died.

'They're coming back down,' Hassan said.

'They've done well,' Jack approved. 'Better than I had anticipated.'

The Mujahidin continued to fire, although in what direction Jack was not sure. A couple of stray shots whistled overhead, with one splintering the facing rock of the sangar. The rumble of the avalanche subsided. *Patience, Jack, wait for your men to return.*

'Sahib!' Fatteh was hardly out of breath despite his climb up and down two thousand feet of rugged rock in the dark and a double crossing of the river. Water dripped from him to puddle on the ground. 'We did it, sahib.'

'You did well, Fatteh. You, too, Alladad; your explosions were successful.'

'Yes, sahib. I planted the flasks under loose rocks, remembering the avalanche we caused at the ridge.'

'Good thinking, Alladad. There's a daffadar in you, at least. I will inform Kerr sahib when we get back to Mardan.'

'Sahib,' Fatteh reminded him, 'the shepherds may expect their gold now. They led us well.'

Jack handed over the second sovereign. 'Thank you, gentlemen,' he said solemnly. 'I hope these coins are sufficient recompense for your lost sheep.'

The shepherds grabbed the money with hardly a glance before scurrying away into the dark in case Jack changed his mind.

'That is more gold than they have ever seen in their lives,' Hassan said. 'They are richer than they ever dreamed.'

'Good,' Jack said. 'Now let's see what's happening across the river. Ursulla, wait here with the horses.' He had another idea. 'Zaman: blow up a couple of these bombs we made. With luck, the Mujahidin will think we are firing artillery at them. The rest come with me.'

Chapter Ten

Pakhtunkhwa, July 1863

The firing from the mujahidin had increased, joined by high-pitched shouts and the occasional scream. Jack led his Guides into the cold rushing water of the ford. He moved slowly, checking every step, holding his revolver ready, feeling very vulnerable in the open. The water was deeper than he expected, reaching to his waist in the middle before receding again.

It was a relief to step onto dry ground, even though he was closer to the enemy. The revived campfires sent flickering light across the ground, revealing groups of men milling around, some firing upwards at the mountain in the belief that the British were there, others not sure what to do. When Zaman's mines crashed out, more of the Mujahidin started firing across the ford, with the bullets whistling past the ears of the Guides. *That was a bad idea I had.*

'They are different tribal levies.' Hassan reeled off half a dozen names that Jack did not recognise. 'This must be a gathering place.'

'That tabla mullah must be calling them all together. I wondered how there were so many armed men at the pass. There are certainly too many for our little group.'

Hassan looked around, holding his Enfield ready. 'Some may not be hostile to the British.'

'Lie down,' Jack ordered. 'We'll watch for a few moments. As far as I am concerned, they all opposed a party of the Guides. That makes them equally hostile.'

'Yes, sahib,' Hassan said.

'That group there,' Jack indicated a large body of men who looked more aggressive than the others. 'On my word, open fire on them.'

Settling down, the Guides aimed, waiting for Jack's command. There was another outburst of firing from higher up the pass.

'The tribal groups are shooting at each other,' Hassan said. 'They don't know who the enemy is.'

Jack grunted. He had seen even the best-trained soldiers fire on their allies in the confusion of battle. He could not expect these tribal levies to maintain their brittle discipline when under pressure at night. That was the weakness of tribal fighters; they may be as brave as hunting lions, but they lacked discipline. That, more than anything else, was what gave the British their advantage in the wars out here. It was not only superiority of arms and equipment; it was not better leadership, although that tipped the balance in the late Mutiny; it was discipline and the knowledge that each soldier could count on the men and the units on either side to keep their position. With tribes who were often mutually hostile, such trust could not exist.

'Fire.'

The four Guides fired on Jack's order. Between the flickering light and drifting smoke, Jack could not see the full effects, although at least one man fell. The others seemed undecided who to blame, with some pointing to another group, while others fired up the hill at the non-existent British army.

'Wait,' Jack ordered. 'Reload.'

His men lay still. They knew as well as he that a man lying still is hard to spot even in the daylight. At night he is next to impossible to see. The Guides watched as the tribal group argued among itself what to do. Jack waited until the argument was at its height. Seeing the Tabla Mullah ride past the fire, Jack took the rifle from Sawan, waited until he had a clear shot, and fired.

His bullet took the mullah full in the chest. The man slumped down on his horse. *Good! That's you out of the way. You won't cause us any more trouble.*

'Fire,' Jack ordered. Two other men fell. Jack could sense the frustrated anger of the warriors as they searched for their attackers, eventually deciding that a group beyond the Guides must be responsible. Jack had no need to order his men to lie still as the various tribes fired on each other. He watched as the gathering broke up in confusion, with individuals and small parties of men running back over the pass, still shooting.

'That leaves the way clear for us.' Jack felt neither satisfaction nor remorse at the scattering of bodies on the ground. If these men had not opposed him, he would have no quarrel with them. 'Sawan, fetch Ursulla, Zaman and the horses. The rest of you, fill the water bottles, and search the bodies for food.'

'There are many dead sheep, sahib,' Hassan pointed out. 'Plenty of mutton.'

'Good thinking, Hassan. We will eat as much as we can before we set off.'

That will give the tribes time to get out of our way, while men do not operate efficiently with empty bellies. Bonaparte was right in that; an army marches on its stomach.

'Has anybody seen the body of that damned mullah I shot?'

'No, sahib.'

Jack grunted. He would have liked to confirm his kill. He had thought that somebody had been rallying the tribes; it must have been that mullah. With luck, the mullah's death would end some of the threat; perhaps it would even end the entire Jihad. It was too early for such speculation. He had his men to feed and to get home to Mardan.

The mutton was a treat for hungry men; augmented by the pieces of bread they found scattered with the other debris of a broken army, Jack's Guides felt they had feasted in the hour before they moved. By that time the night was fading, the sky a leaden grey, streaked with bands of pink that enhanced the rugged beauty of the mountains.

Ignoring the weariness that seemed to accompany any military unit in any campaign, Jack ordered that every Mujahidin weapon should be collected. Knowing how much the Pashtun valued their rifles, he would not leave them to be used against the British at a later date.

'Sahib,' Hassan called. 'This Waziri has an Enfield.'

Jack's had not forgotten the original purpose of his mission. He hurried across. 'Show me, Hassan.'

The Waziri was not dead. He lay apart from the main body with both legs trapped under a huge rock. His eyes glared hatred as Jack approached, and he lifted his rifle threateningly. The Guides formed a circle around him, mocking.

'You have no bullets in your gun, Waziri,' Zaman said. 'What are you going to do, wave it at me?'

'Where did you get that from?' Jack saw the man was in pain. 'Tell me, and we will remove the rock and splint your legs.'

Unable to do anything else, the Waziri spat at Jack. 'If I were able, I would gut you, feringhee!'

'Yet you are not able,' Zaman mocked. He stepped closer, with the tone of his voice becoming more urgent. 'That sword, Waziri; where did you get that sword?'

Jack frowned. The Waziri's silver-hilted pulwar had fallen half out of his scabbard to lie at his side. Light from the rising sun highlighted the flowing Persian script along the blade. 'That is Batoor's sword,' he said. 'The sword of the Khan of the Rahmut Khel.'

Zaman nodded. 'It is, sahib.' Ignoring the Waziri's curses, he lifted the pulwar, holding it reverently in both hands.

'How did you come by that?' Jack asked the Waziri.

'I shall ask him, sahib,' Zaman said. 'He will not talk to a feringhee. He will talk to me.'

'That may be true.' Jack stepped back to listen. 'Find out about Batoor as well as the rifle.'

'It might be better if you are not here, sahib,' Zaman suggested tactfully.

'All right, Zaman.' Jack lit a cheroot and withdrew. One thing he had learned as an officer was when it was best not to notice things. He had no illusions about the methods of persuasion that Zaman would use. Once, as an idealistic young Griffin, Jack would not have believed that British officers would sanction such ungentlemanly practices. The reality of war on the frontiers of Empire had taught him differently.

Leaving Zaman to interrogate the Waziri, Jack checked the horses. He heard the odd muffled moan from behind him, a grunt or two and one stifled scream.

If that mullah was the man rallying the tribes, perhaps we have indeed broken the back of the trouble already? Did I kill him? I saw my shot strike, but there is no sign of the body. Jack tried to concentrate on his duty, while his mind wavered. Batoor had been so proud to show his sword; he would never have willingly parted with it. *Is Batoor dead? I can't think of that laughing, vital man dying.*

'Sahib.' Zaman marched toward him, smiling. He handed Jack the Enfield. 'Our Waziri was most co-operative.'

'I'm glad to hear it.' Jack tried not to notice the blood on Zaman's hands. 'What did he tell you?'

'He bought the rifle from a small village named Tazhak, further to the north.'

'Tazhak.' Jack frowned. 'I have never heard of that place. Do you know it, Zaman?'

'I know where it is, sahib.'

Jack grunted. 'Thank you, Zaman.' He noticed that Zaman had Batoor's sword around his waist. 'And the sword?'

'The Waziri told me he took the sword from a dead Afridi,' Zaman said. 'A tall man with a skull cap. He said the Mujahidin asked a body of Afridis to join the jihad. The Afridis refused and were killed.'

Jack fought his instant distress. He could nearly picture the scene, with Batoor facing up to the Mujahidin on Rahmut Khel land, the altercation followed by a vicious fight.

'Batoor Khan would be happy to die in such a way,' Zaman said.

Jack was numb at the thought of Batoor's death. 'You are right, Zaman.' He shook away his sadness; there would be time to mourn later. Now he had a party of Guides to get to safety and new intelligence to digest. 'We'll put splints on the Waziri's legs and leave him here with food and water. His friends may come back for him.'

'There is no need for the splints, Windrush sahib, or the food and water.'

Jack shook his head. 'The man is injured, Zaman. We must try to help him.'

'The Waziri died, sahib.' Zaman's face was expressionless.

'That is unfortunate.' Jack was not surprised. Suddenly he did not care; that Waziri had killed Batoor. 'How far away is this Tazhak?'

'About two days' ride, sahib.'

Could he take his Guides as far as that? 'Is it rough country?'

'Yes, sahib.'

Jack already knew that he must visit Tazhak. 'Which tribe is there?'

'Tazhak is in Yusufzai territory.'

'Call a Jirga, Zaman.' What Jack had in mind was not exactly a Jirga, but he could think of no other term to describe the meeting he convened.

The six Guides sat around him with the sun fast rising and the inevitable fur of flies covering the bodies of the dead. The vultures that seemed to follow them hovered patiently, aware that they would move on, waiting for their absence to feast on human flesh.

'So far, gentlemen, we have been lucky,' Jack told them. 'We have escaped siege and ambush without taking a single casualty, largely because of your skill in this sort of country.'

The Guides looked at him, nodding sagely as they waited for him to have his say. Jack knew that he was not behaving like an officer of the British Army, but these men were not ordinary British soldiers. He was determined to respect their methods as far as was compatible with his duty to the Queen.

'As you know, we were sent out to gather information about gun smuggling and these Mujahidins. So far, we have not been very successful, until today.' Jack held up the Enfield. 'This is the first example of a British Enfield rifle that we have found.'

The Guides waited patiently. They knew all this already.

'Zaman asked the Waziri where it came from. He said it was from Tazhak, in Yusufzai country. Now, what was a Waziri from the south doing in Yusufzai territory far to the north?'

'Buying a rifle.' Hassan gave the answer Jack had been expecting.

'Exactly,' Jack said. 'These Enfields have been appearing up and down the Frontier. How do they get to Tazhak? Who brings them there? Who supplies them?'

The Guides waited, perhaps wondering if Jack was going to answer his questions.

'I do not know the answer,' Jack said. 'Zaman's discovery of Tazhak may clear up the mystery, it may be the next link in the chain, or it may lead nowhere. We are going to march to Tazhak before we return to Mardan.'

He waited for the groans of protest that his 113th would have emitted. The Guides merely nodded. Hassan took a pinch of snuff.

'Do you know the way, sahib?' Hassan asked.

'No,' Jack admitted. 'But you will.'

'We have to pass through Mohmand and Mamund territory,' Hassan said. 'I have blood feuds with both.'

'We will travel with care.' Jack looked up. 'If we stay here much longer, we will grow roots, or Gulbaz will catch us.'

'That is true,' Hassan agreed. 'Windrush sahib...'

'Yes, Hassan?'

'What are we going to do when we get to Tazhak?'

Jack considered for a moment. 'I'm not sure, Hassan. We'll have a look around and see what there is to see.'

'We look like British soldiers, sahib,' Hassan pointed out. 'I don't think that British soldiers have ever been in the valley of Kot, where Tazhak sits. It would be better if we dressed like Pashtuns.'

'You are right, Hassan. Strip some of these bodies.' Jack could be every bit as pragmatic as his men. Wearing a uniform in Pakhtunkhwa was an invitation to every roaming tribesman to try his marksmanship. 'You're going to turn me into a Pashtun warrior.'

The Pashtun clothes were comfortable and warmer than Jack had expected. He slipped a woollen pakol on his head, adjusted it, and grinned. 'Now I am as Pashtun as you are.' He had not expected the genuine laughter from his men. 'Right, lads, destroy all the old weapons and toss them into the river.'

Acts of destruction seemed as popular with the Pashtun as they were with British soldiers. The Guides worked with a will, laughing as they smashed up the old jezzails. Only when he was satisfied did Jack give orders to move out.

'Alladad, ride ahead to scout. Sawan, you are our rearguard; watch for pursuit or any sign of Gulbaz.'

The two men left at once. Jack felt slightly happier now that he had found an Enfield and knew the location where it was bought. He had justified his mission to an extent. Now he wished to find this Tazhak, riding through hostile territory with a tired group of men he still did not wholly understand.

Jack sighed. He had wanted to be a soldier; now he had to accept the tribulations of a soldier's lot. 'Keep alert boys; we are the Guides.'

Chapter Eleven

Pakhtunkhwa, July 1863

Tazhak stood on a prominent rise within the confines of the Valley of Kot. Protected by a ten-foot-high earthen wall, there was a tall arched gate for entry, with two sturdy watchmen on guard. A stone tower nailed down each corner of the village, manned by armed warriors in skull caps. Under a low, leaden sky, the village looked uncompromisingly hostile. Every so often the distinctive crack of a rifle sounded from within the walls.

'They evidently don't want strangers to enter unseen,' Jack said.

'The Yasufzai take care of their own.' There was pride in Hassan's voice. 'Are we not the sons of Joseph?'

Jack reined up on a ridge overlooking the valley. 'We'll wait here a bit,' he said. 'I want to see how many people enter and leave Tazhak.'

There was a steady stream of visitors, far more than Jack would have expected from a village of that size in such a remote location. He watched as the ubiquitous caravans of camels or strings of mules arrived, together with men in groups or individually. He saw no families, no children. 'It's like a trading entrepot,' he said. 'A place of men. What are the people buying?'

Weapons, he told himself as one mule left with four Brunswick rifles strapped to its sides. *They are buying rifles. How the devil did the rifles get here? I must find the source. I have to find the seller first and then trace the supplier.*

Jack looked over his men. They were as handy a bunch of soldiers as he had ever known, quick in the uptake, expert at mountain warfare and always ready to fight. If he had a company of Guides, he could surround the village to stop ingress and egress, and then search the place house by house until he found the Enfields. With only half a dozen men, such a move was not possible. He would have to think of something else.

The solution was evident if nerve-wracking. During the latter stages of the Indian Mutiny, Jack had disguised himself as a native to enter Gondabad, a city the Mutineers then controlled. It helped that he was naturally swarthy, possibly because he was one-quarter Indian, while since then he had learned some of the languages of the country. All the same, entering a walled village in the heart of Yusufzai territory was akin to putting his head in a tiger's mouth while simultaneously pulling its tail.

Jack took a deep breath. 'I need two volunteers,' he said quietly. 'It will be very dangerous, with little chance of survival.'

'We are all volunteers,' Hassan said at once. Weary as they were, the Guides nodded their agreement.

'I am going into Tazhak to find the gun seller,' Jack said. 'I want two men as escorts. I am going in disguise, but if the locals find out I am a feringhee, we will all be killed.' He waited to see the impact of his words. 'Although I speak Pushtu, my accent may give me away.'

'Yes, sahib,' Hassan said. 'You speak like a feringhee. The moment you speak, the Tazhak people will know what you are. They will flay us alive and decorate the gate with our heads.'

'I'll need your help to look like a tribesman,' Jack said.

While Hassan looked grave, Zaman and Fatteh laughed, as if it was a colossal joke. 'The Yusufzai will spot you right away,' Zaman said. 'You walk like a feringhee, all tense, with your feet nearly scuffing the ground.'

'Teach me,' Jack said. 'I want to find this gun seller.'

Looking at each other, the Guides shook their heads. 'You can't learn to be a Pashtun,' Hassan said. 'You have to suck the milk of a Pashtun mother.' He was the only man who was not smiling.

'I must go in,' Jack said. 'I cannot learn enough by simply observing. If nobody wishes to accompany me, then I shall go alone.' *I won't send a man into danger while I stand in the shadows.*

'If you go alone, we will salute your head as it grins to us from above the entrance gate,' Hassan said. 'I'll come with you.'

'I'd prefer you remain with the men, daffadar,' Jack said. 'You are the best suited to get them to Mardan.'

'No, sahib,' Hassan said. 'You are best suited to get the men to Mardan. That is why I must go with you.' He gave a rare smile. 'Kerr sahib ordered me to look after you, remember? I cannot disobey the orders of a superior officer.'

Opening his mouth to blast Hassan for his insolence, Jack closed it with a snap. 'There is nobody I would rather have at my side, Hassan.' *Except for Batoor, wherever he is, heaven or hell.* 'We will take Zaman as well. He is a good man in a fight.' *He is also liable to cause a war if left unsupervised*, Jack thought. *Zaman is the sort of soldier one wants in one's unit during a battle, but he would be a handful in peacetime.*

Dressed in a shaggy poshteen, and with his pakol pulled low over his head, Jack hoped he looked like a bedraggled tribesman with sufficient funds to buy a rifle as he approached the gate of Tazhak. He rode a Kabul pony rather than the larger Colwell. Hassan rode at his side, erect as always, although his usually steady eyes strayed continually to Jack. A few yards behind them, Zaman held an old fashioned jezzail as if ashamed of the weapon, which he possibly was, Jack thought.

The two watchmen at the gate stepped forward on their approach. One must have been well over six feet, and broad as anybody Jack had ever seen, with a French rifle across his back and a Khyber knife at his waist. 'Your business?'

'We come to buy rifles,' Hassan said.

'You don't look as if you could afford them.' The watchman's eyes were busy on Jack's face.

'That is our business, not yours.' Zaman would not be intimidated by anybody, whatever his size.

'We can afford them.' Hassan pushed past without another word. Jack followed, keeping his head down. Fortunately, his beard had developed over the past few weeks, so he looked the part. Grabbing hold of Zaman's poshteen, he pulled him away from the watchman. 'Come, Zaman, before that fellow decides to cut off your head.'

The watchman laughed, as Jack had intended.

'I will trim his beard,' Zaman growled.

'Not today, Zaman,' Jack whispered savagely. 'We have more important things to do than disposing of an arrogant fool.'

At first, Tazhak appeared like any other large Pakhtunkhwa village that Jack had visited. There was the usual array of walled houses, and the conventional well, with the typical street of small shops and merchants. However, he realised that there was a great preponderance of warriors between the houses, and a constant rattle of metal on metal replaced the usual chatter of children and bleating of sheep.

'Tazhak seems to specialise in metal work,' Jack said. 'And warriors.'

'Yes, sahib.' Hassan looked around. 'I used to know this village before I joined the Guides. It has changed since then. Where are the children? Where are the women? There is no life in a village without them.'

Jack agreed. Tazhak was a place of men. Warriors from seemingly all the tribes of the Frontier plus some from Afghanistan and even further afield wandered the streets, bearing an assortment of clothes and armaments. Buffaloes trundled as if they belonged there, with the occasional small herd of cattle. The main street seemed composed entirely of shops, emblazoned with bright hand-lettered signs, with each one depicting a firearm. Jack glanced at Zaman, swaggering a few paces to the rear. He hoped he could control the Afridi's aggression. Hassan had been correct; he should have left Zaman behind. There was nobody better in a fight, but his hair-trigger temper could make him a liability.

'Ask somebody where we can buy an Enfield rifle, Hassan.' Jack decided to fulfil his mission and get out of Tazhak fast.

'That should not be hard, sahib.' Hassan pointed to the street that stretched ahead of them. 'Every workshop here is making guns.' Between the shops were dirty alleys, too narrow for two people to pass each other, sufficiently dark to make even a brave man hesitate to enter. The sound of hammer on metal was distinct, a background to everything else. Jack flinched as a shaven-headed man emerged from a shop ten yards away, lifted a jezzail and fired it into the air. Grinning, he returned inside.

Jack grunted. 'I don't want somebody to make me a jezzail, Hassan. We're here to find out who is buying British rifles and from where they come.'

Hassan nodded. 'I know, sahib.' He nodded to the nearest workshop. 'Look at that Mohmand, who is leaving the shop, sahib.'

The man was in his early thirties with a ragged turban carelessly tied on his head and a round shield across his back. He emerged from the workshop looking pleased, with an Enfield rifle in the crook of his arm.

'Well done, Hassan.' Dismounting, Jack stalked toward the workshop, with Hassan at his side. 'Look after the horses, Zaman.'

'It may be best if I do the talking, sahib,' Hassan said.

Jack nodded. 'That is true. Enfield rifles, remember, Hassan.'

'I know, sahib.'

Jack did not know what to expect as he entered the workshop. There were four men inside; one was an Afridi customer, another was a man with a red-dyed beard who was apparently the salesman, and the other two were working with a lathe and file. As Jack watched, a grey-bearded craftsman used a hammer and chisel to expertly create the lock of a replica Tower musket. On the wall at the back, the workshop displayed examples of their skill, with four different weapons including a jezzail, an Enfield and a Brown Bess musket.

When the Afridi left, muttering darkly about high prices, Hassan approached the salesman.

'*Salaam alaikum* – greetings, good day.'

'*Salaam alaikum*,' the salesman returned politely. He looked directly at Hassan as he spoke and then took in both Jack and Zaman with a single sweep of his eyes.

'Your fame as a gunsmith has spread from Tashkent to Delhi.' Hassan had a smooth tongue. 'We came from the Vale of Peshawar.'

'I know the accent, Yusufzai.' The salesman glanced at Jack, who said nothing. 'Your friend is not a Yusufzai.'

'No.' Hassan lowered his voice. 'He would prefer not to be known.'

'Ah; blood feud.' The salesman understood at once. 'That is why the Afridi waits outside watching everything. What kind of rifle do you wish?'

'I heard that you have British-made Enfields.' Jack decided to cut short the rhetoric.

The salesman looked confused. 'We have no British-made weapons here. Everything we sell, we make ourselves.'

Stepping to the wall, Jack lifted down the Enfield. 'You did not make this yourself,' he said.

'Yes, we did.' The salesman was hurt by the accusation. 'Am I a liar?'

'No.' Jack had no intention of impinging the man's honour by such an accusation. 'No, you are a Yusufzai, and Yusufzais never lie.'

The salesman accepted Jack's near-apology with good grace. 'That is so. My sons and I made that weapon.'

'You are a skilled man.' Jack examined the weapon, noting the British government stamp and serial number. 'My companion was right to come to you first. Could you make others like this?'

'We do make others.' The salesman nodded to his sons. 'We are making one now.'

Jack wandered over to the two younger men, who had not looked up from their labours. One was punching at the metal of the rifle.

'Forgive me.' Jack lifted the weapon. The stamp and serial number were identical to the first he had handled. 'Thank you. What do you charge for a new Enfield?'

The salesman looked from Jack to Hassan and back, obviously assessing them, working out how much they were worth. When he mentioned a figure, Hassan grunted. 'Too much,' he said. 'You might cheat my colleague; you will not cheat a fellow Yusufzai. Come, cousin.' Tapping Jack on the shoulder, he stalked out of the shop.

'Did you know that fellow made Enfields?'

Hassan gave a small smile. 'Not until I entered the workshop. You must know that the Pashtun are renowned for their skill in copying firearms.'

'So I see,' Jack said. 'One man could not make all the weapons that have been recovered the length and breadth of the Frontier. He is not the man for whom we are looking.'

'No, sahib,' Hassan said.

Jack guessed that Hassan was hiding something. 'We'll keep looking.'

The next workshop was much like the first, with a small group of men busy with simple tools. Again, Hassan made the introductions as Jack studied the weapons on display. He lifted down the Enfield to see the identical serial number. 'Do you have other Enfields?'

The salesman gave Jack a hard look as he produced another Enfield. When Jack lifted the rifle, he thought it was fractionally lighter than the weapons he was used to. A quick check revealed the same serial number.

'I can see a pattern developing here.' Jack looked along the busy street. 'I imagine that most of these workshops produce Enfields?'

'Yes, sahib.' Hassan sounded very patient. 'Are we still searching for the warriors of God? The Ghazi?'

'I hope that we scattered them at the Zargun Pass,' Jack said.

'We defeated some, sahib,' Hassan said. 'But can you not see the men with the red cords around their right arm?' Hassan asked.

Jack had been too busy concentrating on the rifles to notice much else.

'They are Ghazis,' Hassan reminded him.

Jack took a deep breath. Now that he looked, he could see more red cords, with every fourth man sporting one. He felt his tension increase. He had been strolling around Tazhak without thought. 'This village is a hotbed of the Mujahidin.'

'It may be so, sahib,' Hassan said.

'Dear God in Heaven,' Jack said softly, measuring the distance to the gate. *No*, he told himself. *I am here to look for the gun-runner. I cannot allow personal danger to interfere with my mission.* In normal circumstances, he would have lit a cheroot to still his jangling nerves. A Pashtun would not do such a thing. 'Thank you, Hassan. I will watch for them. In the meantime, I still hope to find who sells British-made rifles.'

They spent the morning visiting the workshops, with Jack becoming increasingly alarmed at the skill shown by the gunsmiths. 'These weapons are first class,' he said. 'They are nearly as good as the rifles we make in Britain.'

'Yes, sahib.'

Every workshop they visited displayed a variety of weapons, with about half having the capability to create an Enfield. Jack checked the weapons, finding most had the same serial number. There were only two different numbers, proving to Jack that the weapons had been copied from two originals.

'How many gunsmiths are there in Tazhak, Hassan?'

Hassan glanced along the street. 'About a hundred, sahib.'

'Was it always like this?'

Hassan shook his head. 'When I lived in the valley of Kot, Tazhak was like any other village.'

Somebody has changed it. Somebody is deliberately making modern rifles here and selling them to the Mujahidin. There can only be one reason for that. I must tell Colonel Hook what we have found.

'I don't believe that there is a man smuggling guns to the tribes,' Jack decided. 'Nor do I believe that they have stolen scores of Enfields. I think this village of Tazhak is churning them out like a factory.'

'Yes, sahib,' Hassan agreed.

'If we wish to stop the tribes gaining modern rifles,' Jack said, 'we'll have to shut down this village.'

'These men are only doing what their forefathers have done for generations,' Hassan pointed out. 'They are not breaking any law, Pashtun or British.'

'I know.' Jack could not think of a solution. If the British decided to stop the workshops making weapons, they would be interfering with a centuries-old tradition, which in itself would cause unrest. 'Let's get away, Hassan. We must pass the information on to the authorities.' Colonel Hook would be most interested to hear about the gun-making village of Tazhak. Although it was a relief to know there was no traitor on the British side, it was worrying to realise how skilled the local gunsmiths were.

There was another question: who was behind the gun-making? Who had the power to turn a traditional Yusufzai village into a gun-making powerhouse? Had it been that mullah with the tabla drum?

'I have seen three men that I should kill.' Zaman interrupted Jack's thoughts. 'My family is at feud with them.'

'Not today, Zaman,' Jack said. 'You can have your sport when you are off duty.'

'Sometimes the Queen's service is hard,' Zaman said.

'With that, we can all agree.' Jack thought of Mary, so far away. 'Right, Hassan, we've discovered what we set out for. Let's get back to Mardan as quick as Allah will let us.'

As they neared the gate, a shambling group of mixed horsemen and warriors on foot approached. Even from a distance, Jack could see they were travel-weary, with some limping or carrying injuries.

'Ride round these lads,' Jack said as he came closer.

'Sahib. These are from the Rahmut Khel.' Zaman was a second too late as a tall man pushed forward.

Jack saw the man's hook. 'Gulbaz!' It was too late to escape detection.

'You!' Gulbaz pointed to Jack. 'What are you doing here?' He raised his voice into a roar. 'This is a British officer, a feringhee!'

Swearing, Jack contemplated reaching for his revolver, realised that they were too outnumbered to put up a fight, dug in his heels and thrust forward.

'With me, Guides!'

Now they had been recognised, there was no point in further pretence. Jack hit the Rahmut Khel at an angle, barged one limping footman over, avoided a yelling horseman by luck rather than skill, and at last managed to pull his revolver clear. 'Come on, lads!'

Jack heard a rising tumult of shouts behind him as Gulbaz and his men pressed closer, with some drawing pulwars as they tried to block the Guides' passage. Laughing, Zaman swung his sword at Gulbaz, who parried by lifting his arm. Zaman's blade clattered on the steel bands that held the hook secure. He laughed again and wheeled his horse just outside the ranks of the Rahmut Khel.

'Come on, sahib!'

Glancing over his shoulder, Jack saw Hassan jinking through the mob. 'Come on, Hassan!'

'Ride, sahib!' Hassan said.

'Gallop, lads!' Jack ordered. 'Get out of here.' He kicked in his heels, wishing he had Colwall rather than the sure-footed but slower Kabul pony. A glance over his shoulder revealed that Gulbaz's men had quickly re-organised. He pushed Zaman on. 'The lads will have seen the commotion, and they'll be ready to go.' *I hope.*

The Guides did better than Jack expected. They rode out with rifles in their hands, and the spare horses trotted beside them.

'Well done, Guides!' Even at that emergency, Jack thought how good it was to work with such professional soldiers. 'Fatteh, Ursulla, Alladad, fire on the mob. Try and slow them down.'

'Spur!' He gave the unnecessary order as the Guide's Enfields cracked out. 'Hassan, take the lead; you know the route better than I do!'

Slowing slightly, Jack ensured that all his men were together with no stragglers. Twisting in the saddle, he levelled his revolver and fired two rapid shots. He did not expect to hit anybody, only to unsettle the pursuit. The men of the Rahmut Khel were already far behind. Riding tired horses or on foot, they had not expected to run into the Guides, and the accurate shooting of the Enfields must be discouraging.

'Fatteh, Ursulla, Alladad, reload! Zaman, Hassan, Sawan, fire!' That was all Jack needed to say. Three more shots cracked out with the sounds echoing and fading. The men of the Rahmut Khel were shooting more in anger rather than a serious attempt to hit anything.

Jack organised their fighting withdrawal for another half mile, with the Guides alternately shooting and riding. He could not see any casualties among Gulbaz's men, but they did fall even further behind.

That was unpleasant. I had hoped that Gulbaz had given up the chase.

'Slow to a trot,' Jack ordered. 'Save the horses. Hassan, take us back to Mardan by the fastest safe route.'

'Yes, sahib.' Hassan gave a wry smile. 'This is Pakhtunkhwa, sahib. There is no safe route.'

'So I have learned,' Jack said. 'That firing will have alerted the locals.'

'No, sahib.' Hassan shook his head. 'Listen.'

Jack slowed down his horse. He heard the intermittent crackle of gunfire, single shots interspersed with what could nearly be regular volleys. 'Are they still trying to fire at us?'

Hassan lifted his head a fraction to listen. 'No. That is the gunsmiths testing their new weapons, or those men who have bought a rifle firing it in the air.' He smiled. 'The locals will be used to gunfire. They will pay no heed to a few more shots.'

'I hope you are right, Hassan.' Jack glanced at the surrounding heights. He could plainly see the figures of men, some against the skyline, others sitting on rocks, watching the small body of Guides riding along the valley floor.

'Men are coming, sahib,' Hassan warned. 'Riding fast from the north.'

A minute later Jack felt the slight tremble of the ground. 'Leave the track.' He indicated a group of loose boulders amongst scattered pines. 'We'll wait there.' If the approaching men were hostile, he wanted some solid rocks to shelter behind; they could not hope to run forever.

Within a few minutes, Jack heard the steadily increasing sound of horses' hooves. He glanced over his men; they were well hidden behind boulders, holding their horses close. There was no need to order them to keep alert.

A rising cloud of dust marked the passage of the unknown horsemen. Jack watched them slow down as they neared the rocks where the Guides waited. The dust cleared, leaving the riders visible. There were twenty or so with rifles strapped across their backs and round shields bouncing from their saddles. Jack felt for the butt of his revolver.

'Ghazis.' Hassan placed a percussion cap on his rifle. 'See the red cords?'

'I see the red cords.' Jack felt the tension rise within the Guides. If the Ghazis saw them, they would attack without mercy.

'Cap and load,' Jack said quietly.

'We already have, sahib.' Hassan was equally quiet.

Jack nodded. 'Fatteh, look after the horses. Try and keep them from moving around.'

The Ghazis remained still, looking around as if they suspected that the Guides were nearby. Jack could sense the menace. They were wild-looking men, some with long hair exploding from beneath their pakols, and unkempt, ragged beards, one in chainmail and with a steel helmet. They carried long pulwars and round shields as well as some modern rifles strapped across their backs.

'Allah Akbar!' one of the ghazis shouted. The others joined in, 'Allah Akbar!' One lifted his Enfield into the air and fired it. 'Allah Akbar!'

'God is great indeed,' Hassan said. He breathed out slowly when the Ghazis trotted away. 'He saved us from death there.'

'Were they so dangerous?' Jack wished to hear the opinion of this veteran of the Frontier.

'The men who followed Gulbaz were warriors, yes, but also farmers or craftsmen or herders. These men, these Ghazis, are holy warriors. They know no fear. They fight for Allah, for God, so if they die, they go to paradise. If they kill a feringhee, a kafir, a non-believer, they are assured a place in paradise.' Hassan watched the Ghazis ride away with dust rising in their wake.

'They sound like men it is best to avoid.'

'If the Ghazis take a dislike to you,' Hassan said, 'you have three choices: run forever, for they will hunt you to the end of the earth, allow them to kill you, or kill them.'

'Such men with modern weapons will be dangerous enemies,' Jack said.

'A Ghazi will not stop until he is dead,' Hassan said.

'We have to close down this village of Tazhak,' Jack decided. 'Ghazis with pulwars and jezzails are bad enough, Ghazis with rifles…' he allowed his words to drift away. 'Let's get to Mardan.'

Chapter Twelve

Mardan July-August 1863

'Report, Captain.' Hook sat in the room he had requisitioned, overlooking the parade ground outside Mardan. He had aged in the past few weeks, with new lines of worry engraved on his face. He listened carefully as Jack told him about the situation in Torkrud, the growing numbers of Mujahidin and the gunsmiths of Tazhak.

'Batoor Khan of Torkrud is dead, you say?'

'Yes, sir. We found a Waziri with his sword.'

'He was a friend of yours, I believe. That is a pity; we need every friend we can get out here.' Hook sighed. 'Can't be helped; we'll cope. Now, about these Enfields. Every weapon had the same serial number, you say?' Hook had been scribbling notes as Jack spoke.

'There were two serial numbers, sir. Most had the same.'

'What was the number?'

'771,' Jack said at once.

'771?' Hook took two strides to the rifle that was chained to the wall. 'Even in the heart of Mardan,' he said as he unfastened the chain, 'I keep things secure. We are no distance from the Khyber, and the Khyberies are the best thieves in Afghanistan, and the Afghans are the best thieves in the world.' Tossing over the rifle, he told Jack to check the serial number.

'771,' Jack said.

'Another copy then,' Hook said. 'That is disturbing. We can trace a gun smuggler and plug the leak. It will be more difficult to stop the tribesmen copying. We are dealing with some very skilled men, Windrush.'

'I wonder if we should not destroy Tazhak.'

'A bit draconian, don't you think?' Hook looked amused. 'Technically, the gunsmiths are doing nothing wrong.'

'I can't think of any other solution.' Jack felt his anger rise. 'My men risked their lives a dozen times to get this intelligence, sir.'

'They are soldiers,' Hook said. 'It is their job to risk their lives. They are Guides, so they would enjoy pitting themselves against the wild Pashtuns.'

Jack swallowed his anger. He knew that the colonel was correct, but it seemed foolish to allow gunsmiths to manufacture weapons that would undoubtedly be used against soldiers of the queen.

'There will always be gunsmiths on the Frontier, Windrush.' Hook tapped his fingers on the desk. 'I'll have to think about this village. More importantly, we have to deal with these fanatics, these so-called Warriors of God, the Mujahidin. You have one point, though, Windrush; the Mujahidin will be even more dangerous with modern weapons.' Hook slammed a hand on his desk. 'Damn! If it had been a gun-runner, we could have stopped the supply at source. Your intelligence alters everything!'

'Yes, sir.' Jack did not pursue what he still believed was the most logical course of action. 'I also believe that one man had been organising them.' Jack explained about the mullah with the tabla drum.

Hook grunted. 'You may be correct. We have been plagued by these mad mullahs in the past. As you know, religion is a powerful thing. Even the most sensible of men can become turbulent when somebody taps into his religion.'

'Yes, sir.'

Hook perused Jack over the rim of his brandy glass. 'What we don't wish to do, Windrush, is stir up the tribes. The Pashtun are much like us. They have deep religious beliefs and will defend their land with tenacity and courage.'

'I agree, sir. My own worry is that our own people will become affected. We don't want a second Mutiny.'

'Indeed, Windrush, indeed.' Colonel Hook sighed, looking older than ever. 'I'll see what I can find out about this tabla mullah you think you shot. As always, you have given me worries, Windrush.' He tapped his finger on the desk again. 'With Batoor Khan dead, then this Gulbaz fellow leads the Rahmut Khel.'

'Yes, sir, and he's no friend of ours.'

Hook grimaced. 'That's a shame, Windrush. Again, it can't be helped. We'll deal with him if the need arises. Now, what do you make of this?' He handed over a crushed fragment of paper.

Jack read the ornate Persian script. 'It's like a note from a lawyer,' he said. 'It mentions a lawsuit and a law agent.' He reread it. 'Something about the law agent being the most important person.' Jack looked up. 'That's an interesting coincidence; we picked up a small group of fellows outside Torkrud with a very similar message for Gulbaz. It had the same Persian script and nearly the same message.'

'What sort of fellows, Windrush?'

Jack tried to remember. 'So much has happened since then. There were three of them, one elderly fellow with a dyed beard and two younger men. If they had not tried to run when they saw us, we would not have even noticed them.'

'Were they Mujahidin? Did they have the red cord?'

Jack shook his head. 'Not that I noticed, sir. My lads thought them suspicious, but as they did not try to harm us, I let them go.'

'That is disturbing, but not unique, unfortunately.' Hook opened a drawer of his desk to produce another square of paper. 'Tell me what you think about this one, then?'

Jack scanned the message, translating it from Urdu. 'They seem to say the same thing, sir. I am guessing that they were not all sent to the same person?'

'Your guess is correct.' Hook's fingers began to tap again. 'These messages have been turning up all across North West India, particularly in the Frontier area. These last two I gave you were carried by Fanatics.'

'So they are not from lawyers then,' Jack said.

'I think they are messages from the Fanatics to their supporters,' Hook said. 'Although I cannot think what they mean.'

'Nor can I, sir,' Jack said. 'It reminds me of the start of the Mutiny when chapattis were sent around India to warn that something was about to happen, except these notes seem to contain a more specific message.'

'Carry on, Windrush.'

'Before the Mutiny, the chapattis were general; nobody knew what they meant or who sent them, while these messages are sent to individuals from an individual. Presumably, the recipient knows the sender, or at least knows of him, or what the message might mean.'

Hook poured himself another brandy. 'You are leading up to something, Windrush.'

'I think these messages prove that there is one man behind all this agitation, sir.' Jack reread the notes. 'This word "lawsuit" comes up in all of these messages.' He laid the letters side by side. 'As does the name "the law agent."' He sat back in his chair. 'I would hazard that the law agent is somebody high up; not a lawyer but somebody much higher in the Mujahidin hierarchy.'

'I see your point,' Colonel Hook said. 'The law agent may be the leader of the whole movement, one of those crazed preachers who spread hate and the idea of a holy war against us and anybody else who does not share their ideas. Perhaps the law agent is that mad tabla mullah that you shot.'

Jack frowned. 'Perhaps, sir. I hope so. The Pashtun are as devout to their religion as we are to Christianity, sir.'

'I know that, Windrush.'

'I tend to think of our militant Christians, sir, Cromwell and the like.' Hook's expression did not offer much comfort to Jack, who continued. 'They have their own laws that are different from ours, Sharia law.'

'I know that, damn it!'

'Yes, sir. I am thinking as I speak.' Jack tried to order his thoughts. 'As far as I understand it, Sharia is based on the Koran, and Sharia law must respect life, family, intellect property and honour.'

'Carry on, Windrush. Where are you taking me?'

'Mohammed is the prophet and wrote down the Koran on God's instructions, with the archangel Gabriel acting as intermediary. In that case, sir, Sharia law, based on the Koran, would be the law of God, of Allah.' Jack waited for Hook's nod.

'I know all this, Windrush.' Hook's fingers began to tap again. 'Do you have a point to make?'

'Yes, sir,' Jack said. 'These notes all mention the law agent. I suggest that the law agent, the man who makes the law, is not merely a mullah, but Allah Himself.'

Hook's fingers stopped tapping. He drained his glass, stood up, poured two glasses of brandy, and handed one to Jack. 'That might make sense, Windrush, although I cannot see how it advances our case.'

Jack lifted the brandy. 'Thank you, sir, that is most kind of you. This other word, sir, lawsuit, is also used a lot.'

'Do you have a theory for that, too, Windrush?'

'I may have, sir,' Jack said. 'Is a lawsuit not a legal argument, where one lawyer argues with another?'

Hook nodded carefully. 'I believe so.'

'Then, if we accept that the law agent is what these fanatics call Allah – which is a bit of an insulting term for the great Creator, reducing him to a mere lawyer – then a lawsuit would be a dispute in which he might be expected to adjudicate?' Jack swirled the brandy within its glass.

'You are tiresomely wordy today, Windrush. Carry on.'

Windrush swallowed some brandy to fortify himself. 'As the Mujahidin wish to dispute Pakhtunkhwa, their country, with us over religious grounds, perhaps a lawsuit is their code word for a dispute, or perhaps a battle?'

'We have not had a battle with these fanatics,' Hook said.

'No, sir,' Jack agreed. 'Not yet.' He looked up. 'Perhaps the Mujahidin, or rather the man who leads them, are planning one. Once again, sir, the situation is very much like the prelude to the Mutiny, when all sorts of omens and portents flew about the countryside.'

'Ye shall hear of wars and rumours of wars.' Hook murmured. 'Matthew 24, Verse six. See that ye be not troubled: for all these things must come to pass, but the end is not yet.'

'I hope not, sir.'

'We have spoken of a major rising,' Hook said. 'Yet I have had my finger on the pulse of India for some time. I don't feel any desire to cause upset; the aftermath of the Mutiny with its hangings and blowing-from-cannon seems to have quite dampened the ardour of even the most anti-British agitator. The huge majority wish peace and stability under the rule of the crown.'

'I agree sir, but religion is a powerful motivator.' Jack felt as if they were repeating the same arguments to no purpose. 'A minority will follow any eloquent orator.'

'For the peace of India and the security of the people, let's hope that it is only a small minority.' When Hook looked up, Jack saw the genuine concern behind his eyes. 'This country has seen more than sufficient bloodshed in its history, Windrush, what with petty kingdoms fighting one another, Hindus fighting Moslems, Marathas and Pindaris slaughtering everybody, Moslems slaughtering Sikhs, Sikhs butchering Moslems, Afghan raids, Nepalese raids and the Mutiny. The last thing it needs is a new religious war. Please God, Windrush, any god, that we can have peace now.'

'That would be the prayer of most people,' Jack agreed.

'Well then, let's nip this thing in the bud before it grows even uglier,' Hook said. 'I will paraphrase your intelligence of this tabla mullah and this village of gunsmiths and send it to the Earl of Elgin, our august Viceroy.' He looked up. 'I expect some reaction from the Viceroy. We cannot afford to let this thing grow until we have another situation like the Mutiny on our hands.'

'Yes, sir.'

'In the meantime, you and your men have earned yourselves a bit of a rest.' Hook gave a bleak smile. 'You did well.'

'I'm not sure that I did, sir.'

'You got your men into Torkrud and back out without a single casualty, Windrush. On this Frontier, that is a success. Your Guides are also talking of some very unorthodox tactics. Coming from them, that means a lot.'

'Thank you, sir.' For one moment, Jack contemplated requesting permission to go to Gondabad to see Mary. He knew he could not. He was too deeply involved in this new situation on the Frontier. It was his duty to see it through to its conclusion. At present, he wanted a long bath and a longer sleep.

Chapter Thirteen

Mardan, September 1863

'Did you hear the news, Windrush?' The cheroot seemed incongruous as it thrust from Major Kerr's heavily bearded face. Dressed in an Afghan poshteen and boots, a puggaree adorning his head, he looked more like a Pashtun than anything else. The pulwar at his side completed the image. Sometimes Jack wondered if the Pashtuns were converting the British to their culture rather than the other way around. That idea became stronger when Kerr swore in Pushtu as he barked his shin against the edge of the table.

'Language, Kerr,' Jack rebuked mildly. 'I heard the Mujahidin attacked our camp at Topi.'

'That's right. Damned cheek, attacking a Guides camp.' Rubbing his shin, Kerr perched himself on the edge of the table. He puffed out smoke. 'Impudent beggars! I would not mind if they attacked a Queen's regiment, but not the Guides!'

'We'll have to do something about them,' Jack said. After his expedition into the Frontier, he felt part of the regiment. He knew Hassan, Fatteh, Alladad and the others; they were his men now.

'Oh, we are doing something about them.' Kerr gave a smile that promised bad news for the Mujahidin. 'It's taken time, but that attack has, at last, stirred us up into sorting out these Fanatics once and for all. They'll find that it's one thing to raid and rob unarmed farmers and merchants and quite another when they attack the Guides!'

'What are we doing?' After a period of relative peace on the Frontier, Jack had harboured some aspirations that he might be able to go on his long-delayed leave with Mary. Now that the Mujahidin had caused further trouble, that faint hope withered and died.

Kerr adjusted his pulwar. 'Last time we moved against the Fanatics, Sir Sydney Cotton took five thousand men and chased them from their base at Sitana, burning their villages.'

'You told me that already. That was back in '58, wasn't it?' Jack asked.

'That's right.'

'I was a little busy in Oudh at the time.' Jack did not go into detail.

'I thought that would get you going.' Kerr's granite eyes nearly relaxed into a smile. 'From Malka, the Fanatics have been recruiting again, as you know.'

'I saw some of them,' Jack agreed cautiously.

Kerr nodded. 'When they realised that we would not bother them, the Fanatics moved to a splendidly fortified hill near Siri, but rather than attack them, we only blockaded the tribes that permitted them access.' Kerr shifted on the table, blowing more smoke. 'And sent warnings to those we suspected. That included your friend Batoor Khan, and the Rahmut Khel, of course.'

'I'm not sure if the Rahmut Khel did help them.' Jack tried to defend Batoor.

Kerr raised his eyebrows, pulled on his cigar, and did not pursue that subject. 'Now the Fanatics have returned to Sitana, raiding, plundering and murdering once more. We've had enough, so we have arranged a punitive expedition.' Kerr smiled again, with his eyes softening a little.

'Something seems to be amusing you, Kerr.'

'Something certainly is amusing me, Windrush.' Sliding off the table, Kerr stalked to the far side and opened the drawer. 'Colonel Hook sent this for you.' He held up a folded, sealed document. 'I already know the contents.'

'Thank you.' Jack guessed that the document would not be good news. Breaking the seal, he unfolded the stiff paper and scanned the contents. 'I am to report to Brigadier General Sir Neville Chamberlain as a staff officer with expertise on the Frontier,' he said.

Kerr lit another cheroot. 'That's right, Jack me boy. You, a virtual griff on the Frontier, are to give local help and advice to General Sir Neville Bowles Chamberlain, the bravest of the brave, a man who has fought the length and breadth of the land from Kabul to Baluchistan. Chamberlain, who has collected more wounds than Alexander the Great; why, Captain, once Chamberlain dies, they are going to smelt his body for the lead, he has so many bullets in it. The man is a veritable legend, and you have to give him advice.' Kerr did not laugh often, but when he did, he did not hold back. He roared with laughter at the thought of Jack, with one Frontier expedition to his name, advising one of the most experienced men in the army.

Jack could not help his rueful smile. He had not asked for the posting. He did not want the posting, but orders were orders. He had no choice except to do his duty as best he could.

'*My darling wife,*' Jack penned a hurried note to Mary. '*I am off on my travels again. This time I am posted to the staff of General Chamberlain, who is, I am sure you know, one of the most distinguished officers in India. I still hold out hope of leave once this present emergency is over, so do not despair. As soon as we dispose of the threat of these Warriors of God, I should be back to your loving arms.*'

Jack paused to nibble the end of his pen. He was never very good at voicing his emotions, let alone writing them down. What would Mary wish to hear? What could he tell her about his experiences that would allow her into his life without unduly alarming her?

'*I have had some interesting times out here, which I will tell you about more fully when next we meet. The Pashtun people are entirely different from those we know so well. You will be pleased to know that I was entertained by our old friend Batoor for a while.*

I must close now, as I am due to meet General Chamberlain soon and must get washed and brushed up to look my best.

Give young Andrew a hug from his father, and I send all my love to you.
Your affectionate husband,
Jack.'

Reading the letter, Jack knew it was hardly adequate to express even a tenth of the love he held for Mary. He also knew that she would understand; she was Mary. She always understood. Making a decision, he pressed the blotter over the damp ink, folded the paper, sealed and addressed it.

Please, God, I see her in person soon and don't have to write any more letters. Yet he knew that was a vain hope. The government would not send out a man such as General Chamberlain unless they had a full-blown expedition in mind.

As Kerr had intimated, Chamberlain was a vastly experienced soldier. Wounded five times in the first Afghan War alone, he had since fought through the Gwalior War and the second Sikh War, doing great execution at the battle of Gujerat. More recently he had been wounded again during the terrible fighting around Delhi during the Mutiny. Jack had never met him, although his name had been mentioned on numerous occasions.

* * *

'Well, Windrush.' Looking far older than his forty-three years, Chamberlain had recently fought off a bout of malaria, as the yellowish tinge of his skin proved. 'You are to be on my staff as an advisor.' He smoothed a finger across his neat little moustache. 'Damned nonsense, of course; I have forgotten more about this Frontier than you will ever know.'

'I do appreciate that, sir,' Jack said. 'However, I may have some pertinent information.'

'You may,' Chamberlain said. 'We will discuss that later.' Although he sighed like an old man, Jack saw bright humour behind the weariness. 'I really hoped for a less demanding post, but it looks as if my last days in India are to be spent in fatigue and exposure. I would much rather turn my sword into a shepherd's crook. However, if duty really requires the sacrifice, I cannot repine.' He sighed deeply. 'All right, Windrush, if you are to be on my staff, then you should share the intelligence we have.'

Chamberlain glanced around the room as if fearing one of the Mujahidin may be listening under the table. 'You know that the fanatics are back at Sitani. Evidently, I need to take a more forceful approach if we are to eradicate this poison once and for all.'

'Yes, sir.' Jack studied the map of North West India and the Frontier that Chamberlain unrolled on the table.

'We must attack them from the north.' Chamberlain stabbed down his finger with some force. 'That way the Fanatics have two choices. They can stand and fight us when we will slaughter them to the last man, or they can run across the Indus, where our army in Hazara can destroy them.'

'Having seen some Ghazis, sir; I am sure that they will fight.'

Chamberlain stroked his moustache again. 'You've met our Ghazis, have you? I hope they do fight, Windrush. There can only be one outcome for any native force standing against a British Army; inevitable defeat.'

'The Afghans destroyed Elphinstone's army, sir,' Jack dared to remind the general. 'And the Sikhs gave us plenty hard knocks.'

'I was present at both, and we were ultimately successful.' Chamberlain treated Jack to a chilling stare.

'Yes, sir.' Having said his piece, Jack thought it diplomatic to let the general have the last word.

'We will base our Yusufzai Field Force here, in the Chamla Valley.' Chamberlain indicated a valley about twenty miles north of Mardan, deep in the northern hills. 'Although they can muster some ten thousand fighting men, the Bunerwal tribe there has shown no hostility to us.'

'Yes, sir. I have heard they are a warlike bunch toward other Pashtuns, though. If they are pressed, they retaliate.'

'Yes, indeed. You are holding something back, Captain. Say what you think.' Chamberlain's voice was sharp. 'Your duty is to advise me!'

'Have we ever had an expedition there, sir? I've never heard of one.'

Chamberlain shook his head. 'Not that I am aware of, Windrush. As I said, they have shown no hostility to us.'

'I think they may be friendly because we have left them in peace, sir. From what I have seen of the Pashtun, they want the freedom to live their own lives without any outside interference.'

'You're an opinionated beggar, aren't you, Windrush? What you say may be correct,' Chamberlain allowed. 'However, there is no help for it. We must chance a smaller evil in the hope of averting a greater.' Chamberlain glanced at Jack to ensure he was paying attention. 'To get to the Chamla Valley, we have to cross this range of hills that stretches from the south-western spurs of the Mahabun Mountains to the Guru Mountains.'

Jack studied the map. He was growing used to the tangle of rocky hills that made up the Frontier. 'I can see three passes, sir.' He marked them with his finger. 'There is the Ambela, the Kanpoor and the Daran.'

'That's correct, Windrush,' Chamberlain agreed. 'We know virtually nothing about the Kanpoor; certainly, we lack sufficient knowledge to march an army through it. When Cotton explored the Daran, he thought the tribes extremely hostile and the road impossible for artillery, so that only leaves the Ambela. A two-day forced march should see us through the pass.'

'Which tribe claims the Ambela Pass, sir?' Jack studied the map again. 'Is it the Bunerwals again?'

'It is,' Chamberlain said. 'My local informants tell me that the Bunerwals dislike the Fanatics as much as we do. I presume that they suffer from their raiding; neighbours on the Frontier are seldom the best of friends.'

'That is certain, sir. Most feuds seem to be among neighbours.'

'Quite so, Windrush.' Chamberlain nodded. 'I will command some five thousand men, including one hundred sabres of the Guides and the 11th Bengal Cavalry, plus the 71st Highlanders, the 101st Royal Bengal Fusiliers, six battalions of the Frontier Force, Sikh Pioneers and artillery.'

Jack nodded. 'That is a formidable force, sir.'

'I hope it is sufficiently formidable to overawe the tribes and smash the Fanatics,' Chamberlain said. 'I will advance with two separate columns. I'll send a column to protect the Indus; we'll call that the Hazara column. I will lead the main force, which we'll call the Peshawar column.' Lifting a stick, Chamberlain traced his planned route on the map.

'While the Hazara column ensures the tribes around the Indus remain quiet, the Peshawar column will march to Nawakili, a few miles from the Daran Pass. The Fanatics will think we are emulating Cotton's route and prepare to receive us there. Once we reach the Daran, we will swing around and march for the Ambela Pass.'

'The Pashtuns can move faster than us, sir,' Jack reminded him.

'I am well aware of that, Windrush. We must do what we can. Now, make yourself useful. I want you to collate all the intelligence reports that our spies and agents hand in. I doubt you'll find anything out of the ordinary, but it will keep you occupied. Oh, and find us sufficient transport for 5,600 men plus guns.'

In the Army, Jack knew, he could be attacking a heavily defended position one day and acting as nursemaid to the officers' wives the next. It was typical of the Army to casually order him to do two jobs at once, both vitally important, and one utterly time-consuming. Cursing the gods of fate that had sent him to the Frontier, Jack took a deep breath, reminded himself that he must do his duty, begged Major Kerr to lend him Hassan to do the legwork, and buckled down.

Finding transport for such a large force on the North West Frontier was not easy. Now more experienced in the reality of travelling in Pakhtunkhwa, the first thing Jack did was buy himself a stout Khyber pony that could carry him over all except the sternest of mountains. After that, Jack immersed himself in the commissariat aspect of soldiering. He was aware that although fighting was the ultimate object of a soldier's job, the Army had to get him to his destination and ensure he was adequately fed, watered and equipped at all times.

Just as Jack was getting to grips with the transport situation, the intelligence reports began to arrive. Most were of a routine nature, talking of the difficulties of the different routes, the lack of fodder, and the population of the various villages which the British columns would have to pass. Every so often, Jack found himself reading something more interesting. He placed his reports into two classifications: Group A, which were the mundane, and Group B, which were the significant.

The first of the Group B reports came from a Guide patrol, mentioning a sighting of Mujahidin in the Ambela Valley. Jack put that report to one side. When a second Guide report spoke of a mullah with a tabla drum, Jack became more concerned. *Damn! I thought I had killed that man! He must have only been wounded.* Where that mullah appeared, trouble invariably followed.

Sending an account of the two pieces of intelligence to Chamberlain, Jack ordered the patrols to look for more activity by the Mujahidin in the Ambela Valley, and particularly to watch for the tabla mullah.

It was Hassan who made the next breakthrough. 'I happened to be passing through the villages, sahib,' he said smoothly, 'and spoke to one of the men here.'

Jack translated that as meaning Hassan was engaged in a personal blood feud, and his enemy had given him information under some compulsion. 'What did you learn, Hassan?'

'There is a Jirga planned in the Chamla Valley, sahib.' Hassan stood at attention beside the battered plank table that Jack used as a desk. 'The Mujahidin have sent envoys to the Bunerwals.'

'Do you know why, Hassan? Do you know what they are going to talk about?'

'Yes, sahib,' Hassan said. 'The Mujahidin wish to persuade the Bunerwals to join them in a jihad.'

Jack had expected nothing else. 'I'd like to be a fly on the wall at that Jirga.' He smiled at Hassan's confusion. 'I mean I would like to hear what they say, Hassan.'

Hassan nodded, wordless, but Jack wondered what thoughts were behind his expressionless blue eyes.

Chamberlain's frown deepened as he listened to Jack's report. 'Thank you, Windrush.'

'I could go along to the Jirga, sir.' Jack felt the usual mixture of sick despair and high elation as he volunteered to venture into one of the most dangerous places on earth.

'That would be suicidal.' Chamberlain turned down the idea without a second thought. 'Who do you think you are? Sekundar Burnes? Remember what happened to him?'

'Yes, sir.' Captain Sir Alexander Burnes was a Scottish explorer and diplomat who surveyed the Indus and explored Afghanistan. He was the first British diplomat to Bokhara and advised the British to support Dost Mohammed on the Afghan throne rather than Shah Shuja. If Lord Auckland had listened to Burnes, the disaster of the First Afghan War might have been avoided. As it was, Burnes died heroically when the Afghans rose against the British and the ruler they imposed.

'So we'll have no more clandestine operations among these people, Windrush.' Chamberlain closed the subject. 'There is sufficient evidence to warn us to alter our plans. As you are aware, we were originally informed that the Bunerwals were more inclined to support us than the Fanatics. Now you have found out that the Fanatics are working with the Bunerwals, spreading their idea of jihad.' Chamberlain's grin did not fool Jack for a moment. 'It would be more sensible to restrict our movements.'

Jack nodded. He knew it would be foolish to offer advice to a general. He had already learned that on the Frontier; the situation was always fluid. While part of him was relieved that he would not be venturing into the Chamla Valley, he also felt that the situation was not yet proven. Although he trusted Hassan's information, he would have preferred to hear the mullah's words for himself.

Chamberlain continued: 'Rather than attacking the Fanatics in their valley fastnesses, we will attack the villages they infest.'

'Yes, sir.'

Chamberlain looked older than ever. 'We will rid the country of this particular poison, Windrush, although knowing the Pashtun as I do, there will be other mullahs coming along in their wake.'

Jack nodded. He knew that Chamberlain had made up his mind. Nothing a mere captain said would influence the general's decision.

'We will advance by the Ambela Pass into the Chamla Valley.'

The die was cast, the cards were dealt; now the soldiers, the ultimate expression of Queen Victoria's imperial will, would march. Jack took a deep breath. He was going to war once more. *We belong to God, and unto God do we return.* Jack shook his head. No, he would use the old 113th slogan: *Cry Havelock and let loose the dogs of war.*

Chapter Fourteen

North west frontier 19th October 1863

'It's a shambles,' Jack said. They stood at the base camp with the mountains of the Frontier rising before them. All around, the land seethed with activity, with infantry preparing to march, the artillery checking their equipment, and the cavalry feeding their horses. Great elephants trumpeted as their mahouts fastened the carts and artillery they would have to pull. Camels spat, roared, bubbled and refused to move while the discordant braying of mules sounded everywhere. A host of soldiers, British, Gurkha and Indian, waited in increasing impatience for the order to move. Jack walked over to have a word with the Guides.

'Halloa there, Windrush.' Major Kerr fixed him with his gimlet stare. 'Are you joining us?'

'I don't know what I'm doing,' Jack said honestly. 'I seem to be a bit of everything and a lot of nothing.'

'That's life on the staff for you,' Kerr said. 'Take my advice, man, and get back into regimental duty.'

'I doubt that a Queen's regiment would have me,' Jack said. Not many officers' messes would accept a man with a half-Indian wife, while Mary would live an isolated and uncomfortable life with the other wives.

'Try the Guides, Windrush. My lads liked you, and they are particular who they serve with.'

Jack appreciated the compliment. The Guides did not take to every officer. 'Thank you, Major. I may do that.' He missed the men of the 113th, his old regiment. He would relish that personal contact with soldiers again, being part of the minutiae of their lives, their daily problems and triumphs. With the Guides, he would be part of the Punjab Frontier Force, permanently stationed on or near the Frontier. He would belong. But did he want to belong to a sepoy regiment? Try as he might, Jack could not shake away the memory of the opening weeks of the Mutiny, when regiments who had been part of the Company's forces for a century and more attacked their British officers. He remembered the horrors of the sack of Gondabad where he and Elliot had rescued Mary from the rampaging sepoys. Could he ever fully trust a sepoy regiment again, let alone serve in one and have Mary and young Andrew at their mercy?

'Think about it.' Kerr puffed on his cheroot. 'You look a trifle agitated, Windrush. What's bothering you?'

'I've never been on the commissariat side of the army before,' Jack said. 'It's a blasted shambles. We're advancing into the Frontier, and half the artillery pieces are useless. The general has ordered them sent back, as well as the five-and-a-half-inch mortars.'

'We're weak in artillery then,' Kerr said. 'Not good when we're out here.' He glanced at the heights that frowned down on them. 'Let's hope the Bunerwals have resisted the Mujahidin advances and remain friendly to us. If they turn hostile, we'll have to fight our way through some very ugly territory.'

Jack nodded. 'The general used to think the Bunerwals preferred us to the Mujahidin. Now he is not so sure.'

'My boys are convinced that the Mujahidin have infiltrated the Bunerwals,' Kerr said. 'As Hassan told you, there have been mullahs parading around the Chamla Valley, including your famous tabla mullah.'

'I thought I had killed that man,' Jack said. 'I shot him clear.' He shook his head. 'I have often wondered if one man is behind all this unrest, and that fellow seems to turn up wherever there is trouble.'

Kerr nodded. 'He certainly seems to be a man to watch.' Kerr watched as a troop of Guides cavalry formed up, each man riding proud. 'Religion is a unifying force with the Pashtun. Please, God, it can be a force for good.' He gave a wry smile. 'Did you realise that Caspar, one of the Three Wise Men, was from this part of the world?'

'I did not.' Jack wondered if Mary knew about Caspar.

'The Acts of Thomas in the Apocrypha call him Gudapharasa, and local legend says he founded Kandahar, just a few miles away in Afghanistan.'

Trust an Ulsterman to know his Bible and all facts related to it. Jack looked around. The army was forming up, the Guides Cavalry at the forefront, as was right and proper, with the 11th Bengal Cavalry backing them up. Jack looked at their faces, pushing away the memory of the sepoys running amok in Gondabad, killing civilians. That black day was passed now; these men had proved their loyalty. Hassan, Zaman and the others had not put a foot wrong when they had accompanied him to Torkrud and on that tortuous journey back. He was wrong to doubt them, yet he knew that the shadow of distrust remained.

As officers and NCOs began to bark orders, the infantry formed up, blocks of scarlet and khaki with rifles held ready. The Guides Infantry were there, stolid, proud of the red piping on their uniforms that highlighted the part they played in the Siege of Delhi. Beside the Guides were the 20th (Punjabi) Native Infantry including the Sikhs, to Jack's mind some of the most stolid infantry in the world. The British infantry was nearby, lean, with the nut-brown faces of long-term professionals, eyeing the mountains with neither fear nor favour.

After a single, searching scrutiny of his Guides cavalry, Kerr signalled for his horse. 'Have you been to Taxila, near Islamabad, Windrush?'

'No.' Jack had never heard of the place.

'Take your Mary there, she'll be interested,' Kerr said. 'It was on the old Silk Road. There's a tradition that one of the Magi passed through on the way to the Holy Land.' He mounted his horse. On foot he was a stocky, slightly cumbersome man; mounted, he looked like a centaur, an extension of the horse. 'We won't be as famous as the three wise men, Windrush, but let's try and make a bit of a name for ourselves!' When he grinned, his basilisk eyes brightened with the crazed joy of soldiering. 'You already have a reputation from Sevastopol and Lucknow, Jack-my-lad. Now you can add to it on the Frontier. Ho, now; here's mischief coming our way.'

'So I see.' Jack watched as the galloper pushed through a section of Sikh infantry, and reined up, his face alight with excitement. 'Are you Captain Windrush?'

'I am.'

'General Chamberlain wants you.'

'Who are you?' Jack grabbed hold of the galloper's reins before he rode off.

'Cornet Aubrey Cheshire.' The cornet looked down at Jack.

'You call me sir, cornet.' Jack spoke softly but with an edge to his voice.

About to kick in his spurs, the cornet looked into Jack's eyes, and quickly changed his mind. 'Yes, sir.'

'Now report properly.' Jack knew that the members of some Queen's regiments thought themselves superior to men who served in units of the Indian Army, even the Guides. He made it his business to alter that misconception.

'Yes, sir.' Cornet Cheshire coloured as Kerr also stared at him. 'General Chamberlain sends his respects, sir, and could you attend to him at your earliest convenience.'

'That's better, cornet. You're only a Griff. Don't give yourself airs and graces out here; they won't last long. And you rode through the Sikhs as if they were unimportant. Don't ever treat the Sikhs like that again; they are better men and finer soldiers than you will ever be. Now cut along and try to look like you're useful.'

Red-faced, Cornet Cheshire trotted away.

'Well said, Windrush.' A Sikh officer nodded to Jack. His men were all watching, their bearded faces impassive, yet Jack knew they had heard every word. 'Some of my men were in the Khalsa.'

Jack included the Sikh infantry as he returned the nod. 'I thought they looked like true soldiers.' He saw the grins; the Sikhs recognised his appreciation. 'I fought beside Sikhs in the Mutiny. Few better.'

'None better,' the officer corrected. He shook his head. 'These young ringtail griffs now; they are not the same quality as they used to be.' He lowered his voice. 'Nor are the British regiments, I fear.'

Jack said nothing to that. He had heard similar concerns voiced before. Thinking of the quality of the Highlanders at Lucknow and the Connaught Rangers outside Sevastopol, he wondered if any soldiers could reach these heights again. 'I hope we are both wrong in thinking that.'

'Aye; well, you'd better report to the general, Captain.'

Jack turned to say his farewells to Kerr, but the major had already ridden to join his Guides. Once again, Jack realised that he wished to belong to a regiment.

'Windrush.' Chamberlain looked younger now the campaign had properly started. There was bright humour in his eyes. 'Ride with the advance column; when they meet with the men I have sent to guard the Daran Pass, send a galloper to inform me.'

'Yes, sir.'

'Pray inform the advance column they have to halt at the entrance to the Ambela Pass. They must wait there for the main body to arrive.'

'Yes, sir.' Jack prepared to kick in his heels. 'Sir, Major Kerr informs me that his Guides also believe the Mujahidin have been attempting to suborn the Bunerwals.'

Chamberlain nodded. 'That confirms the intelligence you gathered, Windrush. Let's hope that the Bunerwals have enough sense not to listen to them. The last thing we need is to have to fight our way through the passes.' He straightened his shoulders. 'But if we have to, then we shall.'

'Yes, sir.' Jack rode on. To his mind, cornets carried messages, not captains with a dozen years of experience behind them. However, orders were orders, like it or not.

'General Chamberlain sends his respects,' he reported to Colonel Wilde, in command of the advance force. 'Could you halt the advance body at the entrance to the Ambela Pass?'

Wilde barely nodded. 'Will do, Windrush.' He nodded to the surrounding hills. 'The locals look a bit agitated.'

From the glowering heights, parties of lean men with jezzails sat or stood, watching Wilde's advance force move toward the Ambela Pass. Jack trotted over to the Guides cavalry, at the front of Wilde's men. 'Hassan,' he called. 'Who are these men?'

'Bunerwals,' Hassan said without hesitation. 'They have not fired on us yet. They will if we enter the Pass.'

'Thank you, Hassan.' Wheeling his horse, Jack thought it best to report himself, so galloped back to Chamberlain. 'The Bunerwals have pickets out to watch us, sir.'

'They will have.' Chamberlain accepted the information. 'Do they look hostile?'

'They are all armed, sir, but nobody has fired on us yet. The Guides believe they might if we enter the Pass.'

'Very good, Windrush. Let's hope our main body can get a blasted move on. We have to penetrate the pass by noon, for God's sake.' Chamberlain hesitated only a moment. 'Bunerwals or no Bunerwals.'

'Yes, sir.'

Chamberlain's main body was three hours behind the advance force, struggling to haul the artillery over the ever-worsening road. Jack watched as the elephants failed to find sufficient space, with the mahouts who sat behind the elephant's ears urging them on with the pointed sticks they carried.

'Wilde's men will be isolated unless we push along,' Chamberlain said. 'I don't like to leave a small body alone on the Frontier.'

To Jack, it was evident that Chamberlain's experiences during the Afghan War haunted him. 'Wilde's a good man, sir, with good quality troops.'

'That I don't doubt,' Chamberlain said. 'We'd get on faster if we leave the guns behind, but we need all the firepower we can get out here.'

Remembering his earlier conversation about the failing quality of British infantry, Jack studied the men as they marched past. The 71st Highland Light Infantry moved at a fair pace. Lithe, gaunt-faced men in tartan trews and scarlet jackets, they looked as capable as any infantry Jack had ever seen. But this was a veteran regiment; they had fought in Crimea and in the latter parts of the Mutiny, although Jack had not been associated with them in either of these wars. Looking at their grim, set faces, Jack was glad he was not facing them in battle.

Then came the 101st Royal Bengal Fusiliers, a regiment that the Honourable East India Company had raised in 1652, and which had been transferred to the British Army after the demise of that company. The regiment had a proud history, having fought at Plassey, the first Afghan war and in Burma in 1852 as well as distinguishing itself in the terrible actions around Delhi during the Mutiny. With many experienced men having left in protest at the transfer to crown control, hundreds of ringtails, young recruits now filled the ranks. Jack was unsure whether griffins could cope with the conditions on the Frontier.

Pulling aside Sharbat, his Kabul pony, Jack watched as three battalions of Punjab infantry, stolid, professional and mainly Sikh, marched past. They would fight, whatever the odds. Jack had every respect for the Sikhs. They had not joined in the Mutiny, and nor had the Gurkhas, who came next.

Jack spent the remainder of that day passing on messages or gathering intelligence from unit commanders and scouts. He spoke to the ranking soldiers as well as the officers. The men may have had a limited view of events, and were often starved of information from the top, but an experienced NCO could gauge what was happening. Their comments had always given Jack an insight into their morale, helping him decide what was possible. It was the ordinary men who provided the sharp edge of any army and without them, there was only hot air and ideological rhetoric.

As the main body pushed on, the road petered into nothingness as the surrounding hills increased in size. Jack realised that leading a small body of very mobile horsemen in this terrain was vastly different from forcing through an army. The Frontier could have been designed specifically for defence, with every rock a possible hiding place and every ridge a potential ambush spot.

'Windrush.' Chamberlain seemed determined to use Jack at every opportunity. 'Ride ahead; see if Colonel Wilde has secured the head of the pass yet.'

Once again, Jack kicked his heels, and Sharbat responded willingly. She was not as fast or as attractive as Colwall, but there was no doubt she had a stout heart. Jack waited for the ribald comments that the 113th or Campbell's Highlanders would have shouted as he passed, but neither the 71st nor the 101st responded. Jack frowned, wondering if the Sikh officer had been correct. He hoped that British infantry had not lost their spirit.

The Ambela pass rose before him, narrow, craggy and stern, with towering pine trees straggling up the rocky slopes. When a picket of Guides infantry challenged him, Jack responded with a wave.

'Captain Windrush, sometimes attached to the Guides. I'm off to find Colonel Wilde.'

'He's about a mile ahead, making a secure base for the general sahib.' The Guide was a Mohmand with deep brown eyes. 'Watch for snipers, sahib. The Bunerwals can be treacherous.'

'Thank you, I will.' Jack rode on.

Wilde looked concerned when Jack reined up. 'Pray inform the general that the Bunerwals do not appreciate our presence, Windrush.' He pointed to the crags that lowered over them. 'The Guides have reported an ominous number of them in small parties and large.'

'Have they attacked you, sir?' Jack asked.

'Not yet, Windrush. I think it's only a matter of time.' Wilde looked behind him. 'In this terrain, it's essential we control the heights, and for that we need artillery. I believe we sent some back.'

'Yes, sir. The guns were not functional.'

'Guns that don't work are no blasted good to me.' Wilde preened his whiskers. 'I don't know what this army is coming to. Don't report that to General Chamberlain though, Windrush; he knows what he is doing.'

Jack could feel the brittle tension in the air. Fir trees dotted the slopes, affording cover to any Bunerwal, with date trees and wild figs lower down. To Jack, the combination of vegetation encompassed the region, a mixture of near-Alpine and sub-tropical that typified the Pashtun people themselves, an amalgam of intense fierceness and deep family loyalty. His time with the Guides had heightened his ability to spot movement, so he could observe the tribesmen on the hills. He saw a patch of shade on the wrong side of a rock, a flash on sunlight on metal, the branch of a tree shifting against the breeze. 'This is the most fascinating place in the world.' Jack had not intended to voice his thoughts.

'Aye, and the most dangerous.' Wilde did not flinch at the deep thud of a jezzail. 'Here we go. The Bunerwals have opened the ball; it could be a typical Pashtun shot for shikar or the beginning of something much bigger.' He looked at Jack through jaundiced eyes. 'You'd better warn the general that I expect trouble here.'

By the time Jack returned to the main body, he knew the road between Wilde's force and the main army very well.

Chamberlain grunted at Jack's news. 'If Colonel Wilde expects trouble, then trouble there will be.' He looked backwards, where the elephants were toiling to find space on the narrow track. 'Get these blasted guns moving, Windrush!'

Feeling more like a messenger than a soldier, Windrush carried Chamberlain's instructions.

'Please inform the general that we're as quick as we can be,' the reply came. 'Does he want us to carry the damned things on our backs?'

'Do that.' Chamberlain had followed Jack. 'Do anything that is necessary. I won't have my men exposed to long-range fire without the ability to retaliate.' He turned to Jack. 'I saw enough of this business back in '41, Windrush. The Pashtun are not people you can give an inch to. They are the most perfect warriors.'

'We have better rifles now, sir. Back in '41, the Afghans jezzails outranged our old Brown Bess muskets. Now our rifles are better than theirs.'

Chamberlain replied with one word: 'Tazhak.'

'Indeed, sir,' Jack said.

'Get the artillery moving, Windrush.'

'Yes, sir.' Jack could understand Chamberlain's agitation. Having seen one British army with all its camp followers massacred, he had no wish to preside over the loss of another.

The guns struggled onwards, with the men pushing, carrying what they could, sweating until their uniforms were stained black. Still, the main body made painfully slow progress, so they were much later than planned when the two forces finally merged. Chamberlain called a meeting of his senior officers and staff with Jack, as a lowly captain, standing on the outside of the ring.

Chamberlain surveyed his officers and the surrounding hills. 'Gentlemen, I have decided on a change of plan. With our present slow rate of progress, I no longer intend to penetrate into the Chamla Valley. Tonight we will set up camp at the summit of the Ambela Pass.'

Jack nodded approval. With night fast approaching, it would be foolish to push a cumbersome column into the territory of a tribe that was appearing more hostile by the hour.

'Colonel Wilde, send out pickets to secure these heights.' Chamberlain pointed to surrounding hills.

'I have already done so, sir.' Wilde was an experienced man. Jack saw the khaki turbans of the Guides infantry bobbing among the pine trees and rocks.

'I'll post the mountain guns on the high ground in the morning,' Chamberlain said. 'At present, the gunners are too exhausted to do anything.'

The British camp was just to the right, the south, of the ridge of the Ambela Pass, at the head of a couple of small streams that flowed into a river, presumably the Chamla, Jack thought. On the right was ridge after wooded ridge that climbed to the peaks of the Mahabun

Mountains. To their left, the five-thousand-feet-high Guru Mountains frowned over them, appearing sinister in the gathering dark, with a British piquet occupying an outlying spur.

'That place is like an eagle's nest,' Kerr said.

'That's as good a name for it as any.' Jack was busy with his binoculars.

To the northeast, at the tip of the roughly oval British camp, was Standard Point, from where the multi-crossed Union flag would be hoisted at daybreak. Beyond that, to the southeast, another knoll rose, covered with pines and rocks. The British soldiers had already christened it Crag Piquet, with Water Piquet slightly to the south, and less well-protected. To the south, east of these hills, was a double-peaked conical hill. By the time Jack focussed his binoculars on that hill, the light had faded away.

When the meeting broke up, Jack mounted Sharbat once more and rode to the summit of the Ambela Pass. To the south, dim in the distance, glittering lights sugared the plain of Yusafzai.

I stand on the border between one civilisation and another. On one side I have a gradually improving land of trade and industry under British protection. On the other, there are tribes, wild and free. I am like a Roman legionnaire guarding Hadrian's Wall from the Picts, but what did Calgagus say when he opposed Agricola's army at Mons Graupius? The Romans make a desert and call it peace. Are we seeking to make a desert of Pakhtunwali? Are we attempting to alter a culture that is happier to be left alone?

Riding back into camp, Jack saw Chamberlain frowning at him. 'Windrush, first thing tomorrow I want you to accompany Colonel Taylor of the Engineers and Lieutenant Sandeman on a reconnaissance.'

'Yes, sir.' *It seems that life on the staff does not mean beer and skittles. At least I am being useful.*

Although he knew he might be riding into the open jaws of a tiger, Jack was glad to go. Anything was better than being used as a glorified runner. As he lay on his charpoy, Jack wrote another letter to Mary, sealing it with a sigh. He did not say much, but he felt closer to her when he wrote.

I have no idea when you will get this. I hope this is a short campaign, but I must do my duty.

As always on the Frontier, Jack did not undress and tied his revolver to his wrist. Even deep in the British camp, with guards patrolling the perimeter, he knew that the local thieves could sneak in if they chose to. He sighed; was this what he had missed when working in Gondabad?

Lieutenant-Colonel Dighton Probyn commanded the escort for the reconnaissance. A handsome man wearing the obligatory beard, he stood with his head slightly down and looked to Jack like a brooding eagle. 'So you're Windrush,' he said when Jack reported to him.

'Yes, sir,' Jack admitted. He surveyed the straight-nosed, steady-eyed man who had won the Victoria Cross for acts of incredible bravery during the late Mutiny. *This is another of these iron men we throw up so casually.*

'You did good work at Lucknow,' Probyn said. 'I didn't know you were on the Frontier.'

'I'm fairly new here, sir.'

Probyn nodded. 'Aye; you'll find it's not the same as fighting under Colin Campbell.'

'I've found that already,' Jack said.

Probyn's eyes softened a little. 'We both know that you should be more advanced in rank, Windrush, after your exploits.'

Jack knew he could not afford to purchase promotion. 'Perhaps I have reached my ceiling, Colonel.'

Probyn frowned. 'Perhaps the Bunerwals will welcome us with open arms and psalms of praise, but I doubt that, too, Windrush. Come on.' Kicking in his heels, he inspected his men and took up a position at the head of the reconnaissance force.

With Probyn's green-turbaned 1st Sikh Irregular Cavalry, known as Probyn's Horse, riding loosely around the column, Colonel Taylor led them down the pass and into the Chamla Valley. Jack kept one hand near the hilt of his revolver as he saw the Bunerwals watching from behind rocks, or occasionally standing in the open, not responding to any greetings from Taylor's men.

'They're just watching us,' Probyn said, 'as if they are waiting for something to happen. What do you think, Windrush?'

'I think they're counting our numbers,' Jack said. 'They're wondering how strong we are, and if we are likely to fight, or run.'

'We'll know soon enough.' Probyn pointed to a ridge. 'That saddleback is what we know as the Kotal. On the opposite side is Buner, which these lads call home. If the Bunerwals are as friendly as we hope, it will be nearly empty. If they distrust us, the warriors will have occupied it to prevent us from coming too close.'

Jack saw the flash of sunlight on steel. He focussed his binoculars. 'They're there.' He saw an array of turbans and long robes as the warriors stood on the ridge, making no attempt to hide from the small British patrol. A slight wind ruffled the dun clothes of the Bunerwals, giving a rippling effect to the men who stood watching.

'How many?' Probyn's casual tone did not fool Jack.

'A couple of hundred,' Jack said. 'They are shifting around. Capable-looking lads, however many there are. They're making sure that we can see them.'

'All the Pashtuns are capable lads,' Probyn said. 'Two hundred, eh? And ensuring they're visible. The Bunerwals are sending us a message, Windrush. It's like our gamekeepers, they are saying: Keep out, no trespassing.'

Jack lowered his binoculars. 'Perhaps we should have sent a note asking permission first. "Please Mr Bunerwal, please may we crash through your valley with thousands of men, guns and elephants so we can attack your neighbours."'

'There's no perhaps about it, Windrush. That's exactly what we should have done. I fear that we have turned a neutral tribe into an enemy when God knows we have more than sufficient enemies in this part of the world.' He touched the hilt of his sword. 'Pray that Chamberlain does not do an Elphinstone and lead us to disaster.'

'He seemed to know what he is doing,' Jack said. 'He's very experienced.'

Probyn released his sword. 'Let's hope so, Jack, let's hope so. Pass over your binoculars. There's a good lad.'

The even more casual use of his Christian name alerted Jack to Probyn's concern. He handed over the binoculars without a word as he continued to scan his surroundings. Somewhere on the Kotal, a drum began to throb.

'I thought so.' Probyn spoke without emotion. 'While we've been riding around showing the flag, the Bunerwals have been busy. Do you see that broken ground between us and the head of the pass? Look at that area of rocks and ravines that overlooks the camp.'

'I see it.' Jack felt the sudden surge of mixed fear and excitement that always marked the prelude to action. He wished that the men of his old 113th were around him. He missed the stolid security of O'Neill, the foul-mouthed aggression of Logan, the banter of Thorpe and Coleman. He drew a deep breath. They were not here; with service in the army being what it was, he would probably never see them again.

'The Bunerwals are there, waiting for us. I hope you are ready to fight, Windrush.'

'Oh, aye, always ready.' Jack tried to sound as casual as Probyn. The drumming was louder now. Was the tabla mullah with the Bunerwals? Or was there another drummer?

'Ride in front, Jack, while I get the lads ready.' Probyn's grin was of pure delight. The elemental warrior was at home in this sort of situation. 'Now you'll see why Probyn's Horse is the best in the business.'

Did every unit in the army believe it was the best? Jack did not speak his thoughts as Probyn wheeled away to attend to his men. Jack knew that the Guides considered themselves to be the elite, as did the Guards, while every regiment knew that they were superior to every other. Even his own 113th had boosted their credentials at the battle of Inkerman and during the Mutiny.

Glancing over his shoulder, Jack saw Probyn's Horse forming up, the bearded faces eager as they drew their swords. Taylor and Sandeman pulled back. Probyn kissed the guard of his sword in a melodramatic gesture that belonged to the Middle Ages rather than the industrialised nineteenth century. 'Are you with us, Jack?'

That was a challenge Jack could not refuse without damaging his reputation. 'I've never been in a cavalry charge.' He had to raise his voice above the increasing pounding of the horses' hooves. 'I'll just follow your lead.'

'Good man!' There was sheer joy in Probyn's face as he gave the next order. 'Remember, Jack, slash and cut, don't thrust. If your blade gets deep into somebody, it's hard to disengage unless you twist your wrist and ride on. You are vulnerable at that time. There is nothing a Pashtun warrior likes better than a vulnerable British soldier.' He grinned again. 'If you run a man through on the move, you either break your sword or are unhorsed because you can't get the damned thing out.'

'I'll remember.' Holding the reins in his left hand, Jack clutched the hilt of his sword. It felt rough and clumsy.

'Try to remember. It might save your life.' Probyn raised his voice. 'Bugler, sound the advance.'

Jack remembered watching the Heavy Brigade advance at Balaclava and the headlong charge of the Light Brigade into a valley where Russian artillery dominated on three sides. He had never thought to take part in such an event himself.

The bugle sounded again, the shrill notes raising the small hairs on the back of Jack's neck. He heard the increasing drumming of hooves behind him, the jingle of bridles, the quick snort of a horse, and the subdued laugh of a nervous trooper. 'Let the horse lead, Jack.' Probyn spoke quietly.

Jack did not need to force his smile. 'We're fine, Probyn. We're just waiting for your orders.'

'Canter!' Probyn commanded. The bugler blew again, and the horsemen increased their speed. Now Jack was aware of nothing except the men around him, the feel of the horse beneath, and the land speeding past. Somebody was shouting, the words formless in the air. With the reins in his left hand, Jack tightened his grip on the hilt of his sword.

This exhilaration was different from the slow, impersonal advance of British infantry, or even the terrifying frenzy of a bayonet charge. It felt mediaeval, as if he were a Crusader knight charging the Saracens, or one of William the Conqueror's Normans advancing against the Saxon shield-ring at Hastings. For the first time, he could understand the attraction of the cavalry.

'Sound the charge!' Probyn yelled. 'Follow me, lads! Show them the best regiment in the world!'

The bugler called again, the cords of his neck standing out as he blew the charge. Jack drew his sword. He did not know what he yelled as Sharbat bounded forward with the other horses. *I wish I had Colwall rather than this pony, but too late now.* Riding at his best speed, Jack hardly saw the Bunerwals as they fired their jezzails or rose from cover to face Probyn's Horse, pulwar and circular shields in hand.

As Probyn had said, the ground was broken, with outcrops of rock amidst rough grass, the occasional tree or group of trees and small holes that would trap the ankles of a horse. Jack saw a Bunerwal appear from behind a boulder to lunge at him with a Khyber knife, parried with a swing of his sabre, felt the shock of steel on steel, and then he was past, with the force of the exchange having driven the Bunerwal back a pace. Jack had to tug madly at the reins to avoid a shattered rock, flinched as something buzzed past his ear, heard the deep thump of a jezzail being fired, and swore as the ground fell abruptly away in front of him.

'Steady, Sharbat!' He hauled at the reins as his exhilaration altered to anxiety. He was an infantry soldier, not a cavalryman; neither he nor his horse was trained in this form of warfare.

The Bunerwal rushed at him from the left, pulwar in one hand, shield in the other. Still fighting to control Sharbat, Jack raised his sabre just in time to parry the Bunerwal's swing at his leg. Balancing on the stirrups, Jack twisted his blade, hoping to disarm the Bunerwal, but the warrior was skilled, withdrew his pulwar, and lunged with the point. Jack shifted sideways to avoid the blow, altered his grip on his sabre, and struck back-handed. The point sliced at the warrior's face, opening a long if shallow gash that sent the man reeling backwards. Jack seized the opportunity to steer Sharbat away from the ravine.

'They're running.' Probyn wiped blood from his sword. 'My boys have taken the position.' He looked around. 'I'll leave a few of the lads here and report to the general.'

'I wasn't much help, I'm afraid,' Jack said.

'You fought,' Probyn said. 'In your first cavalry action, nobody can ask more than that. Now you can tell your grandchildren that you rode with Probyn's Horse.'

Jack nodded. Suddenly he felt intensely weary, and that damned drumming had started again.

Chapter Fifteen

Ambela Pass September 1863

General Chamberlain sat on the folding camp chair behind his travelling desk, listening to Probyn's account of the patrol.

'You say the Bunerwals are guarding the Kotal.'

'Yes, sir,' Probyn said. 'They tried to prevent us from returning to camp, as well. I have left a strong picket at the point of action.'

'I'll send a couple of companies of infantry to relieve them.' Chamberlain gave the orders to a fresh-faced runner. 'That way if the Bunerwals try to return they'll find a hot reception waiting for them.' He stood up, stroking his moustache. 'The Bunerwals won't like being pushed aside in their own territory. They'll seek retribution.'

'I agree, sir. They'll attack us,' Probyn said. 'As sure as death, the Bunerwals will come at us either tonight or early tomorrow morning.'

'Then we'll have to be ready for them.' Chamberlain shouted for another runner. 'I'll order that the sentries are doubled and warn the men to keep alert.'

The precautions seemed sensible, although Jack would have preferred a more robust response. With the Pashtun, doubling the sentries hardly seemed sufficient.

'Well, Windrush.' Chamberlain noticed Jack at last. 'What intelligence can you add to what Colonel Probyn has already relayed to me?'

'I heard more drumming, sir. I wondered if the tabla mullah was with the Bunerwals.'

'Did you see him?' Chamberlain asked. 'Did you see him, Probyn?'

'No, sir, but we do know that the Mujahidin have been busy among the Bunerwals. Captain Windrush believes that one man is behind this outbreak and has seen this tabla fellow in various places.'

'You are the only man to have seen him, Windrush. Keep a lookout for him. Do you have anything else?' Chamberlain leaned forward to study the map that was spread out in front of him.

'The patrol proved that the Bunerwals are out in force, sir,' Jack said. 'Hassan, one of the Guides, told me that the Bunerwals believe we are here to annex their lands. That is what the Mujahidin have told them. I wonder if there is still time to talk to their khans, hold a Jirga to explain our actions, or we could have the whole tribe attacking us.'

Chamberlain glanced at Probyn and back to Jack. 'That may be an idea, Windrush, except it would delay us. Anyway, who is to say that the Fanatics have not already influenced them past the point of reason?' He nodded. 'No, Windrush, we will stick to our original plan.'

'Yes, sir.'

'Now, you get some rest.' Chamberlain said. 'I suspect that this campaign is just beginning. That little skirmish you had today will only be a preamble to what is to come.'

Jack thought of the man he had wounded. How many more men will be maimed or killed before this new horror is completed?

'You're looking pensive, Jack me boy!' Probyn appeared outside Jack's tent. 'I have a bottle to kill and nobody to help me drink it.' He looked at Jack closely. 'You're not one of these deeply religious temperance fellows, are you?'

'Not at all.' Jack knew that he should rest but also knew that he would not sleep that night.

'Good man!' Probyn grinned. 'You'll help me then? It's whisky of some sort. I got it from that Sawney regiment, the 71st Highlanders.'

'Trust the Sawneys to find whisky,' Jack said. 'They were the same outside Balaclava, while Campbell's boys at Lucknow used to make their own; only God knows how.'

'Turning water into wine, were they?' Probyn grinned at his weak joke.

'Come into my tent,' Jack invited.

'I sometimes wonder why we're here,' Jack said as he lounged on a basketwork chair with Probyn opposite, the level of whisky in the bottle fast diminishing. 'Oh, I know the theories about bringing civilisation to the heathen and all that sort of stuff, but the Indians had a civilisation when we still lived in caves, and these Pashtuns are happy with their own culture. They will never accept ours.'

'Perhaps not.' Probyn poured himself another glass. 'Would you prefer that we allowed them to raid into India, steal Hindu women and force them to be wives, capture merchants for ransom, burn, rape and plunder at will?' He raised his eyebrows. 'That was a rhetorical question, old boy. We both know that you would not like that. No; we're here, and we have to keep the peace, although history tells us that nobody has ever done that before.' He grinned again. 'Well, these Pashtun fellows have never met Probyn's Horse before, or the Guides.'

'We do our duty,' Jack said. 'As always.'

Probyn sipped at his whisky. 'Could you imagine yourself doing anything else, Jack? Maybe farming back in England, or working in a bank, God help you?'

Jack shook his head. 'I've no lands to farm unless I became a tenant. And as for working in an office, banking, lawyer or what have you.' He shivered. 'I would go out of my mind with boredom.'

'As would I,' Probyn said. 'What do you think of the Frontier, Jack?'

'Hard and hostile,' Jack said. 'I suppose it is necessary to hold it, although I think the best way would be to allow the indigenous peoples to get on with their lives with a minimum of interference from us.'

'You don't agree with the Forward Policy then,' Probyn said.

'No, I don't believe we should keep pushing, just in case Russia may decide to move into Afghanistan sometime.' Jack wondered why

Probyn sounded him out in this manner. Most young officers would never talk shop, preferring to discuss hunting, women or simply pass the time over cards. 'I think we should leave Afghanistan and its environs severely alone. God help the Russians if they ever decide to invade. The Pashtun would wipe the floor with them.'

'Ah.' Probyn took a deep drink from his bottle. The sound of a single shot interrupted whatever he was about to say. He looked at Jack with the glass still to his mouth. 'One shot is merely a man on shikar or having fun with our sentries.'

A second shot sounded, the resounding thud of a jezzail.

'Two shots could be more meaningful.' Probyn's smile broadened if anything.

The third and fourth shots were so close together they merged into a single sound, followed quickly by a high-pitched yell that seemed to encompass the entire camp while penetrating the thin canvas walls of Jack's tent.

'Allah Akbar!'

Then there was silence so intense that Jack thought he could hear the wings of each individual insect humming as they vibrated.

'I think that they're playing on our nerves.' Probyn's smile had not altered.

'If they are, it's working.' Jack felt his breath coming in short gasps.

'Stand to!' That was Chamberlain's voice. 'Bugler! Sound the stand to!'

'That's our call.' Placing the glass on the ground, Probyn stood up, reached for his sword belt, and buckled it in place. 'No rest for the wicked, is there? And they don't come much more wicked than a soldier of the queen on this frontier.'

'Allah! Allah!' The words came clearly through the bustle of men hurrying to their posts. 'Allah! Allah!'

'Here they come, boys!' Chamberlain mounted a rocky knoll to peer around the perimeter of the camp. 'Fire on your officers' command.'

Moon and starlight glittered on the circling blades of swords as the Bunerwals screamed their war cry. With the jezzails giving their hefty thump, the Bunerwals emerged from the trees a hundred yards from the camp.

'Fire!' The command was laconic, followed by the sharp crack of rifles. Muzzle flares revealed brief vignettes of charging tribesmen, of twisted turbans and long robes, of men ducking behind round shields, of waving pulwars and screaming mouths. The Bunerwals covered the ground at an amazing pace, charging straight for the pickets and lines of British and Indian infantry.

Jack heard the calm words of command.

'Fire!'

'Cap and load!'

'Present!'

'Mark your target: fire!'

'Fix bayonets, 71st!'

The British response came with the controlled, calculated volleys of professional soldiers. The same musketry that had smashed the French at Waterloo, that had defeated the Americans at the battle of Camden, that had repelled the Russians at Inkerman and Balaclava. Powder smoke smeared the camp, lay heavy on the men in their scarlet serge, stung eyes, and bit acrid into twitching nostrils.

'Fire!'

The volleys rolled out. Without a company to command, Jack drifted to the nearest body of infantry, the 71st Highland Light Infantry. He heard them mutter to themselves, the lithe, high-cheekboned men in tartan trews who reminded him so much of Logan of the 113th.

Dear Lord! That was a thought! An entire regiment of Logans. Jack shivered at the prospect.

'Captain Windrush requesting permission to join your regiment, sir.' Jack saluted a hard-faced major with a splendid set of whiskers.

'Oh, do join us, Windrush. Glad to have you aboard.' The man's voice was as gravelly as General Colin Campbell's. *Lord Clyde now,* Jack reminded himself. 'I'm Girvan. Find yourself a spot and help yourself. Plenty of the enemy to go around, don't ye know?' Girvan jerked a calloused thumb at the advancing Bunerwals.

'Thank you, Major.' Jack slotted in behind a forward company of the 71st. Two of the men glanced at him, wondering who this stranger was in their midst.

'Who's he?' the nearest man, a gaunt-faced private, asked.

'How should I know? As long as he's on our side.' The second man was red-haired, with china-blue eyes.

'Here they come again!' A wiry sergeant with a sprig of fir in his checked bonnet said. 'Ready with your bayonets, lads.'

'They'll no' get that close, Sergeant Dalgleish,' the gaunt-faced private said. He was clean-shaven, unlike most of his moustached colleagues.

'If they do, I'll blame you, Rougvie.'

The gaunt-faced man spat tobacco juice onto the ground. 'Thank you, Sergeant. I didnae know I was that important.'

'Dinnae worry, Rougie. You're no' important.' The red-haired private assured him. 'Naebody'll miss you when the Paythans slice you up.'

'You'll miss me, Dougie. I owe you a fill of baccy.' Rougvie faced the sergeant again. 'Here, sergeant, what's oor orders when we're on picket duty again?'

'You're not on picket duty, Rougvie. The general doesn't trust you.'

'Aye, but when we are, sergeant.'

'Simple, Rougvie. You don't leave your post til you're killed, and if you see anybody else leaving, you've to shoot them.'

'Aye, that's what I heard. So I can shoot Dougie here.'

'I wish somebody would shoot you, Rougvie, and spare me the bother.'

Jack hid his grin. It was reassuring to hear the black humour of British infantrymen. It made him feel at home. *God, I miss the 113th.*

The Bunerwals had been reinforced for their second charge. Again the cry 'Allah! Allah!' announced their coming as they left the shadowed shelter of the trees to rush directly at the British camp.

'Nae finesse, they lads.' Rougvie shook his head in disapproval. 'Just making themselves targets, that's what they're doing. They think we cannae hear them in the dark.'

Sergeant Dalgleish kicked Rougvie's leg. 'Stop yacking, and start firing, Rougvie; you're meant to be a soldier, not a comedian.'

Unfastening his holster, Jack hauled out his revolver. A few moments ago he had felt fear. Now, in the company of men such as Probyn and Private Rougvie, he did not. For a moment he wondered if more people were like that, bolstering their courage with the bravery of others. Perhaps that was how armies worked, collective courage that made men perform actions that they would never attempt alone. Then the Bunerwals were closing, and he had no time for abstract theories.

Jack flinched at the roar of artillery; grapeshot and canister ripped into the charging Bunerwals, tossing up gravel to add to the confusion as the infantry augmented the guns with rifle fire.

'Fire!' the whiskered major roared.

The Highland Light Infantrymen responded, ignoring the brutal kick of their rifles as they fired into the teeth of the advancing Bunerwals. Again smoke clouded, dense, white and acrid. The yells of 'Allah' ended, replaced by the piteous howling of wounded men.

'Cease fire.' Standing on his knoll, silhouetted against the moon, Chamberlain no longer looked like a tired man. Rather, he was some classical warrior surveying the scene of his latest triumph. 'They've gone. See to the wounded; our lads first, and then the enemy.'

Somebody began to sing, the words and voice unfamiliar to Jack, although he suspected Rougvie was the singer. *Fatteh would approve.*

'When first I went to soldier
With rifle on my shoulder
There wasn't no-one braver
In the Corps boys'

Others joined in, humming the tune or mumbling the words they did not know, and roaring those they did.

'And when I walked abroad
All the pretty girls would wink at me
The ladies can't resist a jolly soldier.'
The words died away as Sergeant Dalgleish glared at them.

'A jolly soldier? You lot? You're about as jolly as a cold November in Airdrie!' The sergeant clamped shut his mouth as Major Girvan lifted a hand.

'That's the spirit, lads!' Girvan roared. 'Sing out! Show the Paythans that we care nothing for their pulwars!'

Most of the regiment joined in the chorus, with men from the 101st Fusiliers also doing their bit, so the valley echoed with the stentorian, if virtually tuneless, bellow of the invading army.

'Bang upon the big drum, clash upon the cymbal
We'll sing as we go marching along boys, along
And although on this campaign there's no whisky or Champaign
Still, we'll keep our spirits flowing with a song, boys.'

Chamberlain remained on his knoll, watching, no doubt listening, remembering the Afghan War as his army yelled out the last verse of their song.

'Then we marched from Chalazan
And we met the wild Afghan
And made him crazy for to run boys, oh
And we marched into Kabul
And we took the Bala Hissar
And we made them to respect the British soldier.'

As the brave words faded away into the dark, Jack saw Chamberlain jump down from his knoll.

'Now we know the Bunerwals mean business,' he said. 'We're a bit isolated out here, so we'll fortify the camp. I'm not marching into their territory to be ambushed and sniped to pieces.'

Jack nodded; Chamberlain was a cautious commander, which was needed out on this wild frontier.

'We'll let them come to us and mow them down. If it was good enough for Wellington at Waterloo, it's good enough for me.'

Jack looked around the already greying heights, wondering how many predatory eyes were watching them and how many messengers were gathering warriors to come to the party. The drumming was soft in the background, a sinister reminder that the Pashtun would not give up after one encounter. Jack knew that they were still out there, watching and waiting, their eyes probing for any weakness to exploit.

'That was round one.' Probyn sounded as laconic as ever. He toured the field of the skirmish, looking at the dead. 'These are all Bunerwals, as far as I can see, but look at this.' Kneeling down, he pointed to the right wrist of one white-bearded man. 'This fellow is wearing a red cord; he is a Ghazi.'

'So is this fellow.' Jack turned over a man whose face had been obliterated by grapeshot.

Probyn stood up. 'It seems that our intelligence was correct. The Fanatics have influenced the Bunerwals. This fight will be like nothing you have seen before.' Jack was unsure if his grin was forced or natural.

Chapter Sixteen

Ambela Pass October 1863

'So it has happened.' Chamberlain stood on his knoll, scrutinising the valley through his binoculars. 'Well, my tactics will not alter. As I said last night, we'll hold here and let them come to us.' He gestured to the pinnacle of the Eagles Nest that stood prominently between the British camp and the Guru Mountains. 'We only sent a piquet there. I want it properly occupied and fortified.'

Chamberlain's staff officers scribbled notes as the general spoke.

'Over there, on the right' Chamberlain pointed to a series of rocky, forested hills. 'I want each of these peaks occupied and strengthened right up to the Crag Piquet. That will see our flanks guarded. Colonel Wilde, you take command of the Crag Piquet, and Colonel Vaughan, take over the Eagle's Nest.'

'Sir.'

Chamberlain continued: 'Where's the artillery? I want it positioned as high as possible, so when the Bunerwals and Fanatics attack, the guns can support the men. We need every advantage we can get out here.'

That day was one of bustle and sweated labour as Chamberlain's force fortified their position. Artillery from the Peshawar Mountain Battery was manhandled up the slithering rocks, with mules giving up halfway up the slope and men swearing as they slogged up with wheels, gun-barrels and ammunition. Jack carried messages from one post to the other and lent a hand where he could.

'I don't think I like these screw guns,' Rougvie said as he fell on his face for the third time. 'They're bloody heavy.'

'You'll bless the guns when the Paythans attack,' Sergeant Dalgleish told him. 'We'll all bless them then.'

'Why are they called screw-guns?' a very young-looking Griffin asked.

'I'll tell you,' Rougvie said until Sergeant Dalgleish silenced him.

'Ignore Rougvie,' Dalgleish said. 'His mind is like a sewer, and his actions are worse. No, it's simple son. If you look closely, you'll see that the muzzle and the breech screw together. That makes them easier to carry and more mobile.'

The sepoys who operated the guns grinned at the young soldier. 'You'll thank us soon,' they said. 'We save your lives.'

Jack fought off his vague feeling of discomfort when he heard the accent of low-country sepoys. He could not rid himself of the prejudices the Mutiny had created.

With the screw-guns finally in position, the 71st looked around, no doubt hoping for a respite, for despite the lateness of the season, sweat coursed down their faces and darkened their tunics.

'Thank God for that.' Rougvie threw himself down behind a rock.

'Don't relax yet,' Jack said. 'I want scouts out to watch in case the Bunerwals creep up on us.' He ordered half a dozen men a hundred yards in front. 'And we'll need sangars if the Bunerwals attack.'

Rougvie looked at Jack, then at the sergeant. 'Is this officer in the 71st, Sergeant Dalgleish?'

'Do as the captain says,' Dalgleish ordered. 'Don't mind him, sir, his mouth works faster than his brain. He means nothing by it; he just speaks before he thinks.'

'As long as he works as fast as he speaks,' Jack said. *There is that regimental pride again. The 71st Highlanders only take orders from their own officers.* 'From what I've seen of the Pashtuns, the more protection we have between them and us the better.'

'Excuse me, sir.' Dalgleish threw a smart salute. 'Are you *the* Captain Windrush?'

'*The* Captain Windrush?' Jack repeated. 'There are at least two officers of my rank and name in the army, sergeant.'

'Yes, sir. Are you the Captain Windrush who was with the 113th at Lucknow, sir? If you don't mind me asking.'

'I am he.' Jack wondered what the sergeant was going to say.

'I thought so.' Sergeant Dalgleish nodded. 'I've heard of you, sir.'

'Then you'll know that I make my men work,' Jack said. 'I want these sangars built above breast height, with loopholes in the rocks to fire through. The Pashtuns are crack shots; they can kill a man at four hundred yards with their jezzails, so make the loopholes small. The less of a target we give them, the better.'

'Yes, sir,' Dalgleish said. 'I'll make sure the lads do it right.'

There was a hush around Eagles Nest Picket, broken only by the click of stone on stone as the 71st built their sangars, the low breastworks that they would shelter behind if the Bunerwals attacked. The hills around seemed to be watching, waiting. *I know this atmosphere,* Jack told himself. *It is the hush before the storm, the lull before the hurricane. The Bunerwals are observing everything we do.*

'I can see them.' Dalgleish placed a head-sized rock on top of a sangar. 'Over there at the fringe of the trees.' A veteran of Crimea and the Mutiny, he had never ceased to study his surroundings, searching for the enemy.

Jack nodded. He could also see the hint of movement within the trees. The Bunerwals were there, watching.

'Why don't the ghastlies attack?' Rougvie asked. 'They could come when we're still building the sangar.'

'They're assessing us,' Sergeant Dalgleish said. 'They're working out how many of us there are, where the weak points are, and how they are going to come.'

'Good,' Jack said. 'The longer they are doing nothing, the stronger we can make the defences. Scoop a little hollow behind each sangar, lads; it gives you a little bit extra protection. Rougvie, you have a lot to say for yourself; go to the Fusiliers and the Punjabis, use your silver tongue to scrounge some more water canteens. Fighting is a thirsty business, so we can never have too much water.' He looked up as Probyn strolled up, his feet making no noise on the stony surface.

'What date is it, Jack?' Probyn lit an oversized cheroot as he perched on a flat rock. Above him, a pine tree shivered as a jezzail bullet smacked into the trunk.

'25th October.' Jack glanced at his now sadly scratched watch. 'Four-thirty in the afternoon.'

Probyn nodded. 'It'll be dark in an hour and a half. Time for the Bunerwals to come again.' He sighed. 'This is a lovely spot; far too pretty for a battle. It's far more picturesque than Gandamak or Jalal-abad or any of these other places we've fought along this frontier.' He drew on his cheroot. 'I think that politicians and kings and queens and what-nots should all gather together in a big room somewhere and decide where to have their wars. They should choose the ugliest places they can find, where nobody lives. That way nobody will care when it gets torn to pieces by shell fire or battered by bullets.'

'If only things were that simple,' Jack said.

'They could be,' Probyn said. 'I mean to say, just look at this valley.' He waved his cheroot around, so a thin trail of blue smoke followed his hand. 'It's as romantically picturesque as the Lake District or Switzerland or the Trossachs. If this were in Europe, there would be a road, and every day a charabanc would unload its cargo of visitors to admire the scenery and gawp at the picturesque locals.'

'The picturesque locals here would shoot them,' Jack said.

'That is a drawback, I admit,' Probyn said with one of his characteristic grins. 'We can't have dead bodies cluttering up our romantic scenery, can we?'

'Windrush,' Chamberlain interrupted them. 'There's a Sikh officer sick with dysentery on Crag Piquet. Take his place.'

'Yes, sir.' *Probyn is correct: there is no rest for the wicked.*

'Look after yourself, Jack,' Probyn said. 'The Bunerwals will come again tonight.'

It was about a mile of rough country from one extreme flank of the British position to the other. Refreshed after her rest, Sharbat took Jack across to Crag Piquet in fifteen minutes, where the Sikhs of the Punjab Infantry welcomed him with solemn nods.

The Crag was a tall, narrow knob of ground, overlooked by higher hills, shielded by open woodland. The Crag itself was so small that it could only hold ten men, with the main Punjabi lines below, and a couple of forward pickets up the south-eastern slopes among the pine trees.

It's not the most secure position in the world, Jack told himself. *The Bunerwals will know that we must hold the Crag, so they will want it back, while the trees give them plenty of cover.*

'Captain, sahib.' A solemn-faced naik gave a smart salute. 'Welcome to the Punjab Infantry and to Kutlghar, the place of slaughter.'

'Thank you,' Jack said.

'Now you will see how the best soldiers in India fight.' Turning away, the naik shouted a string of orders in Punjabi, a language with which Jack had no familiarity. He could only watch with admiration as the Sikhs formed a defensive perimeter and pushed forward a number of piquets.

'Do you know Johnny Sikh?' The major was long, lanky and laconic. He offered Jack a cheroot, lit it from his own and shouted a string of orders in fluent Punjabi.

'I saw them a few times during the Mutiny,' Jack said. 'I fought beside them outside Lucknow.'

'Best soldiers in the world.' The major could not have been more enthusiastic. 'They'll soldier seven days a week, never say die, and kill you for a threepenny bit. If you're lucky, you'll see them in action. God help the Pashtun if Johnny Sikh gets off the leash. They hate each other. What did you say your name was?'

'I didn't, but it's Windrush. Jack Windrush. I'm replacing a man who has dysentery.'

'I know. I sent for a replacement officer. I'm Sinclair by the by,' the major said. 'I met a Windrush once. I was attached to the Cameronians during the Sebastopol business. A fellow named William Windrush serving with the Royal Malverns. I can't recollect his rank. Any relation?'

Jack nodded. 'My half-brother.'

Sinclair raised his eyebrows. 'Was he indeed? He won the Victoria Cross, I believe, for doing something or other. Damned if I remember what. It would be suitably heroic no doubt. So he is your half-brother, is he?' The languid look did not fool Jack. Sinclair was assessing him to see if he was suitable material to serve with his Sikhs, even temporarily.

'He is,' Jack said.

'Ah.' Sinclair peered into the growing dark. 'Are you like him?'

'Not in the slightest,' Jack said. 'I'm no hero.'

Sinclair's eyes ran over Jack from the crown of his head to his feet and back. 'No, perhaps not. Which unit were you with before you became a staff man and general factotum?'

'113th Foot,' Jack said. 'Not quite the esteemed Royal Malverns.'

'No,' Sinclair said. 'The 113th are not the Royal Malverns.' He blew blue smoke into the chill evening air. 'I'd better make sure my lads are all right. My Sikhs can be a little over-enthusiastic at times.' He waved his cheroot around, dropped it and ground out the glowing end under the heel of his boot. 'I wouldn't put it past them to attack the Bunerwals just for the fun of the thing.'

'I'll bear that in mind,' Jack said.

'It's been interesting chatting to you, Windrush.' Touching the brim of his forage cap, Sinclair ambled off into the dusk. He stopped after a dozen paces. 'They'll come tonight, you know. The Bunerwals will come tonight. That's what they do. You'd better get some sleep while you can, old man. Oh, and don't let my Sikhs down. I wouldn't like that one bit.'

Jack's weariness descended on him without warning. Sliding down in the lee of a rock, he slept in a crumpled bundle, with dreams haunted by the throbbing of a tabla drum, and Mary warning him to look after himself.

The drumming continued after the deep chill of pre-dawn woke him. Jack stretched, groaned and breakfasted by lighting a cheroot until Sinclair knocked it from his mouth and stamped the glowing end out.

'The Bunerwals can see the gleam,' he said in a fierce whisper. 'Their marksmen will kill you.'

Jack nodded. Tiredness had made him careless. The Sikh sentries were alert, with the others sleeping in various positions. He heard the whisper of wind in the trees, smelled the sweet scent of pine, and sighed. Probyn had been correct; why did humanity spoil beauty with bloodshed? Thank goodness there was no sound of the tabla drum.

A few minutes before dawn, the Bunerwals attacked. This time there was no warning. They came in a rush, silent except for the swift pad of their feet on the ground and the rustle of their blue cloaks.

The first Jack knew of it was a crackle of musketry through the dark and a shrill cry of 'Allah Akbar!'

'Sahib!' The naik stood at attention as Jack stepped toward the sangar. The naik spoke first in Punjabi and then, realising that Jack did not understand, tried Urdu. 'Major Sinclair Sahib asks that you come to the central sangar.'

Jack was moving before the naik finished speaking. 'Thank you, naik. Please inform Sinclair Sahib that I am on my way.'

The sound of musketry increased, now backed by the rhythmic thunder of war-drums, and the high screech of 'Allah!' Something thudded into the ground near Jack's foot.

The Punjabis were at their posts, waiting for the order to fire. So far the Bunerwals were only attacking the piquets at the summit of the Craig.

'Everything all right?' Sinclair loomed up.

Jack nodded. 'What's happening out there?'

'They've overrun our forward piquets.' Sinclair sounded as calm as if he were discussing the price of tea. 'Damned nuisance in the dark.' He did not flinch as two of the screw-guns opened up, sending grapeshot spattering in front of the Sikh's position.

A messenger ran to Sinclair, speaking in rapid Punjabi. Sinclair replied, sending the man away. 'Change of plan, but this is the Frontier, dear boy,' Sinclair said. 'One must be prepared for anything at any time.' He gestured to the left. 'Take the left flank, could you, Windrush? We have a wounded officer.'

'That was rather silly of him.' Jack tried to emulate Sinclair's nonchalance.

'Rather.' Sinclair sauntered away, exchanging cheerful banter with his Sikhs as the artillery fired again. At night the extended muzzle flares were always spectacular. To the Bunerwals, unused to such sights, they must have been terrifying. *If anything can terrify the Pashtun,* Jack thought as he strode to the left flank.

The Bunerwal came through the dark in a screaming mob, pulwars raised above their heads and circular shields in front of them.

'Fire,' Jack ordered. Perhaps it was the influence of these stolid soldiers, but he felt amazingly calm. He stalked behind his men, speaking in Urdu, wishing he had learned Punjabi, and watching the Sikhs load, cap and fire with a precision that would rival the Brigade of Guards.

The Bunerwal attack slowed, and then the artillery hit them. The screw-guns may only have been lightweight compared to the siege artillery Jack had seen in the Crimea, but their effects on charging men were devastating. Each shot sliced great swathes into the dim shapes of the Bunerwals, cutting men down in ones, twos and groups. The Bunerwals learned quickly, ducking into cover each time they heard the bark of the guns, hiding behind trees and firing their jezzails at the sepoy artillerymen. Jack saw a horseman moving through the fringes of the forest. When he came closer, Jack realised that the man had a long drum in front of him and was beating each side to encourage the Bunerwals. The tabla mullah was back.

Right, you bastard. I missed the last time. I won't miss again.

'Cease fire!' Jack ordered. The space in front of the sangar was empty except for the dead and dying. The Bunerwals had withdrawn to the trees, taking the drummer with them. The reek of burnt powder smoke drifted to Jack, with that incessant drumming in the background. Jack waited, single-minded in his search. The tabla mullah appeared, a vague figure with the smoke veiling his horse, and only his upper body visible.

'Give me a rifle.' Jack lay prone. He placed the cap very carefully, adjusted the ladder rear sight for four hundred yards, and aimed. *I won't miss this time.* A drift of smoke covered the tabla mullah; when it cleared, he had gone.

Damn.

The rifles remained silent. The Sikhs waited. One man began to sing, the words and tune unfamiliar to Jack, whose calmness evaporated. He felt very alien out here with these men whose language and culture he did not understand in this place on the very fringe of Empire. What lay beyond these mountains? There was Afghanistan and then the mysterious lands of Central Asia, the great Steppes that reached all the way to Russia.

Dear God, I am a long way from Herefordshire.

The drumming continued, now joined by the lilting strains of a shpelai, the Pashtun flute.

The tabla mullah appeared again, riding slowly through the fringe of trees. Taking a deep breath, Jack waited until the man's head was squarely in his sights. He slowly squeezed the trigger. The kick of the recoil bruised his shoulder, and when the smoke cleared the mullah's horse was empty. *Got you! At last, I've got you! There was no mistake that time, you trouble-making bastard.*

Jack's shot seemed to activate the Bunerwals into activity. They exploded from the forest, yelling with pulwars raised and shields held in front of them.

'Here they come again.' Jack felt the familiar rush of excitement and fear. 'Fire!' Dropping his rifle, he gave an example by firing two shots from his revolver, with no noticeable effect on the blue-clad mass that erupted from the trees.

Sinclair appeared at Jack's shoulder. 'They've taken the Crag Piquet!' His words permeated the crackle of musketry.

'That's a bugger.' The piquet dominated the sharp point of the hill. With quality infantry and an excellent field of fire, the piquet should have been able to hold out against any number of attackers.

'These lads don't fight like the Russians or even the Mutineers.' Sinclair was as calm as ever as he peered upwards toward the Crag. 'I would not be surprised if they used the frontal attack on us as a cover to take the Crag Piquet. I don't like to think of my lads being overwhelmed.'

'We have to get the Crag back.' Jack knew he was stating the obvious. 'The Bunerwals can overlook our whole position from there. Imagine a dozen sharpshooters with jezzails shooting down.'

'We'll get it back,' Sinclair said. 'Johnny Sikh is the best in the business at hand to hand fighting.'

Finding a small knoll to stand on, Sinclair made a short speech in Punjabi. He ended with a quote, repeating it in English for Jack's sake:

'O Power of Akaal, give me this boon. May I never ever shirk from doing good deeds.

That I shall not fear when I go into combat. And with determination, I will be victorious.

That I may teach myself this greed alone, to speak only of Thy Almighty Lord Waheguru praises.

And when the last days of my life come, I may die in the might of the battlefield.'

'That is powerful.' Jack had listened, trying to pick up the rhythm of the words.

'So are my Sikhs.' Sinclair jumped from his knoll. 'Don't let my men down, Windrush.'

The attack faded away. The Bunerwals withdrew to the trees. The music of the shpelai continued without any drumming.

Dawn cracked the eastern sky, bringing light that gleamed like blood through the drifting powder-smoke. As Jack held the flank against intermittent Bunerwal probes and the occasional more determined attack, Major Keyes of the Guides consulted with Sinclair to organise a counterattack to retake the Crag.

'I spoke to the naik from the Crag Piquet,' Sinclair said. 'He told me that there's a ridge running right up to the summit. The Bunerwals crawled up there at night, and when the piquet was lending its fire to repel the frontal assault, the Bunerwals slid behind them.'

'Clever men, these Bunerwals,' Jack said.

'Aye, sneaky is another word. The Bunerwals have reinforced the Crag.' Sinclair nodded upwards. 'They've jammed it solid with men.'

In the gathering light, Jack saw a horde of Bunerwals beneath the summit peak, busily reinforcing the sangars between them and the Punjabi positions.

'Major Keyes and I are taking up half a company of men to recapture it,' Sinclair said. 'I want you to take command of a platoon to come in support.'

'Yes, sir.' Jack looked up the precipitous slope of the Craig. He wished he knew the men better; he knew the capabilities of his own 113th and had learned the skills of the Guides. He had no idea how to talk to these Sikhs. 'I hope they speak Urdu, sir. I have no Punjabi.'

'Lead by example, Windrush.' Sinclair thrust a cheroot into his mouth. 'My lads will always follow a good officer.'

As soon as it was full daylight, Keyes and Sinclair led the 1st Punjabis in a counter attack. Clad in rifle-green, the Punjabis, mainly Sikhs but with some Pashtuns among them, clambered up the shifting slope to avenge the loss of their position, while Major Brownlow led the 20th Punjabis in support.

Still with the unlit cheroot between his teeth, Sinclair strode to the front of his men. Shouting in Punjabi, he pushed upwards, a distinctively tall figure. As they neared the Crag, the hill became steeper, so the men had to climb up in single file, with the Bunerwals firing down at them from above. As so often in battle, the powder smoke soon concealed the action, so Jack was left fretting with little idea what was happening up there in the trees.

The sound of musketry increased, joined by shouts of 'Allah Akbar' and *Jo Bole so Nihaal, Sat Shri Aka,l*' the Sikh battle cry.

Knowing that this was the largest operation since the Mutiny, Jack was professionally interested to see how the new Indian Army performed. Until 1857 there had been three separate armies of the now dissolved East India Company. Now there was one army, with a new focus on manpower from the so-called 'martial races' of the northern sub-continent rather than the traditional recruiting grounds of Bengal, Oudh and Madras.

Jack saw the Sikhs advance with the bayonet as the Bunerwals and Mujahidin put their backs to rocks and trees to face them with sword and shield. He saw Keyes stagger and fall, with a young ensign leading a determined attack on a group of Ghazis, but then the Bunerwal musketry began to fall on his own position.

We're doing no good here, Jack told himself. 'Come on, Punjabis! Let's get up there!'

Jack clambered up the slope, trying to keep ahead of the Punjabis. They were not natural hill men like the Pashtun or Gurkhas, but what they lacked in agility they made up for in sheer determination, climbing without any outward sign of fatigue. Within a few moments, Jack felt the breath rasping in his throat and his lungs burning. A sudden hammer-blow to his left leg made Jack cry out and fall. He looked down, expecting to see the limb hanging by a frayed thread of skin. However, his leg seemed perfectly normal save for a slight trickle of blood halfway up the thigh.

I've been hit. Jack inspected the wound. A spent bullet had slammed into his thigh on precisely the same spot that a stake had injured him in Burma a decade previously. The skin was hardly broken, yet when Jack tried to stand, the leg would not take his weight.

He slipped, swore and began to slither back downhill again with his arms flailing to help him try to regain his balance.

'Sahib!' A very young Sikh ran across the slope, eyes full of concern. Speaking in rapid Punjabi, he took hold of Jack's arm and hauled him to his feet, deliberately placing his body between Jack and the Bunerwal's fire.

'Thank you,' Jack spoke in Urdu. 'What is your name?'

'Ishar Singh, sahib.' The Sikh stood to attention despite the Bunerwal bullets that pattered down.

'Thank you, Ishar Singh. You'd better leave me now.' Jack saw that his Sikhs were now yards ahead, climbing up with incredible energy. He tried to catch up, staggered again and found Ishar Singh at his side, still smiling.

The youngster stepped backwards, put his shoulder to Jack's backside, and pushed.

'I'll be all right.' Jack hated to look undignified. *I am a British officer, damn it!*

Ishar Singh either did not understand or chose not to as he shoved all the harder until Jack was propelled up the hill at a greater speed than was comfortable. He passed through his men, ignored their undisguised amusement, and drew his sword. 'Come on, Punjabis! *Jo Bole so Nihaal, Sat Shri Akal!*'

As the tree cover thinned, Jack found himself in a battle as desperate as any he had ever seen. Sikh Bayonets and Pashtun pulwars clashed over the tumbled stones of a succession of sangars. As the attackers pushed to the summit, the Bunerwals withdrew, barrier by barrier, and began hurling down rocks. Jack saw a boulder crash into a British lieutenant; the Punjabis shuddered, regrouped and renewed their attack.

'*Jo Bole so Nihaal, Sat Shri Akal!*' Without waiting for orders, Jack's platoon threw themselves up the final few yards of the slope and onto the Bunerwal position.

'Leave me!' Jack ordered Ishar Singh. Drawing his revolver and using his sword as a makeshift crutch, Jack clambered upward into the melee.

The Sikhs were gradually pushing the Bunerwals back, taking sangar after sangar and tree after tree. One of Jack's platoon ducked under the swing of a Bunerwal pulwar, yelled, and thrust with his bayonet. The blade entered the Bunerwal's chest, killing him instantly.

'Sahib!' Ishar Singh was on the ground, his rifle dropped from his hand. One muscular Bunerwal held him down by sheer weight, while another poised ready to lunge with his pulwar.

Levelling his revolver, Jack took quick aim at the warrior with the pulwar. He squeezed the trigger, cursing when nothing happened. 'It's jammed,' he said, tried again, and swore once more.

'Hold on, Ishar!' Jack shouted, balanced on his sword, and vaulted forward. In that instant, nothing else mattered except to save the life of the beleaguered Sikh who had helped him. Using his pistol as a club, Jack swung it at the head of the pulwar-wielding Bunerwal. The warrior staggered, turned around with the pulwar in his hand, and slashed overhand.

Jack did not hear the shot that killed the Bunerwal. He only saw the effects as the bullet hit the man in the head, smashing it open and throwing him two yards back.

'Thank you, somebody.' With the pain in his thigh easing, Jack put his left foot back on the ground.

'Up you get!' Helping Ishar Singh to his feet, Jack handed him his rifle. 'Look after this,' he said. In the few moments he had spent rescuing the youngster, the skirmish had been won and the Punjabis had retaken the Crag. Jack had a momentary vision of the Bunerwals retreating, running down the opposite slope at great speed and then up to the hills beyond, blue cloaks flying.

Sinclair appeared, cleaning his sword as he gave orders in rapid Punjabi. 'Windrush, take your platoon back to camp. I'll leave a strong piquet here. That was a warm morning's work.' He sheathed his sword with a flourish. 'I remember now what your brother was saying about you.'

Jack stiffened. 'What was that, sir?' Whatever William said would not be good.

'He said you were born on the wrong side of the blanket.' Sinclair faced Jack squarely. 'Is that correct?'

'It is, sir.' Jack expected instant sneering.

'Me too, old man, me too,' Sinclair said. 'Your old man was a philanderer, was he? I mean no offence.' He stopped to shout orders at an NCO, waved to a lieutenant, and began to saunter back down the hill. 'Mine was a regular womaniser who chased any filly with a skirt.

My mother was one of his captures.' He pulled two cheroots from his breast pocket and handed one to Jack. 'She was a good woman. Too good for him.' He stopped to acknowledge the salute as a platoon of Sikhs filed past, one with his left arm in a bloody sling. 'Did you know your mother?'

'I met her briefly.' Jack was reluctant to give too much away.

'I know it's not done to smoke while in uniform,' Sinclair said, lighting up, 'but I don't give much of a fig for conventions. Oh, I'm all for the traditions of the regiment and all that, of course.'

'Yes, sir.' Jack remained cautious.

'Your brother spoke at some length about you, now I recall,' Sinclair said. 'He said there was an officer of the 113th that shared his name. He also said that that officer had an Indian mother.'

'My mother was Eurasian.' Jack felt his chin lift in defiance.

Sinclair drew on his cheroot. 'So is your wife, if the stories are to be believed.'

'She is.' Again, Jack waited for the mockery. He knew he would respond with anger if anybody, British officer or not, insulted Mary. He wondered if he should challenge Sinclair to a duel or just punch him in the jaw. Either would see him in front of a court martial.

Sinclair jumped from a rock onto scree below, slithered down a few yards, and waited for Jack to catch up. 'Not many British officers would marry a Eurasian,' Sinclair said. 'Woo them, yes, bed them, certainly, and then discard them as if they were nothing like my father did to my mother.'

It took a few moments for Sinclair's words to sink in. 'I see,' Jack said.

'There are more of us around than people think,' Sinclair said.

They walked in silence for a few moments, with the Sikhs passing them on their return to the camp.

'Before this action,' Sinclair jerked his head back to indicate the Crag, now bright with autumn sunlight, 'we were discussing your brother.'

'We were,' Jack agreed.

'There must be Windrush blood in both of you,' Sinclair said. 'Yet you're nothing like William Windrush. He is undoubtedly a brave man, but he would never stop to help an ordinary ranker, as you did with young Ishar.' Sinclair did not look at Jack as he spoke. 'My men won't forget. If you ever wish to transfer into the 1st Punjab Infantry, mention my name.'

'Thank you,' Jack said. That was an honour, as the Sikhs reckoned themselves an elite regiment. Jack hid his smile; every Indian Army regiment considered themselves elite. They were fighting men with as much pride as any regiment in the British Army, and with reason.

'You were with the 113th, you said,' Sinclair said.

'They were known as the Baby Butchers,' Jack said. That seemed a very long time ago now.

'Were they?' Sinclair shrugged. 'I did not know that. I knew of them as the regiment that fought at Inkerman and marched with Havelock.'

'They did that, too,' Jack said softly. If he had helped the 113th wipe clean their old sordid reputation, then he had done something positive with his life. He breathed out. He was just beginning to relax when he heard his name called.

'Windrush, is that you?' Chamberlain shouted from the back of his horse. 'The 71st need an officer, and you're unattached. Grab yourself something to eat then report to the 71st's colonel. They're on the Eagle's Nest.'

'Yes, sir,' Jack said. He was again moving from one flank of the British position to the other, but at least he was useful, and the 71st Highlanders spoke English, of a fashion. He might be able to understand something that they said.

Chapter Seventeen

Ambela Pass October 1863

The Eagle's Nest was a more extensive scale model of the Crag, an isolated peak at the opposite flank of the British camp, with rugged hills overlooking it. Pine trees, knolls, and a plethora of rocks and boulders provided cover for the enemy. By the time Jack struggled to the 71st's position, it was nearly noon.

'Welcome back, Girvan.' The major greeted him with a sour grin. 'Well, now you're here, you'd better stay, but our lads are not very susceptible to officers from other units.'

'So I've heard, but I'll see what I can do.'

'Aye.' Girvan glanced over his men. 'They're a decent enough bunch. They can fight. The Bunerwals are gathering in the trees over there.' He pointed to the fringe of the encroaching pine forest. 'This country could be made for them.'

'Where do you want me?' Jack agreed with Girvan. The terrain was perfect for the sort of irregular warfare the Pashtun's favoured.

'In reserve,' Girvan was blunt. 'It's a job for an ensign, maybe a lieutenant, but the best I can offer.' He nodded to a platoon of fifteen men. 'There is your command. If any section of the line is hard pressed, I want you to take over.'

The men surveyed Jack without a pretence of respect. The sergeant in charge gave a reluctant salute. 'Sergeant Dalgleish, sir.'

Jack remembered him. 'As you were, Dalgleish. What are the men doing?'

The privates had relapsed into small groups, stuffing small items into glass bottles.

'Making Ambela Pegs, sir. We're a bit short of artillery, so we must make do.'

Crouching beside one of the groups, Jack studied the procedure. While three of the infantrymen ignored him, the third, the red-haired, freckle-faced man in his early twenties that Jack had heard called Dougie, shifted aside to make room.

'I've never heard of them before,' Jack said. 'Are they a sort of grenade?'

'That's right, sir. We got gunpowder from the gunners and added small stones and anything else that might be useful, so when the Paythans come, we can lob the pegs among them.'

'I see you've a pipe in your mouth,' Jack said. 'You'd best be careful not to drop hot ash into the gunpowder.'

'Oh, aye, we'll be careful sir.'

'What's your name?'

'Douglas Lennox, sir,' the freckle-faced man said. 'That's Connor, Rougvie and Burnes.'

'I remember you and Rougvie,' Jack said quietly as the other three privates glanced up briefly. Connor, a broad-faced ruffian in his thirties, gave a brief nod. His eyes were grey and steady.

'Well, if the Bunerwals come, I'm sure these Ambela pegs will come in very handy.'

'Yes, sir.'

The drums started then, fast and low, gradually increasing until the sound seemed to throb around the entire valley. Jack could not hear the distinctive throb of the tabla drum.

'That's their encouragement,' Dalgleish said quietly. 'The pipes will start soon, lads; nothing for you to worry about.'

'Who's worried?' Rougvie wore a fir sprig in his bonnet. 'They should be bloody worried, not us.'

Burns gave a weak grin. He was the youngest man there, an auburn-haired youth with a pencil-faint moustache. 'Will they attack, sergeant? The Sikh lads just cleared them from the Crag Piquet.'

'That they will, lad.' Dalgleish said. 'Their mullahs, their holy men, tell them that our bullets can't hurt them, but if they die they go to Paradise with hordes of virgin women.'

Burns spat on the ground. 'What good is a bloody virgin? You want a woman who kens what she's doing.'

'As if you would know,' Connor said, as the privates jeered.

'Women are not much bloody good if they're deid,' Rougvie said. 'Do the virgins want to be in a paradise with all these beardy Bunerwals? Or is paradise only for dead warriors?'

'You can ask them that yourself,' Dalgleish said. 'Here they come now.'

Don't these Bunerwals ever give up? They are launching one attack after another, probing our defences.

As the Bunerwals surged from the tree cover, the 71st opened fire. Massed rifles, backed by the screw-guns once again created great gaps in the attackers, but sheer numbers saw them reach the British line. All the time, Pashtun marksmen fired at the British, hitting a man here and there, so the defences were weakened by the time the Bunerwals reached the sangars.

Jack saw that some of the Bunerwals carried standards that flapped and flowed above them. One brave man leapt on to the British parapet, thrusting the staff of his red standard between two of the rocks.

'Allah Akbar!' he yelled, seconds before a man of the 71st thrust a bayonet into his belly, twisted and withdrew. The standard bearer slowly crumpled. The bayonet man hauled down the standard, stiffened and fell as a Bunerwal bullet thumped into his chest. He passed the standard to another man, spat blood and died.

Behind Jack, the sepoys of the artillery fired the screw-guns, angling the barrels so the shot passed over the heads of the defenders. He saw one blast mow down a dozen of the attackers as a second Bunerwal wave erupted from the trees. The drumming continued, with the distinctive roll of a tabla as a sonorous background.

You're back, are you? That's twice I've killed you. Maybe there is something in the idea that a sacred charm protects these Mujahidin warriors.

Girvan was on the front line of the 71st, giving orders and fighting with his sword. In their tartan trews and stained scarlet jackets, the men of the 71st appeared like Highland ghosts as they alternately appeared and disappeared in the powder smoke.

'The lads at the sangars are hard-pressed,' Jack addressed his platoon. 'Fix your bayonets. We might be needed soon.'

The platoon left their peg-making, fixed bayonets, hitched up their trews and stamped their feet, getting ready for work.

'Rougvie, your bayonet's rusty!' Dalgleish yelled. 'I've told you before about that! A rusty bayonet can stick in the scabbard, delaying your draw and giving the enemy time to plunge their pulwar into your guts. Do you want that, Rougvie?'

'No, thank you, Sergeant.'

'I thought not. Next time, you'll be on a charge.'

'Yes, Sergeant.' Rougvie did not sound concerned.

'Captain Windrush!' Girvan's voice floated above the clamour of battle.

'That's us.' Jack saw that Girvan was stepping back as a horde of Bunerwals was pushing over the sangar. 'Follow me, lads!'

However reluctant they had been to acknowledge Jack's authority, the platoon ran forward on the word of command. There was no need to give any more orders; these men of the 71st were born rough-house soldiers. They smashed into the Bunerwals without hesitation, fighting with plunging bayonets and flailing butts to meet the pulwars and shields of the Pashtuns.

After his recent experience with his revolver jamming, Jack left it in its holster and drew his sword, although he knew that the Bunerwals were experts with that weapon. He clashed blades with a tall man in a filthy red turban, gasped as the man rammed a shield against his chest, kicked up, missed, swore, and lunged with his sword. The Bunerwal twisted to catch Jack's blade on his shield, grunted, and crumpled with a bayonet in his side.

Jack saw the flare of explosion an instant before he heard the bang. The peg had landed in the midst of a group of Bunerwals, the flash of gunpowder and scatter of small pebbles knocking one man down and injuring three others. As the Bunerwals hesitated at this unexpected twist, a second peg exploded among them, enveloping one man in flames. Jack had not expected the high-pitched screams.

'They're going!' Rougvie shouted, smashing the butt of his rifle on the bearded face of a bright-eyed man. 'Chase them, lads!'

'Stand fast.' Grabbing hold of Rougvie's shoulder, Jack dragged him back. 'Our job is to wear them out, not get ourselves killed.' He saw the tabla mullah emerge from the fringe of the woodland. As before, the man was naked except for a loin-cloth and a dirty turban. He sat astride a Kabul pony with the drum across his waist, pattering his hands steadily as his gaze roamed along the British sangars. For a moment, he looked directly at Jack, his eyes smoky, and then his horse took him away, the Bunerwals streaming past him into the shelter of the trees.

'Who's the best shot here?' Jack asked.

'The lads with the fir sprigs in their bonnets are our marksmen.' Sergeant Dalgleish touched the fir in his bonnet.

'See that fellow on the horse?' Jack pointed to the tabla mullah. 'He is goading the tribes to attack us. Wherever there is trouble, he appears.' *I've shot that man twice. Does he have some divine protection, as some Pashtun claim?*

Dalgleish nodded. 'Yes, sir. Rougvie, Connor, did you hear that?'

'We're ready, sir,' Connor replied for them both.

'Kill that mad mullah,' Dalgleish said.

'Yes, sir.' While Rougvie lay down, Connor took a stance behind a tree with his rifle resting on a branch. The two shots rang out as one. Jack saw the horse fall, taking the mullah with it. 'Good shooting, lads.'

'We missed,' Connor said laconically as the mullah rolled free from the horse, stood up, and stared at the powder-smoke drifting British lines.

'Try again.' Taking out his binoculars, Jack focussed on the tabla mullah. He was not as old as Jack had supposed, perhaps in his late thirties, with a tinted beard and long hair that straggled around his head. He looked directly at Jack through kohl-lined eyes, his stare more direct than anything Jack had seen before. 'That man is dangerous.'

As Jack watched, a group of Pashtuns ran to the mullah, surrounding him. Precisely at that moment, Rougvie fired. One of the Pashtuns crumpled. Another took his place, standing as a human shield between the mullah and the British lines. A man in a dun pakol lifted the tabla drum, faced the 71st, and spat his contempt on the ground.

'That mullah bears a charmed life,' Jack said.

'If kind Sergeant Dalgleish gives me a sixpence I'll melt it into a silver bullet,' Rougvie said. 'It worked for Bluidy Claverhouse at Killiecrankie'

Jack knew the story. When Claverhouse led the Highland charge at Killiecrankie, the British soldiers thought he was in league with the devil, so one of the redcoats shot at him with a silver bullet.

'Maybe his Allah is looking after him,' Connor murmured.

'Maybe he is at that.' British other ranks always could surprise him.

Girvan nodded. 'Keep trying.'

Rougvie settled down again. Taking a cartridge from his pouch, he ripped it open with his teeth, poured the gunpowder down the barrel, licked the bullet to aid lubrication, and rammed it home. Placing the percussion cap in place, he adjusted the back sight. 'Right, you scruffy bastard,' he said softly. 'Let's have another shot at you.' Lying behind the sangar, he rested his rifle on a boulder, aimed carefully at the mullah, and fired just as one of the mullah's guardians moved.

The mullah staggered and fell.

'Got you, you dirty old bastard.' Rougvie immediately began to reload.

Jack focussed his binoculars. Two of the guardians lifted the mullah, who was bent double, holding his thigh. 'He's wounded, Rougvie. You hit him.'

'I want him dead.' Rougvie returned to his previous position as a dozen Pashtuns fired at the 71st's sangars, narrowly missing Jack. 'They've taken him away.'

'With any luck, he'll bleed to death.' Jack was shocked at his own callousness.

'We have forty casualties,' Girvan said. 'That's a heavy price. Only God knows how many men the Bunerwals lost. If they carry on like this, we'll denude the whole tribe of its manhood.'

Jack nodded. Chamberlain's strategy was paying off. When adequately equipped British troops held a defensive position, heaven and earth would not shift them, let alone a few thousand ill-armed tribesmen. The Tabla Mullah, if he survived Rougvie's bullet, would have to recruit many times the number of men. Or find them better weapons. Jack remembered the gunsmiths of Tazhak. *We should destroy that place.*

Probyn joined them, dismounting and stepping elegantly across the camp. He ignored the sniping from the Bunerwal jezzails.

'We might decimate the Bunerwal tribe as Major Girvan says,' Probyn said, 'if it was only the Bunerwals who opposed us. I saw Afridis, Mahmuds, Swats, Hazaras, and even Waziris from the Baluchistan border among the enemy. Some were wearing the Ghazis' red cord on their right wrists. Others,' he shrugged, 'others are just here for the love of the thing or their dislike of us.'

'It's a gathering of the clans,' Girvan said. 'Our presence is acting as a magnet. The longer we are here, the more Pathans will come. This valley will be a permanent battlefield until we smash them, or they overrun us.'

'Let's hope it's not the latter,' Jack said. 'All the Pashtuns need is one decisive victory over us for all the clans to rise en masse, with God knows what effect on India.'

'I wouldn't worry about India, Jack,' Probyn said.

'Why not?' Jack pressed his point. 'Some of the Sikhs will remember the good old days of the Khalsa when they were independent, there are plenty of sepoys who joined the Mutiny ready to take up arms again, and I would not trust some of these rajahs and maharajas as far as I could spit.'

'Still no reason for you to worry.' Probyn was smiling as if at a rare joke.

'Why the devil not?'

'Because you'll be dead, old boy, along with the rest of us!' Probyn burst into roaring laughter. 'Remember Elphinstone's disaster at Kabul? Well, we may be in line to be the next, unless Chamberlain has something very clever up his sleeve.'

Probyn's laugh was so infectious that Jack and Girvan both joined in. *What must the Bunerwals think of us, laughing in the face of death? Batoor would understand.*

Jack had a vision of Batoor lying dead, killed by the tabla mullah and his Mujahidin. *Well, Tabla, I can follow the Pashtun code of badal, as well. Batoor gave me hospitality. I will take retaliation on his behalf, even if that means coming back to the Frontier myself and hunting you down, wounded as you are.* The feeling was so strong that Jack felt himself shaking with anger. He straightened up, staring beyond the British camp to the fringe of pine trees where he had last seen the tabla mullah. *Batoor was a friend. If you are still alive, Tabla, then I will kill you.* Jack shook his head. *Dear God, the Pashtun have converted me to their culture.*

Scattered firing disrupted the night when the Bunerwals and Ghazis tried to infiltrate the British positions, and the Guides and Gurkhas met them on their own terms in the broken terrain of the slopes. In the game of stalk and counter-stalk, the Bunerwals were gradually pushed back. Jack heard the Bunerwals' complain that the British were not fighting in the same fashion they had during the Afghan War. The voice came clearly to the British camp.

'Where are the *lal pagriwalas* (red-turbaned Sikhs) or the *goralog* (Europeans)? They are better sport!'

Jack could not hide his smile. *We are not the Khalsa, boys. We can match anything you can do.*

Chamberlain had his ideas of creating a better understanding that did not include badal. The next day, 27th October, he arranged a ceasefire so that the Bunerwals could collect and dispose of their dead.

'It shows good faith,' the general said. 'The Pashtun people do not like to leave their dead in the hands of unbelievers. More importantly for us, if we leave piles of dead around our camp perimeters, it will attract predators and flies.'

Remembering his ruse at the Torkrud watchtower, Jack could not argue with that. Those corpses which were not already the target of vultures or other creatures were a mass of flies.

The tribesmen were cautious at first as they came to collect their casualties, but when they realised that the British were acting honesty, they became more confident. Men arrived in small groups, with jezzails ready if the British proved hostile. Under strict orders, the British and Indian soldiers held their fire.

Jack wandered over to the Guides position, where Alladad was happily talking to one of the Pashtun.

Jack waited until the conversation ended. 'Do you know that man, Alladad?'

'That is my brother,' Alladad said. 'I told him I would kill him next time he attacked.' Alladad was laughing, as if at a colossal joke.

'What did he say to that?'

'He said he would kill me first.' Alladad laughed all the louder.

Chamberlain waited until the Pashtun trusted the truce then invited them to a Jirga. A group of grey-bearded elders considered the proposal and then agreed.

'We trust your nang, General Chamberlain,' their spokesman said.

'As I trust yours.' Chamberlain gave a stiff little bow. 'You come along, too, Windrush. I want you to identify this tabla mullah fellow if he is still alive.' He nodded. 'You don't have to say anything.'

That was as firm an order to keep my mouth shut as any Chamberlain has ever given, Jack thought as he positioned himself at the edge of the

Jirga, looking at the men who he had so recently been fighting and listened to what was being said. As always, the Pashtuns who attended were elderly, dignified men with grey or henna-dyed beards. They all wore their pulwars or Khyber knives.

'Salaam Alaikum.' They greeted Chamberlain gravely as if they had not been trying to destroy his army only the previous day.

'Salaam Alaikum.' Chamberlain was equally polite. He got down to business at once. 'You have lost many men,' Chamberlain said. 'You cannot possibly win against British infantry fighting behind stone walls. All you will do is incur needless casualties among your people.'

The Bunerwal tribal leaders nodded courteously, long beards wagging, intelligent eyes fixed on Chamberlain or examining the British defences. 'We have lost many men,' they agreed. 'We have lost too many for us to give up the fight against invaders who defile our holy land.'

Holy land? Jack remembered the Russians using similar language when they fought the British in the Crimea.

'Our land, like our women, is kept in purdah,' a man with his beard dyed henna-red explained. 'We cannot allow infidels to trespass here.' He tapped his jezzail to emphasise his words. 'We cannot allow feringhees to take our land.'

'We did not come to make war on the Bunerwals,' Chamberlain said. 'I know your holy men have told you that we came to take away your land. That is not true.'

'Then leave,' the tribesmen said. 'You did not seek our permission before you came with an army. We know the British; they come with smiles and promises of friendship, then they take over and tell us they are doing us a favour by being here. We do not wish such favours. Leave our land, and leave us in peace.'

Chamberlain shook his head. 'I can assure you that we have no intention of taking your land.'

'We have a proverb.' The man looked about seventy, still fit and wiry, with bright, predatory eyes. 'First comes one Englishman, as a traveller or for shikar; then come two and make a map; then comes an army and takes the country. Therefore it is better to kill the first Englishman.' He sat down again, his gaze fixed on Chamberlain.

In that spirit, the Jirga broke up. Proud and defiant, the Bunerwals lifted their dead and departed, leaving the British with a feeling of foreboding. Standing in the shadows, Jack saw the tabla mullah sitting astride his horse unhurt. As long as that man was present, Jack knew there would be no peace on the Frontier. *I have tried to kill him on two occasions, and Rougvie shot him clean, yet here he is. Perhaps he does have a charmed life.* Jack shook his head. *Don't be stupid; that is rank superstition. At least Gulbaz is not here,* Jack thought. *He was sent these notes about the law agent. Perhaps I was wrong in my assessment?*

Probyn pulled his horse beside Jack. 'The worst is yet to come.' He passed over a cheroot to Jack. 'I can feel it.'

'So can I,' Jack said. 'I felt like this before the Mutiny broke out. It is as if the land is waiting.' He looked around at the surrounding hills. 'This is a harsh country, quite unlike the lush plains of India. As that Bunerwal elder said, the Pashtun keep Pakhtunkhwa in purdah against everybody. We have no right here.'

'None at all,' Probyn agreed. 'Yet here we are, and the minute we leave, the tribes will debouch onto the Peshawar Valley, over the Indus to raid and kidnap, rape and plunder to their hearts' content. The Sikhs held them in check for a generation. Now that we've broken the power of the Khalsa, it is up to us to act as guardians of India, whether India likes it or not.'

'Do you think there will ever be peace in this land?' Jack asked.

Probyn shook his head. 'There may be peace sometime in the far distant future when man's attitude has changed to peace-mongering, and all the swords are made into ploughshares.' He grinned. 'I think some fellow said that hundreds and hundreds of years ago. His message has not reached this part of the world yet.'

'Evidently.'

'Not to worry.' Probyn slapped Jack's shoulder. 'Think of the bright side; this is a grand place for soldiering, and that's the life we chose. Could not be better for the likes of you and me, eh? A stern landscape, a bold and worthy foe, brave soldiers as comrades, and all the world before us. What more could we want?'

'What more indeed.' Jack thought of himself as a young ensign, when he sought glory and advancement above all. Back then he would have asked for nothing more than a posting to the Frontier. Now, with a decade of experience, he was not so sure. Experience and marriage had altered him.

'Probyn,' Chamberlain interrupted them. 'Take out a patrol of your badmashes; see what's happening to the east. Windrush; you're at a loose end just now. Do the same on the west. My compliments to Major Kerr, and could he lend you half a dozen of his men.'

'Yes, sir.' If nothing else, this expedition was keeping him from boredom or moping for Mary.

Kerr's beard seemed bushier than ever as he nodded to Jack. 'Take the same lads you had last time, Windrush. You got back in one piece without losing a man. That is unusual out here.' He lowered his voice, his Ulster accent seemingly quite at home amidst the brittle tension of the Frontier. 'Don't push your luck, man. I value my Guides, and this place is waiting to explode.'

'I'll look after them,' Jack promised. *Or they'll look after me.*

The Guides welcomed him as if he were one of their own. Jack looked over them, from grave Hassan, the volatile, dare-devil Zaman, young musical Fatteh, to handsome Alladad with his kohl-rimmed eyes, they were nearly as familiar to him as the men of the 113th.

'Where are you taking us this time, Windrush sahib?' Ursulla asked.

'Only on a short patrol; the general sahib wishes us to see what the Bunerwals are up to on the west.'

'They are up to mischief,' Hassan said. 'The Bunerwals are always up to mischief.'

'Then it's up to us to see what that mischief is, and stop it,' Jack said. 'You men are the shield and sword of India.' Although those words sounded like trite rhetoric, the men seemed to appreciate them.

'We are the Guides,' Fatteh said simply.

Although Jack led his patrol out before dawn, the Bunerwals were already alert. A jezzail thumped the moment the Guides left the camp, with the muzzle flare distinct against the dark. Others followed.

'Ride fast and hard,' Jack ordered.

'We know, sahib,' Hassan murmured.

Jack grunted; he was giving orders to men who had lived in this environment all their lives. As the shrill bugle calls of reveille from the camp faded behind him, he felt the old mixture of excitement and apprehension. He was outside the security of the camp, away from senior officers and all the familiar apparatus of order. Out here in the wild lands, a man had to be able to stand on his own merits, especially if he did not have the framework of clan or tribe as support. Was that the appeal of this kind of life? Or was the British army the equivalent of the family? He had heard it said that British officers were more than a class, yet not quite a caste or a military order like the old Knights Templar. They were a select society of their own. Yet often Jack felt more comfortable with his ranking soldiers than his fellow officers. He shook his head; he was not here to indulge in philosophical debates with himself, yet something about this untamed landscape awoke that desire within him.

He had been aware of the party of Bunerwals moving alongside them in the decreasing dark for the past ten minutes. Although Jack's patrol was mounted, while the Bunerwals were on foot, they kept pace without trouble.

'Sawan, drop back a little and see if they are trying to cut us off.'

'Sahib.' Sawan needed no further instructions. He cantered back a few moments later. 'No, sahib. They are quite content to watch. They are observing us, as we are observing them.' Only a Pashtun trooper would have added the unnecessary words to instruct his feringhee officer.

'Thank you, Sawan. Now it is your job to observe them observing us. If you think they pose a threat, inform me immediately.'

'Yes, sahib.'

They rode on cautiously, with their swords loose in their scabbards, alert for any possible attack. The air had a decided chill, a foretaste of the harsh winter that would soon sweep upon them. Jack remembered his boyhood dreams of India, of heat and jungles and balmy nights. He had no thought of this frontier with its extremes of climate and a population every bit as martial as the British. Jack gave a wry smile; when he was a boy, the Sikhs controlled this frontier.

Jack saw something thrusting from a ridge to his left, with the cold rays of morning sun glinting on the tasselled green. At first, he thought it was a tree, dimly seen in the half-light, but as he drew closer, he realised that it was a standard on a tall pole.

'Something's happening over there, lads. Let's have a look.' Guiding Sharbat to the left, Jack realised that their escorting Bunerwals were moving closer. One levelled his jezzail and fired a shot. The bullet whistled close to Jack. 'They don't want us to find out what that standard means,' he said. 'What do you think, Hassan?'

'I think that if we ride towards the standard, the Bunerwals will attack us.'

'I agree.' Jack peered at the body of Bunerwals still keeping pace with his patrol. His attempts at counting them gave different totals as the Bunerwals ducked behind cover, sheltered behind trees or showed themselves openly, depending on their mood. 'They seem to be playing with us.'

'Yes, sahib.' Hassan sounded patient, like a schoolteacher with a stupid pupil. 'They don't wish us to know how many of them there are.'

'Let's see what they are hiding,' Jack decided. 'We were sent out here to gather intelligence. Perhaps these Bunerwals are only a screen to fool us while the rest retreat, so we will be shadow-boxing nobody as the whole of Pakhtunkhwa mocks us.'

He knew that the opposite might also be true; the Bunerwals could be luring them into a trap.

'Be prepared for anything,' Jack ordered. 'Follow me!'

Veering left, he increased his speed to a trot, with Sharbat's hooves kicking up clods of earth. He saw the Bunerwals spread out, a score of turbans and blue cloaks, with gesticulating arms and the flash of early sunlight on pulwars. He heard the deep roar of a jezzail, but where the shot went, he could not tell.

'Fatteh! Sound the canter!'

This was exhilarating, riding forward towards an unknown number of the enemy on the farthest frontier of the empire. Was this why he had joined? To fight the foes of Victoria, Queen of Great Britain? Or was it to follow the family tradition, as these Pashtuns were doing? Or was it just for the excitement?

The Bunerwals had spread out; some were levelling their jezzails, others holding the long, curved pulwars as they ducked behind the circular shields.

'Charge!' Jack roared, knowing that he would be more sensible to observe and withdraw. *To the devil with that*! He was a soldier, not a spy; his job was fighting, not skulking. With the adrenaline surging inside him, Jack drew his sword. 'Come on the Guides!'

As the thin notes of the bugle sounded out and the Guides galloped forward, the Bunerwals melted away. One or two fired, the shots going nowhere; the others vanished, making use of the plentiful cover the terrain provided. Jack found himself charging nothing except broken ground and the fringes of a steep tree-crowned ridge.

'Canter,' he ordered, 'trot and walk.' He was unsure of the correct commands for cavalry, but the Guides were unconventional at least. They would understand what he meant.

The ridge ran north and south with uneven, rock-and-pine-tree slopes. In a gap on the summit between two clumps of trees, the green standard swayed slightly in the breeze.

'Do you recognise that flag, Hassan?'

'Yes, Sahib. That is the banner of the Akhund of Swat.' Hassan's voice was neutral, although Jack sensed the tension behind the words.

'Forgive my ignorance, Hassan. I do not know the name.'

'May I explain, Windrush Sahib?' Hassan was uncharacteristically diffident.

'Please do, Hassan.'

'He is also known as Akhund Abdul Ghaffur, sahib. You might know that name?'

Jack shook his head. He could see men flitting among the trees. 'No, I don't. Keep moving, boys. We don't know how many of the enemy are there.'

'The Akhund is the Emir of Swat, away up there, deep in the mountains.' Hassan indicated the north.

'Why have I not heard of him?'

'He has been a peaceful man for many years,' Hassan said. 'The British have had no reason to make war on Swat.'

Jack accepted that. He was a soldier; his attention was taken by military matters. Peaceful Emirs did not interest him.

'What is he like?'

Hassan screwed up his face. 'He is an elderly man,' he said. 'Over sixty, maybe even seventy.'

'What is he doing here?'

'He will not be here for his military prowess,' Hassan said. 'He is a mullah, a religious leader, and sahib, although he has been quiet for years, he is no friend to the British. In 1836 he called for a Jihad. He opposed the Sikhs and supports Dost Mohammad Barakzai of Afghanistan.'

Jack absorbed the information. 'Is the Akhund of Swat influential? Would men, Pashtuns, follow him?'

'The Pashtun would follow the Akhund to Paradise or to Jahannam, sahib, to heaven or hell.' Hassan's voice shook slightly.

'I did not know the Pashtun believed in hell.' Jack wondered if the Akhund could influence Hassan's loyalty.

'Some do, some do not. Some say that the entrance to hell is in Wadi Jahannam in Afghanistan.'

Jack nodded. From what he had heard of Afghanistan, the entrance to hell might well be there. 'I want to see what's behind that ridge. I want to see this Akhund fellow.'

Hassan shook his head. 'The Bunerwals will stop us.' He looked shaken.

'I'll go alone,' Jack decided. He had no intention of taking his Guides into danger.

'Then the Bunerwals will kill you.'

'Perhaps.' Jack wondered at his sudden recklessness. 'I want you to create a diversion.'

'Ah,' Hassan nodded. 'The sahib is not quite as stupid as he pretends.'

'The sahib does not appreciate being spoken about in such a manner,' Jack responded, knowing that Pashtuns had their own way of dealing with foolish British officers. 'I want you to take the men and ride north at great speed as if you had discovered something. Give me a full hour. If I'm not here when you return, get back to camp. Inform Kerr Sahib what happened. Tell him I ordered you to leave me.'

'He won't be pleased,' Hassan said.

'You must obey a direct order,' Jack said. 'Major Kerr Sahib understands that.'

Sliding off Sharbat, Jack jettisoned his sword, which would slow him down when he climbed the ridge. Fastening his scabbard over the saddle and carrying only his revolver, he slid into cover as Hassan rode off. Jack understood the magnitude of the risk he was taking; he knew that if he was captured he faced a horrendous death by torture, but the rewards might be worth the risk. Either the Bunerwals were retreating, or the Akhund of Swat had arrived. The news could be very good or very bad; he had to find out which.

Lying still for five minutes, Jack surveyed his surroundings. He saw his Guides trot north with much hallooing and waving of hands. A moment later a dozen Pashtun footmen followed. Jack allowed them another few moments, before sliding from his cover and moving up the hill. Wearing khaki and a turban, he was not dressed much differently from the average tribesman, so from a distance, he would be safe. If anybody came close, it would be another story. Jack felt his heart hammer as he thought again of the consequences. What would Mary think if he was killed?

No; Jack shook his head. Thinking like that would weaken him. He could not think like that. He must concentrate on climbing this hill.

The tree cover grew thinner as Jack climbed with little undergrowth to either hide him or impair his progress. Twice his feet slipped under him, and he fell; once he heard the mutter of conversation and lay still as a couple of Pashtun warriors walked easily up the steep slope. One carried a jezzail in his hand; the second had a Minie rifle, or a copy of a Minie rifle, across his back.

At the summit of the ridge, a length of bleak scrubland stretched between two belts of trees. In the middle of the gap, thrust into a pile of loose stones, the Akhund's green banner ruffled unattended in the breeze.

Why is that there? Jack thought. *Is it a challenge to us? Is it to lure us here?*

Avoiding the bare area, Jack moved cautiously within the trees until he had a clear view of the opposite side of the hill. He stopped, taking a deep breath.

Oh, dear Lord. Oh, dear Lord in heaven. All the Pashtuns in Pakhtunkhwa have gathered here.

On the reverse slope of the ridge, Jack counted scores of different standards flapping in the breeze. Predominately green or black, each thrust proudly above an encampment of Pashtun warriors. Some of the Pashtuns were smoking from hookahs, others talking together, cleaning their rifles or sharpening their swords. Music drifted to Jack from shpelai, sitar or sarinda, or a combination of all three.

Jack tried to count the assembled army, maybe twelve thousand, maybe fifteen thousand men, each one a warrior, each one at home in this rugged country. Chamberlain had encamped and invited the Pashtuns to the ball. They had responded with a vengeance.

'We asked for a piper,' Jack said. 'Now we must pay the bill.'

As he watched, each man stopped what he was doing, knelt on the ground and bowed in prayer. Thousands of men praying together was an impressive sight, something that Jack had never expected to see. He watched, not even sure what to think until the Pashtuns resumed their previous occupations. The music began again, softly.

The sound of drums alerted him, and he swivelled his binoculars. Riding among the different groups was the tabla mullah. *I have shot you twice. I saw Rougvie's bullet hit you clean as a whistle, yet there you are,* he said to himself, *the indestructible mullah, spreading mayhem wherever you appear. Do I need a silver bullet?*

'It is a fine sight, is it not, Windrush Sahib?'

The words made Jack start. The point of the knife pricking the back of his neck forced him to keep still. 'I know that voice.'

'Rise slowly, Captain Windrush, in case your sense of duty compels you to do something so foolish that I will be forced to use this blade, which would deny your lady Mary the man she misses so much.'

Jack obeyed, feeling somebody remove the revolver from his holster. 'I know that voice very well.'

'So you should, Windrush Sahib. We have fought side by side.'

When Jack turned slowly around, he found himself facing the humorous eyes of Batoor.

Chapter Eighteen

Ambela Pass October 1863

'Batoor?' Jack stared at him. 'I thought you were dead!' Unable to hide his pleasure, he lunged forward, grabbing hold of Batoor's upper arms. 'How are you? What are you doing here?'

Jack's initial surge of pleasure faded at sight of the red cord tied around Batoor's right arm.

'I am watching you crawling around.' Batoor pulled back his Khyber knife without replacing it in the scabbard. 'You are a brave man, Windrush. Not many would place their heads in the tiger's mouth. I heard that you had escaped from Gulbaz at Torkrud.' He nodded, stepping back slightly. 'I did not know you were with Chamberlain Sahib until a few days ago.' He grinned. 'Once I learned you were with Chamberlain Sahib, I set this trap for you.'

'For me?'

'Probyn Sahib would come with all his horsemen. Only Windrush would come with a small band of men.' Batoor laughed at his own cleverness.

'I did not know you were here at all. You were going to chase intruders from your land, Batoor. What happened?'

Batoor did not smile. 'I met the Akhund of Swat.'

Jack touched the red cord. 'Why are you with these fanatics? I thought you were dead.'

'Why did you think I was dead?' Batoor asked.

'We found your sword, the sword of the Rahmut Khel. A Waziri told us he had taken it from the dead body of the owner.'

'Ah,' Batoor nodded. 'The khan's silver sword. I did not take that with me, Windrush. It belongs in Torkrud.' He shook his head slowly. 'Ayub always had eyes for that sword. He must have taken it and fallen foul of the Mujahidin.'

'I see.' Jack remembered Ayub eyeing the sword. 'But why did you join the Mujahidin, Batoor? You are not a Ghazi.'

'I am now.' Batoor sounded surprised at the question. He indicated the red cord around his wrist. 'The Akhund of Swat asked me to join the Jihad.'

'You could have said no.'

'You cannot say no to the Akhund.' Batoor spoke seriously.

'Does he ride a horse and beat a tabla drum? Is that the Akhund of Swat?'

Batoor shook his head. 'No, Windrush. Once you meet him, you will know that there is nobody like him.'

The indestructible tabla mullah is not the Akhund, then. Is the Akhund more powerful than a man who cannot be killed?

'Are you going to kill me?' Jack dropped his guard to look as vulnerable as possible. Batoor had saved his life in the past, so Jack gambled that their friendship was stronger that Batoor's new found religious enthusiasm.

'No, Windrush.' Batoor kept the knife in his hand. 'I am going to show you how impossible it is for you to win this fight. I am going to send you back to General Chamberlain with a message from Allah, and from the Akhund of Swat.'

'I would like to meet this man who convinced you to turn against us,' Jack said.

'You shall.' Batoor slid his knife into its scabbard. 'If you try to overpower me, there are a hundred men nearby. They would give you to the women to blind, castrate, and flay alive.'

'I will not try to overpower you.' Jack knew that Batoor was a master of the sword and knife.

Sliding Jack's revolver into his cummerbund, Batoor nodded. 'Come to the standard, Windrush Sahib, and tell me what you see.'

Feeling very vulnerable, Jack stepped to the open space where the green standard fluttered in the breeze.

Previously hidden by a dip in the ground, an elderly, white-bearded man appeared beside the standard, flanked by two large, heavily bearded men who could only have been his bodyguards. On their own, either of the large men would have been distinctive. When next to the elderly man, they were insignificant.

'Is this your Captain Windrush, Batoor?' The elderly man turned his gaze to Jack. 'Salaam Alaikum, Captain Windrush.'

'Salaam Alaikum, sir,' Jack responded. 'Do I have the honour of addressing the Akhund of Swat?'

'Some men call me that. Others know me as Saidu Baba. Only Allah knows my true name, as only Allah knows yours.' The Akhund gave a small smile, his gaze never leaving Jack's face. Jack was immediately aware of the force of the man's personality. Although he must have been about seventy years of age and well past his physical prime, his eyes held Jack's attention like few men he had met. Suddenly Jack knew who had organised this rising against the British. It had not been the tabla mullah. It was this quiet, unassuming man with the serene eyes.

'Stand beside me, Captain Windrush.'

Jack found himself, a British officer, obeying without thought. 'From here we can see right across to the British camp on one side of the ridge and over the massed warriors of the Pashtun on the other. It is a good vantage point, don't you think?' The Akhund's smile was like a benign doctor, not like a man who had raised half of Pakhtunwali against the British. 'I like to think that both sides can view my standard.'

'It is a good vantage point,' Jack agreed. Once more he heard the drift of music on the wind and saw men gathered around campfires. He saw the glitter of sunlight on arms and accoutrements and the constant movement of men. The Akhund must have tremendous influence to gather so many warriors from different tribes together in one spot. It could not only be his personality unless he had visited each tribe individually.

'We have fifteen thousand men gathered here.' There was no pride in the Akhund's voice. He was merely stating facts. 'And more are coming from all across Pakhtunkhwa. Most are Ghazis or *Taliban-ul-ilm*, religious devotees, men dedicated to the cause of Allah.'

'I can see the red cord on Batoor's arm,' Jack said.

'My messages are going out all across Pakhtunwali,' the Akhund continued as if Jack had not spoken. 'Gathering men to the lawsuit, the battle between Allah, the law agent, may his name be praised, and the breakers of Allah's law, the feringhees.'

Jack nodded. So he had been right. The letters were for a gathering of the clans, with religion the unifying force.

'I have issued orders for a jihad against the infidels. We have men from all the tribes between the Kabul River and the Indus; I brought a hundred standards, each capable of rallying forty men. Pashtun warriors are coming from as far as Bajour, the Mullazyes of Dher, and others from the furthest reaches of Pakhtunkhwa.'

'It is a large army for a *lashkar*, a tribal force.' Jack decided to throw in a little dissent. 'Until they remember their blood feuds and start squabbling with each other.'

The Akhund's gaze did not waver. There was wisdom there, as well as infinite sadness, yet there was iron behind all. 'It may look large to you, Windrush, but this is only the beginning. My messengers are everywhere. Soon all the Afridi will join us, and the Waziri, the most fierce and most numerous of the Pashtun. The Waziri can raise 150,000 men, ten times the number you see here.'

Jack tried not to look shaken. He drew on his experiences with the Commissariat for Chamberlain's much smaller force. 'That number of men will need supplied, fed, transported, and cared for.'

'We are not a European army, Windrush, nor yet an Indian one.' The Akhund did not raise his voice, yet every word was clear despite the blustery wind. 'We do not need large baggage trains and thousands of servants. We are the Pashtun.'

'Indeed you are, sir.' Jack tried to find a way to weaken the Akhund's confidence. He remembered the chaos at the Zargun Pass. 'Sooner or later, Akhund, the various tribes in your army will turn against each other. It is not in the Pashtun's nature to stay united for long.'

'That has been the way of the Pashtun in the past. Not this time.' The Akhund gave his gentle smile. 'It is manifest to me that the British have a grudge against Islam.'

'We do not.' Jack tried to break the Akhund's chain of words. 'We have millions of the Faithful living peacefully under British rule.'

Again the Akhund continued as if Jack had not spoken. 'The British, in common with the other feringhee nations, have never forgiven Islam for their humiliation in the Crusades. They cannot bear to see Islam become powerful again.'

Jack could not control his anger. 'Islam attacked Christianity long before the Crusades, and in the shape of the Ottoman Empire and the Barbary corsairs, long after, as well.'

The Akhund looked directly into Jack's eyes. His power was so nearly hypnotic that Jack was forced to jerk his gaze away. *This is the most dangerous man I have ever met. The Tabla Mullah is nothing compared to him. The Pashtun have found their leader, their Saladin, their Montrose, their Washington.*

'There are many good followers of Islam in Chamberlain's army,' Jack said gently. 'They worship the Prophet as devoutly as any in your army.'

The Akhund gave another gentle smile. 'They have been deceived into following a feringhee general who represents the infidels. They would be welcome if they chose to change sides, as your friend Batoor has been welcomed.'

Batoor had been listening intently, nodding at all the right places. 'How many men does your general have, Windrush? We estimate six thousand.'

'You are facing the British army, Akhund.' Jack did not directly reply to Batoor's question. 'You know that no gathering of tribal levies will defeat us. Oh, you may gain a victory here, or ambush a column there, but we will always be back with a larger and more powerful force.'

'Large forces starve in the valleys of Pakhtunkhwa.' The Akhund spoke without emotion. 'And small forces are ambushed. This is our holy land. Allah has given this land to his people. Although all lands belong to Allah, Pakhtunkhwa is especially blessed.'

That was twice Jack had heard that phrase, our holy land. It was troubling, this infusing of religion, nation and the military power of the Pashtuns. He knew enough about human nature to know it was dangerous to interfere with anybody's religion, let alone the belief of a people as warlike as the Pashtun.

'Even so, Akhund.' Jack tried to defend a position he knew was becoming untenable. 'An essentially guerrilla army, however large, cannot defeat a modern nation of trained soldiers with modern weapons.'

'Don't you know your own history, Captain?' The Akhund's gaze never left Jack's face. 'Great Britain lost thirteen of their North American colonies to what you call an essentially guerrilla army.'

Jack hid his surprise; he had not expected a tribal leader from the Frontier to know about British military history. About to mention the French influence in the American war, he closed his mouth. Perhaps it was not wise to argue with a man who could kill him in a second.

'General Elphinstone's army was also defeated by similar tactics.' The Akhund was not finished yet. 'Even the armies of the great Napoleon Bonaparte suffered huge losses by such warfare in Spain and Russia.'

Jack swallowed his pride. 'You are right, Akhund. One must never underestimate one's enemies. I know that General Chamberlain does not, and neither, I am sure, do you. Batoor here knows how dangerous the British Army can be.'

The Akhund gave a grave nod. 'We will prevail if it is Allah's will. Only Allah understands everything.'

'We agree there, Akhund,' Jack said. 'We have different names for the same God.'

The Akhund gave a grave bow. 'That is also the will of Allah.'

Even as Jack spoke, he glanced at Batoor, one of the most dynamic men he knew. The Akhund had turned Batoor into a Ghazi seemingly without any trouble. His calm certainty was unsettling, yet strangely reassuring. Despite the fact the Akhund was an enemy, Jack could not help respecting, even liking, the man.

Batoor tapped the butt of the Enfield rifle that was strapped across his back. 'So far, Captain Windrush, the Pashtun have faced your army with outdated weapons. Now Allah has seen fit to supply us with rifles as good as anything the British Army carries. In a short time, General Chamberlain will face thousands of Mujahidin armed with modern rifles.'

'Oh?' Jack raised his eyebrows. He hoped he would survive to pass this information on to Chamberlain. *In a short time? What does that mean?*

'I think you have seen sufficient, Captain Windrush,' the Akhund said. 'It is the will of Allah that I use you as my messenger for General Chamberlain. Tell him that if he withdraws at once, I will hold back my men from attacking him. If he and his army depart from Pakhtunkhwa and promise that no British Army will return, I will call off the Jihad.' He sighed. 'I am a spiritual leader, Captain Windrush, not a man of war. When I wanted a messenger that General Chamberlain would listen to, Batoor Khan suggested you.' The Akhund permitted himself a small smile. 'His deception was successful. We know the British, you see.'

Jack did not respond to Batoor's smile. He had been very neatly trapped.

The Akhund continued. 'Neither of us wish any more blood spilt on this land, Captain Windrush. Pray tell that to the good general.' He bowed and spoke to Batoor. 'Ensure that Captain Windrush returns safely to the infidel's encampment, Batoor Khan.'

Batoor took hold of Jack's shoulder. 'Your men will be back for you shortly. Remember to inform General Chamberlain that the Akhund of Swat orders him out of Pakhtunkhwa in the name of Allah. If the general remains, the forces of Allah will descend upon him.'

'I will pass the message on.' Jack's mind struggled to process all this new intelligence. He had to tell Chamberlain that the Pashtuns expected modern arms soon. He had a last look at the Akhund, who remained standing beneath his banner, his face grave.

'Come on, Windrush.' Batoor guided Jack away from the Akhund and along the ridge.

'I am glad you are alive, Batoor.' Jack spoke the truth. 'Although I am saddened you have joined the Mujahidin. You can still come back to us. You know you would be welcome.'

Shaking his head, Batoor gave a small smile. 'Will General Chamberlain take heed of the Akhund's warning, Captain Windrush?'

'He is a general, Batoor. Who knows how a general thinks?'

Before he began the descent, Jack glanced again at the Pashtun forces with their flapping banners, drifting smoke and hordes of warriors. For a moment he felt an overwhelming sadness about the futility of war. He was beginning to know these people. They only wanted to be left to pursue their own way of life. He also knew that the average British soldier had no interest in Pakhtunkhwa.

Ill-used men from the back slums of industrial towns, plodding ploughmen from the broad English fields, half-starved Irishmen from impoverished cabins or freckle-faced sons of Highland crofters were not warriors. Oh, they were brave and hardy, but they had not been brought up to war and fighting as these Pashtun had. In some ways, it was unfair to pitch the two peoples and cultures together. In a straight contest, without the army training, weapons and discipline, the British soldier would be no match for these warriors. If the Pashtun had weapons and leadership equal to those of the British soldiers, then the balance tilted in their favour. In the Akhund, they had a charismatic leader. In the village of Tazhak, they had the source of better rifles.

'Come, Captain.' Batoor was watching as the thoughts ran through Jack's head. 'Or your men will return without you.'

Small groups of Pashtun warriors watched as Batoor escorted Jack down the wooded ridge to his agreed rendezvous with his Guides. None tried to interfere, although some shouted insults.

'You cannot defeat the Akhund,' Batoor said solemnly. 'He is favoured by Allah. Every morning, when rising from prayers, Allah deposits gold under the Akhund's praying mat, sufficient gold to fund him through the day.'

Jack grunted. 'Is that true, Batoor? Do you believe it is true?'

'It does not matter if I believe it, Windrush.' Batoor balanced on the steep slope without difficulty. 'What matters is that the warriors of God believe it.'

Jack nodded. For a moment he wondered how sincere Batoor's faith was and why he had told him about the rifles. 'You know you cannot win, Batoor. We will wear down the Bunerwals and smash the Mujahidin.'

Batoor's smile taunted Jack. 'We think of time differently, Windrush. We have patience; to us, a wait of a hundred years is a snap of Allah's finger.'

'What does that mean?'

'It means that you must hustle and bustle and think today's deeds are all that matters. Allah has granted us infinity. A battle lost today can be gained in a year or a hundred years.' Batoor kept his smile. 'I am glad you are still alive, Windrush.' He escorted Jack to the lowest fringe of trees, so the valley was open before them. 'There are your men,' Batoor said as the six-strong Guides patrol trotted along the flank of the hill. 'It is all right; the Akhund has given orders that they are not to be harmed.'

'That was kind of him.' Jack kept the irony from his voice. Remembering the force of the Akhund's personality, he could imagine that the orders would be obeyed.

'Come on, Captain Windrush.' Batoor increased his pace, so he ran down the final slope of the hill, disappearing behind a rocky spur. Jack kept up as best he could, stumbling in Batoor's wake.

Jack heard the voice as a Bunerwal hailed the Guides from within the trees. 'Why are you here, fighters for the feringhee?'

Zaman shouted back. 'We are true to our salt. Run away, Bunerwal, lest true men come for you.'

'Do you seek the infidel officer Windrush?'

Jack started to hear his name so well known among the enemy.

'We seek him,' Hassan answered for the Guides. Although the words carried quite clearly to Jack, the angle of the hill spur prevented him from seeing what was happening.

'He's dead!' The Bunerwal sneered. 'We caught him and killed him.'

'He's alive!' A gust of wind blew away Batoor's words. He slowed slightly. 'Hurry, Windrush, or your men will leave without you.'

'If you have killed Windrush,' that was Hassan's voice, 'we will kill all of you.'

Half a dozen Bunerwals joined in the laughter. 'Run back to the British, servants of the feringhees.'

'Come on, Windrush.' Drawing his Khyber knife, Batoor ran, leaping downhill without any regard where he placed his feet. He stopped at the base of the slope, where a party of some dozen Bunerwals were still jeering at the withdrawing Guides.

'We are too late,' Batoor said as Jack's patrol trotted away, taking Sharbat with them. The Bunerwals watched, sneering.

'Who told the Guides that Windrush was dead when the Akhund ordered him let alone?' Batoor asked mildly.

A young man stepped forward. His kohl-rimmed eyes and lovelocks beneath his pakul contrasted with the pulwar at his belt and jezzail across his shoulder. 'Who are you to ask?'

'I am Batoor Khan of the Rahmut Khel.' Drawing his Khyber knife, Batoor plunged it deep into the man's chest.

The other Bunerwals watched without interfering. Jack wondered if Batoor had just started a new blood feud.

'I will take you to the British camp,' Batoor said. 'You will be safe with me. I am known by both the Bunerwals and the Mujahidin as a friend of Akhund.'

About to refuse the offer, Jack realised that Batoor spoke sense. On his own, he could be a target for any hot-headed young Pashtun or any sharpshooter with a jezzail.

'You might wish this back.' Batoor handed over his revolver. 'I don't like these weapons. They jam too easily and are hard to reload.' He touched the hilt of his Khyber knife. 'I prefer my old friend here.'

'I still owe you a horse,' Jack said. 'And I know where the sword of the Rahmut Khel is.'

Batoor nodded. 'The sword will return to Torkrud when the time is right. Come on, Windrush. You have a message to deliver.'

Chapter Nineteen

Ambela Valley October 1863

'My men told me you were dead.' Major Kerr seemed angry that Jack proved his men to be wrong.

'I'm not.' Jack could see Hassan staring at him as if he had risen from the grave. 'I must see General Chamberlain.'

Kerr touched him with a thick forefinger. 'You are a hard man to kill, Windrush. I've never heard of a man being escorted to safety by a Ghazi before.'

Jack grinned. 'That was Batoor Khan. My one-time host.'

'I see,' Kerr grunted. 'You lead an interesting life, Jack, I'll grant you that. Come on, and we'll see what the general makes of all this.'

Chamberlain shook his head as Jack repeated what Akhund had told him. 'Fifteen thousand men to my six thousand, and more coming. This Akhund; is he a military leader, would you say, Windrush?'

Jack shook his head. 'I would say that the Akhund is more of a spiritual leader, a man who inspires his men.'

'The Ghazis are among the most formidable opponents we have faced,' Chamberlain said. 'They are as courageous as the Sikhs. If they had half the discipline of the Khalsa, they would be a very dangerous force indeed.'

'I can't answer for their discipline,' Jack said. 'I do know that they will soon be better armed.'

Chamberlain grunted. 'A few gunsmiths, even a score of gunsmiths, won't make sufficient rifles to arm 15,000 men.'

'No, sir, although I would calculate there were about a hundred gunsmiths in Tazhak, maybe more.'

'Even a hundred, creating say, one, maybe two rifles a week at most?' Chamberlain shook his head. 'I think we can disregard the Akhund's warning. He was trying to frighten us into withdrawal. That is what happened with Elphinstone in '41. He accepted the word of the Afghans.'

Jack nodded; it was evident that memories of that disastrous campaign still haunted Chamberlain.

'No.' Chamberlain made his decision. 'Thank you for your information, Windrush. I will think about what to do about these rifles. In the meantime, I will stick to my original strategy and stand fast here. We will let the Fanatics and Bunerwals take casualties when they attack us.' Standing up, Chamberlain paced the few paces that his tent allowed. 'However, I will send for reinforcements. The Pioneers have been building roads from here, one forward to the village of Ambela, the other giving us better communications over the lower slopes of the Mahabun Mountains to the Peshawar Plain. I entertain no fear as to the final result if we are supported by more infantry and kept in supplies and ammunition.' He smiled. 'That is what I shall tell the Commander-in-Chief, Sir Hugh Rose. The tribes are losing men and will tire first. In the meantime, when you have rested and eaten, I want you to trot over to the Punjabis. They are still an officer short.'

'Yes, sir.' Once again Jack wished he had the continuity of a regimental officer, rather than being sent to whichever spot he might be useful.

* * *

Major Sinclair welcomed him with a faint smile and a handshake. 'I heard you were killed and came back from the dead.'

'That's right, Major.'

'Useful trick, that. You'll have to teach it to me sometime.'

'I hope I never have to use it again.'

Sinclair nodded. 'Can't say I blame you. Now, I'll give you a company to command. The Bunerwals and all those other interesting chaps have not forgotten about us. They keep things lively with sniping and the occasional raid.'

'I'm sure your Sikhs can cope with that, sir.'

'Oh, it's all meat and potatoes to my boys.' Sinclair nodded. 'We are the best there has ever been.'

'So I've heard, sir.'

'You get settled in with my lads,' Sinclair said. 'You know them now.'

It was next morning before the Bunerwals and Mujahidin attacked again, just as dawn greyed the sky. The first Jack knew was a sinister noise he instantly recognised. 'Can you hear that?' He asked the nearest man, the young Ishar Singh.

'I hear it, sahib,' Ishar Singh said. 'It's a tabla drum.'

I will have to kill that mullah yet again. 'Rouse the men,' Jack said. 'The enemy is coming.'

There was no need to say more. The Sikhs rose willingly, forming up in near-silence with their bearded faces showing a variety of emotions from eagerness to impassivity.

'Here they come, lads! Hundreds of the buggers!'

The Bunerwals and Ghazis came with a rush, heads down and pulwars held high.

Ishar Singh levelled his rifle. The other Sikhs did the same, waiting for the order to fire.

'They're not coming on this front,' Jack said. 'Hold your fire.'

'Ready!' Kerr's Guides were on Jack's left flank, with Hassan closest to Jack. 'Here they come!'

'Stand ready, 5th Gurkhas!' A powerful voice came from the Punjabi's left flank. A dozen standards fluttered above the mass of Ghazis that advanced on the stone breastwork guarding the eastern end of the pass. Unseen behind the warriors, pipes and tabla drum urged them on.

The Ghazis split, with hundreds charging for the Guides, the British infantry and the Gurkhas, yet none approaching Jack's section of the line. He felt his Sikhs fretting with frustration, eager to join in.

'They're scared of us!' Sinclair said.

'Sahib,' Ishar Singh pleaded, 'can we go and help?'

'No. Stand fast,' Jack said.

'Ready, cap, aim, fire!' The precise commands rang out as the men of the 71st Highlanders and 101st Regiment fired volleys into the charging masses, felling Mujahidins and Bunerwals in small piles. Ignoring their casualties, the Pashtun charged on to be met by the stabbing bayonets and clubbed muskets of the 71st and 101st.

'There's my father!' Hassan shouted on Jack's left. Without hesitation, he aimed and fired. 'Missed you that time!'

Jack shivered. What sort of men were these to fire at their own kin? Would he ever understand the Pashtun?

The Pashtun attack faltered at the British line, with warriors at the rear trying to push forward the more reluctant men at the front.

General Chamberlain recognised the hesitation. 'Now, 5th Gurkhas!' he ordered. 'Now's your time! Let them see the blades of your kukris!'

Jack saw the delight on the Gurkhas' faces as they unsheathed their wickedly sharp kukris and vaulted over the sangar.

'Sahib, can we join them?' Ishar Singh said. 'The Gurkhas are having all the glory.'

'Stand still,' Jack ordered.

In an instant the Gurkhas who had lightened the camp with their cheerful good humour altered into one of the most efficient fighting machines that Jack had ever seen. Disregarding the bullets that pattered among them from the Pashtun's jezzails, they charged with their kukris held high.

Although Jack had experienced many hand-to-hand encounters in his career, he had never seen anything like the charge of the 5th Gurkhas. Yelling, they used only their kukris as they pursued the suddenly fleeing Pashtuns. Heads and arms flew in the air; others of the Pashtun were disembowelled or simply slashed to pieces as the Gurkhas chased them hundreds of yards from the British positions. Even when the recall sounded, some of the Gurkhas continued, so that the officers and NCOs had to physically pull the men back.

'Go on, Johnnie Gurkha!' The 71st Highlanders roared their approval.

The firing continued as the 5th Gurkhas returned to the British positions, with jezzails thumping from the Pashtun side and the British sharpshooters and artillery replying.

Sighing, the Sikhs settled back down, evidently disappointed that they had not been allowed to share in the fighting.

'Better luck next time, lads.' Sinclair seemed to share their dissatisfaction. 'There are plenty more of the enemy out there.'

General Chamberlain loomed up, looking as weary as ever. 'I hope you enjoyed your rest with the Punjabis, Windrush. Come with me, please.'

The general had set up his tent in the lee of a small ridge in the centre of the British camp, with a stalwart Sikh sentry standing like a granite statue. Ushering Jack inside, Chamberlain seated himself behind his desk.

'You have been fairly successful in your information gathering so far, Windrush.'

'Thank you, sir.' Jack was unsure what else to say.

'Judging by the casualties and the banners, Windrush, we have tribesmen from half the Frontier opposing us. Until our reinforcements arrive, we will continue to invite the enemy onto our defences and fend off all their attacks.'

'Indeed, sir.' Jack was too experienced to think that Chamberlain had brought him into his tent to keep him apprised of the military situation. The general was merely laying the foundations for some ugly news.

'Now, sir.' Reaching under his desk, Chamberlain produced an Enfield rifle. 'What do you make of this, eh?'

'It's an Enfield.' Jack checked the serial number. 771, complete with crown and cypher. 'With the same number as the weapons copied by the Pashtuns in Tazhak.'

'A patrol of the Guides picked up this from one of the dead out there. It seems that your rifles are indeed filtering through to the enemy.'

'Yes, sir.' Jack thought it diplomatic not to say any more.

'Your Akhund fellow mentioned that his army would soon be supplied with modern weapons, Windrush.'

'Yes, sir.'

'We can take that to mean a shipment from Tazhak,' Chamberlain said.

'I believe so, sir.' *Why are generals so pedantic? Get to the point, man!*

'Very well,' Chamberlain said. 'You know more about Tazhak than anybody else. I want you to take a small force, find and destroy the arms, and make sure there are no more made at Tazhak.'

'Yes, sir.' Jack spoke before the practicalities of the mission struck him. 'How small a force, sir? I'll have to move at night to get past the Bunerwals and Mujahidin, so I'll need men used to clandestine operations.' Once more he wished for his men of the 113th with their vast experience in this type of operation.

'You know best, Windrush. You can have your pick as long as you don't weaken me too much.'

'Thank you, sir.' Mentally scanning the garrison, Jack discarded them regiment by regiment. The British infantry was expert at attacking or defending fixed positions or fighting a conventional battle in the open. In Jack's opinion, there were none better anywhere. They were not as good in irregular warfare or in moving silently in the dark. The Sikhs had the same attributes and failings as British infantry. That left the Gurkhas, Probyn's Horse or the Guides. He had no doubt of the Gurkhas' courage or skill and had recently seen their fighting prowess, but his lack of Gurkhali would be a disadvantage.

'The Guides, sir. I would like a score of the Guides cavalry.'

'I'll speak to Kerr,' Chamberlain agreed at once.

Jack's mind was racing. Now that Chamberlain had finally agreed to his request, he seemed to have a thousand questions and things to do with little time in which to do them. 'Could you set up a diversion, sir, something to attract the enemy's attention while we slip out of camp?'

Chamberlain gave a single nod. 'I'm fully aware of the magnitude of your task, Windrush. I am ordering you into the jaws of a very dangerous leopard. You can take more men if you wish; say, two hundred with a couple of screw guns.'

Jack remembered the Akhund's words. 'That would be a small army, sir, and in the Frontier, small armies are ambushed. No; I'll take the Guides I had before if they are available, and another dozen of the same.' He grunted. 'There are certain things I wish done before we leave, sir. The men might not like them.' He explained what he wanted as Chamberlain nodded.

Chapter Twenty

Pakhtunkhwa, November 1863

The artillery barrage started two hours after dark, cracking open the silence of the night as the guns targeted the ridge on which the Akhund's standard flew. For a moment Jack watched the yellow-white explosions highlighting the ragged pines and wondered how many men would die or be maimed merely to provide a cover for his Guides.

'Right, lads.' Jack had insisted that rather than Guides uniform, the men should wear the local loose top and trousers, with whatever headgear they preferred, and a poshteen against the cold. Even so, his men looked distinctly military as he led them out of the camp and into the valley. All sported the red cord of the Ghazis on their right arm.

'Spread out,' Jack ordered. 'Try to look less like soldiers. You're a mob of Mujahidin, not a troop of Guides cavalry!'

The men grinned at him, teeth white through the dark. For some, years of training in the Guides had become second nature, while others quickly reverted to the less disciplined habits of their previous existence.

After ten minutes the artillery fire died away. Only a few isolated rifle shots punctuated the silence, and when they faded there was silence except for the keen of the wind.

Jack had ordered each man to muffle his equipment, so there was nothing to jingle or rattle as they rode. The horses' hooves were padded to make no sound on the ground, while no man carried anything that might mark them down as fighting for the British. Even their weapons were altered so rather than Enfields, they carried an assortment of captured Pashtun firearms, with Khyber knives or pulwars as side arms.

I've done all I can. Let's see if we can dent these Mujahidin.

Hassan took the lead when they passed close to a Bunerwal outpost. He shouted out a greeting before the Bunerwals challenged.

'Salaam Alaikum,' Hassan said. 'Allah Akbar.'

Jack kept riding as his Guides responded to the Bunerwals with obscene jests. Their combined laughter rose.

'Stop.' Jack turned around in the saddle, removed his Minie rifle from its holster, and fired a round in the direction of the British camp. At this distance, it was unlikely he could do any damage, while the gesture might help bolster an image of a group of Fanatics.

The other Guides followed Jack's example, with the result that one of the British piquets fired back.

'Hey! You Mujahidin are all the same!' One of the Bunerwals complained. 'You start the trouble and leave it to men like us to finish it off! You get away back to Swat and leave us in peace. I've got two wives to support; I've no time for a war with the feringhee!'

Raising a hand in acknowledgement, Jack said quietly: 'Ride on. Hassan, you know this country far better than I ever will. Could you guide us?'

'Yes, sahib.' Hassan pushed forward without any fuss.

They rode until dawn and camped in an abandoned caravanserai that a troop of vultures had made their home. The well contained sweet water for the horses, but the accommodation was timeworn, and alive with insects. Shuddering, Jack stamped on one of the enormous spiders the British knew as jerrymungulums. *What a country; even the spiders want to kill you.*

As he lay on the ground, looking up at the quickly fading stars, Jack wondered anew what he was doing here. *It's like a roundabout*, he told himself. *One of the tribes raids the part of India we protect. We retaliate by attacking that tribe; we burn their crops and kill some of their young men. They need food so raid their neighbours, who then ride into India to plunder for food, and we retaliate. It is a Pashtun blood feud on a larger scale. We are not solving anything by being here; we have been caught up in the local way of life. Am I tired of being a soldier? Has marriage softened me?*

Jack heard the familiar drumming before he was properly awake. He opened his eyes to see Zaman standing over him with an old Brunswick rifle in his hand. The silver hilt of the Rahmut Khel sword glinted at his waist. 'There is trouble, Windrush, sahib.'

'Get the men up.' Jack reached for his Minie. He kicked Fatteh awake. 'Come on, lads. Where is the drummer, Zaman?'

'About a hundred paces from the caravanserai entrance, sahib.'

'Is he the same mullah?' Jack knew the answer before Zaman nodded. Somehow he knew that wherever he travelled, the indestructible tabla mullah would arrive. He sighed. 'Come on then, lads.'

Jack's Guides were still getting ready when the Mullah's men rode into the caravanserai, with two dozen men surrounding him.

I'll kill you yet, Tabla.

For a second the two groups of men eyed each other with hands twitching toward their weapons and eyes wary. At last, supposing Hassan to be the leader of the group, the Mullah reined up in front of him. Jack glanced at his thigh; there was no wound, no sign at all that Rougvie had shot him. What sort of man was this?

'I am gathering warriors for the Jihad against the infidels,' the tabla mullah said.

Hassan indicated the scarlet cord on his right arm, saying nothing.

The mullah turned his smoky eyes on the Guides, studying them one by one. 'You claim to be Ghazi, yet here you are sheltering miles away from the feringhee.'

'We are in the same place as you.' Hassan was calm as he rested his hand on his sword.

The mullah turned until his gaze settled on Jack.

'We have met already, cousin,' the mullah said.

Knowing that he would reveal himself as soon as he spoke, Jack merely grunted. The mullah dismounted, stepping closer. Jack held his gaze, hoping to mirror the confidence of a Pashtun. The mullah scrutinised Jack for what seemed hours, but was probably only a couple of minutes, then looked away. Jack could not read the expression of his eyes.

Jerking his head to his men, Jack made for the entrance of the caravanserai and the covering darkness of the night. He felt the frantic hammer of his heart gradually slow.

'I thought that mullah had recognised me,' he said.

Hassan nodded. 'If he had, we would all be dead by now, or wishing that we were.'

'Let's put some distance between him and us.'

With Hassan in the lead, they rode into the night, following some obscure track that Jack could barely see. Twice he heard a grey wolf howl, the sound bringing some repressed folk memory that sent a cold chill down his spine. Once he heard the rustle of wings overhead and wondered if the vultures were following them, sensing death.

'How far are we from Tazhak?' They had been riding for hours, stopping only to rest the horses.

'We'll reach there at dawn.' Hassan sounded quite comfortable in his role of guide.

Jack looked over his men, wondering if he should have brought more. Twenty men, even such formidable fighters as the Guides, was a tiny force to capture and destroy an entire village as well as a caravan. Ever since he had been given the task, he had cudgelled his mind trying to think of some stratagem to even the odds. He had nothing. His once-fertile brain was blank. He would have to camp nearby, observe the target, and hope for inspiration — that was not reassuring while operating in very hostile territory.

And as for the caravan? Jack took a deep breath. Was the Akhund's information inaccurate? He shook his head: *I was never in worse humour for anything in my life. What's wrong with me?*

With the onset of dawn, Jack recognised his surroundings. They were in the Valley of Kot, only a couple of miles from Tazhak. He looked around; the valley was quiet, with only a few herds of sheep on the lower slopes and no discernible inhabitants. He had to make his decision soon.

'We'll find somewhere overlooking Tazhak.' Jack tried to sound more confident than he felt. 'And observe the village.' As a young officer, he would have ridden straight there and attacked bald-headed. Now, with more than a decade of experience including three wars under his belt, he had learned caution.

Circling around Tazhak and being careful to keep out of sight, the Guides found a position in the hills and settled down. They were in a saucer-like depression, with a fringe of rocks and trees to provide cover from casual travellers. Jack focussed his binoculars on the village. There were some small groups of men arriving but less than there had been on his last visit, which he found odd, given that Chamberlain's campaign should ensure brisk business for gun makers.

'What do you think, Hassan?' Jack passed over the binoculars.

'It is very quiet,' Hassan said.

Jack swept his gaze along the guard towers. The sentinels watched as intently as they had last time, yet he sensed that something was wrong. If anything, the sentinels looked too alert.

'I'm going down for a closer look,' Jack decided. 'If I don't come back, you are in charge, Hassan. Get the men back safely.'

'Yes, sahib.' Hassan accepted the possibility of Jack's death with disturbing equanimity. He hesitated for a moment. 'Sahib, it may be best if you take one of the Guides with you in case you have to talk. Your accent is terrible.'

Jack nodded. 'Thank you, Hassan. I'll take Sawan. You're needed here. Come on, Sawan!'

Slipping down the hill on foot, they sauntered close to Tazhak's only gate. Sawan hummed a little song, fingering his jezzail with more nervousness than Jack had expected. It was quite reassuring to know that the Pashtun were human, with the same fears and emotions as everybody else.

'Steady, Sawan,' Jack murmured as they approached the entrance. A warrior leant against the open gate, sharpening his pulwar on a stone. He gave Jack and Sawan a hard glance before returning to his sharpening.

'Salaam Alaikum,' Sawan said quietly.

'Salaam,' the guard replied.

'Where are you going, cousin?' A second guard looked up from his position inside the gate. His indigo-black clothes and steel cap suggested he came from the Indus Valley, while the buckler across his back was of untanned buffalo-hide. Jack put his age as anything between thirty and forty.

'To look at the rifles,' Sawan patted his jezzail, 'this one was old when your grandfather was a young man.'

'You are wearing the red cord of a Ghazi,' the Indus Valley guard observed. 'Should you not be fighting the feringhees?'

'I shall,' Sawan said, 'as soon as I get a better weapon.'

'You might be a day late.' Grunting, the guard spat betel-juice on the ground, and returned to his post, his hooded eyes never straying from Sawan's face.

A day late? Has the caravan already departed?

Feeling as if he was passing through the gates of hell, Jack stepped inside the village. Only half a dozen steps later he realised why the guards had been so wary. Filling the main street, thirty camels stood patiently, some decorated with colourful cloths and little bells, others old and dull. Their drivers stood at their sides, wiry bare-legged men in dusty turbans and open sandals. Each camel was laden with panniers. As Jack watched, a man emerged from one of the gunsmith's workshops carrying an Enfield in each hand. Without hesitation, he placed the rifles inside the pannier of the nearest camel. Jack had a glimpse of another score of Enfields before the man closed the pannier.

We're not too late.

'That's our caravan.' Jack stopped a few paces within the village.

'Yes, sahib,' Sawan said. 'There are thirty camels, each with two panniers. If each pannier holds twenty rifles, that's forty for each camel, twelve hundred in total.'

The Akhund must have made these craftsmen work flat out. Twelve hundred Enfield copies!

Jack had a mental image of twelve hundred Ghazis armed with modern rifles. Added to their huge preponderance of numbers and their martial skill, that made them an incredibly formidable enemy. If Chamberlain were defeated, the blow to British prestige would be as immense as the Kabul disaster of 1841, weakening the British position in India. 'We have to stop them.'

'Yes, sahib,' Sawan said.

'We can't leave here yet,' Jack said. 'Let's see if they have any Enfield rifles in the first workshop.'

Jack led them in, knowing that every minute could be vital yet aware that if they left Tazhak after only a few moments without purchasing anything, the sentries at the gate would be instantly suspicious, which could jeopardise the entire mission. The gunsmith inside the workshop looked at him without recognition or expression.

'How much are your Enfields?' Jack allowed Sawan to do the talking.

The smith spread his hands. 'Alas, we have only just now sold the last one. Can I interest you in a Brunswick, perhaps? Or a Minie?'

'I only want an Enfield.' Sawan was too forthright for Jack, who wished to purchase something, anything, as an excuse to leave the village.

'The Minie is a fine weapon,' the gunsmith said. 'Your colleague carries one. Do you find that it suits, cousin?' He faced Jack directly.

'Yes,' Jack said shortly. 'We'll take the Minie.'

'I want an Enfield,' Sawan protested.

'You'll take a Minie and like it.' Jack cursed the bloody-mindedness of these Pashtuns. *They're as bad as the blasted Scots.* He glowered at the gunsmith, daring him to make any comment.

Sawan grabbed the Minie with ill grace as Jack parted with far too much money for the weapon.

'My younger brother,' Jack explained as the gunsmith peered at him.

'Family.' The gunsmith shook his head. 'He is a Yusufzai, yet you speak like a feringhee. How is that?'

Jack felt the tension rise within the workshop. 'I was in the feringhee's army,' he said. 'And his jail.'

The gunsmith laughed. 'No wonder you became a Warrior of God.'

The caravan was still in the street when they left the workshop, Sawan holding his Minie as if it was diseased.

'That was a short visit.' The Indus Valley sentinel at the gate recognised them.

'We had it on order.' Sawan was quicker-witted than Jack had expected. He held the Minie up for inspection.

The sentinel spat more betel-juice. 'You'd be better with an Enfield.'

'Next time,' Sawan said over his shoulder as he examined the Minie. 'They're too expensive, with this jihad.'

* * *

'There is a caravan of thirty camels lined up in the main street,' Jack explained to the Guides. 'I think each camel carries about forty copies of the Enfield rifle. That will be a significant boost to the Mujahidin's firepower, so they will be able to do more damage, kill more farmers, kidnap more merchants and attack more posts of the Guides.'

The Guides watched him impassively. Zaman stood up, his right hand on the silver pommel of the Rahmat Khel pulwar that never left his side. 'We know these things, Windrush Sahib. When are we going to attack them?'

'We will attack two hours before sunset when there is still sufficient light for us to see,' Jack said softly. 'If the caravan leaves the village, we will attack earlier. Make sure your weapons are oiled. Make sure your swords are sharp. We are going straight through the front door. Half of us,' he split the Guides in two, ensuring some of his veterans were in each party, 'will cut out the caravan and take it out of the village. The rest will destroy the workshops and wreck the tools.'

The Guides nodded eagerly, understanding at once. Jack knew there was no need to explain further. To such men, bred to the blood feud, a raid on a village came as naturally as breathing. He wished again that he had brought more men.

'Zaman, I want you to command the destruction party.' As the most aggressive of the Guides, Zaman was the obvious choice.

Zaman nodded, grinning. 'Yes, sahib.'

'Don't kill any civilians,' Jack reminded him. 'We are on the Queen's business, not a tribal raid.'

'Yes, sahib,' Zaman agreed, far too readily.

The rest of that afternoon, Jack kept an anxious watch on Tazhak in case the caravan should leave. A few men walked into the village with a single train of mules, but the caravan remained within the walls. Nothing else changed. The guards on the towers were as alert as ever, swivelling this way and that while the sentinels at the gate questioned all who came in.

Jack checked his watch; three in the afternoon. 'That caravan will not leave today,' he said with satisfaction. 'There is not sufficient daylight remaining for it to get anywhere.'

The Guides readied themselves for the raid, sharpening swords, checking and re-checking their firearms. They prayed twice, kneeling on the stony ground to face Mecca. Jack wondered what Mary would say when she learned that he had neglected the worship that she demanded.

I won't tell her, he decided, knowing that she would ask, worming the truth out of him within ten minutes. He grinned, missing her. *I hope that a relief column reaches Chamberlain soon. I hope he can smash the Mujahidin, so we get something like peace in Pakhtunkhwa.*

Jack knew that peace was a false hope as long as the Pashtun held to Pakhtunwali, and the British Empire abutted onto Pakhtunkhwa. He sighed, wondering about the as-yet-unborn generations of British soldiers who would have to guard this Frontier. In the unthinkable future, when the British Empire disappeared, as it would, as every Empire always did, their successors in India would inherit the same clutch of problems, and the same circle of raids and reaction would continue.

Jack sighed. *I hope Mary is right and sometime, somehow, there is a Second Coming to bring peace to this troubled world.*

'Sahib.' Hassan was beside him, proffering a hunk of bread and chicken. 'You have not eaten today.'

Jack looked up. 'Thank you, Hassan. I was just thinking of the future. I was wondering if there would ever be peace in this land.'

'All lands belong to Allah,' Hassan said. 'If He wills there to be peace, then peace will come. If His will is for war, then there will be war. All blessings to Allah.'

Jack spoke through a mouthful of bread. 'I hope His will is for peace, Hassan.'

Hassan smiled. 'Then you and I will both be unemployed, Windrush sahib. Who then will look after our families? Allah's timing is perfect in every matter. We don't understand the wisdom behind it, but we have to learn to trust it.'

Jack nodded. 'The ways of Allah are wonderful.' Mary would have substituted God for Allah with identical sentiments. 'Mount up, Guides.'

'We belong to God, and unto God we do return,' Hassan said, with the others murmuring the words.

Jack led his Guides on a wide detour, so they approached the gate from the valley floor. He had them ride in a casual group, laughing as if they had not a care in the world.

Both sentinels stepped forward, the man from the Indus Valley raising his hand. Without stopping, Jack rode through the gates, barging the men aside, knowing his Guides would follow his orders.

For one moment everything seemed right. The camel caravan stood precisely as Jack had left it, a few people walked around the workshops, and some men turned to stare as Jack's Guides crashed into the village.

'Right, lads!' Jack ordered, just before the world exploded around him.

As soon as the last of the Guides clattered into the village, half a dozen Pashtun warriors raced from the nearest compound to slam shut the gates and drop in the massive securing beam. One shouted, 'Allah Akbar,' and fired his rifle in the air.

The shot was a signal. The men who had been standing casually beside the camels suddenly produced rifles, while more warriors appeared on the watchtowers and poured from the workhouses.

'It's a trap!' Jack yelled. He saw the tabla mullah appear at the tail of the caravan. Jack fired, missed, and swore as the mullah began to thunder at his drum, bringing forth an eruption of warriors, some shooting at once, others levelling their rifles at the Guides. Jack saw one of his men fall, sliding sideways from the saddle. A Yusufzai Mujahidin immediately pounced on him, repeatedly stabbing with a long *pesh-kabz* dagger.

'Get out of here!' Jack drew his sword, wishing it was his own sabre rather than the less familiar pulwar. He slashed at an advancing warrior, missed utterly, felt something crash into his leg, looked down to see a massive warrior with a clubbed rifle, kicked in his spurs, and yelled for his men to join him.

'Come on, Guides! Back to the gate.' There were some recommended responses to an ambush, from sitting tight to charging straight for the centre of the ambushers, but none were possible in such an enclosed space. Slashing at a warrior with an upraised pulwar, Jack rode for the door, cursing to see four Pashtuns standing in front of the massive beam that held it closed.

The tabla mullah was encouraging the Pashtun with his drum, so more warriors surged onto the wall and around the gate.

'Allah Akbar!' It was a call that Jack knew would come to him in his nightmares, the same cry that the Ottoman Turks had used in their assault on Christian Europe, the same cry the Moors had used as they invaded Spain. Richard, the Lion Heart, would have known that call, and now it was his turn to be out-thought and out-manoeuvred by the Warriors of God.

No, by God! The Mujahidin are not quite as smart as they think. They acted too fast; they should have waited until we were split further apart.

'Stick together, lads!'

Jack's Guides mustered around him, firing, slashing with their swords, some with gritted teeth, Fatteh singing, Zaman cursing the attackers, striking with the sword of the Rahman Khel. Jack saw Fatteh fall from the saddle, to be immediately dragged away by two warriors. His eyes were huge.

'Sahib! Help!'

Jack reached out. 'Fatteh!'

A group of the Mujahidin got in his way, angry bearded faces intent on killing. *So this was what defeat felt like.* 'Get away from that man!' Jack slashed right and left, swearing.

'Hassan! Take the men to the gate!' Jack made another push for Fatteh, knowing he could not leave anybody in the hands of the enemy. Wishing he was astride Colwall rather than the lighter Sharbat, he tried to thrust through the mass, feeling his sword-cuts parried by a skilful enemy. Another Guide fell, cut down by a swinging pulwar. More Mujahidin warriors appeared at the gate, blocking the Guides' exit.

What's happening here? Jack asked himself. *They could have stayed in the shelter of the houses and shot us down like targets at a shooting gallery. I have to lead my men clear.*

More shots sounded, and two horses fell, throwing their riders onto the ground. Jack saw a tall man vault down from the gate, land on his feet and shout orders. The man looked directly at Jack.

'Batoor!' Jack said.

Zaman turned his horse, kicked in his spurs, and burst through the Pashtun ranks, cutting down a skull-capped Mahmud. Jack barged into one of the Pashtun warriors, knocking him out of the way. Dismounting, he wrestled with the heavy bar. 'Keep out of the way, Batoor. I don't want to kill you!'

Batoor strode forward, pressing his Khyber knife against Jack's throat. 'I can kill you and all your men,' he said softly, 'or you can surrender.'

Jack looked around. The Mujahidin had his men surrounded, with knives, swords and rifles pointed at each man. Only Hassan and Zaman continued to fight, Hassan shouting some slogan and Zaman screaming in frustrated fury as three men parried his blows. *They are containing Zaman's attack. They could easily kill him. What is this?*

'No!' Lifting his sword high, Zaman thrust it into the logs of the gate, used it as a lever, and threw himself upwards. Without looking back, he vaulted to the top of the gate, reached down, retrieved his sword, and vanished outside.

'Surrender, Windrush,' Batoor said. 'I cannot hold my men back much longer.'

'There will be no surrender, Batoor! You're not torturing my men.'

'You have my word, Windrush. None of your men will be tortured. We will treat you with honour.' Batoor eased the pressure of his knife. 'You know me, Windrush.'

Surrender meant captivity and humiliation. Not to surrender meant death for all his men. Jack could see that the Mujahidin were eager to kill the Guides, arguably the most effective regiment that the British had on the Frontier.

'If you break your word to my men, Batoor, you will have lost your honour forever.'

'I despise the man who does not guide his life by honour,' Batoor quoted Khushal Khan Khattak, the Pashtun warrior poet. 'I do not wish to kill you, Windrush. What would Mary think of me then?'

'You're a bastard, Batoor.' Jack felt the frustration of defeat. He raised his voice. 'Sorry, lads. Drop your weapons. We have Batoor's word that they will treat us well.'

One by one, the Guides threw down their weapons, most with a curse. 'It is the will of Allah.' Hassan stood quietly, counting his men. 'We have lost three men, Windrush. I saw you try to rescue Fatteh.'

'Try and stick together,' Jack said. He could only watch in numb despair as Batoor had his men remove the Guides' weapons. The tabla mullah rode around them, smiling, his drum stilled for once.

'Where is Zaman?' Batoor asked. 'Where is my cousin?'

'He got away.' Jack felt bitter about Zaman's desertion, yet pleased that at least one of his men had escaped.

'A pity,' Batoor said. 'I was going to hand him to my women.'

'You gave your word,' Jack said.

'I gave my word that none of the Guides would be tortured or killed. I did not give my word that my cousin would live. We are at feud, as you know. That is Pakhtunwali.'

Jack grunted, understanding why Zaman escaped. It was not cowardice or treason but simple self-preservation, the pragmatism of a man who lived with the realities of life in Pakhtunkhwa.

As the Mujahidin herded the Guides into one of the compounds, Batoor led Jack away to another of the houses. Three sturdy Mujahidin followed, never taking their gaze off Jack.

'Chain him.' Batoor gave rapid orders. 'This is Captain Windrush of the 113th Foot, and now of the Guides. He is a most dangerous man.'

'Was this trap your idea, Batoor, or was it that madman with the drum?'

Batoor smiled. 'We knew that the British knew about the rifle making, so they would eventually decide to end it. We thought it better to tell you about the caravan so that your General Chamberlain would send a column to stop it. I guessed he would either send Probyn or you.' Batoor gave a small frown. 'Allah heeded our wishes, although I had hoped for a larger force to weaken the British position.'

'You were right, Batoor,' Jack admitted grudgingly. 'Your trap worked perfectly.' He lifted his arms, not resisting as the warriors placed heavy manacles on his wrists. *Keep him talking. Learn all you can. There will be a way to escape. Don't give up hope. Find out why they want us captive when they could easily have killed us.* 'You're a clever man, Batoor.'

'I know how you work, Windrush, so setting an ambush was easy.'

Jack grunted. *Am I so predictable? I will have to change my methods if I survive this ordeal.* 'What are your plans with us now, Batoor?'

Leaning over, Batoor checked to ensure Jack's chains were secure. 'The Akhund will convert your men. If you had brought me British, Gurkhas or Sikhs, we would execute them. British-trained men will help us to understand the enemy even better.'

Jack nodded. *That made sense. Why kill men when they could be persuaded to join the Jihad?* 'My Guides are not so easily converted,' Jack said.

'The Akhund will guide them to the truth,' Batoor dismissed Jack's words. 'You, Windrush, I will hand as a gift to the Akhund of Swat. I do not know what he will do with you.'

Jack did not pursue that line of thought. 'Your camels will soon tire of standing here waiting for Probyn or whoever General Chamberlain sends to find what's happened to us.'

Batoor shook his head. 'No, Windrush. I will take the caravan to our forces opposite Chamberlain. I will also send a message to him from you that the village and caravan are destroyed in case he decides to send a larger column.' Batoor frowned. 'Why only bring twenty men, Windrush? We hoped for a much larger number.'

'If I had, Batoor Khan,' Jack rattled his chains, 'we would have burned your village to the ground and destroyed your caravan. As it is, nobody will believe your message.'

'Perhaps they will. Perhaps they will not. Allah will decide,' Batoor said. 'It is no longer your concern.'

'Perhaps it is not. Perhaps it is.' Jack returned Batoor's words. 'Why have you joined these fanatics, Batoor? You know that they cannot win. Your position of Khan was secure; now it is under threat from Gulbaz. He moved against you the moment you left Torkrud.'

'It is Allah's will,' Batoor said. 'Position in this world does not matter when compared with the paradise of the next.'

'You have been smitten with religion, haven't you? Well, that's probably the will of Allah as well.' Jack forced a smile. 'We were friends once, Batoor.'

'We are still friends.' Batoor sounded surprised at Jack's statement. 'We are friends on opposite sides of a war.' He stepped up to Jack, crouching at his side, speaking urgently. 'If you embrace Islam, Windrush, what a team we would make. I would ensure you had all the earthly things a man could want, while Allah would take care of you in Paradise.'

'I thought you religious types did not believe in such material matters,' Jack tried to test Batoor's commitment to the Jihad.

'I can ensure you have horses and hawks for shikar.' Batoor's eyes were bright. 'We can hunt every day, Windrush, you and me, and talk about old campaigns. We can raid for women if you wish, or boys if you prefer.'

'I have Mary,' Jack reminded him. 'My wife. I have no use for boys or other women.'

Batoor was not affected by Jack's attempts to unsettle him. 'You could send for Mary, Windrush. If she does not come, I will send men to bring her here as your senior wife. She will soon become used to our culture.'

This man, my captor, wishes to remain my friend. Our concept of war is vastly different. 'I do not think that Mary would wish to be kidnapped, Batoor. Nor would she be willing to share me with other women.' For a moment Jack toyed with the idea.

'She would be with you,' Batoor said simply. 'Would you not do the same for her?'

Jack closed his mouth. *Would I? Would I change my religion for Mary, if she embraced Islam?*

'I can see you are considering that.' Batoor stood up. 'I do not like to see you in chains, Windrush. Think what times we could have! Think what campaigns we could wage, what stories we could tell our children!' He stepped to the door. 'Your men will be well cared for, Windrush, whatever they decide.' He left, closing the door behind him.

Although it was not the first time that Jack had been held prisoner, it was the first time that he had been captured by a man who considered him a friend. Unsure what to think, Jack leaned back. He knew that sleep and hope were vital to a prisoner. *Without rest, I will be gradually worn down; without hope, I will descend into a slough of despond, as Bunyan would say. So sleep and allow your mind to recover, Jack, my boy. Things look bad, but you're not dead yet.*

Calming himself down with thoughts of Mary, Jack heard the drum of the tabla mullah. He knew his men would remain loyal. They were Guides.

What a mess.

Sleep was fitful with the chains dragging at Jack's wrists and ankles and the sounds of the village now more alien. After a while, the hypnotic drumming of the Tabla faded away, to be replaced by the snorting of camels.

The door opened with a crash. Two unsmiling Mujahidin handed a hunk of fresh bread and a leather bottle of water to Jack. 'Eat and drink, feringhee.' They waited until Jack was finished before unfastening his chains and leading him outside the compound.

'Salaam Alaikum.' Batoor was waiting in the main street. 'I hope you have reconsidered your position, Windrush.'

'You know I won't change, Batoor.' Jack watched the tabla mullah lead the caravan out of Tazhak, the shuffling of feet and tinkling of bells replacing the beating of the drum.

'There, you see?' Batoor touched Jack's arm. 'Some of your Guides have already embraced Mujahidin; they are now Warriors of God.'

Jack lifted his head. He felt a twist of despair when he saw Hassan and Ursulla among the escort of the caravan. Ursulla looked directly at him, then away again, quickly.

'Aye, you should feel guilty,' Jack shouted. 'You have betrayed your salt!'

Hassan faced Jack. 'It is the will of Allah,' he said quietly. 'You could join us, Windrush Sahib.' His eyes were pleading. 'Join us, sahib.'

For an instant, Jack contemplated singing God Save the Queen but decided that such a display would be crass and clamped shut his mouth. As he watched the caravan leave the village at a steady pace with a dozen of his Guides among the escort, he felt as if his world was collapsing. If even the Guides, the elite of the Indian Army, could be suborned to the Mujahidin cause, how vulnerable was India to such attacks?

The camels glided past, each one with its laden panniers, each one holding rifles that could kill British or Indian soldiers, each one carrying a cargo that could end the fragile peace in India and allow the Mujahidin to debouch from the mountains into the vulnerable plains to rape, raid, kidnap and kill. He had been sent to end such occurrences, and he had failed.

The tabla mullah rode up to him, now tapping lightly on his drum. He circled Jack three times, staring at him through these strange smoky eyes. 'Embrace Islam,' he advised. 'Come to Allah.'

Jack said nothing. He held the gaze of the mullah, seeing nothing there except contempt. 'I am going to kill you,' he said flatly. There was no bullet wound on the mullah's chest or thigh.

'If Allah wills.' The mullah circled Jack again, always beating his drum. 'You will be welcome in our ranks, Captain Windrush.'

'Damn you for a troublemaker,' Jack said.

The mullah rode away, following the caravan.

'You can join us, Windrush,' Batoor said. 'You are more like us than you know.'

'I am an officer in the British Army,' Jack reminded him. 'I cannot join you, even if I wanted to.' He knew that his refusal probably meant he was consigning himself to a very unpleasant death.

Batoor looked genuinely sorry. 'Then I must leave you, Windrush. I am taking the caravan to its destination. We may meet again, in peace or war.'

'If it is in war, Batoor,' Jack said, 'I hope you choose the right side next time. If it is in peace, then I shall shake your hand and give you the horse I owe you.'

'May Allah go with you.' Batoor raised his voice. 'Take this man away! Keep him secure until the Akhund gives orders what to do with him.' He sighed. 'Your jailors are not warriors, Windrush.' He tapped his forehead significantly. 'I have given them orders to look after you. I have done all I can for you.'

Jack nodded. 'If we meet in war, Batoor, I will try to kill you. I hope we meet in peace.'

'It will be as Allah wills.' Turning around, Batoor strode away. He did not turn back.

Two burly Pashtuns grabbed hold of Jack and marched him back into the compound he had just left. Within minutes he was pushed to the ground, his chains were looped around a staple in the wall, and both men had landed a couple of hefty kicks that left him in no doubt that he was not a welcome guest.

'I hope the Akhund wants you dead,' the younger man said. He spoke slowly as if forming the words was a great effort.

'The women will castrate you,' the older man added, equally ponderously. 'Then slowly flay you as you scream for mercy.' He seemed to enjoy the idea, for he hovered over Jack, savouring his words. 'They will peg out what is left of you and urinate in your mouth until you drown.'

'I will take your skin and make it into a coat,' the younger man said.

Jack forced a smile, although he knew that nothing these men said was exaggerated. *Don't let them see that I am scared. Bullies feed on the fear of their victims.* 'Come closer,' he said. 'Help me up.'

'Help you up?' The first man said.

'Yes, I have something to tell you.' Jack waited until both men hauled him roughly to his feet. 'Do you want this jacket I am wearing?' He indicated his poshteen. 'It is a very special jacket. It is an English jacket.'

'An English jacket?' The second man repeated. 'It looks Afghan.'

'Help me take it off.' Jack had worked out that these men were the Pashtun equivalent of the village idiots. They were not sufficiently sharp-witted to join a raiding party.

'He is trying to escape,' the first man said. 'It is a trick.'

'It is no trick,' Jack said. 'It is a special English jacket.' His hope that he may escape as they released his chains died as one held a knife to his throat as the other stripped him of the poshteen.

'It's not made from goatskin or sheepskin,' he said. 'It is made from an animal that only lives in England. You will know by the smell.' He hid his satisfaction as the younger man grabbed a handful of his coat and inhaled.

'What is it?' The older man asked.

'The great Malvern swine,' Jack said. 'Our own brand of pig.' He laughed openly as both men recoiled from the skin of an unclean animal. 'What's wrong, lads? You have both pawed my pigskin coat.'

The older man kicked at him, while the younger contented himself with a mouthful of oaths foul enough to earn him praise in any barrack room in the British Army. Jack was still laughing as his guards left the house, slamming shut the door. It was only a tiny victory but one that raised his morale slightly.

Keep your head up, Jack. There are rough times ahead, but I'm not defeated yet.

Waiting until he was sure he was alone, Jack began to work at his chains. After searching them for any weakness, Jack scraped the links of his chain against each other, hour after hour until his fingers bled with the strain. *I have little chance of releasing myself, but I'm damned if I'll just give up without a struggle.* With no window in the room, and Batoor having helped himself to his watch, Jack was unable to keep count of time. He worked on until fatigue overcame him, then he dozed, to wake with a start, unsure where he was. At one time he thought he was back in Jayanti's dungeon; at another he thought he was in that hellish Burmese hut.

I've been in worse positions in the past. Work on. I'll get home to you, Mary, somehow.

As time passed, Jack became weaker. With nobody checking on him or feeding him, he thought he would be left to die of hunger and thirst. He scraped on, making little impression on the links but keeping some hope alive.

When the door eventually opened, Jack blinked in the unexpected light. 'Who's there?' He lifted his hands to shield his eyes.

'You're going to meet the Akhund. He wants you alive.' The older man had returned, bringing a third jailor with him.

'Best take care of me, then.' Jack heard the rasp of his own voice.

'Drink.' The third man, heavily bearded, thrust the end of a leather bottle into Jack's mouth. The water was warm, flavoured with goatskin, and tasted like nectar. Jack gulped it down greedily until the bearded man took the goatskin away.

'Take him outside.'

A bevy of Mujahidin hustled Jack into full daylight, where cold rain washed some of the filth from him. He looked up, blinking, to see a dozen horsemen waiting, their predatory faces glowering at him. One man brought forward a horse.

'I can't ride with these on.' Jack indicated the chains around his ankles.

'You aren't going to ride.'

When two of the Mujahidin grabbed his arms, Jack made a clumsy swing at them with his chained arms. Weak from lack of food, he missed completely. Lifting him bodily, the men threw him face-down over the saddle.

After a few moments, Jack knew he was in for a supremely uncomfortable ride. He only hoped that the Akhund was not too far away. Unable to move with the chains weighing him down, bouncing up and down on the back of a horse, Jack gritted his teeth as cramps hit him. He endured, thinking of Mary. What would she think of him now? He saw himself, the once-proud British officer, chained and helpless across a Pashtun's horse. There was no dignity in this position. There was only pain. Jack drifted into the abyss of agony, only dimly aware what was happening around him. Every part of him screamed for release, yet he refused to make a noise. His captors would love to hear him moan; he would not give them that satisfaction.

Jack did not know how long that ride lasted. He was drifting into unconsciousness when the motion finally ended. The pain continued. He heard men talking, a gruff laugh, then the sound of men at prayer. Twisting his head, he could see his captors on their knees, praying.

If Jack had not been chained, he would have slipped off the horse and tried to run. As it was, he could not move. After a while, the Mujahidin stood up. One approached him, hauling him casually off the horse so he fell in an untidy bundle onto the ground. The man stepped over him as if he was a bale of straw and led the horse away. Somebody kicked him, grabbed his hair, pulled back his head, and shoved a hunk of what tasted like mouldy bread into his mouth.

'Eat, feringhee. The Akhund wants you alive.'

Jack chewed. It was so long since he had eaten that he found it difficult to swallow. Struggling onto his side, he forced himself to sit upright. They were in a bowl of the hills with a rapid river running between bare rocks. Pine trees straggled close by, some sprinkled with slowly falling sleet. Jack closed his eyes; he remembered snow coating the gentle slopes of the Malvern Hills back home. He remembered the square tower of Mathon Church and the squeak of the gate as he entered the hushed graveyard. He recalled the reassuring sound of carols ringing out on the Sunday before Christmas and suddenly felt very homesick. What was he doing in this alien land so far from home?

'Water.' The Pashtun dropped a goatskin bag in Jack's lap and walked away. Jack lifted it clumsily. The water was fresh and cold. He choked, spewed out water, and drank some more, looking around, trying to assess his position. The geography was unfamiliar; the faces less so. He could be anywhere from Kabul to Chitral; somewhere in the north of Pakhtunkhwa to judge by the pine trees. If he was being taken to the Akhund, he might be returning to the Ambela Pass. The thought of being close to British troops was heartening.

Perhaps the idea stimulated Jack's mind, for he heard the crackle of distant musketry. He killed his initial surge of hope that it could be British troops; on this Frontier, it could be any two rival tribal groups fighting among themselves, or even a wedding party celebrating by firing in the air, or at each other. Captivity had sullied Jack's growing liking for the Pashtun.

'Here they come now,' one of the Mujahidin warriors said. He tipped back his skull cap and spat on Jack. 'The Akhund will know how to treat the feringhee.'

'He is a Christian, isn't he?' a young man with a skimpy beard and liquid brown eyes said. 'Maybe the Akhund will order him crucified. I've never seen a crucifixion.'

Jack said nothing, although the horror crept through him. He remembered the mild eyes of the Akhund. Surely that man would not order the torture and death of a British officer? Then Jack remembered that nobody knew where he was or even if he were still alive. To General Chamberlain, he was only another junior officer, one of the hundreds he had seen killed in his career. Jack knew his life or death depended on the humanity of the Akhund.

'That's not the Akhund coming.' The young man reached for his pulwar. 'There's no standard.'

'Maybe he's sent some riders to take the kafir.' The second man gave a wide grin. 'The feringhee would not ride here.'

The Guides, Jack thought. *Kerr has heard about my predicament and has sent a squadron of horse to rescue me.* He looked up as a large troop of horsemen clattered into the Mujahidin's camp. The leader dismounted without hesitation and strode up to Jack.

'I know this man. Give him to me.'

Jack looked up with all his hope quickly draining away. Gulbaz Khan stared down at him with no expression in his vicious eyes.

Chapter Twenty-One

Pakhtunkhwa, November 1863

'You are Captain Jack Baird Windrush.' Gulbaz lifted his hook.

'You are Gulbaz Khan.' Jack tried to show no fear, although he knew his life with Gulbaz was likely to be short and agonising.

Gulbaz's stare did not falter. 'You blew up my watchtower.'

'Your men tried to kill me.'

'It seems that they failed,' Gulbaz said.

'Yes.' There was little else that Jack could say. He saw Gulbaz's men clustering around, some looking curiously at him as they fingered their weapons, others watering the horses or talking to the Mujahidin who had brought him this far.

Jack grunted as one of Gulbaz's followers strode up to him. 'Zaman! So you made your choice.' He injected venom into his words.

'I did, Windrush sahib.' Zaman stood at attention out of pure habit. 'I had a choice to remain with the Guides and have Batoor Khan hand me to the women, or escape and bring Gulbaz an end to his feud with Batoor once and for all.'

'And your oath of allegiance?' Jack could not hide his contempt. 'Do you remember that you took an oath of loyalty to the Guides?'

Zaman grinned. 'You don't understand us yet, Windrush Sahib.'

Gulbaz grunted. 'Take off his chains.'

The Mujahidin guards protested, until Zaman lifted his Khyber knife and killed the first. After that, the Mujahidin obeyed Gulbaz's order. Jack raised his wrists, surprised how light they felt with the shackles off them. He kicked out as the guard unfastened the chains from his ankles. 'Thank you, Gulbaz.' *He must have some trick planned. Keep alert.*

'I would kill you.' Gulbaz touched the hilt of his pulwar. Jack noted with surprise that it was the silver-mounted sword of the Rahmut Khel. 'I am honour-bound by a pledge to your man Zaman.'

Jack grunted. 'What's this all about, Zaman?'

Gulbaz spoke before Zaman could open his mouth. 'Zaman has renounced all claim to be Khan of the Rahmut Khel in return for your freedom.'

Dear God! Zaman did not betray his allegiance. These Pashtuns can always have the capacity to astonish me. Suddenly humble, Jack bowed to Zaman. 'You have my gratitude, Zaman.' It was a new situation for Jack. *Indeed,* he told himself, *it was probably a new situation for any British officer.* Bending, Jack lifted the dead guard's pulwar and jezzail. The sword was well balanced with an ornate handle. The jezzail was of poor quality, but better than nothing.

'The river is there, Windrush Sahib,' Zaman wrinkled his nose. 'Your scent is offending the horses.'

Jack nodded. Unable to wash for the past days, he would stink. 'Thank you, Zaman.'

The river water was so cold that it stung Jack's skin. He emerged, discarded his old clothes, and stripped the dead guard, wondering if he probably had fleas, lice or both. *I don't care. I can deal with that later.*

Gulbaz had been watching, wordless.

'What happens now?' Jack fastened the pulwar around his waist.

'Now we find Batoor Khan.' Gulbaz lifted his metal hook. 'You can ride the horse that carried you, Windrush. If you endanger my men or fail to keep up, I will have you killed.'

Grabbing a stale loaf from the baggage of the dead man, Jack adjusted the saddle and mounted his horse. Surrounded by men who would kill him in a heartbeat, riding through a hostile country without any idea what he was doing or where he was going, Jack felt helpless. Only Gulbaz's honour and his word to Zaman kept him alive.

'What's happening, Zaman?'

'Gulbaz is going to find Batoor,' Zaman said quietly. 'When Batoor took his followers to join the Mujahidin, Gulbaz chased us out of Torkrud, as you know.'

Jack nodded.

'We lost him in the hills, so Gulbaz returned to Torkrud and called for a Jirga of the Rahmut Khel. He showed them the message he got from the Akhund of Swat, the one we intercepted when we first came here.'

'I remember,' Jack said.

'Gulbaz told them that he had rejected the jihad and questioned if Batoor Khan should lead the Rahmut Khel. The Jirga decided that the Rahmut Khel should not join Akhund's Jihad, although individuals could do so if they wished. They removed Batoor from his position.' Zaman dropped his voice to a whisper as one of the Rahmut Khel inched suspiciously closer. 'Or rather Gulbaz persuaded the elders he was the better man.'

Jack tried to grasp the tangled skein of Pashtu politics, where religion and Pakhtunwali struggled for supremacy. 'I see. How did you know where Gulbaz would be?'

'I didn't,' Zaman admitted. 'When I left Tazhak I rode to Torkrud to see what I could do.'

There is so much left out there, so much I will never know. 'You gave up your hope of being Khan for me.'

Zaman grinned. 'I've not given up anything yet, sahib. Gulbaz is temporarily using my sword. The future is unwritten.'

'The future depends on Allah's will and the hands of the Pashtun,' Jack murmured. He felt rather than saw Zaman's sideways look.

'That is so, sahib.'

Jack jerked his head up as Gulbaz lifted his hook. 'What's happening?' The Rahmat Khel slowed down as more riders erupted from the pine trees on the slopes above. The men galloped down towards them with swords and rifles raised, yelling and firing.

Zaman stopped Jack from reaching for his sword. 'It's all right, sahib. These are also the Rahmat Khel.'

Jack estimated a hundred warriors were charging down the hill. 'I thought that Batoor took the bulk of the fighting men with him.'

'No, sahib.' Zaman shook his head. 'Batoor only brought the men of Torkrud who followed him. Gulbaz has raised men from all the lands of the Rahmat Khel.'

'I hope they all know that we are on their side,' Jack said.

'You are a guest of the Khan,' Zaman reminded him.

'Now we will remove Batoor, the man who claims to be Khan,' Gulbaz shouted. 'Come with me, men of the Rahmat Khel!'

Carried along with the Rahmut Khel, Jack could do nothing except ride. The Mujahidin had defeated his Guides; he had failed in his mission. He was only alive because of Zaman's selfless act and the Pashtun code of honour. Fighting away the wave of self-pity, Jack lifted his chin. *I am still alive, damn it. I am still a British officer. All is not lost. Fight on!*

'We're in the Chamla Valley,' Zaman said. 'The caravan is ahead.'

Peering through the dust haze raised by the Rahmat Khel, Jack nodded. 'I see them.'

'Batoor must be a hard taskmaster to push them so hard.' Jack heard respect in Zaman's voice. 'Camels are slow animals.' The caravan was at the inner lip of the Ambela Pass, within a couple of miles of the scattered Bunerwal position. From where he stood, Jack could see the Akhund's standard flying proud on its ridge, a host of supporting standards on either side. The head of the caravan was on the final rise leading to the pass, each camel toiling under its load, while the escort looked casual, not expecting any trouble so close to the Akhund's army.

'Oh, Batoor.' Jack shook his head. 'I thought you were better than that.' He felt a lift of hope. Even the best of the Pashtuns could make mistakes.

Gulbaz did not waste any time. Forming his riders into a rough vee formation with Jack near the tail, Gulbaz gave brief instructions. 'Come on, Rahmut Khel, follow me, get rid of the false Khan, and take these Enfields for ourselves.' Folding the reins around his hook, Gulbaz headed straight for the caravan. Still weak, Jack sat his horse with difficulty, unsure how he should act when he met Batoor. *Is he an enemy or a friend? I do not know.*

The caravan escort looked stunned as Gulbaz's cavalry appeared over the ridge. While some of the guards tried to wave, others realised their danger and drew their swords. Jack noted with some satisfaction that his Guides were among the latter. Only when he was about ten yards from the caravan did Jack shake off his intense weariness.

'Guides!' Jack croaked the name. 'To me, Guides!' At last, drawing his pulwar, he slashed at the nearest of the Mujahidin. The man parried Jack's weak blow and stared open-mouthed in complete incomprehension. 'To me, Guides!'

This situation was the ultimate test of the Guides' loyalty when their officer was virtually helpless beside them and three rival forces competed for their swords. Would they follow Batoor and the Akhund, would they choose to fight for Gulbaz in his private war with Batoor, or would they return to their salt? If they chose either of the first two options, Jack knew that his life was precarious, at best.

'To me, Guides!'

'Captain Windrush!' Hassan pulled toward Jack. 'It's Captain Windrush!'

Sawan and Ursulla were next, with the other Guides rallying as the news spread.

'Shabash, Windrush Sahib!' Alladad shouted, waving his pulwar. 'Shabash the Guides!'

As Gulbaz's Rahmut Khel crashed into the escort in a welter of bodies, slashing swords and yelling, bearded faces, Jack gave rapid orders to his men. 'Scatter the camels! Drive them towards the British lines.' Levelling his jezzail, Jack fired it at one of the Mujahidin escorts. The noise was deafening, the kick nearly unhorsing him. He had no idea where the shot went, except it did not hit his target.

It was a three-way battle with nobody sure who the enemy was. Jack slashed sideways at one of the escorts, roared at a camel driver, who fled in terror, and smacked the flat of his sword against a camel's rump to make it increase its speed. With the Mujahidin more intent on facing Gulbaz's warriors than tending to their caravan, Jack's Guides could concentrate on the camels.

'Come on, Guides!' Jack encouraged. 'Herd the camels!' He looked for Batoor in the mass, dodged a riderless horse, cut loose the reins of a camel, and kicked out at another.

One by one, the camels began to break their formation and lope forward, grouping together as they covered the ground. A steel-helmeted tribesman pushed his horse in front of the group until Sawan shot his horse. The man fell, screaming as the now panicking camels trampled him underfoot on their mad dash onwards.

'Drive the camels; forget the rest!' Jack ordered. The two factions of the Rahmut Khel were fighting, the Mujahidin supporting Batoor or standing aside to watch. Jack left them to it; his duty lay with the camel caravan. Batoor and Gulbaz were no longer relevant.

'Come on, Guides! Drive them to the camp!' Jack could see British soldiers lining the sangars, their forage caps and puggarees bobbing as they tried to make sense of this new force galloping toward them.

'Hold your fire!' Jack roared, knowing the thunder of feet and the noise from the battle would drown out his words. 'We're the Guides!'

'Fire!' Somebody shouted. The 101st Foot greeted Jack's onrushing camels with a spatter of musketry. The forward piquets in their circular sangars fell back, thinking they were under attack, with support coming from the main wall until a hirsute major roared an order.

'Stand fast, damn you! It's only a bunch of camels. Shoot the damned Pathans.'

'You leave the damned Pathans alone,' Jack shouted. 'We are the Guides!'

'What?' The major mounted the wall, waving his hand in front of him in a futile attempt to clear the dust. 'Cease firing!'

'Bring the camels in,' Jack ordered as lack of food caught up with him and he collapsed on the British side of the wall. 'They're carrying rifles.'

Ten of the camels had died in the crazed rush to the British lines. The Guides rounded up the remainder, bringing them to Jack as if to apologise for their earlier defection.

'Here are your camels, sahib,' Alladad said.

The 101st watched, some with amusement, others alarm, as if they would have to dispose of these unruly beasts.

For the first time, Jack had the opportunity of counting his men. Of the original twenty he had taken out, he had lost Fatteh and five of the new men. Two of the fourteen who remained had been wounded.

Jack glanced beyond the wall. The battle between Batoor and Gulbaz had ended, leaving a score of casualties on the ground. Jack could not tell which faction had been the victor. At that second he did not care.

'I've sent a runner to the general,' the hirsute major said. 'Windrush, isn't it?'

'Yes, sir.'

'You'd better get yourself and your badmashes cleaned up. You look like a bunch of scallywags rather than soldiers of the queen. My men nearly shot you flat.'

'We are the Guides,' Jack retorted. 'We don't need to dress in scarlet to look like soldiers. We are soldiers.'

The major gave a small nod. 'Windrush, eh? I'll remember that name.' Turning on his heel, he stalked away.

More trouble in the future, Jack thought. *That can wait. I have things to sort out here first.*

'Before we go any further,' Jack glared at his men, 'you had better decide where your loyalties lie.' He spoke Pushtu, guessing that few, if any, of the watching 101st spoke that language. 'You deserted your salt in Tazhak.'

'We did not, sahib. We are Guides.' Hassan seemed more puzzled than hurt.

'You joined the Mujahidin,' Jack said flatly.

Hassan raised his hands to still the Guides protests. 'Captain Windrush, what would you have us do? By pretending to join the Mujahidin, we saved our lives so we could return to our duty.' The other Guides nodded.

That was plausible. But was it true? Jack pondered. He wanted to believe these men. He had ridden and fought beside them; he had trusted them with his life, and they had not let him down until Tazhak. He had already heard Zaman's story and seen the proof with the arrival of Gulbaz with the sword of the Rahmat Khel.

Jack took a deep breath. Were these men lying to him? Was there a cultural difference that he did not understand, or was he being too hard on them because of his lingering distrust of sepoys since the Mutiny? These Guides had certainly rallied to him in the skirmish around the camels, and Zaman had probably saved his life with his agreement with Gulbaz.

'All right.' Jack counted his men. 'Including me, we have thirteen fit men. I don't know how many of us died in Tazhak, but I believe that we have left some behind as prisoners.' He nodded grimly. 'That will be the men who did not join the Mujahidin. I don't like leaving men behind. We're not finished with Tazhak yet.' He turned and walked away.

'Where are you going, sahib?' Hassan asked.

'I am going to report to the general,' Jack said. 'And if he agrees, we are going back. We failed in our mission. I dislike failure.'

* * *

Chamberlain listened to Jack's story, scribbling the occasional note on a pad of thick paper. 'How well do you know this fellow Batoor Khan?'

'I thought I knew him very well, sir. We fought side by side in the Mutiny. He was the Khan of Torkrud before he joined the Akhund of Swat. Until this last incident, I would have trusted him with my life.'

'Religious fervour is a terrible thing,' Chamberlain said. 'Whatever religion it is.'

'Yes, sir. Can I have permission to return to Tazhak, sir? I'll take a larger force this time.'

'You brought back the Enfields, Windrush.'

'Yes, sir, but I did not destroy the workshops, and I left some of my men behind.'

'They'll be dead by now,' Chamberlain said. 'If they are lucky.'

'I'd like to see for myself, sir.'

When Chamberlain looked up, his eyes were dark with compassion. 'I understand your concern for your men, Windrush, but we are under siege by thousands of Pashtun warriors here. Why should I send you again to try what you already failed to do?'

Jack lifted his chin. 'I don't like failure, sir. I want to redeem myself and try to rescue my men.'

Chamberlain sighed, stood up and paced the interior of the tent. 'You are a bit of a loose cannon, Windrush. I don't know what to make of you. Your men like you, but Colonel Snodgrass of the 113th got shot of you, and only an hour ago another officer complained about your attitude to him. Perhaps you are not officer material.' He stopped. 'I knew your father when he was out here. He was a good man.'

'I hardly met him, sir.' Jack saw any hopes of career advancement sliding away. He was destined to remain a captain for the remainder of his life.

'No?' Chamberlain shook his head. 'That's a pity, Windrush. You could have learned a lot from him.' He sat down again. 'All right, Windrush. You may have another opportunity to do what you failed to do the first time.' When he looked up, Chamberlain looked very old. 'I am doing this for your father's memory and for the sake of these poor men who may still be in Pashtun captivity.'

'Thank you, sir.'

'Get your men together,' Chamberlain ordered. 'Get rested and re-equipped, then wait for my command. Don't let me down.' He mused for a moment. 'I won't tell you not to let your men down, Windrush. That is one thing of which you are not guilty.'

Was that back-handed praise? Unfortunately, the opinion of rankers did not win an officer promotion.

Chapter Twenty-Two

Ambela Pass 20th November 1863

The runner arrived at Jack's side. 'The general wants you, Captain Windrush.' He was gone before Jack could reply.

Leaving his position behind the 1st Punjabi's ranks, Jack strode to the mound on which General Chamberlain stood. 'You sent for me, sir?'

Ignoring the odd bullet that whistled past, Chamberlain scanned the entire perimeter before he replied. 'Since we moved our camp to the south side of the pass two days ago, the tribesmen have attacked with even greater ferocity, but our men will hold them.'

'Yes, sir,' Jack agreed. From Chamberlain's knoll, he could see the ebb and flow of battle, with long clouds of grey-white smoke where the defenders were firing volleys in response to the massed charges of the Bunerwals and their Mujahidin allies.

'We expect reinforcements any day; the 7th Fusiliers, 93rd Highlanders, 3rd Sikhs, and 23rd pioneers; all good fighting men. How many of my Guides Cavalry are you taking?'

'Thirty, sir.'

'More than last time.' Chamberlain nodded. 'How long will it be before they are ready?'

'My men are waiting for your word, sir.'

'You have it. Take them out the moment this present attack wanes.' Chamberlain turned to a runner, giving him explicit orders to carry to the left flank.

'Yes, sir.' Fighting his lift of elation, Jack called together his Guides. Deliberately parading them inside the British camp, he walked along their ranks.

'All right, Guides. Conditions out here may be different to anywhere else, but the basics remain the same. There is us, the Army, the Guides, and there is the enemy. We stay together, fight together and support each other. Rank, race, religion is secondary to our bond within the regiment.'

The firing was increasing. Jack knew he would have to lead his men out soon after the defenders had repelled the attack. With Chamberlain in command, watching everything, the Bunerwals and Mujahidin would never overrun the British positions. Chamberlain might look old, but his mind was acute, and his military intellect as sharp as the point of a rapier.

'We're going back to Tazhak. Make sure you are ready.' Jack ignored a stray shot that whined overhead. 'I'm taking a chance on you all. Don't let me down. Regain your nang. Rescue our colleagues.'

Jack could feel the hurt from the Guides. He had insulted them in the worst possible way by hinting they were dishonourable. They could react by killing him once they were clear of the British camp, or they could attempt to prove him wrong. He did not yet understand the Pashtuns well enough to know which avenue they would choose.

The firing increased, volley after volley crashing out.

'Cease fire!' That was Sinclair's voice. 'They're on the run!'

'Sir!' A breathless Cornet Cheshire nearly tugged at Jack's sleeve. 'General Chamberlain's orders, sir, and could you ride out directly.'

'Thank you, Cornet. You delivered that message very well.' Jack added a wink to his words. There was no harm in being friendly to this youngster now that he had learned how to deliver a message.

'Mount up, Guides.' Jack kept his voice deliberately hard. 'Follow me.'

Leading from the front, Jack rode out of the British camp. He ignored the spatter of musketry; there were sufficient British, Gurkha and Sikh soldiers to take care of any number of tribesmen. Having seen them in action, Jack now had no doubts about the loyalty or fighting prowess of the Sikhs or Gurkhas. It was only his Guides, the elite, he questioned. Well then, he would give them a chance to prove themselves.

With Sharbat sturdy underneath him, Jack increased his speed from a walk to a trot.

'The men are faithful, sahib.' Hassan rode beside him, his face concerned.

'We'll see, daffadar.' Jack had not forgotten the time that Hassan had rescued him on the ridge when Gulbaz's men were pressing hard. 'I hope that you are right.'

'You insulted their honour.' Hassan did not give up. 'My honour, too.'

Jack did not immediately reply. He remembered too well the carnage at Gondabad when the sepoys mutinied. He recalled the horror of the well at Cawnpore where the mutineers thrust the mutilated bodies of the murdered women and children of the British garrison. He could never forget such things; the actions of the Guides at Tazhak had not been a hundredth as bad, yet they had awakened that niggle of distrust.

'Keep up with me,' Jack snarled.

Riding hard, they pushed through the retreating Mujahidin and Bunerwals and ignored any shouted challenges. Jack watched his men as they passed the Akhund's banner, flying from the summit of its ridge, the green fabric now tattered and stained with powder smoke. He was glad to see his Guides barely glanced at it as they passed out of the valley, and into the semi-wooded hills beyond.

That's one test passed. Well done, lads.

Twice marksmen fired at them, the shots going nowhere. The wind was keen now, biting into them as a harbinger of the bitter winter to come. Jack pulled his poshteen closer, hauled his pakol over his forehead, and spurred on. After his previous visits to Tazhak, he knew the way as well as any of his Guides.

They camped at night, lighting a small fire close to one of the many rivers, and moving a quarter of a mile away to sleep. On this Frontier, only a fool would advertise where they camped.

'Sahib,' Hassan said. 'The men are unhappy.'

'Are they indeed?' Jack was in no mood to pander to the *nang i pukhtana*, the honour of the Pashtun. He listened to the rush of the river and the distant howl of a wolf. He also fought a gnawing headache.

'They wish me to speak for them.'

'Then speak, Hassan.' Jack spoke shortly. With his head pounding and sweat soaking his clothes, he found it hard to concentrate.

'They want you to know that they were always faithful.'

'Thank you, Hassan.'

The next day Jack would lead these men back to Tazhak, where his missing men may be held captive, or they could be dead. The men of Tazhak might expect his arrival; if Batoor had survived the battle with Gulbaz Khan, then he would undoubtedly expect Jack to return. There could be a great deal of tough fighting ahead. He could not fight with men he did not trust. Jack closed his eyes; he had to forget the Mutiny. These men had not been involved in that old war. Their behaviour at Tazhak had been unusual from a British perspective, but perhaps not from a Pashtun point of view.

I have no choice; I must put aside my distrust. If I am wrong, well, death is a soldier's lot. Fight this feeling of lethargy.

Sighing, Jack stepped over to the Guides. They sat in a circle with their eyes the only mobile things in the dim. Jack squatted among them.

'Right, gentlemen,' he said quietly, very aware that his voice could carry far in the night. 'I have already said my piece about disloyalty. I will not repeat my words.'

'Do you no longer trust us, Windrush sahib?' Hassan asked the direct question.

In answer Jack unbuckled his sword belt, handing the weapon to Hassan. He took the revolver from its holster next to his skin and placed it on the ground at Zaman's feet. 'I am now unarmed,' he said. 'I am standing without a weapon in the midst of the biggest collection of rogues and badmashes between Kabul and the Khyber.'

Some of the Guides smiled at that, as Jack had intended.

'If I did not trust you, would I do such a foolish thing?'

The gesture appealed to the Pashtuns' sense of drama. Zaman was first to laugh, with the others following soon after.

'All right then. Now we have to destroy the gunsmiths of Tazhak,' Jack said. 'More importantly, we have to rescue any Guides still in the village.'

'They will be dead,' Hassan said. Jakub, the second daffadar that Jack had brought, nodded his agreement.

'They might be. We won't know until we get there. If we rest for three hours now, we should reach Tazhak just before dawn.' Jack took a deep breath. 'I want every workshop destroyed and every Enfield copy located.'

'Shall we kill the gunsmiths too, sahib?' Zaman asked the question that Jack most wanted to avoid.

'No.' Remembering the elderly men and their sons who made the guns in the first workshop he had visited, Jack shook his head. Even though he was aware the smiths were every bit as dangerous to the British as warriors were, he could not condone killing civilians.

'They will merely set up shop elsewhere.' Hassan was always the pragmatist.

'I know.' Jack remembered the aftermath of the Mutiny when furious British soldiers had hanged anybody who might have been a mutineer. Hundreds of innocent men had died in that orgy of vengeance. Jack swore he would never be guilty of such practices. 'Destroy all their tools and equipment.' It was not a perfect solution but the best that Jack could devise… 'If there are any warriors…'

'There will be few warriors,' Hassan said. 'The mullahs have swept the Kot Valley clear for the jihad.'

Jack nodded. He had noticed the lack of men in the valley. The Akhund and his mullahs were gathering everybody they could to defeat Chamberlain. 'Shoot only if you have to. Try and take the craftsmen alive.'

Tazhak was in darkness. Even knowing where the village was, Jack could hardly make out the walls against the dark of the overcast night. He knew his Guides were behind him, watching from the same bowl in the hills that they had occupied on their previous visit.

'You know what to do,' Jack said. 'We belong to God, and unto God we do return.'

'Yes, sahib.' Hassan spoke for the Guides.

With the horse's hooves and all loose equipment muffled, Jack led them slowly downhill. He had no idea of knowing how large the garrison was or if the Mujahidin had set another trap. He only knew he had to succeed.

As the gate was on the eastern side of the village, the sentinels on the watchtower would face into the rising sun, giving Jack's men a slight advantage. 'Halt.' He spoke in a whisper. 'Zaman, Alladad: Kill the sentries, and open the gate.'

Without a word, the two Guides dismounted and moved toward the village. Jack felt his tension mount, knowing that he had sent the two men best suited for the task, fighting his guilt at not accompanying them. Commanding men was never easy; sending men into danger while one waited in comparative safety was harder than advancing into enemy fire.

'Sahib.' Alladad's voice was soft at Sharbat's shoulder. 'The sentries are gone, and the gate is open.'

'Well done, Alladad. Mount up.' Jack walked on with the Guides a few steps behind. Sharbat stepped delicately over the body of one guard just within the doorway. Zaman stood casually a few paces deeper into the village.

'There were three guards,' Zaman said.

'Well done, Zaman.' Already the light was increasing, making Jack's job slightly easier. 'You four.' He pointed to Jakub and four Guides. 'Take over the watchtower and gate. Don't let anybody in or out.'

Jakub nodded. 'Yes, sahib.'

'Shut and bar the gate.' On their previous visit, Jack's men were trapped when the Mujahidin slammed the gate on them. Now that he controlled the entrance, he had a secure escape route.

'Sahib.' Hassan touched his arm. 'Up there. Fatteh is watching us.'

'What?' Jack's surge of hope ended when he looked up. Fatteh's head adorned the top of a stake, staring out of empty eye sockets, his genitals thrust into his mouth. At his side were the heads of the other Guides that Jack had hoped to rescue. The Mujahidin had treated them all in the same manner.

'Bastards,' Jack said. 'The dirty, murdering, torturing bastards.' He tried to fight the anger that sought to take over from his rational mind. 'Destroy this place,' he said. 'Tear it to the ground.'

'Hassan, take fifteen men to the far side of the village, evict the gunsmiths, and destroy the workshops. If anybody shows fight, shoot them.'

'Yes, sahib.' Hassan understood Jack's anger.

'You have three minutes to reach the far side, and we'll start at this end.' Those three minutes seemed to stretch to eternity before Jack gave the order to start work. By then the light had strengthened so he could see what he was doing.

'Two men to each workshop,' Jack ordered. 'Bring the people out, break all the equipment, and burn the place down.' He did not need to give any more orders. The Guides were naturals, zestfully kicking the doors down before thrusting into the workshops, smashing up all the tools, and throwing any gunsmiths who lived there into the street, where Jack had five men waiting to keep them under control. The occasional gunshot showed that some of the smiths resisted. Jack grunted; he could trust his Guides to deal with them.

The prisoners were restive, protesting to their captors, waving their hands in the air as they saw their livelihoods destroyed before their eyes.

'Who killed these men?' Jack asked, pointing to the heads of Fatteh and his companions. 'Who murdered my men?'

Shocked at the destruction of their homes and businesses, the men gave the same response. 'The mullah ordered it.'

'Which mullah?' Jack already guessed the answer.

'The mullah with the drum.'

The tabla mullah. The man I have already killed twice. That man is the epitome of evil. I must hunt him down. My mission is not complete as long as that murderer is loose.

The explosion took Jack by surprise. He looked up as one of the workshops at the far end of the village blew up, coiling smoke into the sky. 'What the devil has happened?'

Gunpowder! Each of the workshops would have a supply of gunpowder. A second explosion followed the first, and then a third as the flames spread from building to building. By now the entire village was awake, with crowds of men running back and forward, unsure in which direction to run.

'Gather the gunsmiths,' Jack shouted. 'Get all the others out of the village.' He gave rapid orders that saw his Guides clearing the streets as workshop after workshop exploded in a welter of fire and fury. He had not intended to blow Tazhak up; the destruction was far more significant than he expected. *There will be no more guns made in this village. That is fitting for the murder of Fatteh. Sleep easy, my friend. I have extracted badal for your murder. I will extract more.*

'Get out, lads!' Jack shouted. 'Leave the village.' He waited, counting his men out one by one. Some carried loot in the shape of rifles or food. He said nothing. Looting had been the perquisite of soldiers since time began. No doubt the men who followed Darius of Persia or Alexander the Great had scoured this very valley. *The people of Tazhak watched while the tabla mullah murdered Fatteh; they deserve no pity.*

'That's us.' Jack counted the last of his men. He had brought thirty in, and he would bring thirty out. That was a success. Now there was only that blasted indestructible mullah. Jack swayed, holding a hand to his thumping head. 'Zaman!'

'Yes, sahib.' Zaman was smoke-blackened but smiling.

'That mullah is not here. One of these men will know where.'

'The mullah that had Fatteh killed?' Zaman nodded. 'I will find out, sahib.'

'Daffadar!' Jack roared. Hassan and Jakub appeared.

'I want you to check the prisoners. Hold the master gunsmiths, but let the apprentices go.'

'Yes, sahib,' Jakub said.

'Why, sahib?' Hassan had served with Jack long enough to ask questions.

'You will be taking the master gunsmiths to General Chamberlain,' Jack said. 'He can decide what to do with them. I have other business to attend to.'

Hassan gave Jack a sidelong look. 'You are going after the mullah who killed Fatteh.'

'I am,' Jack said. 'I am leaving the Guides in the hands of one of the most capable NCOs I have ever met.' Jack did not often give praise. He thought this was an excellent time to break his habit.

'You do not know Pakhtunkhwa as we do,' Hassan said. 'You will die on your own.'

'That is my choice.' Jack gave a twisted smile. 'It is Allah's will if I live or die.'

Hassan looked away. 'That is true.'

'Windrush Sahib.' Zaman marched over, smiling. 'The very first man I spoke to was accommodating.'

'What did he tell you, Zaman?'

'The mullah has his headquarters in a cave near the Chamla Valley.' Zaman cleaned blood from the blade of his pesh-kabz knife. 'The cave is at the Jaromgar waterfall.'

'Chamla?' Jack tried to order his chaotic thoughts. 'That's in Bunerwal territory.'

'It is the heart of Bunerwal territory,' Hassan confirmed. 'You will never get in alone, sahib.'

'I can only try.' Jack knew that his smile was crooked. 'I want badal for Fatteh.'

'You are not Pashtun,' Hassan said.

'Fatteh was Pashtun, and he was one of my men,' Jack said. *I wonder if I should try a silver bullet to kill the tabla mullah, as Rougvie had suggested. Nothing else seems to work. The Tabla Mullah's wounds even miraculously heal.*

'How about the prisoners, sahib?'

'We will bring them to Chamberlain sahib,' Jack said. He could accompany the Guides as far as he could before striking off alone. 'He can decide what to do with the master gunsmiths. I am sure he will find jobs for such skilled men in the armoury.'

Taking a deep breath to combat his growing dizziness, Jack kicked in his heels, with Sharbat responding willingly. Leaning forward, Jack caressed the horse's ears. 'Well done, thy good and faithful servant. You can rest soon. When we get back to Mardan, you will get a long rest.'

'Somebody is following us,' Hassan said.

'I know.' Jack had been aware of the small body of horsemen ever since they left Tazhak. 'Let them follow.' Out here on the Frontier, he expected nothing less.

Chapter Twenty-Three

Ambela Valley December 1863

'This is where we part company,' Jack said. They stood at the head of the Ambela Valley with the British encampment in the far distance, hazed by powder smoke. The intermittent rattle of musketry informed Jack that the siege continued. 'You are as capable as I am of taking the men in, Hassan.'

'That is so, sahib,' Hassan agreed.

'Then do so,' Jack said. 'Pray convey my respects to Major Kerr, and tell him that I will join him at my earliest convenience. No, hang it all, I'll write this down.'

Finding a scrap of paper, Jack wrote that he had ordered Hassan to bring the men home while he pursued the Tabla Mullah, who he considered too much of a threat to India to leave alive.

'Thank you, sahib.' Hassan held the scrap of paper as if it were gold dust. 'I will ensure this reaches Major Kerr.'

'I know you will, Hassan.' Jack returned Hassan's precise salute. *Hassan does not expect to see me alive again.* Turning Sharbat, Jack checked he had ammunition and caps for his Enfield rifle and touched the revolver inside his poshteen and the pulwar at his waist. He was as prepared as circumstances permitted.

All right, tabla mullah. I've seen you shot at least three times before. If bullets cannot hurt you, I will cut off your blasted head. You murdered my men. Swaying slightly in the saddle, Jack allowed the sure-footed Sharbat to pick her own way along the rough terrain. He did not know where he was going; he only knew that the Chamla Valley was over the ridge on which he rode and that the Tabla Mullah lived in a cave in a small valley near the Jaromgar waterfall.

Ridge followed ridge, with a keen wind biting at Jack's face. He shivered, delving into his poshteen.

I will exact badal on this mullah. Jack repeated the words as Sharbat plodded on, upwards to the summit of the ridge and over to the opposite side. *I will extract badal on this mullah.* Jack swayed again. *What the devil is wrong with me? I am a British officer; I cannot give in to weakness.* He halted there, overlooking a broad valley with the path stretching before him, a huge drop below, and copses of pines scattered all around.

'Sahib.' The voice came as from a fog. 'Sahib.'

Zaman caught Jack before he fell. 'Sahib.'

'Zaman?' Jack peered into Zaman's face. 'What are you doing here?'

'You are not going alone into the Chamla valley, sahib.' Zaman looked concerned.

'I ordered you to take the prisoners to General Chamberlain.' Even saying these few words was exhausting.

'Yes, sahib,' Zaman said. 'You have a fever. You must rest.'

'Damned if I will,' Jack said. *I won't give in to fever!* 'Do you know this cave, Zaman?'

'I know a cave near the Jaromgar waterfall,' Zaman said.

'Take me,' Jack ordered. 'Take me quickly before this damned fever takes full control.'

'Can you keep up?' Zaman sounded genuinely concerned.

'Take me, damn it.'

'You are not well…'

The rider galloped from the shelter of a group of trees, long sword raised in his left hand, yelling. With the fever dulling his reactions, Jack barely registered the man before Zaman pushed Sharbat away.

'Gulbaz!' Zaman reined his horse to one side, drawing his pulwar in the same movement. The blades clashed, held, and parted as Gulbaz spurred on. Zaman laughed. 'I wondered who was following us!'

'I'll kill you,' Gulbaz roared, 'and then the feringhee.'

'We were allies once,' Zaman reminded him.

'Of necessity, not choice!' Gulbaz attacked again, riding his horse directly at Zaman, who waited until the two animals were nearly touching before jinking aside in a display of horsemanship as neat as any Jack had ever seen.

Swearing, Gulbaz clattered by, the hooves of his horse kicking loose stones from the path into the fearful abyss below.

Drawing his pistol, Jack aimed at Gulbaz until Zaman shouted, 'No, sahib! This is about honour. The best warrior will win.'

Lowering his pistol, Jack nodded. It was the Pashtun equivalent of a duel, man against man. He understood, although he had not expected such chivalry on the Frontier.

Turning on the very edge of the precipice, Gulbaz sheathed his sword, lifted an old-fashioned single-barrel pistol, and fired. The bullet crashed into Zaman's horse, sending it staggering. As Gulbaz quickly dropped the pistol and drew his sword, Zaman leapt agilely from the stricken horse, landed on his feet, and parried Gulbaz's slash.

Again Gulbaz trotted past, but this time Zaman followed. As Gulbaz turned, Zaman leapt on the back of his horse, thrust his sword into Gulbaz's side, twisted the blade, withdrew, and jumped back down. Gulbaz turned, his eyes wide.

'Zaman Khan of the Rahman Khel,' he said. Wordless, Zaman thrust his sword through Gulbaz's chest.

'Now I am Khan.' Lifting the silver-hilted sword of the Rahman Khel, Zaman removed the scabbard from the body of Gulbaz and attached it to his belt. 'I will take better care of this than the previous two owners.' Tipping Gulbaz's body over the edge of the ravine, he adjusted the stirrups of Gulbaz's horse and mounted. It had taken less than two minutes for the Rahmat Khel to lose and gain a khan.

'Are you still fit to continue, Windrush Sahib?'

'I am still fit,' Jack said.

'Then let's find this mullah.'

Jack nodded, barely able to sit his horse, let alone register all that was happening. He allowed Zaman to lead him down the dizzying slope into a surprisingly fertile valley.

'Where are we?'

'In the Chamla Valley, the heart of Buner.' Zaman looked around. 'Normally this place would be filled with people and animals. As you see, it is empty. The men are either fighting Chamberlain Sahib or are already dead.'

'So much the better for us.' Jack fought waves of dizziness. 'How far is this waterfall, Zaman?'

'About an hour's journey,' Zaman said. 'Can you manage that?'

'Take me.'

Jack gripped the reins tightly, fighting to stay in the saddle as Zaman led him through the most fertile valley he had yet seen in Pakhtunkhwa. Around them, snow-smeared mountains soared above the line of dense pine trees, reminding Jack of pictures he had seen of Switzerland. Perhaps the tabla mullah had discovered his paradise while still alive.

'Sahib.' Zaman put out a hand to prevent Jack from falling. 'We are nearly there, sahib. It would be better if I met this man.'

Jack shook his head. 'No, Zaman. I must do this. It is my duty. I must get badal for Fattah.'

Zaman looked at him sideways. 'This way, sahib.'

Jack heard the rush of the waterfall before they crossed the spur of a hill to a dell that would have delighted the most demanding of Romantic artists. A thread of water eased over a rocky ledge to plummet toward a small pool, from where it overflowed into a dramatic drop of some hundred feet into a turquoise lake. Even Zaman stopped to appreciate the beauty.

'This is the Jaromgar Waterfall,' Zaman said.

'Where is the cave? Where is the tabla mullah?' Jack felt for the hilt of his pulwar. 'Show me.' He felt his strength draining minute by minute. He had to act quickly before he was too weak. 'Take me to him, Zaman.'

'Down here, sahib.' The track was pencil thin as it spiralled down the side of a grass-and-scrub slope towards the lake.

'Come on, Sharbat.' Jack allowed the horse to take control, concentrating on remaining in the saddle. The further down the slope they rode, the more the noise of the waterfall dominated until all he could hear was the hammer of falling water. In his head, the sound altered to the rolling of the Tabla drum, so the two sounds became indistinguishable.

The mullah belonged to this place; perhaps both his holiness and his drumming came from the waterfall? Jack shook his head. *No. That was the fever talking. Keep rational, Jack; fight this thing.*

'Over here, sahib.' Zaman dismounted.

'I can't see a cave.' Jack nearly fell from the saddle. He recovered, took hold of the hilt of his sword, and looked around.

'The spray from the waterfall hides it.' Zaman stepped forward. 'Look.' He pointed to a group of Kabul ponies standing under an overhang of rock. 'This way, sahib.'

The entrance was little more than one man wide with a muddy puddle underfoot. Jack blinked into the darkness, trying to ignore the sickeningly familiar stench as he entered. Handing his rifle to Zaman, he drew his pulwar. 'Bullets don't work with this mullah,' he muttered. 'Unless they are made of silver.'

Zaman also drew his sword. 'May Allah guide our steps.' His voice trembled. 'We belong to God, and unto God we do return.'

Jack stumbled over the uneven surface. 'I am Captain Jack Baird Windrush of the Guides!' The echo of his voice mocked him. 'Show yourself, if you are here.'

'I should go ahead, sahib.' Zaman's voice was weaker than Jack had ever heard.

'No, Zaman.' Jack pushed on, nearly gagging at the stink of death. 'What is happening in here?'

'There's light ahead,' Zaman said. 'And the smell of smoke.'

'I see it,' Jack said. 'Somebody has lit a fire.'

The light diffused from a crack high in the roof of the cave, spreading out as the cave itself widened into a cavern. Jack stopped. In front of him, the tabla mullah sat beside a small fire that was as smoky as his eyes as he looked up.

'Salaam Alaikum, Captain Windrush.' He remained sitting.

'You murdered my men,' Jack said.

The mullah stood up. Stark naked, snakes of lank hair coiled past his shoulders. 'Everything is the will of Allah.'

'You had him murdered.' Jack's sword felt so heavy he had difficulty in lifting it. Swaying, he tried to thrust, slipped, and crumpled to the ground. He lay still for a moment, gathering his strength to push himself to his feet.

'You cannot kill me,' the mullah said. 'Allah has blessed me. Your bullets cannot hurt me; your blade will not part my flesh.'

'Mine will.' Lifting the sword of the Rahmat Khel, Zaman sliced sideways, taking the Mullah's head clean from his shoulders. 'That was for Fatteh,' he said. The firelight gleamed from the sword's silver hilt.

Jack pushed himself upright. 'He might come back to life. He's already been killed twice and wounded once.'

'No.' Zaman shook his head. 'That is impossible. Only the Yusufzai would believe that.' Lifting a brand from the fire, he stepped into the darker recesses of the cavern. 'Here, sahib. Here is your answer.'

Using his sword as a makeshift walking stick, Jack followed.

'Here, sahib.' When Zaman lifted the burning brand higher, the light showed three bodies lying on the floor of the cave. Each man was identical, a copy of the Tabla Mullah. One had been shot in the head, one in the chest, and the third in the leg. The stink from the rotting bodies was appalling.

'Quadruplets,' Jack said. 'I did kill them after all.'

'Yes, sahib. That was how this mullah could appear after you killed him. There were four of them, each identical.'

Jack nodded. 'Let's get back to the camp, Zaman. I can do no more here.'

There had been no need for a silver bullet. The tabla mullahs had been mortal, like everybody else. Jack sat astride Sharbat, barely aware of his surroundings as they rode to the Ambela Valley. He heard the firing as if in a dream.

'Who is shooting, Zaman? Wait! That's British artillery — screw-guns!'

'I don't know what's happening yet.' Zaman had a hand on Jack's reins, leading him slowly onward. 'Something is burning, as well. I can smell the smoke.'

The first of the fleeing warriors arrived a moment later, running along the floor of the Chamla valley. The drift of smoke increased, together with the high crack of the screw-guns. The musketry continued, both in regular, controlled volleys and the heavy thumping of jezzails.

'There's a regular battle going on.' Jack's sense of military duty surfaced through the lassitude of his fever. He saw a retreating tide of warriors, some in organised units, others individually. 'I think the British have advanced from the camp at last.'

'Be careful, sahib.' Zaman pulled Sharbat's reins, trying to take Jack away from the valley floor.

'No, hang it, Zaman.' Jack fought the fever. 'Leave me be.'

The horsemen rode in a purposeful group, ignoring the chaos around them. The green banner fluttering above them told its own story. 'It's the Akhund of Swat,' Jack said.

'This way, sahib.' Zaman's voice was urgent as he attempted to guide Jack away from the oncoming Akhund. 'Stay still, sahib, and say nothing.' Zaman stopped when a horde of fleeing warriors blocked their way, some firing over their shoulders, others intent on escape. 'He's seen us!'

The Akhund's horsemen slowed as they approached Jack. Their banner was in the centre, still proud despite the fly being faded and frayed.

Drawing his sword, Zaman edged closer to Jack. 'Stay with me, sahib.' Holding the pulwar across his chest, he faced the Akhund's two huge bodyguards.

The Akhund pushed closer with a third man close behind. 'Salaam Alaikum, Captain Windrush.'

'Salaam Alaikum, Akhund.' Jack gave a little bow from the saddle. He fought to clear his fever-muddled brain. 'It seems that the tide of war has turned against you.'

The Akhund was as calm as ever. 'Allah willed that British reinforcements should bring victory to them, this time.'

Jack realised that the Akhund's third escort was Batoor. 'Do you intend to raise another army, Akhund? Batoor Khan there will be a good general.' He heard the exhaustion in his voice.

The Akhund gave a small smile. 'It seems that Allah intends me to be a spiritual leader rather than a man of war, Captain Windrush. Without the modern rifles, my warriors fought at a disadvantage.'

Jack felt Batoor's gaze on him. 'Perhaps it is not yet the Pashtun's time.'

'Time does not end, Windrush. Empires, even the British Empire, always do. Allah is with the patient.' The Akhund glanced at Batoor and back to Jack. 'We will not meet again, Captain Windrush. Peace be upon you.'

The words came into Jack's head from some half-forgotten text. *Respect the enemy; he is a man doing what he believes is right.* 'Peace be upon you, Akhund.' Despite all that had happened, Jack could not bring himself to dislike this courteous, dignified man.

The musketry continued with a shell exploding fifty yards away, scattering dust and pebbles in a wide diameter. Jack saw a charge of Probyn's Horse and Guides scatter a force of Mujahidin. At the call of a bugle, Probyn's men headed for Jack, no doubt attracted by the Akhund's green banner.

'Akhund.' Jack pointed to Probyn's approaching horsemen.

'Thank you, Captain Windrush,' the Akhund said gravely. 'Batoor, I wish you to remain with Captain Windrush. Your time with me is at an end. You and Zaman Khan have things to discuss.' Unhurried, the Akhund cantered away with his two bodyguards close behind. Jack watched his standard for a moment. He felt as if he had gone back in time and met a great man. He knew he would never see his like again.

Batoor and Zaman glared at each other, each with his hand on the hilt of his sword. Jack pushed between them.

'I will fight the first man to draw his sword.'

'You, Windrush?' Batoor laughed. 'You are as weak as a day-old kitten! You are sick with fever.'

'Then you will have to kill me.' Jack knew that Batoor was correct. He could barely lift his sword, let alone fight with it.

'Zaman Khan. One of us will be Khan of the Rahmut Khel.' Batoor did not flinch as Probyn's horsemen closed around him. Hassan was in their midst, with Alladad Ursulla and Sawan slightly further back.

'Hold!' Jack lifted his hand. He did not want any of his Guides to start a blood feud. He did not wish any of his men to face Batoor.

'I killed Gulbaz Khan.' Zaman tapped the hilt of his sword.

Batoor smiled. 'You will find me harder to kill, Zaman. I have two hands.'

'I want no killing.' Jack forced Sharbat between the two men.

'There will be none, sahib,' Zaman said gently. 'I have no need to kill you, Batoor. You are the Khan of the Rahmat Khel, and I am a trooper of the Guides. A sword for a sword.' Zaman drew the sword of the Rahmat Khel, reversed it, and presented the hilt to Batoor. 'Take care of your sword, Batoor, and the people of the Rahmat Khel.'

Unbuckling his sword belt, Batoor handed over the Khyber knife he carried, replacing it with the sword of the Rahmut Khel.

Jack stared, unsure what he had just witnessed. 'Next time we meet, Batoor,' Jack said, 'I hope it is in peace. Go now, before my Guides decide you are an enemy.' Then he fell from Sharbat.

Chapter Twenty-Four

Gondabad February 1864

Jack lay on his charpoy, fighting the last of the malaria germs that had racked his body. He looked around his world. Mary was sitting with Andrew on her lap and a book in her hand, her eyes stern with concentration. Jack took a deep breath, knowing he wanted nothing else. He read the official letter that a smart Rajput had handed into the bungalow. 'That's my home leave confirmed, Mary.'

'That cheered you up,' Mary said. 'You've been lying there feeling sorry for yourself for weeks.'

Jack scanned the letter again before handing it to Mary. 'We're going Home, Mary. You'd better dust down your list of where you want to go.'

Holding young Andrew in her arms, Mary stepped to the side of Jack's charpoy. 'Before I do, Captain Jack, there are things you should know.'

'Oh? What sort of things?'

'Do you remember that Sergeant O'Neill gave us a wedding gift?' Mary said.

'I do.' Jack smiled at the memory. 'I think it was four pounds ten shillings.'

'That's right,' Mary agreed. 'Do you remember there was also a small packet with my name on it?'

'No,' Jack said. 'That was years ago, Mary. A lot has happened since then.' He fondled Andrew's blond hair. 'Like this little chap.'

'I know. I was there at the time,' Mary said. 'That small packet was a wedding gift to us, and it was very kind of the sergeant. You should remember such things, Jack. Anyway, here it is.' Mary lifted the packet. 'Do you want to open it, or shall I?'

'We both know that you opened it years ago.' Jack did not hide his smile. 'The seal's already broken. You haven't stuck it back very well.'

'Of course I opened it.' Mary re-broke the seal with her fingernail and emptied the packet. 'Look.' Lantern light sparkled from the small shower of jewels that cascaded downward onto Jack's charpoy.

'Now that's interesting.' Jack lifted the closest jewel. 'That's a fine ruby, Mary.'

'Yes, indeed. All these jewels are of top quality. I wonder where Sergeant O'Neill got these.'

'He didn't,' Jack said dryly. 'O'Neill had nothing to do with these. I'd wager a thousand pounds to a pinch of tea these came from Private Riley. He and Logan tried to steal a wagon of loot from Lucknow. I'll have a word with him if ever I meet him again.'

'They were stolen?' Mary said.

'Yes. How else would a ranking soldier get anything like this?'

'We can't keep them of course,' Mary said. 'That would be dishonest. We should return them to the legal owner if you know who that is.'

Jack saw his jewels sliding away from him. 'The convoy was bound for the coffers of the Honourable East India Company,' Jack said, 'so as the government took over John Company, and India indeed, I presume that they should go to the Crown or the governor general, whoever that may be.'

'Sir John Lawrence is the present governor general.' Mary pursed her lips. 'He doesn't need the money, and nor does the government.'

'We need the money,' Jack said. 'We could sell one of the rubies and buy my majority. I can't see any other way of me getting my step.'

'I like you fine as a Captain,' Mary said.

'A major has more responsibility and higher wages.' Jack indicated the walls of their bungalow. 'We could get a better house, maybe a promotion to lieutenant-colonel in time.' That exalted rank seemed an impossible dream.

'No.' Mary shook her head. 'The Book says we should not build our house on sand, and stolen jewels are not a good foundation for anybody's life. If we sell these, the money could fund an orphanage.'

'They could pay for a house back Home.' Jack tried to regain the jewels.

'No.' Mary replaced the jewels in their packet, folding it up securely. 'Jack, did you not hear the other news when you were out on the Frontier?'

'I was a little bit busy.' Jack had been too fever-stricken to tell Mary about Pakhtunkhwa. 'What news should I have heard?'

'We already have a house back home.' Mary put a hand on Jack's shoulder. 'Your grandfather, old General Baird, died when you were away.'

Jack nodded, saddened but not surprised. 'That's a shame. He was a decent old stick.'

'He was.' Mary allowed Jack a moment to absorb the news. 'You'll miss him.'

'I will miss him,' Jack said. 'But he lived his life as he wanted to. He was the last of his kind, I think, a British man settling in India, taking Indian wives and living like the natives. That's all changing now.'

'We live in unsettling times.' Mary was watching Jack closely. 'I read the general's will. I know I should have waited for you.'

Jack did not have to force his smile. 'It's as much for you as for me. What does it say?'

'It says that your grandfather has left you just about everything, including his properties back home.' Mary pushed Jack back down onto the charpoy. 'You own two modest houses, Captain Jack, a small house and a slightly larger house.'

'Oh.' Jack stared at her. 'I did not think that the general had anything back home. What are our houses like?'

'The smaller one is in the north somewhere. The larger one is smack in your area. It's in Herefordshire, Jack, at the Malvern Hills.'

'Oh, dear God.' Jack felt the increased hammer of his heart. 'We'd better start packing, Mary. I want to see our house.' He was going Home. After twelve years abroad, he was going back to Herefordshire.

Historical Notes

PASHTUNS AND THE NORTH WEST FRONTIER

Many historians have written about the Pashtuns of the North West Frontier. They were, and are, a uniquely independent people occupying one of the most hostile pieces of land in the world. The Pashtun know their land as Pakhtunkhwa, while their preferred way of life was Pakhtunwali, a strict code of hospitality and revenge.

Harry Lumsden, one of the great early British commanders of the Guides, said of the Pashtun: 'Everywhere family is arrayed against family, and tribe against tribe, in fact, one way and another every man's hand is against his neighbour.'

In 1898, the Army believed there were around 200,000 tribal warriors with approximately 48,000 rifles. Ownership of a rifle gave a Pashtun warrior great prestige, and the British tried all they could to stem the flow of modern weapons to the area, including a naval blockade of the Persian Gulf.

The North West Frontier was a constant source of trouble to the British, who launched scores of expeditions to try to keep the peace. Even as late as the 1930s, the British Army was active here, with mixed success.

THE AMBELA CAMPAIGN

The Ambela or Umbeyla campaign of 1863 against the Mujahidin, or so-called Hindustan Fanatics, was one of the larger expeditions on the North West Frontier between the First Afghan War of 1839-1842 and the Second Afghan War of 1879-1881. General Chamberlain led 5,600 men on to the Ambela Pass, camped there and endured wave after wave of Bunerwal attacks. When Chamberlain was wounded attacking a Bunerwal position, Major General John Garnock took command of the expedition. With the expedition now reinforced to 9,000 men, he advanced out of the Ambela Pass into the plain of Chamla. He moved in two columns, taking the fanatic stronghold of Conical Hill and the village of Lalu.

With the infantry having cleared the way, the vastly experienced Probyn led 400 horsemen to attack the Mujahidin in Chamla Valley with the infantry close behind. During this set-piece victory over the fanatics, the Bunerwals watched without getting involved. Realising they could not defeat the British in open warfare, they asked what the British wished of them. The British asked them to destroy the headquarters of the Mujahidin. The Bunerwals did so, not without drama, and the British withdrew.

The campaign had lasted three months but is largely forgotten now. It cost the lives of 15 British officers, 34 British and 189 Indian, Sikh, Pashtun and Gurkha soldiers, with another 24 British officers, 118 British soldiers and 541 Sikh, Pashtun, Indian and Gurkha wounded. The casualties among the enemy are not known but probably run into several hundred.

THE GUNSMITHS OF TAZHAK

Tazhak is purely fictitious but based on a real village. Darra Adam Khel near Peshawar is a village whose primary industry is making copies of commercial firearms. Working with primitive machinery, the thousands of craftsmen of Darra Adam Khel can produce a copy of virtually any firearm within a few days. The weapons are useable but lack the quality of the originals.

THE AKHUND OF SWAT

In his day, the Akhund of Swat was one of the most respected spiritual leaders of northern India. In 1835 he led a small army of Yusufzais against the Sikhs, who brushed him aside. Returning to Swat, the Akhund reverted to a peaceful, religious life of piety to Islam. It was not until 1863 that he returned to military action against Chamberlain's force. The Akhund was said to feed the poor, cure the sick, and work miracles. As early as the 1850s, the Akhund was calling for an Islamic state that would stand against the British, who he said were 'fast laying the foundations of their rule deep in our homelands.'

The Akhund lived to the age of 84, dying in 1871, with his tomb becoming an important Pashtun shrine.

SIR NEVILLE CHAMBERLAIN

Born on 10th January 1820 in Rio de Janeiro where his father was consul-general, Chamberlain was one of four brothers. Educated at Woolwich, he was commissioned in the Bengal Native Infantry at the age of 17. He fought in the First Afghan War of 1839-1842 where he was wounded at least four times and took part in the 1843 Gwalior Campaign. He was also present in the Sikh Wars, being notably active at the battle of Gujerat.

In 1849 he was Assistant Commissioner at Rawalpindi, then Hazara. In 1852 he relaxed by hunting lions in South Africa, following this by becoming brigadier of the Punjabi Irregulars, watching the North West Frontier. Never idle, in 1855 he led two expeditions against the Pashtun, and another the following year. He was active in the Mutiny, being wounded in front of Delhi. In 1858 he was back on the Frontier to stop a Sikh rebellion, with another expedition on the Frontier in 1859, this time against the Waziris. In 1860 he was facing the Mahsuds, and then in 1863, he commanded the Ambela expedition, his final duty, where he was wounded for the ninth time.

After he retired, honours came to Chamberlain. He became KCSI in 1866, GCB in 1875, and a Field Marshal when he was eighty years old. More curiously, he is perhaps better remembered for inventing the game of snooker than for all his fighting prowess.

* * *

We hope you enjoyed reading *Warriors of God*. If you have a moment, please leave us a review - even if it's a short one. We want to hear from you.

Want to get notified when one of Creativia's books is free to download? Join our spam-free newsletter at www.creativia.org.

Best regards,
Malcolm Archibald and the Creativia Team

About the Author

Born and raised in Edinburgh, Malcolm Archibald was educated at the University of Dundee, a city to which he has a strong attachment. He has experience in many fields and writes about the Scottish whaling industry, as well as historical fiction and fantasy. His grandfather and great-grandfather both fought in Queen Victoria's Army.

Books by the Author

- Jack Windrush -Series
    - Windrush
    - Windrush: Crimea
    - Windrush: Blood Price
    - Windrush: Cry Havelock
    - Windrush: Jayanti's Pawns
    - Windrush: Warriors of God
- A Wild Rough Lot
- Dance If Ye Can: A Dictionary of Scottish Battles
- Like The Thistle Seed: The Scots Abroad
- Our Land of Palestine
- Shadow of the Wolf
- The Swordswoman
- The Shining One (The Swordswoman Book 2)
- Falcon Warrior (The Swordswoman Book 3)
- Melcorka of Alba (The Swordswoman Book 4)

Printed in Great Britain
by Amazon

47648039R00187